CURSE OF MIDNIGHT

AMELIA IVES

A.P. DESWICK
PUBLICATIONS

First published in Great Britain in 2025 by **A.P Beswick Publications**,

Publishing rights are held by **A.P Beswick Publications** under license from the author.

ISBN (Paperback): 978-1-916671-48-5
ISBN (Hardback): 978-1-916671-49-2

Edited by Quinn Nichols – Quill & Bone Editing

Cover Design by Krafigs Design

A.P Beswick Publications
Oswaldtwistle Mills Business Centre, Clifton Mill, Pickup Street, Accrington, BB5 0EY

To Nadine, who always trusted me to cut her hair when the world shut down. Ginger Snips lives on.

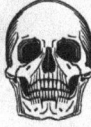

The Woes of Family

Noah Kiers hated this house. It had been his prison for well over a hundred years, and its novelty had worn off long ago. The manor stood nestled in the rolling hills of Northern England, with two symmetrical wings and more than enough rooms to get lost in. Ivy had long ago claimed the exterior, and a battered slate roof protected tall windows that overlooked the manicured lawn. To the back stretched acres of woods, hiding the history of the land beneath twisted branches. There was a timeless quality to the property, but the house had lost its grandeur before the turn of the twentieth century, if Noah was being generous.

He currently stood in the east wing on the ground floor in a well-loved library. The room was cosy, a particular favourite of his. The walls were lined floor to ceiling with books, and a large Chesterfield sofa sat before a worn fireplace, where flames licked the stone. Noah loved to read in here when he didn't have anything else to occupy his time. Right now, he had something to focus on.

He looked out from one of the windows, his hands

tucked neatly into his pockets. He stood, cast in the glow of the early evening light, waiting. The east wing gave him one of the best views of the expansive front yard and the house just across the street.

"Is she coming by today?" a woman's voice asked Noah from behind.

He turned sharply on his heel, annoyed to take his eyes off the garden and beyond. He would miss *her* if he weren't careful.

"Aye. I believe so." His voice was clipped, edgy for him. Makenna hadn't been by in two weeks.

"I won't keep you from it then." The woman, Maryam, slipped back into the hallway, and Noah rubbed at his forehead. Maryam was a lovely woman and never deserved his ire. He would be sure to apologise to her later.

Turning back to the garden, Noah watched the street. It was around the time Makenna typically came home from work. However, the last two weeks had been anything but typical. From what Noah could gather from the others in the house, Makenna was away visiting family in Wales. But today, she was set to return.

Across from the manor sat a humble house made of stone. It was cut off from the estate by a thick, black gate and a street not built for cars. The house lacked the architectural grace of Noah's prison, but the word comfortable came to mind. The view of it never got old. Or perhaps it was the girl pulling up in a beat-up Nissan that never lost its appeal.

Noah leaned forward, careful not to smudge the glass. Makenna parked in the driveway and kicked the car door open with her boot. It swung back with force and nearly slammed on her ankle. Noah could practically hear the curse from her lips as she struggled to haul herself out. She had a few bags of luggage heaped over her arms. Their

2

weight threw her off balance and nearly landed her on the ground. It was incredibly disorganised, but the girl didn't slow down. In all the years Noah had watched her, she had never taken a second trip back to the car. Not for groceries, luggage, or anything else that might require a second trip. She was stubborn. But Noah knew that. He had known that for a long time.

~

MAKENNA FELT the stare of someone watching her as she exited the car. It was a familiar feeling. There was something almost reassuring about it, like a guardian angel poised over this very spot, waiting for her to come home safe and sound. She had tried for years to put a name to the feeling. A nosy neighbour, perhaps? Although the only building near her was the manor across the street. Ownership had changed multiple times over the years, so Makenna had stopped paying attention long ago. Whoever was there now kept to themselves, so she kept to hers. One of the perks of living so far from the village was the privacy it afforded, privacy for everyone. This feeling of someone watching over her was something else – something other.

Now wasn't the time to dwell on it. Makenna has spent the last few hours in a cramped car with nothing but junk food to snack on and her own shitty company. She was in a foul mood after spending two weeks with her extended family in Wales. They never gave her any space, always concerned for her well-being. It was exhausting.

With the last of her luggage, Makenna kicked the car door closed and headed for the house. The late afternoon sun had long ago disappeared behind the clouds, and the threat of rain was high. Makenna would be pissed if the skies opened up in the few seconds it took to get from her car to the front door. She *was* pissed when she realised her house keys were buried somewhere in a pocket, well out of reach with all the bags in her arms.

Home. She was so close to her bed, and food, and a TV that she could zone out to. All she wanted was to turn her brain off and speak to no one. God, her family had hounded her the entire time. Too many questions, too few answers Makenna could give in response. Their eternal disappointment was exhausting.

In one motion, she dropped the luggage at the foot of the door. The rain was coming down now, and her blond curls would be a mess in no time. Finding her key, Makenna groped the slick handle and shoved it in. There was no satisfying click as she turned her wrist – the door popped open without resistance. Inside, Makenna could see the lights on in the kitchen at the back of the house. The smell of dinner wafted through the hall. Shepard's pie. Her mother's favourite.

Makenna's back went stiff as she took in the smell, the lights, the inevitable presence that was her mother. It was bullshit enough that Makenna had had to visit with relatives who smothered her. It was worse now she had to deal with her mum, too.

Jacqueline Grace was one of the scariest people Makenna knew. No one won an argument with her; she simply let you play along until she got bored and tore you to shreds. She never had a kind word for Makenna or her sister Paige, either – not since the passing of their younger brother, Rory, a few years back. It was Jacqueline's world, and they were lucky to be living in it.

Makenna's house was supposed to be a sanctuary. She had been privileged enough to spend her summers here with her grandmother before she passed away some years ago. Upon Makenna's eighteenth birthday, she had said goodbye to her mother and packed her bags to move here. Her younger sister hadn't so much as waved to Makenna as she drove off. Their sense of family had died the day they buried their brother.

In a few days was her twenty-first birthday. Makenna would have been more than glad to spend the day alone. She had zero plans to celebrate with her mother.

"Hello?" Makenna called out as she kicked the luggage through the blue-painted door, chipped away at the edges.

"Good, Makenna, you're home. I was beginning to worry." Jacqueline stepped out into the hall, her thin figure illuminated from behind.

Closing the door behind her, Makenna flicked the lights on, illuminating a dull, yellow-painted hall. She could feel her mother's disappointed stare before she even saw it. "There was some traffic on the motorway. I was later than I expected."

Jacqueline clicked her tongue and turned back into the kitchen she had come from. "I told you to leave early, but you never listen."

"I wanted to leave before breakfast, but Rayna insisted I stay and leave after." Makenna peeled off her wet plaid jacket and dropped it on the floor, as was habit.

"You better not have dropped your jacket on the floor, Makenna dear. There are coat hangers for a reason. A closet even, should you be so inclined to keep clutter out of the doorway."

Closing her eyes, Makenna counted to ten. It stopped her from saying the first crude thing that came to mind and made her settle on the fourth or fifth. These latter ones were usually less creative. They didn't stir the same rage in Jacqueline as Makenna's first choice of words.

Picking up the coat, Makenna yanked a hanger from

the closet and did her best worst job of hanging the garment. It would be enough to satisfy her mother while undermining the act as much as Makenna could. It was the little victories.

With shoes off and keys placed on a secure hook, Makenna thumped her way into the kitchen and braced for her mother's inevitable disappointment. "Mum, what are you doing here?"

Jacqueline stood near the stove, a sharp knife cutting into the sheperd's pie and two plates pulled out for serving. "It's your birthday in a few days. Why can't I visit my daughter on her birthday?"

"You could have called and saved yourself the trip." Jacqueline was a woman of practicality. If Makenna could appeal to that nature, maybe she could get her mother out of the house faster.

"I wanted to see my daughter's lovely face. Is that so hard to believe?"

Yes. "You could have FaceTimed."

Jacqueline slapped a piece of pie onto the first plate. "I shouldn't have to have an excuse to see my daughter on her birthday."

Makenna tightened her lips. Practicality wasn't going to win this one. "It's nice to see you, Mum. Thank you for stopping by and making me dinner."

"See, that wasn't so hard." Jacqueline passed a plate to her daughter. There were forks already set on the tiny table shoved into a corner.

Makenna didn't bother waiting for her mother as she sat down and dug in. "Are you just here for dinner?" she asked around a mouthful of food. She knew full well it didn't become her to talk with food in her mouth, but Jacqueline let it pass.

"I figured I could stay for the next two nights since

your birthday is coming up. I never get to see you anymore, and I know your dad certainly won't come by. Probably off with a new wife. I wouldn't be surprised." Jacqueline's fork hovered above her plate as she stared at her daughter. "I worry about you," she added.

Here we go. "Oh?"

"Are you taking your meds? I know you have a habit of forgetting."

Makenna forked in another bite. "Yes. I have been." Lies. Makenna had stopped taking her pills for depression months ago. She had conveniently forgotten to tell her mother that. The meds always made her feel like the dead, shuffling around like a zombie or ghost. They had never lifted her spirits. "Since you're staying, I'll make up the guest room once I'm done with dinner."

"No need to make up the room. I've already done it." Jacqueline took her first bite of food. She chewed slowly, and when she swallowed, her attention was back on Makenna. "Are you sure you're taking your meds? I don't want a repeat of what happened after Rory's death. Your little episode put us all through quite the scare. Nearly taking your life like that, honestly."

Makenna bit down on her back teeth to keep herself in check. "I'm fine, Mum. I've not done anything to hurt myself in a long time."

"Humph."

It was hard to satisfy Jacqueline even on a good day.

"Have you talked to Paige lately?" Makenna asked to fill the silence.

Jacqueline set her fork down on the table after swallowing another small bite. "I'm concerned about your sister."

Better her than me. "What has she done this time?"

"She won't return my calls. She's away at that damn

school, doing who knows what." Makenna knew the next words out of her mother's mouth before she said them. "But at least she's at school."

Another thing Jacqueline was worried about. Nearly twenty-one years old, and Makenna still hadn't applied to university. Maybe if she redirected the conversation, she could avoid the lecture. "I heard from Paige a few days ago, actually. She mentioned this girl she was seeing. I can look into her if you want."

"I don't know why you're so concerned about your sister's love life when you should focus on your own. Maybe if you went to school, it would help with your mood. It would get you out of this house, too."

Makenna played with the potatoes on her plate, no longer hungry. "I'm just not ready."

"Perhaps this will change your mind." Jacqueline pushed back from the table as she excused herself. Makenna could only guess what her mother had up her sleeve as she rummaged through her comically large purse on the counter, then slid an envelope across the table towards her daughter.

"What is this?" Makenna asked. She picked up the page with stiff fingers, eyes glazing over what was clearly a school logo. "A school application form?"

"It's time to apply for uni. You've been putting it off far too long." There was no room for argument in Jacqueline's voice. Just a command that was expected to be followed.

Makenna barely read through the page before setting it back down. "I told you, I'm not ready."

"You can't rot away in this house forever," Jacqueline said, her lips a thin line. "I want you to apply by the end of the week."

"Is this why you came?" Makenna asked. "To get me to fill this out? 'Happy birthday, Makenna. Here's my gift to you: mandatory education. Don't squander your future away. Love Mum.'" She could feel the rage begin to burn, igniting whatever dull ache usually settled in her chest.

"I'm not going to let my oldest daughter throw her life away when there's opportunity. This school is online. You want to stay in this house, that is the price you pay for it. Take it, or get out."

Makenna could only blink as the words settled. "You're giving me an ultimatum?"

"No, I'm motivating you." Jacqueline's face was cool, calm. No emotion whatsoever. Did this woman feel anything outside of disappointment? "You go to school, and you can stay here. Otherwise, it's time to pack up. The real world is calling, Makenna. It's time to be an adult and answer it."

"This isn't even your house. This was Grandma's place. *You* have no right," Makenna said, her tone rising.

"Grandma left this place to me, actually, so I have all the right."

Makenna couldn't handle it anymore. She didn't want to be here, not in this room with this woman who claimed to be her mother. Didn't mothers feel the need to protect? How was this helping anyone?

"Where are you going?" Jacqueline asked as Makenna shoved her chair back. "You've hardly touched your food."

"You know, Mum, I'm not very hungry. I'll finish this later when I'm filling out my application and answering the call of the world. I'm going to go shower." Makenna didn't bother waiting for Jacqueline to respond. Before her mother could speak, she was already out of the kitchen and up the creaky stairs to her tiny, outdated bathroom, a nightmare of teal and yellow paint. Turning on the shower, Makenna stripped and threw herself in. It wasn't quite hot yet, but she didn't care. The water calmed her. It had been a safety net for years – an escape.

Jacqueline always had a way of doing this to her – of breaking Makenna down until she had no other option but to retreat. Makenna had become good at that over the years. Hell, she had moved her life to escape Jacqueline. And yet somehow, her mother had shown up today, and this time, with an ultimatum.

When Makenna ran past the acceptable amount of time to hide in the shower, she finished up in the bathroom and headed downstairs in fresh clothes. Jacqueline's head swivelled to her daughter as she entered the living room. "You take an awfully long time to shower."

"So I've been told."

"Your dinner is in the fridge. You can reheat it in the microwave."

A dismissal. Odd. Makenna had come bracing for the worst. She certainly had no plan of telling her mother she could piss off and take the application with her. That was tomorrow-Makenna's problem. Maybe even next-week-Makenna's problem. Right now was all about survival. Get through the next few days, and when Jacqueline was gone, Makenna could rip up the application form.

"I also brought dessert. It's by your dinner."

Makenna wasn't sure how to fill the silence that fell over them. Insulting her mother never went over well.

"I'm going to bed soon. I want to finish this programme first." Jacqueline turned her head back to the TV, and for once, Makenna got off relatively unscathed. Truly a birthday miracle.

"Sounds good, Mum. I'll see you in the morning."

The sheperd's pie tasted almost better than it had straight out of the oven. Perhaps it was the fact that Makenna had survived the night with her mother, and the hours counting down to Jacqueline's departure were even closer. Or maybe Makenna was just starving, and even stale bread sounded appetising at this point.

As Makenna finished the last bite, she heard the TV shut off and her mother's quiet steps as she headed upstairs. Moving to the empty living room, Makenna sat on the worn couch by the window and stared through it blankly. Outside, the rain came down heavily. Resting her head against the glass, Makenna let her eyes drift to the manor across the street. There were lights on, and shadows passed the windows in a flurry of activity for a usually sleepy house. Was something going on? What had everyone up in a tizzy? Makenna focused harder, noticing someone standing in the window of the right wing on the ground floor. She could just make out their shape – a young man, by the looks of it. She knew only a few people resided in the house, but she had never seen him before. Could he see her as well, through the gloom that seemed to settle over Northern England? He was gone before she could work it out, vanishing as quickly as he had come.

Whatever was going on in the house tonight seemed to be causing quite the commotion. Makenna let her mind wander to the strange man before drifting into a light sleep.

2

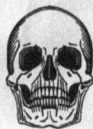

The House Across the Street

"What time is it?" Noah asked. He paced around the library, his gaze darting out through the window to the house across the street.

"It's nearly noon," the only other person in the room said to him. Lydia sat on the leather couch, her lips pulled into a frown. She was a beautiful young woman, currently picking at the ends of her blond plait as she spoke. "Really, Noah, I wish you wouldn't pace like that. It makes me nervous. You're just working yourself up."

Lydia had been Noah's voice of reason for a long time. He tried to focus on her words now, though they didn't soothe him today, not like in the past.

He tried to relax himself. "She's too close." His voice nearly broke as he spoke, his Scottish accent thicker with his heightened emotions.

Stopping in front of the fire, Noah pushed back his wavy dark hair. He had even darker eyes – the colour of midnight, his mother used to say. He had come by it naturally. He even had the same angular facial structure his mother had, both with soft lips.

"I know, hun, but there's nothing else we can do right now. She's safe at home." Lydia wrapped her arms around her narrow waist, her blue eyes focused on the fire. She was dressed in a delicate white nightgown, covered by a rich maroon robe.

Noah chewed on his lips, his fingers locked behind his neck. "I've not done enough."

"Noah, you're stressing yourself out. Come sit down, and we can work through this together," Lydia suggested. She patted the spot beside her on the couch. "Maybe we can try the crosses again. I still have that rosary upstairs. We can—"

Noah was already shaking his head. "We tried that, it didn't work."

Lips in a thin line, Lydia nodded. "I know. I just thought it was worth a second shot. I wish I knew what to do here, Noah. I swear we've tried it all."

The deep seed of panic stuck in Noah's chest threatened to push him over. "Have we, though? Have we done everything we can?" He pulled at his shirt, the room becoming very hot suddenly. He hadn't tried everything *just* yet. There was still the book up in his room, but he had written it off as just another gimmick.

Lydia was on her feet, her arms outstretched to pull Noah into a tight hug. She was almost as tall as he, a woman of impressive height. "Shhh, I know, honey. I know. It's been so tough on you."

The weight of Lydia's arms did little to relax him, but Noah let her comfort him. "Thank you." He settled his head on her shoulder before his eyes caught someone new enter the room. Maryam stood in the doorway to the library, her thick black hair resting over her shoulder. She looked as concerned as Noah felt, and the panic that Lydia had tried so hard to quell bubbled again.

"Noah, dear, would you?" Maryam's voice drifted across the room. It was deep, rich, and comforting, a touch of her Kannada accent from southwestern India flavouring her words. She was older than both Noah and Lydia, somewhere in her mid-fifties. The few times Noah had pried for her actual age, Maryam had batted his arm hard and told him a woman never revealed such things.

Detaching from Lydia, Noah excused himself from the room and followed Maryam into the hall.

"I want to talk to you about something." Maryam seemed to glide across the floor. A talent he had not seen anyone in the house master.

"Where are we going?" he asked. He felt more lost when he couldn't see the house across the street, as if his constant surveillance would slow the inevitable.

Maryam gave him no answer, and Noah didn't ask a second time. Together they climbed the grand stairs branching off the main entrance until they were in the west wing near his room. Maryam pointed to his door with a straight finger. "I think you should use the book," she said matter-of-factly, always a strait-laced woman. There was no wasting his time.

Noah felt his back stiffen. He had only told Maryam about it in a moment of weakness, as a man out of options. He had found the book in the attic, risking the wrath of Harriet, who dominated the space, in hopes of uncovering anything that might help.

"I'm surprised she hasn't noticed it missing," Maryam said as an afterthought. Harriet's attic was sacred to her, full of knick-knacks she had collected over the years. "Last time she thought one of us took something from her, she threw a fit and tore apart one of my children's journals."

A look of grief passed over Maryam's face; her children were long gone. Harriet indeed had a bad habit of destroying people's property when she felt threatened. "Tell me more about the book," Maryam said, eyeing his door.

Noah had known Maryam long enough to know she wouldn't relent. With a sigh, he pushed open the door to let her in. "It's on my bedside table."

Maryam scurried past him into his room to snatch the book. The room was spacious, with tall, arched windows draped in burgundy velvet curtains. Shoved into the corner was an opulent four-poster bed, its frame crafted from dark mahogany and its thick duvet decorated with numerous plush pillows. A part of Noah both resented and cherished that bed. It had kept him warm on his most miserable nights, yet was just one more piece in the prison that was his home.

"It's dated to the 1970s – a text on ancient Greek history."

"Show me the page you were speaking about," Maryam said, thrusting the book towards him.

Noah crossed the floor to take it from her. The book was thin, its pages yellowed from years of age. It represented many things Noah hated: rituals, prayer, belief, religion. Things that had never helped him before. He flipped open to the page he had been glossing over earlier.

"Read it to me," Maryam encouraged him.

He cleared his throat before reading aloud, "Women in ancient Athens would bury tablets that called on the goddess Athena for protection. By invoking her spirit, they walked with the goddess's blessing."

Maryam nodded vigorously. "Yes, yes. Very good. So?"

"So?" Noah snapped the book shut. "I went hunting through the attic to find something that would help me, and this is all I could find. What do you want me to do here?"

Maryam reached for the book, which Noah held loosely in his hands.

"We already tried the Catholic and Christian god, the Hindu deities, Celtic spirits, and everything else we could think of. Do you think the Greek gods will be any different?"

"I don't know, but is it not worth a try?" With one eyebrow raised, Maryam nodded to the window over-looking the house across the street. "Harriet will probably burn your precious books for taking this from her, a risk you were willing to take. Would you really not try this now? What if it protects *her*? Or is a tablet beneath you?"

Leaning back on his heels, Noah considered Maryam's words. Beggars couldn't be choosers. He had risked Harri-et's wrath for something, anything. Was this it? Was this the answer? "Where do I even get a tablet? I don't suppose you have one lying around?"

With a satisfied smile, Maryam crossed her arms, tucking the book against her chest. "No, of course not. But I don't believe you need an exact tablet as the text describes. It's not what you use to perform the ritual. It's the intention behind it."

Noah's fingers found the hem of his suspenders and began to fidget with them. "Do I have to write it in Ancient Greek? I'm a little rusty."

Tapping her heart with stubby fingers, Maryam reminded him, "The intention, my boy. That is all you need. Find whatever feels right for you."

Giving Maryam a curt nod, Noah removed himself from the room with new purpose. Whatever felt right to him. Simple enough. Find an object, write his intention on it, invoke the spirit of Athena, and bury it in the ground. He had certainly never tried anything like it before.

As long as it wasn't *magic*. Religion he could do. Magic was simply out of the question.

What *did* feel right to him? Noah hadn't the faintest clue. But he needed to figure it out fast. Books? Books meant the world to him. They had been his favourite pastime over the years. But books weren't a clean slate. They had pages filled with plots and characters with motives and heartbreak. Noah didn't want someone else's baggage attached to his object. He wanted something he could serve with his own intention, so nothing blocked it.

He racked his brain thoroughly, trying to find something that met such a high criterion. It was nearly impossible. This house had over a hundred years of memories, ranging from dull to painful to pure elation. Maybe that wasn't the right angle to come from. What Noah needed was something that evoked his desire to protect. Something filled with love.

He knew immediately what that was.

～

MAKENNA WOKE up on the couch in a cold sweat. Her body shook from the dream that still gripped her, a nightmare that had plagued her since she first stepped into this house as a child.

It was always the same: Makenna standing in front of the manor across the street when a piercing scream cut through the night. It would morph and twist into sobs and moans, haunting the air. Makenna could never place the wail. She was always rooted to the spot on the perfectly manicured lawn, unable to search for who was crying. The scream drifted through her dreams like an echo, sometimes more loudly than on other nights. The dream seemed to haunt her more than usual, almost every night this last week. Makenna couldn't remember a time it had been this bad.

The early sun woke her from the couch, and as she crept up to bed, she tried to shake the scream from her mind. It was some miracle she managed to fall back asleep until eleven. It was even more miraculous when Makenna found her mother gone when she came down for breakfast. Jacqueline had left a note on the counter saying she would be back after lunch and to eat without her. Makenna didn't have to be told twice. There was leftover shepherd's pie, and she felt no shame eating it for breakfast. One less meal to think of. It would be even better to get out of the house before her mother returned. Venturing on a walk would give her a few more hours of peace. Only puddles remained of the downpour yesterday, and she was never one to waste an opportunity for her wellies.

"Makenna, my dear," a voice boomed out as she locked the front door behind her. "How are you?"

Makenna turned to find Huxley out in the manor's garden. He was maybe the best-dressed caretaker Makenna had ever seen, always wearing the same clothes every time she saw him. An older gentleman, he was nearly as tall as he was wide, with salt-and-pepper hair. He had a big, booming voice and was always curious about the comings and goings of the village. Quite the gossiper, really.

"Hello Hux, how are you?" Makenna crossed the road at a leisurely pace and leaned against the gate.

The man beamed at her. "I am good. What are you up to today? Any big plans for your birthday tomorrow? I remember when you were just a wee lass, running around the front yard. How time flies."

"No big plans. Probably going to keep it quiet. Might order some Chinese. My mother's visiting, but I hope she doesn't stay long."

Huxley's lips tightened. "A girl your age should be going out. Staying home on your birthday, sheesh." His eyes lit up as a thought seemed to occur to him. "You should get out of here. Maybe go to the city. Drink whatever the kids are drinking these days. Kombucha, wasn't it?"

Scrunching her face, Makenna shook her head. "I'm quite pumped to keep it simple. I plan to eat my weight in cheese and crackers as an appetiser to the Chinese food. Then cookie dough for dessert. I'm going to be sick for the next three days. A gift to myself, really."

Huxley patted his belly with a jovial laugh. "That sounds delightful. How I wish I could enjoy some good cuisine like that. It never quite agrees with me."

"I can bring you a cheeky plate if you'd like?" Makenna offered. "I'm sure a bite or two wouldn't hurt."

Huxley waved his hands at her. "Please don't bother. I've actually got quite the busy day ahead of me. We've new guests moving in. It's going to be rather chaotic here over the next few days. I would suggest steering clear of the house while everyone gets settled."

Makenna nodded. "I thought I saw someone in the window I didn't recognise. You seem to have your work cut out for you."

"Ah yes, the new master of the house," Huxley said with a weary smile. "I haven't quite decided what to think of him. Best to avoid him until I can properly 'suss him out' as you young kids say. You never know with people these days."

Makenna stretched her neck to get a better look at the

manor over Huxley's broad shoulders. "Duly noted. I will avoid the man at all costs."

Huxley shot her another smile. "Perfect. Now, I don't want to keep you from your afternoon. Say hi to your mother for me and remember—" Huxley gestured to the garden before shaking his finger.

"Right, I won't venture near the property. Goodbye, Hux." Makenna waved at the man as he went back to fussing over whatever he liked to fuss about.

Strange, how in all her years, Makenna had never been beyond the gates. There had just never been an appeal to venture over there. Not one to dwell on things, she focused on her walk, her solitary plans for her birthday, and just how much longer she could avoid her mother.

～

WITH PURPOSE BEHIND HIS STEPS, Noah stormed his way through the house – a man on a mission. He almost made it to his room before being stopped. Huxley, the second oldest in the house, stood in front of his door. The man's expansive size took up most of the hallway.

"Ah, Noah. So good to see you. I just saw Makenna. She's out for a walk. I told her not to come to the house for the next few days. New people moving in, I said. How clever." Huxley twirled his moustache, quite impressed with himself. He had a fantastic beard that Noah had been jealous of on more than one occasion. Between his beard and finely pressed coat, Huxley looked to be quite the distinguished gentleman, especially considering he saw himself as the caretaker of the property.

"Hux, brilliant plan. And as good as it is to see you, I don't have much time. I'm in a bit of a rush."

Huxley waved nonchalantly. "Of course you are. But I

have something for you that might be of interest." The old man pulled out a brass pocket watch, its once polished case now adorned with small scratches. "And you have time. Surely you can spare a few seconds, especially when it could benefit you and you-know-who."

Noah longingly peered over the man's shoulder to his door. The perfect item was sitting in his room, just waiting for him. The look in Huxley's eye was promising, though. This man could sell water to a fish. "All right, five minutes."

"Atta boy." Huxley clapped Noah on the back. "This way." Leading him out of the house and to the back garden, Huxley stopped just short of an ancient oak tree. "Here," he said cryptically.

"A very nice tree, yes. But you see, I have some things to attend to." Noah tried to resist the urge to scurry back to the house, his mind still stuck on the idea of the tablet.

Huxley tsked and waved a finger like a schoolteacher chastising a child. "If I wanted to look at trees with you, I would have brought you here another time. Better to observe each curve of the flora when you're not stressed. No, no. I brought you here to show you this." With a large hand, Huxley pointed down to the earth where a ring of mushrooms grew. "Fairy rings. Good luck, you know."

Noah racked his brain, something not quite clicking with Huxley's words. "I thought fairy rings were a bad omen?" He took an involuntary step back. The last thing he needed was more bad luck. "My mum always told me if you stepped into a fairy ring, you would die young."

"Nonsense. Perhaps if you ate one, it would be good luck?"

It was hard to stop Noah's eyebrows from disappearing into his hairline. "While I appreciate the idea, I don't think eating mushrooms is going to help. If it was that simple, then I'm an idiot."

Huxley rubbed at his whiskered chin. "Maybe if you danced in the mushrooms first. Better yet, dance in them naked. I'm sure the fairies would love that."

Slowly, so as not to be rude, Noah backed away from the man and his precious mushrooms. "A lovely idea, but Maryam has given me something else to try first. If it doesn't work, I promise I will dance naked amongst the mushrooms next time."

Huxley looked only half put out. "I suppose it is a stretch, but you never know with these things. It is always the last thing you think of, isn't it?"

"Fantastic suggestion, really. The creativity alone is promising. I shall get back to you on it." Noah was already halfway back to the house. He was on a mission, and he'd be damned twice if someone stopped him again.

No one interrupted him as he beelined it to his room. The manor had been built in the Tudor era on a beautiful property. One could easily spend years discovering secret rooms and treasures. Noah had memorised every inch of this house a few years in. Nothing surprised him anymore.

Locking his door behind him with quick fingers, Noah headed for his bookshelf tucked against the wall opposite the window. He scanned the beloved books for the one his heart desired most. It was high up. Sometimes people liked to peruse his private collection, and out of sight meant out of mind. Stretching to his tiptoes, he found the one: a leather-bound book with the cover stained red. It was a small text, fitting nicely into his hands. He had read it a thousand times: *The Damned Thing* by Ambrose Bierce. It had been a gift given to him on a reckless night back in Edinburgh. He flipped to the middle of the book, his fingers gracing the item he knew would make a perfect tablet. Talisman felt like a better word for it.

From the pages, he plucked a picture faded from over a hundred years of viewing. The photograph had been taken on the same night the book was gifted to him by her; Meredith. The love of his life, not long before she died.

The picture was of the two of them, a few nights before they had journeyed to England. In the photo, Noah sat on a stiff chair, wearing a suit far too dapper for himself. Behind him stood Meredith, her hair brushed up in a loose topknot and wispy curls framing her face. She had complained her royal blue dress was too heavy that night. Neither of them smiled in the photo, but Meredith's arm draped over Noah's shoulder. The photographer had asked them if that night had been their wedding. Both had burst out laughing and struggled to maintain a serious face as the photographer did his job.

This photo meant more to him than anything in the world. He had cried over it, agonised over it, loved every inch that it represented. Tonight, though, he would sacrifice it – anything to save Makenna.

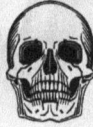

3

The Boy Lost in Death

Wasting time outside was easy enough. The weather cooperated, and when Makenna returned home, it was well into the afternoon. Jacqueline was fussing about in the kitchen. From the sweet scent that wafted down the hall, Makenna could safely assume a cake was being made. How generous of Jacqueline.

"Mum, I'm back," Makenna called out as she shucked off her jacket and boots. She was more mindful when putting them in the closet this time. Being outside always did wonders for her mood, and tomorrow was her birthday. Maybe she didn't have to be so defensive with her mother.

"You were gone a while," Jacqueline called. "I came back after lunch, and you weren't here."

Entering the kitchen, Makenna pulled out a chair from the table and plopped down. "Sorry. I went for a bit of a walk."

Jacqueline stood over the counter with a plastic mixing bowl in her arms. She whisked the batter fiercely, her eyebrow raised as she looked at her daughter. "Do your walks often take hours?"

"Sometimes, when the weather is nice." On the table were a few envelopes. "For me?" Makenna asked as she pulled them towards her.

"Birthday cards. You'll have to call your aunts and uncles to thank them."

Makenna bobbed her head as she tore through the cards. They were mostly from her dad's side of the family. Her mother's had already given their gifts when Makenna visited in Wales. "Oh, did you know Fran is having a baby?" Makenna asked as she read the last of the cards. "She said she's due in the spring."

Batter sufficiently whisked, Jacqueline poured it into a pan before turning to the oven. "I didn't know." Jacqueline wasn't much of a gossip, and after Rory's death, she seemed to shut down around any baby talk. Makenna chastised herself for forgetting. She had been too excited about the news to filter it.

"When I was in Wales, I talked to Christopher. Did you know he's moving to Canada for university? I told him to pack an extra jacket. Last thing we need is a Chris-ticle." Makenna waited for her mother to respond, but she was far more concerned over the cake.

"Damn oven. I forget it runs hotter. Remind me to take the cake out a little bit sooner." Dusting her hands on an apron older than Makenna, Jacqueline took a seat beside her daughter. "My train leaves early tomorrow. I would have preferred to spend the day with you, but I couldn't get off work at the hotel."

"That's fine. I have plans."

Jacqueline raised an eyebrow. "Do you?"

"I plan to do nothing."

Tucking a piece of hair behind her ear, Jacqueline

shook her head. "To each their own on their special day."
It was remarkable how similar the two looked, Makenna
thought as she took in her mother. Both had loose blond
curls, though Jacqueline's looked like the sun had bleached
out the last of their colour, turning them almost white.
They were both on the taller side too, each with a slim
build. While most would consider Jacqueline willowy,
Makenna was more muscular; boyish, her mother had
called it.

"Might as well do nothing now while I can, before I
apply to school," Makenna said with a false smile.

"It's for your own good," Jacqueline said. "You can't
work in a silly little flower shop forever."

Makenna didn't bother telling her mum those flowers
were the only colour she had left in her life. It was so
damn hard to see past the grey, the haze she felt permanently stuck in. At least the tulips and roses brought some
colour into her world. Seeing beyond the shop, beyond
the little corner of England she was trapped in, felt
impossible. Maybe Makenna should be more motivated.
Maybe she should want to go to school, but it was so
damn hard to picture a future that wasn't swamped in
grief.

"Whatever you say, Mum."

"You'll thank me one day, when your future is bright
and full of opportunity."

Makenna could only nod, a heavy silence falling over
them as they waited for the cake to bake. Jacqueline occupied herself with a newspaper she must have picked up
from the village, while Makenna browsed her phone.
When the cake was ready, the two ate their weight as re-
runs of *Gilmore Girls* played in the background. Chinese was
ordered when cake could no longer sustain them, before
Jacqueline turned in for an early night.

"I'll be long gone before you wake up," Jacqueline said on her way to the stairs. "But happy birthday."

Makenna wasn't sure if she should get up from her spot on the couch to hug her mother good night. Jacqueline already had one foot on the bottom step. It decided things for Makenna, so she stayed where she was. "Sounds good, Mum. Thanks for coming."

Jacqueline seemed to linger before her hand tightened on the banister. "Good night, Kenny. I love you." Without another word, Jacqueline disappeared upstairs.

Kenny. Only Makenna's brother had called her that. It felt odd coming from her mum. There was something bittersweet and final about it. It tugged on a small amount of guilt Makenna had long ago buried – guilt over leaving her mother after Rory died, guilt for not saying 'I love you' enough.

Turning her attention back to the TV, Makenna tried to let her mind fall back into the squeaky-clean world of *Gilmore Girls*. The hours seemed to drain as the evening turned to night. Maybe spending her birthday by herself was a little on the lonely side, Makenna thought as she watched the clock inch closer to midnight. But lonely didn't have to mean sad.

If there was one thing Makenna didn't handle very well, it was sadness. Angry she could do. She had been angry at the world since her parents divorced. Happy, Makenna could plaster on her face when the occasion needed it. But sadness was too raw. It ate away at her, ruining her until she felt completely numb. It had gotten far worse after her brother died.

Her birthday seemed to compound these feelings tenfold. Another year older, another year to suffer without him. She didn't like the thought of people celebrating her alive-ness. Others were dead. Sometimes, she wished she had taken after her brother. Death seemed so quiet, so peaceful. No pain. Being alive was suffocating.

So, when the clock hit midnight, Makenna let the pain settle in. This birthday would be just like the rest of them. There was simply nothing else to it.

～

NOAH SPENT the day focused on the shrine, scouring for anything to sacrifice. He didn't have much, for he had brought very little with him to the manor when he first arrived. Just a leather bag with a few clothes and some personal items stuffed in it. He had shoved the bag in a drawer in 1899 and never opened it since. He hadn't expected to be here for so long.

Finding a lovely alder tree near the stream buried in the woods, Noah settled into the dirt. He had never built an altar before. What did one usually consist of? A few things to sacrifice? He placed one of the few trinkets he had brought with him onto the twisted roots of the trunk – a rusted compass that had belonged to his mother. She had always been staring at the skies. He added some of her jewellery as well, a pair of earrings he had taken when he left home. Was that enough? He didn't have much more to spare. But the sun had begun to set, and the evening was ticking away. Noah felt the panic start to build. How could he be sure the goddess was listening to him? This all felt very similar to a magical ritual. He wasn't sure he liked the idea of that.

But desperate times called for desperate measures. Pulling out the photo of him and Meredith, Noah went to work on his talisman. It felt wrong to scribble on the back of the picture, but he hoped the goddess understood it as the sacrifice it was. *Goddess Athena, protect her.*

When the ink had dried, and there was nothing else to do, Noah buried the picture in the ground before the tree, along with the compass and earrings. It pained him to cover the photo with dirt. It was the one thing he had of Meredith, and it felt like a sin to bury it in the ground.

With the last of the dirt packed, Noah bent his head down to the earth and prayed. He wasn't a religious man. His mother hadn't raised him to believe in organised religion. Tonight, though, he would call on any deity, spirit, and mystical force he could think of. One day, he just had to get through one day. So long as Makenna didn't come to the house, everything would be fine.

"What are you doing?"

Noah whipped around at the sound of a voice. Behind him stood a young boy, aged twelve years old, wearing a baggy comic book shirt and blue jeans. "Cody, what are you doing here?" Noah pushed off the ground to his full height and he took in Cody. The boy had a toothy grin, his bright red hair dishevelled and always in his eyes. If a person were patient enough, they could count the freckles on his nose.

"Are you just going to stand there?" Cody said when Noah didn't answer him. "It's kind of weird, but whatever, dude."

"I'm just—" How to explain it?

"Were you crying?" Cody asked. There was no mockery in his voice, just pure curiosity.

Noah wiped at his face, streaking dirt on his cheek. "No."

Closing the distance between them, Cody leaned awkwardly into Noah's side and hugged him. Noah must have looked to be on the verge of tears. "I hope you feel better, man." Noah's arms hung in the air before wrapping around Cody's thin shoulders.

"Me too, *man*."

"I have this comic in my room if you want to read it," Cody offered as he pulled away. "It's X-Men. If you want something to get your mind off of—" Cody's sentence was cut off by the tensing of his body. A distant look came into his eyes as he focused on something Noah couldn't see.

Noah immediately dropped to his knees and grabbed the boy by his scrawny shoulders. "Cody, can you hear me?"

The boy was miles away. "Please don't," Cody whispered. "Please." The word was long and drawn out, laced with absolute fear.

How many times had Noah tried to pull Cody out of his nightmare? It had been a long while since he'd been trapped in one. Of everyone in the house, Noah was most likely to pull Cody out of them, if he was lucky. It was often that once an episode started, Cody was doomed to relive his trauma in its wicked entirety.

Digging his nails into Cody's shoulders, Noah hoped to pin the boy to his spot before he entered another part of the memory. It wasn't always chronological. Cody seemed to relive various parts of his trauma in random order, sometimes reliving the same event multiple times.

"Cody, stay with me," Noah breathed. Cody had had an episode last night, though it had been short. How long would this one last? An hour, maybe two? It was hard to tell sometimes. Wherever the nightmare took him, it was hard for the others to follow. And tonight, of all nights, with Makenna so close. Noah couldn't risk anything going wrong. He needed to protect her, but he couldn't do that when Cody was in an episode.

"Cody, don't—" but the boy was gone. He bolted into the night, too quick for Noah to hold him down. *Shit*.

Noah turned towards the house before pivoting back to

his shrine. Had he done enough? Were his prayers and talisman enough to keep *her* from this cursed house? He hesitated for a moment before an ear-splitting scream echoed through the air.

Cody.

Noah threw one last silent prayer to his shrine and took off for the manor. The screams continued as Noah whipped through the back door and into the kitchen. A woman in her early thirties stood by the island, creating a display of cut flowers from the garden, their colours delicate. Rose's hands twitched over the flowers as she looked up above to where the screams echoed through the floor.

"He's doing it again," Rose said, her voice flat. She looked almost bored, more focused on the flowers at hand than the boy reliving his trauma upstairs. "He was here for a second. I tried to grab him, but he was gone before I could." Abandoning the flowers, she smoothed a hand over her dark brown hair, perfectly coiffed. "He's upstairs."

Without a word, Noah passed Rose and dashed out of the kitchen. Every step he took felt like a delay in protecting Makenna. What if Cody's cries stopped Athena from hearing his prayer? How could he protect Cody and Makenna at once? He was just one man. Clamouring up the stairs, Noah darted into the first room on the second floor. The room belonged to no one simply because it was one of the places Cody frequented during his flashbacks. There was no furniture, the windows were always drawn with thick velvet curtains, and dust had collected on the empty shelves. Throwing the door open, Noah found Cody backed into a corner, tears streaming down his face.

"Cody, it's me. It's Noah." He inched closer in the room when he heard someone else follow him in. It was Maryam. She sidestepped Noah, her demeanour far calmer and reassuring than his.

Cody wasn't looking at either of them. "I can't," he kept saying, his chest rising and falling rapidly. "I can't bring her back." He sobbed harder, trying to burrow closer into the corner as Maryam approached him.

"My dear," Maryam said. Her voice was soft and warm, like a heavy blanket on a cold night. "You are safe. You are among friends here." She stretched out her hands, palms up as she inched closer to the boy.

For a moment, Cody seemed to come back to them. His eyes focused on Maryam, rather than the figure who haunted his nightmares. "Maryam?"

She smiled at him. "Yes, my love. Noah is here too." She twisted slightly to give Cody a view of him. "Can you tell me what day it is?"

Cody blinked a few times before his eyes darted down to his hands. "It's October fifth," he managed to get out.

"Good," Maryam reassured him. "And what time is it? There's a clock on the wall above the closet. Can you read it?"

The boy's eyes darted to the clock frantically. "It's nearly midnight."

The smile on Maryam's face was kind. "You are doing so well, my boy. Now, can you tell me what year it is?" She moved closer, but the movement seemed to spook him. His focus drifted again, and before Maryam could catch him, he darted from the spot. The boy was as fast as the wind, avoiding Noah's outstretched hands a second time in one night. Maryam cursed under her breath. "When did it start?" she asked, hands gripping the air.

"Just now. We were out in the garden when he began to slip." Noah clenched down on his back teeth. "I had him in my hands, Mar. I had him, and I still couldn't keep him from slipping. And now Makenna – I can't protect both of them at the same time. Not today."

The woman took in a measured breath. She didn't bother reassuring Noah. Everyone had had Cody in their grasp at some point when he began to slip. No one had managed to stop it. "I'm going to look for him." She passed Noah, leaving him alone in the room. Why did it feel like he had disappointed Maryam somehow?

Slowly releasing his jaw, Noah listened hard. The best way to look for Cody was to hear him and follow the sound. His screams were like a macabre breadcrumb trail. Moving out into the hall, Noah closed his eyes, thoroughly divided between what he should do. The manor was large. It creaked and moaned of its own accord, cast in shadow most of the time. When he couldn't hear anything, he moved down the hall and began checking room by room.

His own was the last he checked. Not a usual place for Cody to pop up in an episode, but Noah was a thorough man. Then he heard it, the scream. It was muffled and came from beyond Noah's bedroom, out in the garden below. Racing to the window, Noah nearly slammed his face into the pressed glass to see outside. The air escaped his lungs, and his heart stopped beating when he saw him. Out on the lawn, Cody stood, caught between a scream and a sob; only this time, he wasn't alone.

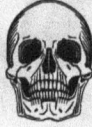

4

The Freaking Gate

The scream echoed through Makenna's dream like a knife splitting the night air. It was sharp and ear-splitting, loud enough to rock her soul and shake her awake. She sat bolt upright, sweat dripping down her forehead. She felt disoriented as she tried to find her bearings, her environment cast into darkness. It took a second for her eyes to adjust as she remembered; she'd fallen asleep on the paisley couch in the living room.

What time was it? After midnight, most likely. *Time for bed, proper*. Makenna was about to peel herself off the couch when the same blood-curdling scream from her dream stopped her in her tracks. It was a horrifying sound, one that ricocheted off the walls and made Makenna cover her ears.

The scream pierced through the night again, laced with pain and sorrow. It shredded any sense of sleepiness she might have felt. Twisting to the window, Makenna tried to peer through the darkness when the wailing stopped. Heart pounding, she leapt from the couch to the front door, yanking on her Converse as she hurried out of the warm house and into the chilly night air. The door slammed shut behind her as she bolted through the yard, the screaming starting again. It reverberated through the darkness, and Makenna chased after the sound. It seemed to come from across the street, beyond the gates guarding the manor. She paused for a hot second at the end of the road, before the iron gates that guarded the manor's property and cut into the dark night. Huxley's words from earlier echoed in her head. He wasn't sure about the new owner and had expressly told Makenna to stay away. Was the groundskeeper's hunch right? Was Makenna walking into danger she had been warned about?

The scream shattered the stillness of the air again, and any thought of self-preservation vanished. Someone needed help, and Makenna was the only one nearby by a long shot.

The iron gate before her was locked, and rattling its thick bars proved useless. It wasn't too high to climb, though. Mustering her wits, Makenna scrambled to the top before slipping, her right hand slicing open on one of the sharp pickets. She cried out but quickly stifled it. The pain seemed inconsequential as the screams echoed through the grounds. Throwing the rest of her weight over the top, Makenna dropped and hit the compact earth hard. Her ankles tingled as she made impact, but she shook it off before continuing towards the screams. They seemed to radiate closer to the manor.

Now that Makenna was further in the property, the lights from the house added some illumination to the grounds. On the grass before the manor's grand doors was a boy, his red hair lit brilliantly from behind. It circled him like a halo, making him look like an angel. The scream that ripped from his mouth was anything but heavenly.

Racing towards him, Makenna noticed he had blood

on his hands. She slid to a halt on the wet grass, nearly tumbling backwards before catching herself. Was someone here? Were they both in danger now? The boy stopped screaming and dropped to his knees, a deep sob racking his chest. His agony was enough for Makenna to throw caution to the wind. She closed the distance between them, ignoring how the sprint left her gasping for air. Frantically, her hands ran up and down his arms to assess the damage.

"Hey, hey. Can you tell me where you're hurt?" she said between breaths.

The boy let out another sob. "They're all dead." He was frenzied, trying to get to his feet to push Makenna away. "All of them."

The thumping in Makenna's chest pounded in her ears like a thunderstorm. "Who's dead? Are you hurt? Who did this to you?"

"I'm next," the boy agonised. "He's coming for me. I can see him." His voice was shrill as he let out another wail. She didn't think twice as she grabbed the boy and pivoted back towards her house. She didn't get far, for a middle-aged man stood not but twenty feet away from them on the manicured lawn. He held his hands out, his dark eyes wide as he approached them. Oh god. Where did Makenna go? Her path home was blocked by a murderous man.

There was little thought as she swirled around and raced to the manor with the boy still wrapped in her arms. She wanted a thick door standing between them and the man that terrorised them. She could lock the man out, use a phone to call the police, and hide while they waited.

With the boy still securely in her arms, she seized one of the brass door handles and jerked it open. It was heavy but swung with enough force. Dropping the boy on tiled floor, Makenna turned around to yank the wooden door closed before locking it securely. Her chest heaved as she waited for the man to pound on it. However, it wasn't the sound of a psycho killer on the other side of the door that made her jump.

"Stop!" a deep voice cried out from above. Makenna whipped around, no longer sure if the danger was outside or in this very room with them. The voice belonged to another man, and for a second, Makenna wondered how many threats were on this property. He flew down a set of grand stairs that wrapped around the room, coming right at them. Makenna backed into the door, feeling for the lock behind her. What was safer – remaining here or escaping back outside?

The man stopped himself short at the bottom of the staircase, his hand holding onto the railing with white knuckles. He couldn't seem to let go, as if it was the only thing holding him up.

Eyeing the crazed man with great trepidation, Makenna noticed how young he looked, perhaps only a few years older than her. His hair was incredibly dark, and from where she stood, Makenna could see his eyes matched his hair's deep tones. He seemed to embody the shadows. It was as if they clung to his shape as he moved. Aside from his appearance, the most remarkable thing about this man was the way he looked at her. It was with pure agony.

Makenna stood frozen in place. She didn't have any words to fill the dreadful silence, so she pointed to the boy that had brought her here. He no longer stood before her, though. In fact, he seemed to have vanished from the very spot Makenna had set him down. She baulked, not sure how he had slipped away from her. "There was a boy," she breathed. It was hard to look at the man before her. His gaze was too intense, his breathing too hard.

"He was right here." Her voice barely came out a whisper.

"You shouldn't be here," the man accused. "I did everything." His tone was cold as the look in his eyes changed. It wasn't agony anymore; it was anger. The look frightened Makenna, and she pushed further back into the door. She couldn't hear the psycho killer on the other side, and the fact the boy had vanished into thin air spooked her a great deal. Feeling blindly behind her, Makenna grasped the lock and slowly undid it. She felt better having an exit strategy.

"Don't come any closer." Her voice came out remarkably loud as she held out a hand to stop him. "Or I'll call the police."

"Will you now?" the man spat, his words laced with animosity. He looked almost feral.

"Let me go, and there won't be a problem. Just give me the boy, and we'll both leave." Pushing the door open a crack, Makenna popped her heel outside.

The man finally let go of the railing, and he inched closer. "You think this is a joke? That you can just leave?"

Makenna swallowed the panic in her throat that cut like glass. This man scared her. This entire house scared her. It felt wrong. All of it. "Where's the boy?"

Another presence cut the man off before he could respond. A middle-aged woman with lovely brown skin and thick dark hair stepped into the room. She wore a traditional red dupatta over clothes that would have been stylish in the seventies. "Noah, I found Cody in the study. He seems to have settled for now," the woman said as she walked into the entranceway. When she spotted Makenna, she halted. All colour drained from her face. "Oh, Noah. I'm so sorry."

Makenna had had enough of this. When the man

seemed distracted by the woman and her misplaced condolences, Makenna slipped through the door. She would tackle the man outside if she had to. At least it would be one on one, not her against a full house of potential killers. There was no one outside though, no man threatening her escape. This whole situation was beyond her now. The cops needed to get here as soon as possible. The boy was still in danger, wherever he had scurried off to hide in the house.

They're all dead. All of them. His words echoed in her mind, driving a spike of fear. She prayed he would remain hidden until the police arrived.

The air was brisk as she sprinted across the lawn. She had never run this fast in her life, her eyes continuing to scan for any other threats as she pumped her legs. She ignored the sting in her hand as she plotted out her escape. The cut was the least of her worries for the moment.

She was close to the gate now and the path seemed clear. The screaming from earlier had stopped. Makenna didn't dwell on what this might mean. When she got home, she would call the police immediately. Then she and her mum would drive as far away from these deranged people as possible.

The gate was far enough from the manor that the porch lights didn't reach. It didn't matter; the sky was clear and the moon was full enough that Makenna could make her way through the shadows. She would leave the way she came. Across the street, she could see her house, tucked away behind some lush trees. She could be off this insane property in a minute or two.

Grabbing the gate, Makenna hoisted herself up and kicked off the ground. She got a fair bit of air, but the minute she nearly had herself over, she tumbled backwards. She had never been a climber as a kid. It was pure luck she had made it over the first time. Plus, her palm ached fiercely. Wiping her hands on her leggings and smearing blood on them, Makenna launched herself again. She couldn't seem to get a grip on the bars, though, and again, she landed back on the ground.

Holy hell, she was wasting time. Peeking over her shoulder, Makenna stifled the scream in her throat when she noticed the first man. He stood a good fifty feet from her, watching, like a harbinger of death. Was he plotting her murder too?

With a mangled croak, Makenna threw herself at the gates a third time, only to slide down the poles pitifully. Good god, was going over the gate out of the question? She would crawl her way out of this nightmare if she had to.

"It's not going to work."

Makenna let out a half shriek as a young girl approached her. She couldn't have been more than sixteen, with crimped black hair in a deep side part that hung at her shoulders. She was Asian, with thick smudged eyeliner under her eyes. While her makeup may have been dark, her clothes were loudly patterned and baggy. They echoed the eighties, at least as far as fashion trends went.

"Who are you?" Makenna asked, though her voice didn't have the authoritative tone she had hoped it would. There had been enough people popping in and out of thin air this evening.

"The Ghost of Christmas Past," the girl drawled. "Who do you think I am?"

Jerking her head between the girl and the gate she was having a hard time climbing, Makenna squeezed her eyes. "I can't get over the gate. And there's a man trying to kill me. And I lost the boy. Oh god." Her eyes flew open again, scanning the lawn to assess how far off the man was now, though he was nowhere to be seen. She whipped her head around, searching for him.

"Am I going crazy?" she whispered, more to herself than anything.

The young girl stood by and watched, her arms crossed over her loud eighties jumper with a bored expression on her face. "No one is trying to kill you. And you're not going to get over the gate. I can't promise a lot of things, but I can promise you that."

Makenna ignored her. Maybe this part of the gate was just bad. What bad meant, she didn't know. She needed to try another section, though, or maybe get her hands to stop shaking. Back on her muddied feet, Makenna followed the property line, sprinting further down. The girl in the bright clothes kept close while still giving Makenna enough room to attempt another jump.

"Damn it." Makenna's palms stung as she flopped back and landed on her palms. "What the hell?"

"Hell is a good word for it," the girl said.

Turning on her, Makenna jabbed a finger at the iron bars that kept her from freedom. "There's a murderer on the loose, possibly two. We need to get out of here. Is there a key? Do you know where one is? Can you open the gate?"

"Would you like me to turn water into wine while I'm at it?" The girl raised a thick eyebrow. "Who do you think I am, Jesus? No. No one gets out. There is no key. There aren't any murderers, and the gates never open. You're stuck here just like everybody else."

Makenna shook her head violently, her heart sinking in her chest. "That's ridiculous. It's a freaking gate. Why won't it open?" she said breathlessly.

The girl ran a hand over her face. "Has no one explained it to you yet?"

Something about the girl's tone felt ominous, and Makenna's panic changed. It wasn't the same panic as earlier, when the child was screaming or the strange man was charging at her. That was adrenaline-filled panic. It moved her body from fight to flight. This panic was more profound, more menacing somehow.

"Explained what?" Makenna demanded.

The girl dropped her arms to pop a hand on her hip, her dark hair blowing across her face as a breeze picked up. "You're trapped here. We all are. No one leaves, ever. Including you."

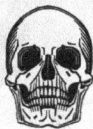

5

I'm Here

"I've been here since the eighties." The girl pulled at her clothes and hair as if it were obvious.

Something between a laugh and cry caught in Makenna's throat. "That's stupid. I've been coming to my gran's house for years before I moved in. I think I would have noticed the neighbours not ageing."

The girl cocked her head to the side. "No one else can really see us. It's part of the curse."

Curse? Makenna let out a ridiculous laugh. "I'm not cursed."

"If you say so."

It was too much. The girl, the house, the stupid gate that wouldn't do as gates should do. Why wouldn't it just open for her already? Makenna turned her back on the girl and began pacing alongside the fence again, exhaustion settling into her bones. She just needed a sweet spot to get out. There had to be something.

"You're not going to find anything. I've been trying for nearly forty years," the girl called after her.

Makenna wouldn't stop. She was shaking now as she

jogged further along the fence, leaving the girl and her silly delusions behind. This was a dream, a nightmare. Makenna would wake up tomorrow in her bed, cosy and warm with leftover cake to eat for breakfast. Whoever this girl was, she was playing a cruel joke on Makenna. She didn't look a day past sixteen. There was no way she had been here for nearly four decades.

Finding no weak points in this direction, Makenna pivoted on her heel to try the gate's entrance again. Her legs were barely keeping her up at this point as a terrible sinking sensation pulled on her limbs. When she got to the entrance, she found the latch to be as securely locked as it had been from the moment she first jumped over. Makenna grabbed at the cool bars with both hands and shook them violently. "Help, please," she called. "Anyone! Someone let me out." Her voice carried through the night. It seemed to echo in the dark but had little to no effect. No lights popped on in her house across the street. There was no movement or any sign that the only person in a two-kilometre radius had heard a disturbance. Makenna raised her voice louder, pushing it to the point of breaking.

"Mum, I'm here!" She rattled the bars as hard as she could, blood dripping down from the cut on her palm and staining her sleeve crimson. She felt frantic as her calls faded into the night. Soon they turned to sobs, riddled with desperation. "Please, Mum, I'm scared." Her chest ached from the effort as she sank to her knees. How could her mother not hear her? Makenna had heard the boy's screams so clearly.

"She isn't going to come," a new voice said. It was the woman from before, the one who had walked in on Makenna and the strange man in the manor. "She can't hear you." The woman came up to Makenna and slowly bent down to her level. Behind the woman stood the teenager. She didn't look as smug as she had earlier. Her eyes were wide and her lips downturned.

"Siobhan, would you leave us?"

"Fine," the girl said with a huff as she sulked away.

"I'm sorry, my dear. Siobhan can be a lot sometimes, but she means well." Closing in on Makenna, the woman put a warm arm around her.

Makenna tried to inch away, but she was already backed up as far as she could go. The iron gate loomed above her, imposing as its pointed spears shot up into the night.

"I know, but I'm not going to hurt you. And you can't stay out here forever. Let's get you inside and get that hand taken care of." The woman was surprisingly strong as she lifted Makenna to her feet.

"I want to go home," Makenna pleaded. "I want my mum."

The woman said nothing to that, just gave her a small smile. "It will be warm inside. The air is so chilly, isn't it?"

"The boy. He was hurt," Makenna said, resisting the woman. "There's someone in the house, two maybe. They're dangerous. I could hear the screams. The boy was screaming so loud." She choked on the end of her words. It was hard to speak right now.

The older woman rubbed Makenna's arms soothingly like a mother would console a distraught child. "Cody has episodes, flashbacks, if you will, from a deeply terrible time for him. He is quite all right now, I assure you. You were very brave to jump the fence to come to his rescue." She nudged Makenna forward, but she didn't move.

"He had blood on his hands."

"He tends to scratch himself in his episodes. It's not uncommon for him." The woman tugged Makenna again. "Come now. Let's get you inside."

"Do I have a choice?" Makenna asked. Tears hovered on the edge of her lashes. She batted them away. "I can't seem to get out. I can't get home."

The woman took a step forward and Makenna followed on shaky feet. "I'm sorry, dear. There is no other choice. Come inside and we can get you settled and explain it all."

Makenna twisted her neck to stare back at her home. It looked so tiny, so sleepy. It had no idea a terrible tragedy was happening right across the road. "Okay."

The walk back to the manor was a blur as the woman guided her. Makenna felt as if she were floating as they passed through the grand doors. There was a word for this feeling; numb. It didn't feel human.

Inside the entrance stood a small collection of people: the two men and the young girl from earlier. Every fibre in her being told Makenna to bolt, but the older woman tightened her grip on Makenna's shoulders. "They will not hurt you," she whispered soothingly. "All of you, be gone," she hissed to the others.

Makenna closed her eyes as their footsteps drifted away. When she opened them again, only one person remained: the man who had yelled at her earlier.

He stood at the bottom of the stairs, his face unreadable. He didn't say anything as the woman directed Makenna into an ornate room left of the entranceway. Makenna felt suddenly exhausted as she was ushered into what looked like a private library. A great fire roared in a hearth, its flames licking blackened stone and filling the room with a warm glow.

"My name is Maryam. Take a seat on the couch. I'm going to go get something to treat your hand. I'll be back in a second," the woman said.

Maryam disappeared through a set of wooden doors,

leaving Makenna alone in the chilly room. The fire did little to warm the shadows. That, or Makenna couldn't stop shivering from disbelief. Finally, by herself, she felt the numbness pass. It was quickly replaced by a deep-seated sadness and the strangest sense of déjà vu. Had she been here before? What had the young girl, Siobhan, said outside – that they were all trapped in this house, and no one was getting out?

Unsure of what to think or do, Makenna made her way to the large bay window. Pressing her head against the glass, she felt the coolness of it against her cheek. She was beyond exhaustion, the adrenaline wearing off and leaving a shell of a person behind. Maybe this was all just a bad dream. Maybe all she needed to do was wake up.

6

Memories

"You made a real mess of that one, didn't you?" Maryam scolded Noah as she brushed past him to collect some first aid essentials.

They were in the kitchen, a large room that had last been remodelled in the 1960s. Maryam rummaged through the pantry. Finding some gauze, she added it to her growing pile on the island counter. Noah sat on one of the plastic bar stools, his head in his hands as Maryam berated him.

"How bad was I?" he moaned. Noah looked up at Maryam, only to find Charles had joined them in the kitchen. The man leaned against the end of the island, eyeing Noah. Charles was the epitome of what it meant to be a gentleman; he was easily the most forgiving person Noah had ever met and by far one of the kindest in the house. He was Black, of short stature, and made entirely of muscle. His coarse hair was shaved close to his head, and his kind eyes had only begun creasing at the corners. Charles leaned back from the counter and began rolling up his plaid sleeves in his typical fashion.

When Maryam refused to answer, Charles cocked an eyebrow. "It was that bad when she got in the house? I didn't mean to spook her on the lawn."

"He yelled at her," Maryam finally said. Seemingly satisfied she had collected all the appropriate first aid supplies, she gathered her bundle to take to the shaken girl in the library.

Noah whipped his head towards the older woman. "I did not."

"You were like a dog on the attack. You frightened her." Maryam dropped all the supplies onto a metal tray before filling a glass of water. "In all my years, Noah, I have never seen you like that."

With a groan, Noah dropped his head back into his hands. "She caught me off guard. It was barely after midnight. I thought I had more time."

Charles rounded the corner and gave Noah a solitary pat on the arm. "I didn't think she'd be here so early. I would have camped out in the house otherwise."

"I should have known she'd be here right at midnight. I was going to man the perimeter." Noah thumped his hand on the table. "The veil between life and death is always thinnest for a person on their birthday. She could hear Cody because of it. I – I should have made sure she didn't get in."

"And how were you going to do that?" Maryam questioned. "Were you going to run up and down the gates like a guard dog and bark at her if she came near?"

Noah laid his head on the table. "I don't know what I would have done. I would have figured it out when the time came. I would have been damned not to try."

"I think you're damned enough," Charles said with a shrug.

"I should go talk to her. Apologise." Noah stood up

straight in his chair, feeling energised suddenly. He pushed himself away from the counter, but an arm shoved him back down.

Maryam was on him like a cat on a mouse. "Oh no, you don't. You have made quite the mess already. Throw Siobhan and Charles in there, too, and you've all done a right good job of scaring the poor girl. Honestly, all of you."

Noah stayed where he was. "You think I've scared her?" That had never been his intention. Truth be told, when Noah had seen Makenna through the window on the lawn, he had blanked. All he had felt was anger at the universe for dragging her into this. He hadn't meant to take it out on her. "Surely I should apologise?"

"Indeed, you will. But for now, give that girl a second to breathe. Let her accept her surroundings before you overwhelm her with all *this*." Maryam pointed at Noah from head to toe.

"But that's all of me," he blanched.

"Exactly." Maryam balanced the glass of water on the tray and gave the two men a nod. "Now, if you'll excuse me, I'm off to do damage control." She backed out of the kitchen and let the door swing closed behind her.

Silence settled over the two men as Charles tried to look everywhere but at Noah. "You don't agree with her, do you?" Noah finally asked. "You don't think I overwhelm people with all this?" He pointed to himself in much the same way Maryam had.

"I think you feel things very deeply," Charles said. It was the perfect, dignified response. He always had the right answer for everything. Noah wasn't quite so diplomatic. He tended to wear his emotions on his sleeve, as Siobhan liked to tell him.

"I didn't mean to frighten her." Noah reached for the

vase left by Rose on the island. "I would never intentionally hurt her. But she shouldn't be here." He felt better having something to occupy his hands, even if he made a mess as he plucked at the flowers. Better to destroy a bouquet than destroy a girl's life.

"I know," Charlie reassured him. He was about to say something else when a loud bang echoed through the walls. It was deafening, and Noah had to fight the urge to cover his ears. When the sound died out, both he and Charles were on their feet, already moving. They didn't want to wait for another.

∽

WAKE UP, Makenna thought, but this nightmare would not end. Her entire being felt drained and yet wired at the same time. Her body ached for her bed, yet her mind would not settle. She was having a hard time sitting still. It was one thing being in this house; it was another being told she was trapped in it.

Part of her didn't believe Siobhan. People didn't get trapped in houses. That sounded like a curse, and curses belonged in fairy tales. Makenna's dad had often read those types of stories to her and Rory before bed. He had grown up with a German mother, and no one wrote horrifying tales quite like the Germans. Those stories had meant to frighten misbehaving children who lacked manners. While Makenna was not a badly behaved child, she was positively frightened. Something about the walls around her felt *final*. It was an odd word to describe it, but the sense of finality in this house was so prevalent, it made her skin crawl.

Beyond the sense of finality, Makenna wondered at the creeping suspicion that she had been here before. The feeling was distant, like she had visited the manor in a dream. There was an ethereal quality to this house, and despite never having stepped foot on its property before, the walls were familiar.

Shaking her fingers out, Makenna began to pace the room. The man, this house, the déjà vu; it was overwhelming. Maybe this was an elaborate joke. It was October, after all. Could someone have orchestrated this as a sick Halloween prank? It was far beyond Jacqueline to pull off. Too cruel even for her. Paige, maybe? But she was off at school doing god knew what. Maybe Makenna going off her meds had been more detrimental than she realised. Perhaps she was just straight crazy.

A prank seemed like the most obvious answer.

Makenna stopped her pacing and stood in front of the roaring fire. The heat felt good on her cold skin. She was only wearing leggings, a thin shirt, and a blood-stained jumper that had soaked up the chilly night for the last hour. Had it even been an hour? What time was it?

If only she had her phone, she could call someone. It was probably best to get the police involved now. They could break the gates open easily. This whole thing had gone on for long enough. Makenna needed away from these crazed people and their ridiculous claims they were all stuck in the house. She didn't feel safe here. There was no point wasting time being scared when she could be doing something about it. Abandoning the fire, she went in search of a phone in the expansive room.

"Looking for a phone?"

Makenna froze as the older woman from before returned, a tray of supplies in her hand. Maryam, Makenna remembered. "Excuse me?"

"A phone. That's what you're looking for, is it not? You won't find one. Not in the entire house."

Makenna smacked her lips. "I'm going to call the police." She pointed a stiff finger in the direction of the entrance. "Wherever that little boy is, he needs help. Professional help. And I'm going to get it."

Depositing the tray on the coffee table, Maryam smiled at Makenna. It wasn't a cheerful smile she wore, but neither was it condescending; it was weary, if a little sad. As nice as she seemed, Makenna kept her distance from Maryam. "We could all use help. Trust me. When I first realised I was stuck, it took a great deal of time to get used to the idea."

"I don't mean to be rude," Makenna said with a new edge to her voice, "but I'm done with all this. I want to go home."

Maryam took a glass of water from the tray and circled the couch. She was only the coffee table's length away from Makenna. It felt too close. Stretching out her hand, Maryam offered the glass to her. "Please have a drink. I realise how stressful this all is. The water will help calm you."

"I don't want a drink; I want out," Makenna spoke slowly and precisely.

"I know. And I wish I could help you. I will do everything in my power to try and help you, but for now, it's best to remain calm." Maryam held the glass out further.

Makenna was tempted to knock the drink from her hand. "You're scaring me."

Maryam dropped her hand and took in a steady breath. "I realise this is scary, Madilyn, but——"

"That's not my name," Makenna interrupted her. "I never said my name."

The older woman tightened her lips. "I apologise. You just remind me of someone I once knew."

"I think I better be going," Makenna said, dropping all

pretences of propriety. She had no patience for this anymore. "This house isn't safe, and I don't want any part of it." She skirted around the couch and headed for the double doors Maryam had brought her through.

Maryam called out to her, but Makenna was well over it. Grabbing the door handles, Makenna yanked on them. They flew open with the loudest bang Makenna had ever heard. It seemed to shake the house and everything in it as it rang in her ears. She nearly turned around to apologise to Maryam, as if she had been the one to cause the sound. Then her eyes caught movement at the top of the stairs.

It was a boy, *the boy*, clawing his way down the velvet runner on the steps, inching his way towards the door. He was on his hands and knees, thick blood oozing from his shoulder – or what was left of it. Behind him, at the top of the stairs, stood a man holding a rifle. He wore a torn bomber jacket and had the same ginger hair as the child. Each had red smeared across their faces. The boy cried out as he pulled himself down the stairs with one arm, trying to put distance between himself and his assailant. Makenna lunged forward, unsure of what to do but knowing something had to be done. She made it halfway through the entrance before the man pointed the rifle at the boy.

The scream that left Makenna's lungs burned her throat as she bolted for the boy. She didn't get far before a pair of arms wrapped around her, stopping her momentum and yanking her back. It was the young man from before, the dark-haired one who had stared her down on these very steps. He had an iron grip on Makenna as he dragged her away from the horror show on the stairs.

"No!" Makenna wailed as she tried to claw her way out. The man's grip was unyielding. She was just about to bite down on his arm when a second bang ricocheted through the room. The sound was deafening this time. The boy gurgled as blood began to seep from the open wound on his neck. He was a mess of mangled flesh, covered in crimson and gore.

The man on the stairs cocked his gun for a third time, aiming to kill. Makenna couldn't move, and if the raven-haired man didn't have her locked in his arms, she would have sunk to the floor.

"We have to let it play out," the man said in her ear. "Otherwise, Cody can't get out of the memory."

Memory?

The gun shot off, clocking the boy in the head. He stopped moving, having crawled only halfway down the stairs. The ginger-haired man stared down at the boy as he dropped the gun to the floor. It hit the ground with a horrible thunk. With a blank expression on his face, he made his way down the stairs, stepping over the body as he headed for the doors. He opened them with a new sense of humanity he hadn't had a moment ago and let them shut behind him.

Makenna let out a sob. This time her legs did collapse beneath her.

"I've got you," the man said. His grip on her tightened as he held her up. "Look at me, okay?"

But Makenna couldn't pull her eyes away from the scene. The boy lay still, his body a ghastly sight as blood poured down the stairs, a crimson trail of brutality. Makenna couldn't breathe. He had been in her arms just earlier, fearful for his life.

"Makenna, look at me," the man before her said again. He stroked at her hair that had fallen loose from its bun. "This is a memory. He's dead. Cody's already dead and has been for a long time now."

His words pulled her from the shock that had riddled her useless. "He's what?" Her voice was barely a whisper.

"He's already dead. He's a ghost. Look." He pointed back to the stairs. The blood, the gore, the absolute trauma was nowhere to be seen. Only the boy remained, sat in the very spot he had been blown apart in. He was perfectly put together now, not a drop of blood tarnishing his clothes. It was as if the whole thing had never happened.

Makenna tore herself out of the man's arms and this time he let her go. She fell to her hands and knees and crawled to the wooden stairs, inching up them one at a time until she was in front of the boy. She was dearly afraid he would revert to whatever Makenna had just witnessed.

"You're new," the boy said. He looked at Makenna with confused curiosity. His eyes were heavily lidded, and his shoulders hung with exhaustion. He couldn't have been older than eleven or twelve, with his crooked teeth and thin limbs. He took a second to better look at her. "Oh wait, you're the girl from across the street."

Makenna tried to keep her face even. She had to bite down on the back of her teeth before she could answer him. "I am. And you must be Cody."

What had the man said, that Cody had been reliving a memory – reliving his death?

"I am," Cody said. His face brightened up slightly at the mention of his name. "What's your name again? I have trouble remembering things sometimes."

"I'm Makenna. And I think I might be going crazy."

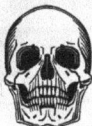

7

Not Dead Yet

"I don't think you're crazy. I'm the crazy one. Ever since I died." Cody shrugged, his eyes a little distant as he and Makenna sat on the stairs.

"I—" Died? The word *dead* was being tossed around a lot in the last few minutes. How was that even possible? Ghosts didn't exist. They didn't haunt houses, and they certainly didn't relive their deaths in traumatic flashbacks. Makenna felt she was losing her grip on reality. Had she hit her head recently? Horrific car crash on the motorway while visiting family? Maybe she was laid out in a hospital bed, fantasising vivid illusions in a coma. Her mother probably stood over her body, no tears to be spent on the wasted potential of her daughter. Just eternal disappointment. Maybe Makenna badly needed those meds she had so heedlessly chucked in the bin.

Supposing Cody was actually dead, what did one say to a deceased child? "I'm so sorry you had to go through that."

"I can't help it. The others try to stop me but – dying's not very fun, is it?"

It was getting hard to keep her face straight. Makenna could feel her lips quivering. "I don't think so. No." This boy reminded her so much of Rory.

Cody inched closer to her and dropped his voice. His eyes were so full of earnest. "When it gets too much, I focus on what I loved when I was alive. I think that helps."

Makenna lowered her head. She was having trouble looking Cody in the face. It was incredibly draining to focus on what she loved in life, not when there was so much death around her. "You're very brave," Makenna said more to fill the silence than anything.

"It doesn't feel that way. I just don't have a choice."

Makenna was about to respond with another superficial answer when the two were interrupted. The raven-haired man cleared his throat to draw their attention to him. He stood at the bottom of the stairs, his stance far less aggressive than before. "Cody, would you mind if I talked to our new guest for a little while?"

The boy shot up, fingers twisting together. "I'm sorry, Noah. I didn't mean to—" he waved his hand in the air. "I know this night was important to you. I'm sorry for interrupting." Cody's eyes darted back and forth between the two. "I didn't mean to miss her coming here."

Before Makenna could ask what the boy was talking about, he stood up and bolted from the spot. She watched him scurry up the stairs before disappearing down a hall.

She turned to the man next. His eyes darted around the room, unsure of where to look. He seemed jittery. Where had all the aggression gone? His nervousness made him seem softer, though, more approachable now.

"So, I'm crazy," Makenna said for him. "That's it, isn't it?" She stood up slowly and wrapped her arms across her chest.

"No," the man, Noah, said. "You're just trapped, like me."

Makenna took a step closer to him. He was a handsome man with a strong jaw and soft lips. His lashes nearly touched his eyebrows. Who gave boys the right to be so pretty? "You better start talking, Casper, or I'll put you in a second grave."

Noah rolled his shoulders out. "We should probably sit for this conversation."

"I don't want to sit," Makenna argued. *Lies*. She wanted so badly to sit. The adrenaline had worn off and she was running on nothing.

Noah opened his mouth and closed it again. "This is a conversation better held in a more private setting. I don't really want to have it out here in the open."

Did Makenna continue to argue for the sake of being argumentative? Something about this man irked her, but she couldn't quite put her finger on it. Maybe it was the way he looked at her? There was a weightiness to his gaze. No man had any business looking at her the way he did. Pushing her hair back and out of her face, Makenna watched his eyes follow her hand. She dropped it immediately as the cut on her palm burned. "I nicked it on the gate. It's fine."

"That's why you just smeared blood on your cheek?" There was that tone again, accusatory, angry, frustrated. Noah lifted a finger towards her. "We have very different definitions of *fine* if that's your standard to go by."

Makenna was sorely tempted to rub at her cheek but kept both hands by her side.

"If you come to the library, I can treat your wound and explain things to you. Plus, you look like you really want to sit."

Makenna was already marching down the stairs past

him. "It's not because I want to sit. I could stand all night if I wanted to."

"I'm sure you could." Noah let her lead him into the library. Where the others had disappeared to, Makenna did not know. She tried to listen as she took a seat on the plush couch by the fire but couldn't make out any sounds in the surrounding rooms. Noah grabbed the tray with supplies where Maryam had left it and settled himself in front of Makenna on the coffee table. She tried to ignore the closeness of him and instead, focused on her hand as she held it out to him, palm up.

It was the first time she had gotten a good look at the wound. The skin was split from the bottom of her thumb to her fourth finger and caked with dirt. She had spent what felt like an eternity attempting to climb over the gate while Siobhan watched on in morbid fascination. How many times had Makenna hit the dirt just to pick herself back up and try again?

"It's dirty," Noah said as he inspected it. He held her hand in his, his long fingers turning her hand to better catch the light of the fire. "You need stitches."

"Don't suppose I'll be getting a ride to the hospital, then?" she hissed as her wound throbbed with the movement. Leaning back to access the tray beside him, Noah kept his lips tight. He readied what looked like a suture kit, and Makenna instinctively pulled her hand back. "Oh, no. I don't need Doogie Howser bandaging me up. I need a real doctor."

Noah took the time to clean his hands with some rubbing alcohol before prepping a needle and thread. When it was ready to go, he placed it on a bandage and turned his attention to her again. "I need to clean and sterilise the wound first." Noah picked up a bottle of hydrogen peroxide and shook it slightly.

"That looks like it's going to hurt," Makenna whined as she pulled her hand into her chest. "And what exactly makes you qualified to do this?" She wasn't sure if insulting the man with the needle was a good idea or not, but she felt better for it.

"I'm medically trained," Noah said matter-of-factly.

"In what decade?" Makenna eyed him up and down, noting his out-of-fashion clothes. "You look like a Victorian ghost who haunts children in their sleep."

Noah reached for her throbbing hand and pulled it towards him. She let him take it, more out of fear he would haunt her dreams if she didn't comply. "You're only half wrong," he said as he doused the wound with the antiseptic. She tried not to squirm as the pain burned, hot and fierce. Noah had her wrist clamped between his fingers so she would show no weakness.

"I was training to be a doctor in my time, and while I haven't had much practice, I've kept up on theory and advancements as best I can."

"Your time?" Makenna said, just a tad out of breath from the pain.

Satisfied with the cleaning, Noah went to work on the stitches. If Makenna thought the hydrogen peroxide was terrible, the needle weaving in and out of her flesh made her eyes tear. She bit down on her teeth to keep her moans of pain in check.

"I may not be the most current medical professional, but this is simple enough."

He hadn't quite answered her question, so Makenna pried. It was better to have the distraction anyway. "You're all dead, aren't you?" she said, just for clarification. "How long have you been here? Just how out of practice are you?"

Noah was gentle with his movements, his eyes focused

on the task at hand. "I'm not dead like the others. I'm cursed, stuck between life and death, I guess you could say. I've been here for 126 years, to be exact."

That wasn't the answer Makenna had been expecting, and she jolted with surprise. The motion made her hand twitch out of his careful grasp.

"Careful," Noah said, though his tone was softer.

"You look good for a cursed 126-year-old," Makenna said as she tried to keep still.

"Technically, I'm 149 years old. I was twenty-three when I got stuck here." As he came to the end of the wound, Noah tied the thread off skilfully.

"I think I might be ill," Makenna said. A queasiness settled into her stomach, her head tingling with an airy sensation. "Or I'm about to pass out. You can handle both, right? You're qualified enough for that?" The joke didn't land very well, for Noah's eyes shot up to her face with deep concern. It made her uncomfortable how intensely he looked at her.

"Do you need to lie down? I can fetch a cold cloth for you."

"No, no," Makenna placated him. "I just feel very weird. This is a lot to take in." Her body temperature was well above normal too, and Makenna resisted the urge to tug at her jumper's collar. Noah would just fuss even more if she told him. Why was she so damn hot now? "I just don't like the idea that I'm stuck here." Makenna focused her eyes on Noah's hands. His stitches were rather precise considering he was an out-of-practice, half-dead physician. "Where exactly is here?"

Noah set the needle and thread down to begin wrapping her wound, his eyes still not meeting her face. "Hell. Purgatory. Limbo. Some combination of all three?" When her hand was wrapped, Noah dropped it and pushed back.

He seemed to want some distance between her and him. "Those who die here become trapped. No one has been able to escape or move on –whatever you want to call it."

"I don't remember dying," Makenna said. Her body felt heavy now that her wound was dressed and taken care of. She could have drifted off to sleep right here and now. "I heard a scream and hopped a fence. So why am I stuck?"

Noah hesitated, pursing his lips together before he spoke. "You broke the barrier between life and death when you helped Cody, a ghost. The living and the dead don't mix, but you crossed that line. Now you're stuck in the same force that holds all the spirits here, just like me."

"And you haven't tried to escape?" The question hung between them for an awful second.

"Of course I have," he finally said. "But I've been here for so long. Even though I'm not dead, my touch on humanity has *faded* over the years." He held the word with so much distaste that it unnerved Makenna. "I don't think I could leave if I wanted to. Maybe if I had found a way when I'd first become trapped."

Makenna's shoulders dropped. She hadn't even hesitated when she heard Cody scream. Seeing him on the lawn, so afraid – he had reminded her of Rory so much. "Getting trapped seems like a shitty price to pay for trying to help someone." She would have done it again if it had meant saving Cody. "So, who did you help that got you stuck?" Makenna said with a yawn.

"You need some sleep." Noah stood up from the table. "We can talk about this in the morning."

"I didn't think the dead slept," Makenna said. "It seems like such a living person thing to do, being tired, I mean."

"You're not dead. Just stuck." He held his arm out to

her like the proper gentleman she supposed he was. "I'll answer any questions you have in the morning."

Makenna gave him her good hand and let him help her up. "Where are you taking me now? Am I about to witness another execution?" There was no humour in her voice. She caught the grimace on her escort's face before he turned from the fire to lead her out.

"There are more than enough rooms here. You can have your pick in the morning. For now—" he led her out of the library and to the grand stairs that swept up from the tiled floor. The velvet runner seemed too pristine for the horror that had occurred on these steps tonight. Makenna felt almost queasy as she stepped around the spot Cody had bled out on.

"How do a bunch of ghosts manage a house? Are there no actual living people here? All the lights are on." Makenna let Noah steer her through the upper level, her curiosity the only thing keeping her awake.

Directing her to the west wing, Noah stopped in front of a wooden door. Makenna nearly bumped into him, too distracted by the ornate design of the house. Everywhere she looked, she saw a mix of luxuries from different time periods. It seemed both confused and charming at the same time. "Humans have lived here on and off for the last few centuries. There haven't been any since Cody's time. No one wants to buy a house—"

"—That a little boy was murdered in." Makenna wrapped her arms around herself. "I don't remember hearing about a boy who was murdered here. My nan must have kept that from me. I always swore I saw people living here. Turns out it was just ghosts."

With a nod, Noah opened the door. "There's a certain level of mysticism. We've always been able to turn the lights on, hold and move objects – interact with the house, you could say. The afterlife doesn't exactly come with a manual."

Noah gestured her in, letting her take the lead into the bedroom. It was cosy, if a little oversized for one person. A large window looked out onto the back garden with a four-poster bed nestled in the far wall. The sheets were clean and pressed, crimson red dominating the colour scheme. There were more pillows than Makenna knew what to do with. Opposite the bed was a large dresser and a door to a private bathroom. To her left was the loveliest vanity set Makenna had ever seen. It was marbled white, the mirror carved with delicate detail.

"If this is the afterlife, I'm already doing better than I was alive." Makenna furthered into the room. She let her hand dance across the vanity before turning to the bed. One could get lost in the pillows if they wanted to.

"You're not dead," Noah said again. He stood in the door, seemingly unsure of what to do with himself. "There are clothes in the dresser if you desire a change of attire. I can have some food brought up to you if you like?"

With a flop, Makenna sunk into the bed face first. Everything was luxurious. The sheets even smelt of lavender, rather than the old musty scent she had been expecting. She had never been in such opulence before. "I'm not hungry. I ate my weight in cake this evening. But I could do with some water." Her voice muffled as she spoke into the duvet. How had she not realised how thirsty she was? Her throat felt ragged. Probably from all the screaming she had partaken in this night. She felt numb as she wrapped the blanket around her.

Noah indicated to a glass already on the vanity. Makenna had missed it in her go-round of the room. "Maryam was here. The tap water is safe to drink should you need more from the bathroom sink."

Pushing up from the bed, Makenna twisted until she faced Noah. His face looked sharp in the dim light of the room. "I think I'm in shock," she said, surprising both her and Noah with her honesty.

"It's been a big night for you," Noah answered. He seemed to teeter on his heels. Was he debating coming closer to comfort her? In her exhaustion and delirious state, Makenna wasn't opposed to the idea. She had never had a handsome man comfort her before. She had pushed all away who had even tried to get close.

"I feel numb, but at the same time, I feel like I've been electrocuted. It's like my body wants to go to sleep, but I know something terrible has happened. I don't think I could sleep if I tried. Does that make sense?" She searched Noah's face for something, anything to make this unusual feeling stop. "I know I need to get out of this house, but I don't think I can move from this spot right now."

Noah held his hand out as if to offer her some profound piece of advice. Makenna leaned forward, eager to hear it. "Just try to get some sleep," he said after a few seconds of posturing. "If you're in shock, your body needs time to rest. You've had a lot of adrenaline in your system tonight."

Smacking her lips, Makenna nodded. "A true doctor, through and through. If only you had been a psychologist. I think my head is fucked."

"Good night, Makenna." He didn't linger a moment longer. As he backed out of the room and closed the door gently behind him, Noah never once broke eye contact with her. There it was again. That same feeling she somehow knew him already.

Turning to the vanity, Makenna pushed herself from the bed she had sunk into to drink the water. She gulped it down greedily and headed to the bathroom for a second glass. Her thirst quenched, Makenna crawled back onto the mattress with stiff limbs.

How odd her actual bed was just across the street, now entirely out of reach. What would her mother do when she woke up to find her daughter missing? Would Jacqueline call the police? Would she search for her daughter herself?

Throwing the decorative pillows off the bed, Makenna settled into the mattress and pulled the thick blanket over herself. They would probably look for a body and never find it. Such a strange way to end the day. After all, how many people got to spend their birthday with the dead?

∼

THE DOOR CLOSED SOFTLY behind Noah. It took every fibre of his being not to crumble against the wood and weep. With whatever strength he could muster, he pulled himself from the door –and Makenna – and found his way to his room. It wasn't far from hers, just across the hall. Noah had strategically chosen that room for her. Any disturbances, and he would be the first to know.

"You outdid yourself tonight."

Noah nearly jumped out of his skin as he closed his door behind him. By his prized bookshelf stood Lydia, touching his books with far less care than he would have preferred. "Lyd, I'm tired."

Stretching on her tiptoes, Lydia tried to grab a book on the top shelf, her blond plait falling over her shoulders. The book was a hair above her reach. "Help me, would you? That one, please." She pointed to the desired text.

"*Moby-Dick*," Noah read as he came over to pull the book down. "It was your husband's. I thought you hated anything that reminded you of him?" He held it out to

Lydia but pulled his arm back just before she could grab it. "How exactly did I outdo myself tonight?"

Lydia's eyes rounded. "I did hate my husband. But this isn't about me. You went from an angry stranger to the perfect gentleman in less than one hour tonight. That poor girl must not know what to think of you. I thought I told you we would figure it out? Overreacting doesn't help anyone."

Lydia swiped for the book again, but Noah held it just out of reach. "I've already had this conversation with Maryam. And so far, no one has figured anything out. Now she's stuck."

Lydia gave him a sympathetic look. "I know, Noah. I'm just saying that screaming at her might not have been the best way to go about it. And then to come in like a white knight to fix her hand right after. You're confusing her. You need to give her some space."

Pondering Lydia's words, Noah forgot to yank the book back a third time. Lydia snatched it. "I was upset." His lips pulled down.

"You should have let Charles stitch her up. He did his fair share of stitching men in the Second War. He could have sewn her up just fine." Thumbing through the pages of the book, Lydia bit her lip. "You just want to be close to her whether it's good for her or not."

Noah was tempted to rip the book right out of her ghostly hands. "I just want what's best for her."

Lydia moved to the door, having secured her prize. "As you should. Just ease her into things. Don't rush her. You're still a stranger to her, remember that." Lydia was almost out of his room.

"I know. And I'm trying. All I do is try—" Noah choked on his words and Lydia stopped to bow her head.

"Of course, Noah. I know you are. We'll keep an eye

on her while you sleep. She'll be here in the morning. I promise. She'll be safe."

"How do you know that?" He couldn't hide the ache in his voice. This house was a curse, a stain on the earth. It hurt anyone who stepped foot in it. Why would Makenna be the exception?

"You just have to trust me. We won't let Makenna suffer. I promise." Drumming her fingers on the book, Lydia offered him a sad smile. "Good night, Noah. I'll see you and Makenna in the morning."

Lydia let the door close firmly behind her, shutting Noah alone in his room. How many times had they had this conversation? How many people had gotten trapped in the hellhole that was this house? No one had been saved. And as much as Noah wanted to believe Lydia's words, they felt empty to him. He just didn't have the heart to tell her that.

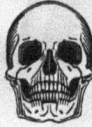

8

Milady

The bed was comfy but unfamiliar. Makenna peeled herself from under the covers and tiptoed across the cold floor to the window. She surveyed the garden below while rubbing the sleep out of her eyes. It was a beautiful landscape that stretched out from the house, lush with trees and paths that crisscrossed lazily. There was a gazebo off to the left, next to a sleepy creek that disappeared into the trees.

Makenna didn't know the lay of the land yet, not on this property. But she would explore. The gates might have had some weird mysticism that kept her locked in, but it was a big property. There had to be some way off it. Noah's little story last night didn't sit right with her, and sitting still and accepting her fate was a no go. It made her skin itch. And she'd be damned if she faded over the centuries like Noah had.

Maybe if she followed the river? Surely the gates didn't circle the entire property. With little else to do in her room, Makenna set out to explore the house. If it was going to be her new prison until she could escape, she would get to know it well. It took her mind off the idea that she was trapped here with the dead. That was a novel thought she wasn't about to get used to.

She wondered how old this place was as she explored the upstairs. Her hand throbbed, and she gave in to the urge to shake out the pain. It still ached something fierce as she looked around the long, winding hallways.

Anytime she had asked about this place growing up, she had been warned to stay away. There had always been a certain allure to the house, but Gran had done a good job of keeping Makenna on the other side of the gate. *"The manor is old and falling apart. You'll get hurt if you go in there. The neighbours are unfriendly and do a terrible job of keeping up the place. Stay out."* Gran's voice rang clearly in Makenna's head. But Huxley had always been there, always monitoring the gate, and he had never been unkind. He had always been a warm presence when Makenna chatted with him by the fence.

Oh Huxley. What had Noah said last night? Everyone in the house was dead except for himself? It couldn't be true. Not Huxley, the jovial man who always begged her for the town gossip. Not the man who always offered her a smile on her worst days when she passed by.

She had to find him.

Her search didn't last for long; after a few ventures down corridors that led to rooms Makenna felt uneasy snooping through, it was on her fourth roundabout in the upstairs hallway that she heard the familiar voice.

"My girl." It came from behind her, as warm and inviting as the day they had first met. Turning around, Makenna was greeted by the most charming smile. "It seems you didn't stay away, after all." Huxley opened his arms and Makenna raced to close the space between them. His was the first familiar face she had seen. She had never had many friends growing up, especially not since moving to her grandma's house. Huxley had been that quiet but constant presence across the street. His hug nearly brought her to tears.

"I just couldn't stay away from you," Makenna said before backing up and clearing her throat. "I've had an awful night." She couldn't hide the crack in her voice, or the way tears welled in her eyes.

Huxley was quick to brush them away with his thumb, a smile still tugging on his lips, though touched with a hint of sadness now. "Ah, but look at you, already on two feet, out and about. Nothing slows you down, does it?"

"I met Noah."

"Did you now? He's quite the man, isn't he?"

Makenna shook her head, still in disbelief. "He told me everyone here is dead. Except for him."

Huxley's smile finally faltered. "I'm afraid he's right, my dear."

"So, you're—"

"Indeed I am. I died in 1912." He spread his hands and gave a soft "Boo" before wiggling his eyebrows. "Not scared of me now, are you?"

Makenna sprung forward to wrap her arms around him again, the tears flowing freely now. "Huxley, no."

He gave her a moment to mourn as he rubbed soothing circles on her back. "Hey now, I've been dead a long time. There's no need to cry over it. I've long ago accepted it."

She clutched on to him harder before finally releasing him.

"I'm still as dapper a dude as ever, as the kids say."

"Forever a dapper dude," Makenna said with a strained laugh. "Is that why you always wore the same outfit?" She looked down to his regal attire, a smart coat and nicely pressed trousers. He had always looked more like a bellman than a groundskeeper. Makenna had just assumed it came with the territory. The manor always spoke of wealth, even for those who managed the property.

"I'm just glad I died wearing a respectable outfit. Imagine if I had passed wearing slippers. The horror," he said, properly scandalised. "And now you've come from the outside world in." He hesitated, and unspoken words were shared between them. Makenna was trapped. Both of them were stuck in this house now, one in life and the other in death. "How about a tour?"

How lovely to have someone show her the ins and outs of the place. It would save Makenna the time exploring and getting lost. She could devise her escape better this way. "Please, lead the way."

Offering her an arm, Huxley directed her down the hall. He pointed out various points of interest and gave Makenna a history of the house as he did so. "This manor was built in the 1700s, you know. It has belonged to many families, often changing hands when tragedy struck." They were on the grand stairs now in the foyer. How different the entrance felt in the daylight. The chaotic energy from last night had dissipated.

"How many of you are here?" Makenna asked. *How many have died here?* "I've met a few of you so far. Are there others?" The two had yet to run into a single soul yet. "Do ghosts just hang around? I feel like that would get boring."

Huxley waved his hand. "There are nine of us in the house. Fear not about being bored. Time passes differently for the dead. You don't realise how much of it has passed until the living come to remind you. Their hair and clothes change, and their gadgets advance. I must say, you'll have to explain to me all about the internet. I've heard Cody talk about it a few times, but I don't quite grasp the concept."

"The internet is complicated to explain," Makenna said. Upon seeing Huxley's face fall, she changed her tune. "But I'll do my best."

Seemingly satisfied with her answer, Huxley pulled her deeper into the house. "These are the stairs to the attic, though I encourage you not to go up there." He pointed to a narrow passage that led up into darkness. A heavy presence seemed to seep down the steps, polluting the area around it. "Harriet, one of the oldest ghosts in the house, occupies that space. She's very . . . territorial, if I may. Best to avoid it."

Makenna made a mental note not to venture up the shadowy stairs. They didn't look inviting to begin with.

"The library you've seen, but the kitchen is a marvel in and of itself. I watched them install the highest of technologies back in the sixties. You will simply be blown away. Come, come."

The two chatted amicably as they moseyed down through the house and into one of the most outdated kitchens Makenna had ever seen. The colours clashed, the patterns were obnoxiously loud, and the appliances looked to be one step from complete failure. Huxley looked mighty proud as he showed her around the room.

"You must be starved. There's quite the supply of canned goods in the basement. Shall I fetch you something to eat?" The man looked more than eager to please, and Makenna could not refuse such an honest face. He reminded her of the grandpa on her dad's side, a kind man who made sure no grandchild went unfed or unloved.

Makenna bobbed her head, even if she didn't feel hungry. "Of course. I haven't eaten yet."

"I would be careful with his food. He doesn't have the best track record."

Makenna swivelled on her heels. A third person occupied the kitchen now, sitting in one of the chairs tucked against the island.

A woman with a thin face and brown hair that was curled short and pinned at the back glared at Makenna. She wore a lovely pale pink dress, her neck adorned with a delicate necklace. She twisted the necklace between perfectly manicured hands, her lips pressed together.

Huxley stood in the doorway to the cellar. He seemed offended at first, but then cracked a devilish grin. "Rose, you rascal." He laughed as he dipped into the basement. That left Makenna alone with Rose, who ripped into Makenna inch by inch with her eyes.

"I've always wondered about the fashion of this decade. What do you call those things covering your legs? Not much left to the imagination, is there?" Rose continued to pick at her necklace. "I would never be so bold."

Makenna resisted looking down at her black leggings. She felt relatively modest. Her burgundy jumper nearly covered her bum and left much to the imagination in her own opinion. Besides, Makenna had been at home about to get ready for bed. She hadn't been trying to win any fashion awards when she ran to help Cody. "They're called leggings. All the rage these days. Comfort and mobility." Makenna squatted so deep her mother's personal trainer would have been proud. "And sweat wicking too."

Rose sat up straight and let go of her necklace. Scandalised, she covered her mouth with a delicate hand. "I have never seen a woman behave as such."

Rose was going to be in for it if it was this easy to rouse her. Jacqueline always chided Makenna for her ability to rile people up. "You can lunge in them too," Makenna stressed with a large step forward. "Really activates the quads."

With a huff, Rose pushed herself away from the counter. "If this is how society is raising the modern woman, I am terribly concerned about the future of this country."

"Just wait until you see American women." Makenna was sure to give Rose a cheeky wave as the woman huffed her way out of the room.

"Did Rose leave?" Huxley asked when he returned from down below. He had several cans of food stuffed under his arm. Makenna didn't want to know when they had expired.

"She had other things to tend to." Taking the seat Rose had abandoned, Makenna leaned on the counter with her forearms as Huxley went to work. "So, the room Noah gave me overlooks the back garden. I was wondering how far this property goes? I couldn't see much beyond the trees." Any information was helpful for finding a way out. The sooner the better.

Huxley tossed a pot on the stove and emptied a slop of food into it. The sound of it hitting the bottom of the pot was rather unpleasant. "The property is quite large – about 300 acres. There's a church. And a stable, for horses were the primary mode of transportation once, you know. Unfortunately, there was a fire in the 1940s, and it was severely damaged."

The smell of something peppery hit Makenna's nose. "And the gates, do they go all the way around the property?"

"They end at the creek. It's a natural barrier. The property ends with the water."

"A creek?" Makenna would press for as much information as possible. This could be a viable way out.

"A creek that empties out to a lovely pond," Huxley answered. Makenna noted it as the man continued stirring the pot. Huxley inhaled deeply, his eyes closing. "Oh, to be alive and to eat again."

Makenna didn't have the heart to tell him the smell was less than favourable. "How does death work? Are you capable of feeling touch? Smelling? What can ghosts do and not do?"

"We are here but not fully. I can catch whiffs of smells, feel the slightest of textures. It's as if there is a thin veil cloaking everything in the living world, separating me from it by just enough to know its loss." Huxley had a distant look in his eyes, the wooden spoon he had been using to stir the food long forgotten. "If there's one thing I miss most, it is the taste of food. I have tried to eat a few times over the years, but it turns to mush in my mouth."

"I'm sorry," Makenna said. "I never thought much about death growing up, not until my brother died." In truth, she hadn't thought much about death since. She had been so focused on the loss of life and not the actual death itself. What happened to her brother after his passing? Was he stuck wandering the hospital halls he had died in, missing the taste of food as Huxley was? Makenna had never returned to the hospital after she said goodbye to Rory. What if he was still there, waiting for his family to return? Had she left him there all alone, wondering if his family would ever come for him? She turned her head away from Huxley and squeezed her eyes at the thought, a sick feeling settling in her stomach. If she ever got out of here, she would return to the hospital and search for him. She made that promise to herself.

Finishing with the food, Huxley set a handcrafted bowl in front of Makenna. It was filled with some form of chicken noodle soup, though it looked suspicious. She was almost tempted to push the bowl away, especially with the nausea hitting.

"Eat, please," Huxley said, eyes wide to encourage her. "I haven't cooked in a very long time. I do hope it tastes good."

Makenna gave him an appreciative thumbs up. It was hard to disappoint this man.

"Does every soul get trapped when they die? Is there no direct way to—" she pointed upwards. "I don't even know if that's right. Is there a heaven or afterlife where people truly rest?"

Huxley shrugged after giving the question some thought. "I wish I had an answer for you. Everyone who has ever died in this house has become trapped in it. I don't know if that applies to death in its entirety. What a cruel thing that would be."

Makenna picked up the silver spoon and swirled the noodles, unsure of the bite she was about to take. Huxley would be none the wiser if it tasted bad. "Very cruel indeed."

～

NOAH PACED the library with renewed anxiety. Makenna was here. She was in the house, and danger wasn't far behind. This house took from everyone who stepped onto its property, like a greedy leech hungry for the misery of others. Makenna wasn't safe as long as she was here. And every minute she spent on these grounds, she was closer to the house taking *everything* from her. Being trapped was one thing. Dying here was another. But as long as she was alive, Makenna still had a chance of breaking free. Noah had been half alive for too long. His touch on humanity had slipped long ago, taking his odds of breaking free with it. But Makenna – she had a fighting chance.

"You'll wear a hole in the carpet," Maryam said from the couch, her head buried in a well-loved book. The pages had begun to fray decades ago. "And I like that carpet. It's vintage."

Noah halted his frantic pacing long enough to scowl. "Are we more concerned with the antiques of the house than the person's life we are trying to save? We must have missed something. We should devise a plan to keep an eye on her, so nothing else bad will happen."

"*We*, is it now? And here I thought I had just come to watch you ruin the carpet."

"Maryam," Noah said, slightly exasperated.

"What if we just killed her ourselves? Maybe death by ghost cancels it out somehow, you know? Cause we're already connected to death? It could set her soul free so she escapes the curse," Siobhan offered. She lounged in the bay window, watching the low-hanging clouds that threatened rain any minute.

Noah pinched the bridge of his nose. "You are not suggesting that we try to prevent her death by straight-up killing her ourselves?"

Siobhan shrugged her shoulders. "No one's tried it before, so who's to say it wouldn't work?"

"I didn't expect purgatory to be filled with such nuts," Noah moaned.

"And in your hundred-plus years here, you've come up with a better idea?" Siobhan sassed. "You've clearly never heard the saying, 'It's so stupid, it just might work.'"

The heavens unleashed their fury then, rain cascading down in a violent rush. It pounded the windows mercilessly.

Maryam set the book down on the coffee table. She had dog-eared a page once, and after the earful Noah had given her, she never did it again. "I don't think that would work. The dead killing the living just makes more dead. There's enough of us around here."

Siobhan swung her feet off the window seat and leaned forward. "As if you would know. I say we do it, and if it works, you'll all thank me."

"No one is killing anyone. I don't want to have to repeat myself." Noah leaned against the handcrafted fireplace. How many times had he stood here, pondering this damn house and the spell it held over everyone? "If we can keep a twenty-four-hour watch on her, maybe we can prevent anything from happening. And I don't want anyone to tell Cody it was him who brought her over the gate, either. We don't need to trigger another episode or make him upset. There's enough pain in this house as it is."

"Do you blame Cody for bringing her over the gate?" Siobhan asked, eyebrows raised.

Noah's mouth turned to a thin line. He hadn't wanted to admit it, but some small part of him did. He didn't like that part. It was ugly, but he couldn't shake the feeling that Cody was responsible. Any other night. Cody could have picked any other night to have an episode. Why on her birthday, when the curse was in full force and everything was at stake?

Noah ran a hand over his face to shake the resentment settling into his chest. "Makenna is here now. That's all we need to focus on. Keep her safe in this damned house."

"Are you going to tell her how dangerous the house is?

Or are you just going to babysit her for the rest of eternity?" Siobhan asked.

Noah maintained his composure. "I don't want anyone telling her anything," he said, shoulders tense. "Not yet. For now, we'll just watch her and keep her safe, somehow. And figure out where it all went wrong so it doesn't happen again."

"If that's all you're doing, you're doing a shit job of it. She's been up and wandering the house for hours without you," Siobhan said matter-of-factly.

Noah's head whipped around. "What? You mean she's up?"

"Relax, Noah. She's in the kitchen with Huxley," Maryam said, her hands out to calm him.

Noah didn't wait. He was already zipping his way through the room and into the kitchen. He probably didn't need to kick the door open with so much enthusiasm, but he had long ago appointed himself as Makenna's guardian angel. To know she was running around without his protection pained him deeply. Both heads in the room turned to face him as he entered; Huxley was busy cleaning some dishes while Makenna finished the last bite in her bowl.

She looked as sleep-deprived as Noah felt, but in the daylight, he was struck by her beauty. Makenna was all sharp angles, fair hair, and light grey eyes. The complete opposite of him. Daylight and Midnight.

"Morning," Noah said in an attempt to make a smooth recovery from his rapid entrance. "It's raining outside."

Huxley raised an eyebrow, managing some serious second-hand embarrassment. That was a term Noah had learned from Cody. It felt rather fitting right now.

Makenna twisted in her seat to peer out one of the bay windows. "You're not wrong."

"Noah, the way you burst into the room, I was sure something was on fire," Huxley said, his second-hand embarrassment turning to concern. Was the old man trying to help Noah or hinder him?

Grimacing slightly, Noah tried to make a smooth recovery. "I thought something was burning." He would work with what Huxley gave him.

The older man turned to Makenna and frowned. "Did I burn the food? I'm so sorry. I thought I'd cooked it as the instructions indicated. Was it that bad?"

Lifting her bowl, Makenna showed him the empty dish. "No, no. I ate it all up, see?" She turned to Noah and shot him a dirty look as if to scold him for insulting Huxley's cooking. Would Noah need a third try to recover? Perhaps it was best to abandon such thoughts and change the subject.

"Since you're done eating, I thought I could give you a tour of the place," Noah offered.

"Huxley has shown me most of the house. We only stopped so I could eat," Makenna said. "He's a lovely tour guide, my good sir."

The older man puffed out his chest, smiling at her compliment. "Well, I had a lovely guest. Very attentive, milady." He touched his fingers to his brow and bowed slightly, Makenna doing the same back to him. There was a strange twisting inside Noah's chest, and he knew immediately what it was: jealousy. A little monster that didn't belong there, but Noah couldn't shake it.

Clenching his teeth, Noah tried to ease the pain in his lungs. "I'm sure Huxley wouldn't mind if I finished off the tour, would you?" Noah walked over to him and gave Huxley a good clap on the back.

"I think that's up to the lady," Huxley offered. He

swung a dish towel over his shoulder and popped out his hip, his hand resting on it.

Did Noah feel his eye twitching? This morning was off to a bad start. "Of course." He looked at Makenna, trying not to appear too hopeful.

The girl stretched in her chair, tipping her neck to each side in a stretch. "I kind of wanted to go off on my own for a bit, if that's okay? Maybe explore outside. I like being in the rain, and it would be good to get some fresh air after last night. But thank you for the food, Huxley." Makenna shot him a kind smile, and that jealous beast in Noah's chest roared a little louder.

More than a little defeated, Noah gave her two thumbs up. It was another cue he had picked up from Cody. He hoped he was using it right. "I'm here if you need anything or have any questions."

"Thanks," Makenna said as she hopped off her chair and put the bowl in the sink. "Guess I'll see you all around. Not like there's far to go." She gave a small, awkward wave as she exited the room. Did Noah imagine it, or had she given him a wider berth? He wished he could accompany her, but Lydia was right. He was still a stranger to her. She didn't know she wasn't to him.

"There she goes," Huxley said after Makenna left.

Noah frowned, confusion in his voice. "What do you mean?"

"She's going on a rampage to break free. It's heart-breaking to watch."

Noah ached at the thought of Makenna desperately trying to find her freedom. This house was scary, full of strangers, and she had just been told she was trapped for eternity. It was an overwhelming fate to accept. She didn't even know death was in the cards, solidifying her fate here. Being alive was the only chance of breaking free. While Noah had accepted his fate long ago, he needed to give her the chance to do the same. "All we can do is try and keep her safe. Let her figure things out on her own and help her when we can."

"I promise, we'll do our best to keep her safe," Huxley said, his eyes soft and full of a hope that Noah struggled so hard with. He at least felt better knowing Makenna had a group of guardian angels protecting her, whether she knew it or not.

9

Try, Try Again

The creek Huxley had mentioned earlier was far closer to a river, if Makenna were being so generous. It indeed snaked through the back of the property, but the water rushed at a rapid speed, its levels coming up high above the banks and pouring out into a pond. The river's width was substantial, and there seemed to be no bridge in sight. In the hundreds of years this house had stood, had no one thought to build a bridge? The torrential rain had done a good job of nearly flooding the whole area. It was far too dangerous to swim across and try the other side.

With a huff, Makenna was forced to abandon her watery escape and instead trudged her way back to the front lawn and to the towering gates that locked her in. Wind and rain lashed at her body as she tried to get a grip on the iron bars. Was this part of the curse? Makenna couldn't even get a hold of them as the rain came down with a vengeance. Maybe it would be better to wait it out and try the gates when the weather had cleared. Makenna had felt so confident she could get over them today.

Had her mother realised she was missing yet? It was early afternoon. Jacqueline would be wondering why Makenna hadn't gotten up by now. What would she do when she found Makenna's bed empty? Would Jacqueline search the house, call the police? Maybe she would just assume her daughter had gone out for another long walk and think nothing of it. But enough time would pass that Jacqueline would grow suspicious. If Jacqueline came out of the house right now, would she see her daughter banging at the hell gates?

Makenna's hand stung as she wrestled with the bars to try and get over them. Would everyone just assume Makenna had been kidnapped? How long would it be before they held her funeral, while Makenna stood perfectly alive but trapped across the street?

She was so close to home.

The house was less than a minute's walk over the road. All Makenna had to do was get over the gate. She tried once more and slipped in the gritty mud forming at her feet. With a frustrated scream, Makenna kicked at the bars from her spot on the ground. Her clothes were soaked and covered in mud, her hair plastered to her face. She had been scared and frightened last night. Now she was just angry.

Back on her feet, Makenna began to pace the length of the fence. Her teeth chattered, body shaking as the cold seeped into her bones, but she wasn't done yet. She was just getting started. Dragging her hand along the iron, she continued her way down the property. Occasionally she stopped to shake the bars – to try and hop them again. When they didn't budge, and she couldn't find her grip to pull herself over, she let the obscenities fly. They were colourful and desperate. The longer she tried, the more exhausted she felt. She was out in the open, but the property felt increasingly smaller. There was a weight on her chest, and it grew the longer she searched for her freedom.

She was almost in a panic now. How long had she been out here? The rain hadn't let up any, and she had long ago lost feeling in her fingers. She didn't even process the pain from her cut anymore. She was so tempted to crumble down and give up. Her anger had waned and turned to a mixture of fear and grief. With a final scream, she sank to the ground, her back against the weathered gate that had become her prison guard.

Makenna couldn't tell if she was crying; the rain had drenched her completely. She had no sense of time, either. It was possible day had turned to night and back again. All Makenna knew was that she was cold, and this house had become her personal hell.

"My dear, come inside."

Makenna looked up to see Maryam standing above her. She wore a kind smile and had a towel in her arms. At some point, the rain had stopped.

"I don't want to." Didn't want to or couldn't? If this house was Makenna's prison, this spot would be her grave. If only she could sink into the ground and become one with the trees. Being a fern seemed better than being human and dealing with all these emotions.

"I insist." Maryam outstretched the towel to Makenna. "Come inside. I've drawn a warm bath for you. You look positively frigid."

Eyeing the house behind Maryam, Makenna hesitated. "If I'm trapped, I would rather spend my time out here. At least the sky isn't suffocating." She sounded whiny, but Makenna was far past caring. The last day felt like a waking nightmare, and she would be as bratty as she wished.

Maryam crouched down until she was eye level with

Makenna. "You can come back out here when you're all dry and won't catch your death from the cold. Let's get you warmed up, and you can come right back to this spot."

Logical, and yet it still catered to Makenna's emotional needs. "Okay." She let Maryam help her up, the short woman bundling her in the fluffy towel. "I can't remember the last time I had a bath," Makenna said as she let Maryam guide her across the lawn to the house. "The one in my house doesn't work. I always have showers instead." It seemed like such a random titbit to share with Maryam. At least it brought Makenna out of the emotional low she was riding and back to the present.

"My daughter loved baths when she was a little girl. It was the only time she let me brush her hair." Maryam smiled at the memories and brushed some wayward strands out of Makenna's face. Makenna's mother had never been so tender. "Her hair was so thick. Such a tangled mess all the time."

They were back in the house, and Makenna began to shiver violently as they walked through the front door. She had, at some point, become disconnected from her body. Only now did she feel the cold. Upstairs the two walked until they were in Makenna's room. For a property that had been vacant the last several years, the manor was relatively warm. There wasn't a chill to the air, despite a ghost helping Makenna through the house.

Maryam had been good on her word as she directed Makenna to the startlingly white bathroom. The bathtub was full of steaming water, and fresh cotton towels had been folded neatly on the sink. "There's some soap and a brush for you to use. I'm afraid we don't have the luxury of many products to choose from." Maryam was already backing out to give Makenna her privacy. "If you need anything, I won't be far. There's some antiseptic on the sink for you to wash your wound with. Please be more mindful of it." Before Makenna could offer her thanks, Maryam was gone from the room. It was awfully quiet without another person to keep Makenna's thoughts occupied.

Stripping off her soaked clothes, Makenna placed them above the radiator to dry. They were her only clothes now, and it would do her well to treat them with care. She tested the water next and found it pleasantly warm, her skin tingling as she slipped in. It was like a hug she had been too stubborn to realise she needed. Sinking in until the water came to her neck, Makenna squeezed her eyes shut.

The emotional rollercoaster was draining. Angry one minute, sad the next, okay for a few minutes, then rinse and repeat. Sucking in her breath, Makenna submerged beneath the water in an attempt to drown out her sorrows.

The anger from before had spent itself, and now there was only grief. Why did it feel much more overwhelming? The anger had been hot and fierce but burned itself out fast. Grief was capable of hanging on for so much longer. Makenna knew. She had dealt with her depression for years, then her brother passed, and she had lost the will to live. It seemed grief had permanently moved into her heart then. Now it was time to grieve the loss of her own life, and Makenna was woefully unprepared to do so. She had never handled her emotions well.

Her lungs burned, and finally out of air, Makenna resurfaced. The bathroom hummed with the electricity from the lights, outdated just like the rest of the house. How long before Makenna aged out of relevance? Would she become like one of the many ghosts here or something more like Noah? Each seemed lost in their own time. Was this where hers stopped?

She had never gone to school. She had never fallen in love. She had barely lived. So much life, and she had missed out on all of it. And it had been her choice up until this moment. How did you grieve that which you were once so ready to throw away? Now she didn't have a choice. It had been made for her.

Makenna took another breath in and sank beneath the water once more. Peace. This was the only peace she had at this moment, and she would stay as long as she needed.

~

THERE WAS something about the rain that bothered Noah. It was as if he had forgotten something, and the downpour pulled at his mind because of it. He couldn't think of what it was and brushed it off.

For now, he could only focus on what he could control, and that was safety-proofing this house, including locking away all sharp objects that could potentially harm Makenna.

He was in the formal dining room with Huxley and Cody. The room exuded elegance, with a long, mahogany table set beneath an ornate chandelier that bathed the space in soft, golden light. He had every kitchen knife and sharp object he could find in the house laid out in front of him. Each was to be wrapped and tucked away in a chest at the end of the dining room table where it would be locked. He should have done this before Makenna arrived, but a part of him had hoped she wouldn't arrive at all, that the curse would have failed, and she never would have gotten trapped. All of this would have been unnecessary. Alas, here he was.

"She's really pretty," Cody said as Noah wrapped a bread knife in a ratty kitchen towel. He was being thorough. Anything that could harm Makenna. Huxley perched in one of the richly upholstered chairs, kept busy by a newspaper from the 1980s while Cody perused some comic books.

Noah had done a good job of quelling his anger towards Cody, though a thin line of irritation still bubbled beneath the surface. It wasn't Cody's fault, he kept reminding himself. If he said it enough times, maybe he would believe it.

"You mean Makenna?" Noah asked. The boy nodded. It caused his hair to flop in his face. He badly needed a haircut. There was no changing the appearance of the ghosts, however. They became stuck in the last positive image they had of themselves before their death. Only did they reverted to their true death form when emotions got high. "She is, isn't she?"

"A sight for sore eyes," Huxley said as he flipped the paper to the next page.

"She's a lot taller than I thought," Cody said, trying to gauge Makenna's height with his hand.

"Just as tall as usual," Huxley said. "Though she's let her hair grow out since the last time I saw her. The Rachel look, is it not called? I recall reading that in a magazine once. Lots of layers."

Cody dropped his hand, his eyes squinting as if trying to recall a memory. "I remember that show. I think Makenna's prettier than Rachel."

"I will take your word for it," Huxley said with a nod.

Noah reached for a pair of cutting shears he had gathered from the garden, a towel prepped to pad it safely. He couldn't stop his mind from wandering to the blond currently running about in the rain. He sorely wanted to pull Makenna back inside and warm her up, to let her know they would take care of her.

"What say you, Noah?" Huxley asked him. Noah had zoned out and missed the question.

"Sorry?" He felt foolish for not hearing the other two.

Huxley gave the young man a coy look. "I asked if we should have a game tonight to welcome Makenna to the family."

Family. Huxley had thrown that word around since he died and became a ghost. It drove Rose crazy. She argued the dead were stripped of their families and that Huxley shouldn't use it so nonchalantly.

"That sounds like a good idea." It was rather brilliant. Noah could spend some time with Makenna in a casual setting. She clearly was uncertain of him, maybe even avoiding him, but in a group setting, he could ease her mind.

"I quite enjoy the girl," Huxley gushed. "Such a personality. She'll keep everyone in check." He folded his paper down with the grace of someone handling an antique. Huxley's newspapers were as precious to him as Noah's books were to himself. Harriet had torn up a few in a particularly nasty rage in the sixties. Noah wasn't sure Huxley had ever forgiven her. The dead clutched on to what little pieces of the living they had with an iron grip.

"I like how brave she is." Cody had given up on his comics. "Maryam told me how she came running up to the stairs when I was having a flashback. My dad's gun didn't even faze her."

Noah tensed at the mention of it but kept silent.

Huxley nodded in agreement with the boy. "And how she came for you out in the front lawn. She hopped the fence and ran to you without a second thought. Not a moment spent considering the danger."

There was a pause before Cody responded. "What do

you mean on the front lawn? I thought she came into the house, then saw me?"

Huxley's mouth hung open before he closed it quickly. "Did Maryam not tell you? Makenna was in her home when she heard you just after midnight. It was her birthday, after all. She thought you were in danger while you were having a flashback."

Cody's head immediately swivelled to Noah, a look of pure horror on his face. "I – I didn't know. I didn't mean to bring her here."

The shears forgotten, Noah was beside the boy before he could dash off. Every ounce of anger Noah harboured rushed to the surface, but the look on Cody's face quelled it all. "Cody, it wasn't your fault. You were in a flashback." Could Cody hear the resentment in Noah's voice? He tried hard to speak softly, reassuringly, but Cody refused to look at Noah, his eyes red-rimmed. "You've had flashbacks before, and Makenna's never heard them. She could only hear you because it was after midnight on her birthday. The veil between life and death was thin for her. It could have been any one of us to draw her over. You know that, don't you?"

Huxley seemed to realise his mistake and joined Noah in the consolation. "My boy, I promise it was not your fault. The house is nefarious that way."

Cody was beyond listening to them. He struggled to get out of Noah's arms, and when Noah finally let him go, Cody bolted from the room.

"I'm a fool." Huxley's head was in his arms. "I shouldn't have said that."

Noah squeezed his eyes shut before taking a moment to breathe. "No, I should have told you not to tell him." Standing up from the table, Noah cleared his throat. "Watch these, will you? I don't want Makenna finding them before I can properly store them away. I'll go calm Cody down."

Why did it always feel like Noah had to choose between Makenna and Cody? Leaving a room full of weapons piled on the table didn't sit right with Noah, but Cody needed him now. Abandoning Huxley, Noah exited the hall and headed for the one place he knew Cody would be.

Outside, near the back garden, stood a large beech tree. Noah remembered the day a grieving widower had planted it. Noah had watched it grow over the decades. In the nineties, an exceptionally skilled craftsman had built his daughter a beautiful treehouse in the twisting branches. Cody frequented it often after his death, whether in good spirits or not. It was his private space, so it felt unfair that Noah would climb up the tree and invite himself in, especially when Cody wanted so desperately to be alone.

"Go away," Cody said as Noah pulled himself up the ladder and closed the trapdoor beneath him. Cody was curled up on some pillows close to threadbare. There was a single light above them that cast the room into eerie shadows. It made Cody look older than he was.

Sitting himself down, Noah tried to gauge how best to address the boy. "I just want to make sure you're okay."

Cody's lips quivered as he pulled his legs into himself, his face resting on his knees. "I'm fine."

"I appreciate the lie, but I do want to make sure you understand that it wasn't your fault." His voice hitched, and Noah took a second to let the anger subside. In the dull lighting, Noah could see the tears on Cody's face. Why was he punishing Cody for this? It wasn't fair to the boy nor the situation. The curse was bigger than all of them, and Noah seemed to keep forgetting that. Perhaps having a target, someone to blame, was just easier than the lack of control he had always been dealt. "I mean it, Bub." It was a nickname from one of Cody's favourite comics, X-Men. "It was the—"

"Does it matter what did it?" Cody asked, his voice rising as he twisted to face Noah. "I played into it. I let it happen. She's here because of me. And you know it."

Noah shook his head, his own eyes beginning to well with tears. "It could have been anything," Noah said, though his words sounded hollow. "But we'll figure it out. We'll keep her safe."

"And when you don't, guess who you'll blame for bringing her here in the first place?" Cody's face darkened, his eyes wet from tears.

Noah didn't want to think about the inevitable. He wasn't ready to think about how it might end. "No one blames you. I – I don't blame you. Maybe for a second, but it's just wasting energy to think about such things when they simply aren't true."

"And will Makenna not blame me when you tell her I brought her here?" Cody's anger turned bitter. He no longer looked like a weeping angel, cast in the ghostly light from above. He was stone-cold marble, or maybe that was just a reflection of Noah. He was working overtime to keep his emotions in check for Cody's sake.

Noah's words were tight as he gritted the back of his teeth. "No one is going to tell her because she doesn't know about the curse yet, not the full extent. She thinks she's just trapped. I won't have a repeat of last time."

Cody's cold exterior cracked. He wasn't as practised as Noah at keeping his emotions in check. "You won't tell me what happened the last time. None of you will. You don't trust me around her, do you?"

"That's not true. You're just a child and you don't need

to know about some things." Noah's words were calm and measured, yet he was crumbling on the inside.

Leaning forward, Cody crawled on his hands and knees to Noah, begging him. "Please tell me. Let me know so I understand. I don't want to cause you any more pain. I don't want to cause *her* any more pain."

It was Noah's turn to crack. He could feel the overwhelming pain as Cody spoke to him.

"I've already done so much, Noah. I don't want to do anything that would cause what happened then to happen now, whatever it is."

Noah sucked in a haggard breath. "I can't, Cody. Not yet. I'll tell you when the time is right, though. I promise."

Cody reeled back from Noah to wrap his thin arms around his knees. "You still don't trust me."

"No, of course not," Noah baulked, his hand out to soothe the boy, though Cody flinched from him. "It's too dangerous. If I tell you, and it slips to her, it might cause a repeat of last time. I can't have that. I won't survive it. Please, trust me when I say I can't tell you yet, Cody. For her sake. I beg of you to understand me."

Cody's lips quivered and his whole body trembled. "But I want to help." His voice was so small, it nearly broke Noah.

"And you can. We can all keep an eye on her. Anything suspicious happens, and you come running to me. Aye? This is my curse to bear, not yours or anyone else's."

Cody shook his head. "I shouldn't be around her. I already brought her here. Who knows what else I'll do."

Noah's heart cracked as the boy retreated in on himself. "Cody, no. That's not what I'm saying. You're not a danger to Makenna. This house is. I need your help to protect her. That's all I'm asking."

Cody shoved himself as far into the wall as he could

get, putting as much space between him and Noah. "I'll stay away from her. I won't cause any more harm." His lips trembled as he made himself this promise.

Noah stretched out a hand but dropped it. "I'm not asking you to do that." His anger broke as he watched the boy curl up into a shell. It had never been Cody's fault, the sweet boy who didn't have a malicious bone in his body. Noah had been wrong to blame him. If it wasn't Cody, it would be something else that drew Makenna over. There was always something that Noah couldn't plan for.

"I'll stay away," Cody repeated, his voice muffled by his arms. "I can do that for you."

Noah rocked back on his heels, a pit in his stomach. He hadn't intended for this to happen, for Cody to take on all the blame. This was Noah's burden to bear. He hadn't meant to pass it on to Cody. "This isn't your fault," Noah said, and for the first time, he believed it. "Tell me you understand that?"

Cody turned his head away from Noah. "I think I want to stay here for a while. Can you close the door on your way out?" It was a dismissal, clear as day.

I have failed you. Keep Makenna safe but hurt Cody in the process. Or the other way around. He couldn't seem to save them at the same time. Always one or the other.

"I'm sorry, Cody," Noah said as he began to back out of the treehouse. "I'm so sorry." He gave the boy one last look before retreating down the ladder, his hands grimy from the descent. It never got easier, Noah thought as he traced his steps back to the manor. This house. The curse. Just existing. It was all too much. Too many people kept getting hurt. And like many nights, Noah would have to sleep knowing he had no control over any of it. And that was a tragedy in and of itself.

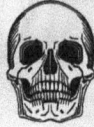

10

Kitchen Wisdom

There weren't any pros to balance the cons of being stuck between life and death. Noah didn't age, but he certainly couldn't die. He had tried more than once. Whatever attached him to this house kept him from death fully. How sweet would the release be? He had spent over a hundred years stuck in this treacherous limbo, his body functioning at some half capacity of living. He still needed sleep, yet he could forgo food and water. He dreamt but only of past dreams, never of anything new. While his body was caught in between, his spirit yearned for freedom – freedom from these walls, freedom to live a life he had been robbed of. He would take death if it meant escaping this hell. If only he would be so lucky.

"Where's Cody?" Charles asked as Noah returned to the kitchen from the garden. His clothes were soaked from the rain that had picked up again. "I just saw Huxley packing up sharp objects on your behalf. He explained what happened." Of all the dead who wandered this house, Charles had been the most at peace with his passing. It hadn't been an easy death, but the man had lived a hard life and found solace in the house. Nothing could ever touch him or hurt him again. He had already made it through the worst of it. That was what he always told Noah, at least.

"Cody's in the treehouse." Noah went over to the fridge and pulled the doors open to stare at the inside. There was nothing in it; it wasn't even functioning. He had watched the living do it enough times that it felt right – at least when he was stressed or bored. He let the fridge door close before pacing around the kitchen. He needed something to busy his hands, and started pulling out drawers, looking for more items he might have missed in his earlier round. God forbid a pair of kitchen scissors be Makenna's downfall. He would collect every sharp and blunt object if he had to.

Charles lounged in the breakfast nook, a thin book in his hand. The dead were fantastic readers. "What did you tell him?"

Was a wooden spoon too risky? Noah held it up to the light, imagining what damage it could do. "That it wasn't his fault. He kept asking about the curse, but I wouldn't tell him anything. It's too risky with Makenna here." He set the spoon down, deeming it survivable.

Charles raised an eyebrow. "I figured as much."

Noah went for a spatula next and ran his thumb over the smooth edge. That felt safe. "I can't keep it from him forever, especially not after he felt so responsible for bringing Makenna here. Now he thinks he has to hide from her or he'll bring about her doom." Noah tried to swallow the guilt that he had put that pressure on Cody. It wasn't going down well.

"Cody's been around long enough that we can't treat him like a kid forever." Charles flipped to the next page.

He had the fantastic ability to read and hold a conversation at the same time.

Noah settled his hands on the counter and stared at Charles as he leaned back in his chair. "But he is, and always will be."

"Just because we're dead doesn't mean we aren't capable of growing. Maybe not physically, but as people, we can. We've all done it. Even you."

"How so? Isn't death stagnant?" Noah asked. He had spent so much time with death, he hadn't given it much thought.

Charles shook his head. "Maybe don't think of death with the sense of finality that most people do. Your body has died, but your spirit lives on. Consider death as post-life. You've had all these experiences while alive that formed you as a person. In death, you get the chance to reflect on them, grow from them, and transform your spirit because of them."

This sounded like something Noah's mother would have said. It directly contradicted the teachings of the Church, which had been so prevalent in Noah's day. There was nothing Noah's mother had loved more than contradicting the Church.

He began fumbling with a stuck drawer, popping his hip against it until it came out. Inside were a few knick-knacks and a rolled-up ball of thick twine. Noah instantly snatched it. Makenna would never lay eyes on this. "That's a rather radical idea."

Charles shot Noah a knowing look. "Most people don't even get living right. Why would they get death right too?"

Before Noah could answer, a rather large yawn passed his lips.

"You look like shit," Charles said.

"I didn't sleep well." In Noah's defence, he wouldn't

have ever slept again if it meant more time with Makenna. But he was trying to do his best to give her space this time, all while proofing the house and protecting Cody from his own blame. It was exhausting.

"Go take a nap, Kiers. She'll be here when you wake up."

Noah fidgeted with the ball of twine in his hands. It scratched at his skin, the material abrasive. "You can't promise that." No one could. Whenever the curse decided it was *time*, it seemed to create a stranglehold on the house.

Charles flipped to the next page in his book. "No, but there's not much else you can do about it tonight. Huxley and I can continue proofing the house." He held his hand out for the rope, which Noah handed over, his fingers tense.

Of all the languages in the world, this man spoke nothing but the truth. It didn't help that Noah's eyelids felt heavy. He had spent the day stressing over that which he could not control while doing his best to control everything. "I'll see you in the morning," Noah said, heading for the stairs. "Keep a watch over Cody, will you?" He didn't wait for a response.

Noah made it to his room and was just about to slip in through the door when he heard a creak. He stopped immediately and swivelled on his heel. There she was, Makenna, in all her glory. Her hair was wet and tied up in a bun, her clothes not her own but of a different decade: burgundy trousers and a loose, burnt orange paisley shirt fashionable in the seventies.

She hesitated when she saw him. "I'm hungry." It was defensive – like she needed a reason to be out here.

"Of course," Noah said. He tried to relax his posture. "There's food downstairs. Charles is in the kitchen. He can help you if you need it. There may be a lack of forks and knives, though."

Makenna furrowed her brow before smacking her lips. "Thanks?" While there was more than enough room between the two in the hall, she kept as much distance between Noah and herself as possible. "You going to bed? It's so early."

Noah didn't have a watch on him, so he felt rather foolish when he checked his wrist. Another thing he had seen the living repeatedly do. "I, uh – I didn't get much sleep last night. I just need to close my eyes for a bit. I'll be down later."

The girl nodded. "Cool. Cool, cool, cool. I'll see you around then."

Noah was incredibly tempted to say he no longer felt tired. "Most definitely." He gave her a tight smile as he opened his door and slipped into his room. It was tough to do, but Noah had to have faith in Charles's words. Makenna would be here when he woke up. Things would be different this time. They had an eye on her. At least that's what he told himself.

~

MAKENNA HAD BEEN afraid to live her life. That was the last thing her brother had said to her before he passed. The words still haunted her to this day, creeping in the back of her mind like a persistent shadowed beast, its talons digging further into her thoughts as the years went by. She had rejected the statement. She wasn't afraid to live life, she just hadn't found a reason to live it yet. Those were two separate things. So she told herself.

This house and its occupants had a way of bringing up Rory's words. They danced in front of her, testing her will to survive. For now, though, survival came down to the very basic need of hunger. How convenient someone had anticipated this need, for there was already a can of ravioli left out for her in the kitchen. All Makenna had to do was pop it in the microwave. She hadn't even realised there was a microwave in the first place. When Huxley made her food this morning, he had done so on the stove. She wondered this out loud.

"It's because he doesn't like the microwave. It's too modern for him," a man answered her. His voice spooked her, causing her to turn around. She had taken an involuntary step back when she realised it was the man from the lawn, the one who had been watching her try to escape yesterday. He was nearing the end of a book, his legs propped up on the chair beside him as he lounged in the breakfast nook.

"You're the infamous Makenna, then. Our newest recruit. A pleasure to meet you. I'm Charles." He had a smooth voice and deep chocolate eyes. Any woman would be flustered to have a man like him look at her.

Makenna gave him a quick wave. "I saw you yesterday, on the lawn, didn't I? I thought you were a murderer, the way Cody was screaming at you. You and Noah both, actually."

Charles's face twisted with a grimace. "My deepest apologies for scaring you. Wrong place, wrong time."

"That seems to be my entire reason for being here," Makenna said, letting her shoulders relax. She hadn't realised they'd become so tense. "Apology accepted. It was a rough night. Not sure I've recovered fully." She forced out a chuckle. "Charles, you said?"

"Indeed, I am." He gave her a warm smile.

"Nice to meet you," she said before facing the cabinets to rummage through them on the hunt for a can opener.

Maybe some sweets if she could find some. "There seems to be a lack of utensils in this kitchen. Not even a single fork or knife. Is that too modern for Huxley as well?"

"Most things are too modern for all of us. I see you people on those small devices all the time. What's so great about them that you can't walk with your heads up?"

"It connects people to the world through the internet," Makenna said. It took snooping through three drawers to find a can opener.

"How so?" Charles put his book down and gave her his full attention as she prepped dinner. "Cody has tried to explain it to me. I regret to say I still don't understand."

How did one describe the internet? "It's like this cyberspace that anyone with a device can access. You can talk to people all around the world – share photos, videos, and more. Most people post things they regret later because nothing ever dies on the internet."

Charles had a far-off look in his eyes as if he were trying to imagine such a thing. "Death, I understand. You lost me on everything else."

Right. Charles was a ghost. He was dead, just like everyone else in this house, aside from Noah. But Noah was a prisoner – as was Makenna now, too.

He seemed to sense the change in her mood and changed the subject. "You know, back in my day, TVs were black and white."

Makenna was glad for the new topic. "Really? I can only imagine."

Charles was about to elaborate when a noise of disgust made Makenna jump in her seat.

Rose stood where Makenna had been preparing her food. The thin woman was bent over the bowl as if smelling the pasta, her face twisting with distaste. "Beef ravioli. How unfortunate."

Something deep within Makenna stirred. It was her own sense of distaste but towards this woman. Something about Rose irked Makenna to no end. "Beggars can't be choosers," she said lightly.

Rose straightened herself and smoothed down her pale pink dress with stiff hands, an air of haughtiness to her. "Thank the heavens I don't have to worry about food."

Makenna blinked a few times. "Are you life-shaming me?"

"I don't know what you mean." Rose's tone was haughty. "I am simply not tied to earthly needs like you are."

There were so many things Makenna could have said at that moment. They flashed through her mind, violently and quickly. Instead, she chose to stay her tongue. If she was stuck here until she broke out, she was going to make nice. "How lucky for you. What's your secret? Eternal damnation?" Well, it was the thought that counted.

Rose puckered her lips and popped her hip. Her jewellery clinked together as she moved. "If hell is a place on earth, it certainly involves you."

Before Makenna could retort, Rose slithered out of the room. Makenna was far too impressed to say anything, not until she processed the insult. "Damn, she gives as good as she gets."

"And it never gets old," Charles noted. Makenna saw the smirk on his lips before the man smoothed his face out.

"What's that supposed to mean?"

Charles shrugged and picked his book back up. "All in good time."

"I get it," Makenna said, the pieces clicking together. "You're the wise one of the bunch. Rose is the resident bitch. Maryam is the mother of the group, while Huxley just likes to appreciate nice things. Cody and Siobhan are the literal children, and Noah and Lydia I can't quite get a grasp on yet. They're still pending. Not sure about the ninth ghost? Maybe a secret lover? Am I close?"

Charles tilted his head back to laugh. "You are good, aren't you? That tongue of yours never tires, does it? Even after all these years."

That was the second thing Charles had said that made no sense. "Have we met before?"

"In another life." Charles winked at her. "Now go heat up your food before Rose comes back and insults you again. As for the ninth ghost, I wouldn't worry about her. You'll probably never even see Harriet, and that's a blessing."

Makenna smacked her lips closed as her stomach growled. "Touché, old man. Touché."

The two fell into a comfortable silence as Makenna heated her dinner. When it was ready to go, she took a spot beside Charles, the breakfast nook rather cosy for such a haunting place. "There are nine of you here, right?" she said after taking a mouthful.

Charles put his book back down. "Yes."

"And you all . . . died." Makenna didn't know how to be tactful about it.

"Yes," Charles said. "Is there something you'd like to ask?" His tone wasn't unkind but straight forward.

Clinking her spoon around her bowl, Makenna tried to phrase her question without coming off as rude or invasive. "Do you remember your death? With Cody, he does that thing. Is it the same for all of you?"

Charles laced his fingers together, his face thoughtful. "We do remember our deaths, but no, we don't all relive them as Cody does his. His death was particularly violent. It was also rather recent in the grand scheme of things. I don't think his spirit has come to terms with it yet."

Makenna bobbed her head. She was close to asking Charles how he had passed, but it didn't seem entirely appropriate. Instead, she asked, "What was your life like?"

Charles cracked a smile. He was a very handsome man. Makenna wondered if he had had a family. "I worked. That was my life. My mother immigrated to the UK from Liberia in 1925. I was four years old, and I remember nothing about my home country. However, my mother made the best fried eggplant. I can still smell it from time to time."

"What kind of work did you do?"

Charles shrugged. "Whatever I could get. I worked for production during the war and did a lot of fixing injured men in the factory. As a Black man, though, no one really wanted me around."

"That's awful. I'm so sorry." Makenna knew it would never be enough, but she had very little to offer besides an attempt to learn from Charles what he would impart to her. "Should I be afraid of death?" she finally asked. "Is it so bad?"

Charles shot her a warm smile, though it didn't reach his eyes. "You have much to live for, if that is what you're asking."

Was it? Makenna wasn't so sure. She had longed for death her entire life, and now she was surrounded by it, having a conversation with it. "You've seemed to make peace with your dying."

"Then make peace with your living," he offered her. "Now, your food is getting cold." Charles pointed to her bowl.

Charles's words echoed in her head. She had fought her entire life to make peace with it, only to ever come up short. Peace of mind was nonexistent or fleeting at best. Would she be able to find it now, as Rory had so desperately wanted her to on his deathbed? She felt a flicker of a flame ignite at Charles's words, even if it was small.

"Oh, right." Makenna picked her spoon back up. The ravioli didn't taste nearly as bad in her mouth as Rose would have had her assume. It didn't taste wonderful either, but Makenna would savour every bite. "I'd like to hear the rest of your story sometime," she said around a mouthful. It wasn't very ladylike of her, but Charles didn't seem to mind.

"And I would love to share it."

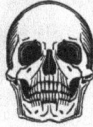

11

I'm Here

Noah had tried to sleep, but the look on Cody's face in the attic had haunted him. In his attempt to save everyone, Noah had only hurt those he was trying to protect, once again. So, instead of tossing, turning, and ruminating, he launched himself from his bed and began to pace his room. He was missing something. What hadn't he tried? How could he break Makenna free and assuage Cody's guilt at the same time?

Then he heard it. The moans, low at first, and then they echoed through the halls outside his door.

Harriet.

The only time she ever left her precious attic was to weep through the corridors, late at night, the most ghostly of any in the house. She haunted the shadows like a plague, spreading her misery one wallow at a time. But it meant the attic was empty, and the attic was full of a hundred years of collected items. Things went up there to die, as Maryam liked to say, with Harriet forever their crypt keeper. But she sat on a treasure trove, so if there was something in the house to help save Makenna, it would most likely be there.

Noah crept to the bottom of the narrow stairs to the attic, washed in darkness and the stale stench of must. His hand hovered on the thin railing, barely hanging on to the wall. Was he really going to do this again? He had risked the attic only a week ago, and that felt like tempting fate. Venturing into Harriet's space was a minefield, but now would be the only chance he got, before she returned from her haunt, a dragon guarding her treasure.

Swallowing the lump in his throat, Noah dashed up the stairs before he could think better of it. The door at the top creaked open on rusty hinges, exposing a forgotten realm, suspended in time. Light struggled to pierce through the gloom, seeping in through small, cobweb-covered windows that framed the night outside. The rafters overhead cast long, crooked shadows that threatened to swallow Noah. Every corner of the space was cluttered with the remnants of lives long past. Wooden crates half open were filled with faded letters, stacked haphazardly. An old gramophone sat silent in one corner, its brass horn tarnished, while beside it, a pile of forgotten records waited, their music unheard for decades. This place was like a graveyard for the living, and Noah had little time to find anything useful.

He began rummaging through the nearest pile of yellowed parchment, scanning the words with his eyes. Deeds and birth certificates, love letters and sales receipts. He was careful not to move anything out of place, lest Harriet return and see something was amiss. When he found nothing useful, he flittered across the room to a bookshelf, scanning the antique titles no one had read in years. Harriet kept all these bits of life prisoner in the dark, and it was a damn shame. But nothing caught his eye. He wasn't even sure what he was looking for, and a daunting feeling began to creep into his bones. He was helpless, directionless, and once again, useless.

He turned in a circle, scanning the expansive room cluttered with memories that didn't belong to him, his hands pulling at his hair. Another dead end, that's what this was. Hope had come to die again, as it always did.

With a frustrated sigh, Noah sunk into green velvet chair shoved into a corner, its fabric worn away by age. He had dropped his head in his hands and was staring at his shoes with wide eyes when something caught his eye. Just a corner of flattened leather that peeked out from under the chair. Without thinking, Noah reached for it.

It was a small leather-bound notebook, bearing the marks of time. Its once supple cover was now cracked, the pages frayed and the corners curled inwards. A simple brass clasp, tarnished with age, held the pages closed. Noah was about to open it when he heard a moan reverberate through the halls below. Harriet. He needed to move.

Shoving the book in his coat pocket, Noah abandoned the chair to bolt out of the attic, his heart pounding at the thought of running into the old crone. Luck must have been on his side, for he was down the narrow stairs and back in safe territory without any incident. He skidded to a halt and had bent over to catch his breath from the adrenaline when a voice called out to him.

"Ah, Noah. You're still up. Harriet keeping you awake?"

The sound jolted him in his spot, though it was no terrifying woman hell-bent on his destruction for thievery. It was just Maryam, sauntering down the hall with Siobhan in tow.

"We've been keeping a watch over Makenna after we

thought you went to bed. Were you up in the attic?" Maryam's eyes shot above, an impressed whistle blowing through her lips. "Did you find something?"

"Please tell me you found something good," Siobhan begged, clapping her hands together at the potential for new gossip. "If Harriet had it, I bet it's kinky."

Patience. Noah hadn't spent much time with teenagers before getting trapped in the house, but Siobhan was teaching him many lessons on them. They required a great deal of patience. "I sincerely hope not." He reached for the book tucked away in his coat and held it aloft. "I don't know what it is. I got nervous and ran before I could assess."

Maryam's lips quirked up in the corners. "That's my boy. Risky, but I like it. Let's take a look, shall we?" She plucked the book from his long fingers and waved the two after her. "But not here. Don't need Harriet to walk up with us guiltily holding anything of hers. Come."

Maryam led them down the stairs and into one of the drawing rooms on the ground floor, a place Noah didn't spend too much time in. It was rather stuffy for him. Lined with faded tapestries on the walls, the room was over-crowded with antique furniture. A heavy scent of polished wood lingered in the air. Quite pretentious really.

Sitting on one of the overstuffed couches, Maryam unclasped the book and began to filter through it as Noah paced the room. Siobhan occupied herself next to Maryam by picking at her nails, humming a song Noah wasn't familiar with. After a long minute, Maryam finally spoke. "Hm, this seems to be a book of spells."

Noah halted his steps instantly. *Spells.* That was a word he hadn't heard in a very long time. "What do you mean spells?"

"Come look instead of standing there like an idiot. The lighting is hitting you all wrong. Your face looks ghastly." Maryam flipped through the pages some more with Siobhan reading over her shoulder.

"How old is this book?" the girl asked. "It looks ancient."

Maryam's eyes raced across the pages. "Yet they're full of detail. Look at all the notes scribbled in between the text." Together the women flipped through the book with far more interest than Noah was comfortable with.

"I've never seen a book on magic before. I mean, like practical magic. I read *The Fellowship of the Ring* in school, but it nearly put me to sleep," Siobhan said.

"We should get rid of it." The words were out of Noah's mouth before he could stop them. Both women's heads turned to him, and he immediately regretted saying anything.

"Why? It's a book." The younger girl pulled the text closer to her as if concerned Noah would snatch it from them.

Quite frankly, Noah didn't want to go near the book. He didn't like anything that even smelled of magic. "If it's a spellbook, then it's dangerous."

Maryam side-eyed him. "It's a book, Noah. Would you relax and come look at it?"

"We shouldn't mess with spells." Noah tried to keep his tone even. If there was one thing that boiled his blood more than anything, it was magic. As someone caught between life and death, he hadn't had to think about it since becoming stuck in this house. He preferred it that way.

"You seem to have forgotten you're in a house full of ghosts and haven't aged in 126 years. I think magic has already messed with you. I surely doubt this book can do any more harm," Maryam said.

Noah pinched his nose. Maryam had never seen what he had seen. She didn't know the extent to which magic could be used to destroy someone's life. It was toxic. He would feel better if that book was gone, especially with Makenna in the house. He couldn't take that risk. Not again. "We shouldn't be so careless with it. Magic is dangerous." He tried to soften his voice so that they would hear his plea.

"And who made you the expert on magic?" Siobhan asked, raising her chin. "You holding back on us, Kiers?"

Clenching his fists, Noah tried to pick his words carefully. "I knew someone who used magic. Quite recklessly, I might add. It nearly destroyed them. It nearly destroyed me to watch them waste from it. My advice to you is don't play with what you don't understand."

"Can ghosts even use magic?" Siobhan asked Maryam, purposefully tuning Noah out as she scanned the book. "The first page here says that magic is a form of life force. Do you think we count?"

Maryam pulled the book from Siobhan to read over the same paragraph. "That is a fascinating question, my dear."

Noah almost grabbed the book from the girls and threw it across the room. It could go into the fire for all he cared. He would watch it burn gleefully. "Look, I beg of you. Please forget about the book. It could be a danger to Makenna. Please, let us destroy it."

"I get you're trying to dissuade us and all, but I'm just more intrigued than ever," Siobhan admitted. "Like, look here, a spell to start a fire? That's pimpin'."

"I don't think 'pimpin'' means what you think it

means," Noah said impatiently, "but I digress. That book is a danger. Burn it, throw it in the pond, tear it to shreds. I don't care. Just promise me you'll get rid of it."

Maryam closed the book but left her hand on the cover to guard it. "I thought this might be an answer to your problems. Surely magic got you stuck here. What if it's the thing to release you? What if it's the thing that could set you and Makenna free?" She pointed upwards to the floor above them where Makenna currently slept. "Is it not worth trying for her?"

Noah squeezed his palms. They were suddenly very sweaty. "You don't understand how dangerous magic is. It will harm before it ever solves anything. We'd tie us to a worse fate just by using it."

"And yet you won't even look at the book? You're not even curious to see what's inside? This could be your answer."

Noah shook his head. "Magic is temptation, a cruel temptation. It will give you what you want, but at a price, and the price is always worse in the end. Please, get rid of it." He would hear no more of it. He had seen enough pain from magic to last him a lifetime. The best thing for them all was to forget about it. They would find a different way. Magic was simply too risky.

For the first time in over a hundred years, as Noah looked at that book, he felt something more than the highs and lows of grief; he felt afraid.

∾

THERE WAS A MAN BEFORE HER – *no, he was on top of her now, yet she couldn't see his face. His cold hands wrapped around Makenna's throat and tightened. She couldn't breathe. Harder she struggled, her arms flailing as her legs kicked up. The man had all his weight on her. She was pinned, and her head swam. Was this what it felt like to die? She fought harder, but the edges of her vision turned black. It crept in on her like an eternal void. There was something else in the room, a light that shone through the darkness. Makenna could see it standing above her, hovering over the man. She tried to reach out to it, but the dark was all-encompassing. It took the rest of her vision and the light with it. And then there was nothing.*

Makenna woke in a sweat, her heartbeat pounding a mile a minute. She could almost feel the hands around her throat. The terror had been dreadful. She had been utterly helpless as the darkness took her, and then she was completely empty.

The morning was relatively young as she peeked out the window. The clouds hadn't quite claimed the sky yet. There was a peak of sunlight over the horizon, and it fuelled Makenna with energy.

Today was the day she was going to break free of this prison. She had spent the last two days in a weird haze – almost like she had succumbed to the fate the ghosts had laid out for her. Again, there was that odd sense of familiarity the house brought her. It didn't sit well with her, and she didn't want to get comfortable with it. Yesterday had gotten her nowhere close to escaping, but now she had a general lay of the land, which would help her decide the best spot to try next. And after her chat with Charles, she felt more motivated than she had in a long time to live her life, outside of these damn walls. She would do her brother proud.

Makenna was sorry she wouldn't get to hear the last of Charles's story. She was genuinely curious to listen to his tale, but she had spent two nights in this house, and that was two too many. The gate was out. She had twice tried to leverage herself over it and been unsuccessful. That left the back of the property where the river acted as a natural perimeter. The fence didn't cut through it; all Makenna would have to do was swim across. Easy enough. She had learned to swim at a young age.

If she cut through the front doors and went around the house, she wouldn't get lost in the maze that was the back garden. She was so close to freedom. Hopefully, her hand wouldn't slow her down when she swam. It ached, but she had wrapped it tight.

She was at the front doors now, glad she hadn't run into anyone. Makenna wasn't in the mood to talk. She had no desire for her plans to be dismantled, or to be persuaded that she couldn't get out. She was leaving this property today.

"Out for a morning walk, are we?"

Makenna froze on the spot before turning around. "You must be Lydia, right?" The blond woman stood at the bottom of the stairs where Makenna had been moments ago. "Such a lovely morning, isn't it? I'd hate to waste it inside."

Lydia gave Makenna a weary smile. Her maroon night-gown clung to her curves in a way that made Makenna jealous. She would never have looked like that in such clothing. It would have hung off her like a wet towel. "If you're going outside, be careful. The property is ancient. It's easy to be careless."

Makenna hoped her smile came off as easy and not insane. "Of course. Appreciate the advice." She turned for the door. Lydia was, quite frankly, wasting her time – precious time that could be spent earning her freedom.

"How's your hand?" Lydia called out, stopping the girl in her tracks again. "Has Noah looked at it? It probably needs a new dressing."

Makenna didn't make polite conversation. She had

never mastered it quite like her mother. "It's fine. Healing nicely."

"I really think Noah should look at it." What was Lydia getting at? She seemed agitated, her voice a little hitched at the end.

"Honestly, I'm fine. Some fresh air is all I need." Makenna wasn't going to let Lydia stall her any longer. Noah wasn't going to get a chance to look at Makenna's hand because she would be long gone before the poor sucker even woke up.

"Makenna, wait—"

Subtly be damned. Makenna threw the door open in her attempt to be rid of the blond. It wasn't the smell of fresh air that hit her first but the sight of flashing lights. Across the street, parked in her driveway, were two police cars.

Makenna had never run so fast in her life. As hard as she could, she pumped her legs, flying across the grass as if her feet had wings. She was at the gates in record time, just as her mother opened the front door to their quiet house. There Jacqueline was, her face distraught as she spoke with the cops she was saying goodbye to.

Throwing herself at the iron bars, Makenna yelled at the top of her lungs. "Mum, Mum, I'm here!" She might have been mute for all the good it did. Jacqueline didn't seem to hear a thing. Makenna wasn't sure she could yell any louder, but she tried. "Please, stop! I'm right here."

The cops waved to Jacqueline as she stood in the driveway. She watched as they got into their cars and drove off, her arms close to her body and her hair dishevelled. Jacqueline looked wholly unkempt. Makenna had never seen her mother like that in her entire life. Jacqueline did not do unkempt. Not even after Rory had died.

Makenna didn't think her mother had it in her body to

weep, but Jacqueline crumpled over. She held her head in her hands and sobbed as she called Makenna's name out, over and over. Makenna lunged at the bars, her hand throbbing with the action. She didn't care. She would have cut her hand off if it meant getting to Jacqueline. "Please, Mum. I'm right here!"

Makenna could no longer hold it in. Her words turned into violent shrieks. She was a banshee, a demon. Her screams would haunt the night and wake the dead. Louder she got, thrashing against the gate with her shoulders, again and again. She would brute her way out of this prison. She would make it across the street and to the arms of her mother. She had never wanted them around her so badly. Only her mother's cries cut through her own as Makenna lost her energy, and the hysterics turned to devastating sobs.

It wasn't her mother's arms that pulled Makenna from the gate but a pair of strong hands. They gripped her shoulders and pulled her back, preventing her from ramming into the gate another time.

"Makenna, please. Look at me." Noah was behind her, but he might have been a thousand miles away for all Makenna cared. Her mother was across the street, buckled on the ground and broken from the loss of her children. If only she knew Makenna stood not fifty feet away.

"Mum, I love you." Makenna's tears were hot on her face. She had never said it enough when she had the chance. "I'm so sorry," she wept, vision blurry from the tears. "I'm so, so sorry." For everything, for not saying *I love you* enough, for not being a better daughter, for getting trapped in this damned house and leaving her loved ones behind. She had never felt so sorry in her life.

Noah was in front of Makenna now. He cupped her face, pulling her vision from her mum to him. "Makenna, she can't hear you. It's just us, okay? It's just us from now on."

It was too much, his words, her mother calling for her daughter – so close but a world away. This feeling was worse than death. "I want my mum," Makenna said between the breaths that shook her core. "She's right there. Why can't she see me? What did I do? Why is this happening to me?" Her voice broke, shrill in her panic and grief.

"I know," Noah said with a soothing tone, though his eyes were wet. "It's not fair. It's never fair, and I'm sorry this is happening to you. I wish I could make it stop. I truly do."

"I don't want this pain," Makenna groaned, her hands flying to her chest. She pulled at her shirt to get at the skin underneath. She wanted to tear it away, all of it; her flesh, her heart, the terrible weighted feeling that pulled her under. It was familiar but more intense than ever. Suffocating. If she could claw away at her body, maybe she could finally rid herself of this ache.

Noah grabbed her hands and pushed them down. "Makenna, stop. You're hurting yourself."

"She's there; she's right there." Makenna tried to catch her breath. "I can see her. Why can't she see me?" She didn't have the energy to pull at Noah anymore. Instead, she let herself fall to his chest. She had cried once to mourn her freedom; now, she sobbed to mourn the loss of her family. She couldn't overcome the gate that divided them, and now her mother was paying the price.

From over Noah's shoulder, Makenna could see her mother pick herself up off the ground. Jacqueline brushed her knees, straightened her white pressed shirt, and wiped at her eyes to collect herself. Then she turned on her heel and returned to the house. Makenna let out a gasp as

Jacqueline shut the door behind her. What if that was the last time she'd ever see her mum?

"Oh god." Makenna pushed herself off from Noah and crawled away from him. She was going to be sick. She could feel it. Noah tried to close the space between them, but Makenna held up a hand to stop him. Her body racked as she dry-heaved on the grass, but there was nothing in her stomach to bring up. When her body had nothing left to give, she sunk onto the grass, her head in her hands.

She hadn't been sick like this since her brother died and she decided she no longer wanted to live. She had been in the room when the doctors declared him dead. Today, at this very moment, she felt the same sense of panic – the anxiety that she would never see someone she loved again.

Noah was on her once more, this time gentler. He wrapped his hands slowly around her to pull her up while not rushing her. "Let's go inside."

She didn't want to go inside, but she was exhausted now. Makenna scrubbed at her face, her eyes swollen and her cheeks puffy. Whatever despair that had just rocked her to the core was long gone. Now, she only felt numb. She was on autopilot while Noah led her into the house and up the stairs to her room. He was kind enough to push back the covers of the bed and let her crawl in. He was even kinder when she didn't say thank you, for she didn't have it in her.

He was almost out the door when Makenna called out to him. "Noah."

He stood in the doorway, his silhouette softly outlined in the morning light. "Yes?"

There it was again, that strange sense of familiarity with him. It clashed with the numbness. "I don't want to be alone." Such an odd thing for her to say. She had been on her own for years. It was all she knew, and she had become comfortable with it. But now, with him standing there, the idea of him leaving almost brought her to tears again. "Will you sit with me for a while?"

"Of course."

12

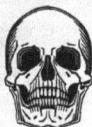

The Voices in My Head

The armchair made an awful clunking sound as Noah pushed it towards the bed. As he lowered himself into it, his fingers gripped the emerald fabric of the arms tightly. How terrible was it that Noah had become so elated when Makenna asked him to stay? She needed comfort, and here he dared to take it as a small personal victory. He should feel ashamed, but he would worry about that later. All he wanted was to spend time with her, to speak to her, to show her that he would help in whichever way she needed it. But he had to remind himself not to say too much, for her own sake.

"I'm here." He hoped his voice was calm.

Makenna's lips pressed down in a thin line as she lay on the bed, facing him. Her head rested on her arm with the pillows pushed back so they were out of the way. "Am I ever going to see her again?"

"Your mother, you mean?"

She nodded, and her lips quivered. He didn't want to give her false hope, but he wanted to provide her with comfort. "When I got trapped here, I thought about my life back home for a long time. I often wondered if anyone would come looking for me."

"Did they?"

Noah released the arms of the chair from his death grip and instead folded his hands. He had to pick and choose his words carefully. It was just so easy to speak to her, so easy to let something slip. "No. I left home at a young age, and I didn't have any relatives, just people I had met in the city. Constance, my mother, raised me off the beaten path. We were very isolated in rural Scotland – rarely ventured into town. People came to us for her services and never the other way around. It was a wild and yet very sheltered upbringing."

Makenna shifted to make herself more comfortable in the bed. "But you became a doctor."

"I did. When I was old enough, I left home for Edinburgh. I wanted proper training. I wanted to heal with science rather than—" he cut himself off, worried he was saying too much. "Rather than natural ways."

"So, you went to Edinburgh and then what? What brought you here to England?" Makenna seemed to finally settle. Her breathing had returned to normal, and the dazed look in her eyes faded slowly.

Noah felt his chest tighten. "I met a girl and fell in love." He couldn't help but lock eyes with Makenna, until the words felt too heavy, and he turned away. "After a few years, I learned I had some family property down here, and we both agreed to come for a better life. I intended to work here since there weren't many physicians in the area. The opportunity was too good to pass up." He felt tense speaking on his past, exposing this part of himself to her, but the words were flowing. He would give her whatever she wanted. All she had to do was ask.

Noah laughed to himself then, the irony of the situation never lost on him. "My mother was very adamant I never go to England, all throughout my childhood. She was convinced I would meet my end here. She hated the English more than anything."

"Do you hate the English?"

Noah chuckled heartily this time. "Dear god, no. I can blame the English for a lot of things, but whatever is tying me here isn't their fault."

"Good. I wouldn't want you to hate me." Makenna pulled her head back as if surprised to have said that.

Noah's eyes flashed up to hers. "Never," he said, his tone losing all humour.

Sitting up, Makenna crossed her legs and tucked the blankets tightly underneath her. "Where are you from in Scotland?"

"A town called Pitlochry."

"I've heard of it," Makenna said. "Do you miss it?"

"Every day. I miss the hills, the lochs up north, the forests."

Makenna leaned forward, her face nestled in her hands. "How do you not go crazy being stuck in this house? I think I'd go crazy spending the rest of my life here. Especially when my home is right across the street."

Noah hadn't meant to make her think of home. He had grieved his over a century ago. "It takes time. Good company doesn't hurt either."

"Why have I never seen you before?" Makenna asked after a beat. "All this time you've been here, why could I see everyone else but you?"

Noah rolled his shoulders. *Don't say too much.* "The living are very resistant to death. They simply don't want any part in it. They fight it, even subconsciously. That's why it's hard for the living to see ghosts. It rarely happens. But just like anyone who's passed through this house, you

125

couldn't see me because I'm something other. I'm not dead, but I'm not fully alive. I'm an abomination, so the living reject me completely."

Makenna's eyes widened. "That's terrible. Is the same thing happening to me? Am I becoming an *abomination*?" She tried to make the word light, but he could hear the weight behind it.

"You're not an abomination," Noah said, his eyes hard. "But you'll start to fade from the living world until you're just like me, caught somewhere in between."

Makenna looked away, and Noah cursed himself for being so blunt. He didn't want to lie to her. He owed her that much of the truth. "We have shitty luck. Don't we?"

The conversation seemed to die between them. It was a knock on the door that brought them out of the silence. "Let me get that," Noah said, rubbing the back of his neck. Makenna sunk back into the bed as he zipped across the room, regretful to leave her side. When he swung the door open, he was surprised to see two very antsy children on the other side.

"Huxley made Makenna breakfast again. He said I could bring it up to the room," Cody said with a tray of food in his hands. He eyed the room with trepidation as Noah closed the door behind him. "Here you go." He shoved the tray forward into Noah's hands, who caught at it ungracefully.

"Do you want to bring it to her yourself?" Noah asked, careful to not knock over the spoon precariously balanced on the tray.

"Nope," Cody said, tucking his hands behind his back and bouncing from one foot to the other. "I'm good."

Noah was about to counteract when Siobhan stretched her arms out, a glass in each hand. "Huxley wasn't sure if she wanted tea or water, so he made me bring her both."

She plunked them down on the tray, nearly upsetting the whole thing.

Noah rocked to the side to accommodate the new weight. "Ach, okay. Thank you very much. I'm sure Makenna would love it if you brought this in for her, the both of you."

Cody shook his head back and forth violently. "I'm not going anywhere near her."

"I think she would like to see you," Noah urged.

The boy took a step back from the door. "Uh-uh. She'll never see me again, not after what I did."

"What did you do? Is it because you stink?" Siobhan asked without missing a beat. "Or because you never stop talking—"

"—I do not talk too much." Cody threw his hands in the air, immediately distracted from his woes.

"Yeah, you do. You, like, never shut up. God, it's so annoying."

Cody shot her a devastating frown. "I'm not annoying. At least I'm not gushing over boys who are far too old to be attractive anymore. Always staring at your pop magazines from the eighties. John Stamos? I googled him once. He's got to be like fifty now."

Siobhan audibly gasped. "Don't you dare sour the name of Stamos in this house. I will find a way to kill you again if you do."

Cody stuck his tongue out at Siobhan the same time she gave him the finger. "Whatever. Jon Bovi called. He wants his crimped hair and bad music back."

Noah was sure he had never seen such rage flash across Siobhan's face. "For the last time, it's Bon Jovi." Her scream hurt Noah's ears as she dashed down the hall in dramatic fashion, leaving him with a very full tray of food and a distressed boy.

Noah set the food down on the floor before it could topple over. "Cody, I think you should see Makenna. I can come with you, and we can do it together."

The boy had his arms crossed over his chest, his lips pressed in a thin, angry line. "Siobhan hates me. Makenna hates me. You hate me. I can't do anything right."

"Cody, no." Noah wrapped his arms around Cody before he could dash off, smooshing the boy into a giant hug. "Makenna doesn't blame you. You can go in and ask her yourself. I strongly encourage it."

Cody's eyes began to well up, the anger dissipating into grief. "But I brought her here."

"Listen, will you? It's not your fault. It never was. There's nothing else to it. Please, go speak to her and ease your mind."

But Cody only pulled himself from Noah's grasp. "I hope she likes the food," he said quietly. "Huxley also told us to tell you he's planning a game night tonight. I won't be there." Before Noah could say anything else, Cody slipped from the hall, disappearing in the opposite direction Siobhan had gone.

Noah sagged over, a tight feeling taking over his chest as he picked up the tray and pushed back into the room. Makenna sat up instantly, her hand running over her hair to smooth it. "Dinner is served," he said, trying his best to sound light as he placed the tray on the bedside table.

"Is everything okay?" Makenna eyed the door he had just come through.

Noah rolled out his shoulders to relax himself. "Teenage angst with a little bit of bad luck on the side."

Makenna picked up the plate of ravioli, then tucked into it with the spoon. "Do go on."

"It's Cody. He thinks he's responsible for bringing you over the gate. He's taking a lot on himself right now."

"It's not his fault," Makenna said without missing a beat.

"I know that." *Now.* "I'm doing what I can to make sure he knows that too. It's just not going so well. He's avoiding you because he thinks he'll hurt you again."

Makenna pushed around her pasta, her lip twitching. "He's protecting me."

"In his own way," Noah agreed.

"Just like you are," she said slowly.

The comment caught him off guard, probably without her realising it. All he had done to keep her safe, and she didn't even know the half of it.

"Cody shouldn't have to avoid me. I don't want him to," Makenna said.

"I'm sure he'll come around." Noah wondered at this new break in tension between them, glad for it either way. Makenna seemed far more at ease around him now. Maybe being a bit vulnerable wasn't the worst thing he could do. Maybe he had been stressing over keeping her in the dark a little too much.

"Thank you for the food," Makenna said, filling the silence that fell over them.

Noah nodded and stepped back from the bed. He didn't want to press his luck. "I should let you eat and rest." He was suddenly aware of just how comfortable he was becoming in her presence. "But I'll see you around?"

Makenna met his eyes, filled with more intensity than he expected. "I'd like that."

"Good. Okay." He gave her an awkward wave before giving her her privacy. As he closed the door behind him and stood in the hall, his heartbeat thumped wildly. There had been a shift in that room, a positive one. And he would take all the positivity he could find.

MAKENNA SPENT the majority of the day in her room. Maryam had come by to offer her conversation, but Makenna politely declined. If she wouldn't have company, then she at least needed a book, Maryam insisted. Makenna wasn't a huge reader, but there was something inherently cosy about curling up in bed with a book.

Seeing her mother cry for her daughter nearly broke Makenna. She thought she had known grief; she had dealt with it long enough after her brother died. Seeing someone grieve over herself, though, had been an entirely different experience. There was something profound about it — like being invited to your own funeral. There was no closure beyond the tears of those who wept for you.

Was this what would have happened if Makenna had gone through with suicide after her brother died? Is this what the aftermath would have looked like? Her mother, weeping on the ground, a broken woman. How much death could one parent take?

"*Hold on,*" a voice whispered in her ear. "*Don't leave me again.*"

Makenna dropped the book she had been holding, her head whipping around to find the voice. It had been so close. It had tickled her ear.

"Hello?" she called out as she peeled herself off the mattress.

"*I can save her. I know I can.*"

Makenna spun on her heels. The voice was on top of her now, coming from above. "Who's there? Hello?"

"*You have to let her go.*" A new voice. "*There's too much damage, Noah.*"

Noah? He wasn't in the room. No one was. Was Makenna going crazy? She suspected if she remained stuck on the property long enough, it was bound to happen. This was too soon. She had only been here for a few days.

I can't. Not again.

Before Makenna could call out a third time, her vision went black, and she hit the floor like a dead weight. Every inch of her body vibrated as if an electrical current coursed through her from head to toe. The feeling dissipated slowly, though her limbs felt tingly as she came to.

What in the hell? She had clearly heard Noah's voice. He had been in the room with her; she would put money on it. There had been another person too, but Makenna was breathing too hard to put a face to it. Her heart felt like she had run a marathon, it thumped so violently in her chest. She had never fainted in her life, had hardly been physically sick beyond the common cold. Indeed, she was having a psychotic breakdown.

"Makenna?" There was a knock on the door.

Scrambling, Makenna tried to find her balance as she got to her feet. There were still stars in her eyes as she opened the door to find Huxley on the other side.

"Ah, good, you're up. I have a surprise for you."

Makenna peered over his shoulder, half expecting to find Noah and the stranger right behind him. Coming back to Huxley, Makenna sucked in a breath. She wasn't really in the mood for a surprise, but she couldn't refuse Huxley if she wanted too. "All right. Lead the way."

The older gentleman held out his arm for Makenna and began leading her through the house. He kept the conversation light as they went.

"Huxley, can I ask you something?" Makenna said, interrupting the small talk after a few minutes.

"Ask away," the older man said.

"What do I do when the food runs out? I don't suppose

there's a limitless supply of ravioli in the basement. My own personal Tesco."

Huxley's eyebrows creased as he hummed and hawed. "I suppose you'll do as Noah did. His human needs slowly faded. One day, he just stopped feeling hungry."

"How does Noah do it? How has he managed being stuck here for so long?"

"He hasn't," Huxley said simply. Makenna raised her eyebrows, and Huxley continued for clarity. "It was around the early 1940s, I believe. Rose was the newest addition to the house, her death a result of multiple tragedies. Poor Noah was going through a rough patch after the demise of – Rose. Too much death will do that to a person."

"So, what did he do?" Makenna asked.

"He took inspiration from Rose's death and tried to carry out his own."

Makenna stopped mid-step, Huxley nearly pulling her off her feet with his continued momentum.

"My girl, what is it?"

Makenna wasn't sure what to unpack first. "Are you saying Rose died by suicide? And that Noah tried to do the same?" Rose, the ghost who had given Makenna nothing but attitude? It didn't seem right. Neither did the thought of Noah taking inspiration from it.

Straightening his shirt, Huxley held his arm out once again for Makenna to continue on their way. "You seem very surprised by death, considering how much you're surrounded by it. Do not forget we have had decades to come to terms with it. Now, we're going to be far later than we already are if we dillydally."

Makenna took her place once again on Huxley's arm. Rose had died by her own hand, and Noah had tried to do the same. Clearly, he had failed. Had he failed because he couldn't go through with it, or did the curse prevent him from dying even by his own hand?

Makenna lost herself in her thoughts. It wasn't until Huxley directed them down a plain hall that she came back to. "Huxley, where are we going?"

"You shall see." The luxuries of the manor stopped beyond here. "These are the servants' quarters. Game night is always held in the servants' hall. In case things get a bit rowdy, you know."

"Game night?" Makenna asked as they weaved their way into a simple kitchen. It wasn't half as impressive as the central kitchen, clearly lacking the technologies of more recent decades. Beyond it was a small, open space with a table where everyone but the mysterious Harriet sat. It was the only ghost Makenna had yet to see.

"Indeed," Huxley said, his famous wicked grin on his face. "It's time for games, and you're going to love it."

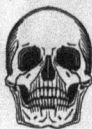

13

Winners and Losers

"You're here," Maryam said with a clap of her hands. "We were beginning to worry."

"I was not," Rose said. She sat at the furthest end of the table, Charles on her one side and Siobhan on the other. "I was simply growing tired of being left to wait."

"You were not," Siobhan said, her hands shuffling a deck of cards skilfully. "You were too busy complaining about the paint in your room. 'It's too stuffy. Why did the owners renovate in the nineties? I liked how it was before.' If you hate it so much, find another room."

Rose picked an imaginary piece of lint off her dress and flicked it as Siobhan. "That has been my room for almost a hundred years. I will not relocate just because someone had bad taste."

"I think the wallpaper has character." Charles scrunched his shoulders up. "I'm sure it'll grow on you. Just give it another decade."

"Thirty years of listening to her complain about wall-paper, and yet your optimism is admirable, Charles," Lydia said. She was sitting across from Noah. That left two chairs for Huxley and Makenna at the head of the table. Makenna was about to sit next to Lydia when Huxley shooed her over to Noah's side.

Makenna settled into the stiff seat, a creeping feeling in her chest that a game night felt like a giant waste of time. She had already wasted much of the day in bed, too unnerved by her mother to go looking for an escape. She should be using this time more productively. Casually hanging around with the dead was jarring enough as it was.

"Hello, everyone, sorry for the delay," Huxley said with a smile. "Siobhan, I see you have the cards out and ready to go. How wonderful. What are we playing tonight?"

Siobhan began dealing out the cards, her actions smooth and precise. Makenna had never been skilled with cards. They had a bad habit of flying everywhere when she was left in charge of the shuffle. No one ever thanked her when they played an impromptu game of Fifty-Two Pickup.

"Egyptian Rat Screw."

"Have you ever played?" Noah turned to Makenna, his eyes rather bright tonight. They had been so dark earlier when he helped her to the house. He looked far less serious now; his lips were cracked in a smile as if she had interrupted a joke when she entered the room. It was rather endearing.

"I haven't."

"It's fast, but once you play a few rounds, you'll get the hang of it."

Siobhan dealt out the entire deck of cards until everyone had a sizeable pile, face down.

Noah pointed to Makenna's hand. "We go clockwise. When it's your turn, you flip a card from your pile and place it in the middle of the table, on top of the last drawn card, face up. If two of the same numbers stack up on top of another, doesn't matter the suit, you can slap the deck. The first person to slap the deck gets all the cards in the pile. The object of the game is to get all the cards."

"Slap the deck?" Makenna motioned to the table, hitting it with some force. "Just like that?"

"Exactly like that." Taking his haphazard pile, Noah gracefully shimmied the cards until they were stacked neatly in front of him. Was everyone in this house capable of handling cards but Makenna? She tried not to mess her hand as she brought the cards close to her body. "You can also slap on sandwiches. So, say you get a five, seven, five, you can slap on that, too." Makenna kept repeating the rules to herself, hopeful she wouldn't forget them.

Siobhan was the first to place a card down in the middle of the table, and the game began. It moved incredibly fast, and Makenna watched until she felt confident enough to jump in. It didn't take long before she was slapping cards and building up her own hand. It didn't take long for the yelling to begin, either.

"I slapped first," Lydia cried as she smacked her hand down right beside Charles's.

"You're not even on the card." Charles dropped his head to the table to inspect it. "Aha! I get the hand. I'm touching the deck."

Lydia stood up from her chair, passion heating her voice. "I still slapped first."

"Rule is your hand needs to be on the card," Siobhan said. "It goes to Charles."

The man pumped his fist in the air while Lydia fell back to her seat. "Rigged. All of it." She gave Makenna a quick wink when the girl caught her eye. It was hard not to giggle. The group's antics were rowdy at best and uncivilised at worst, especially as the night wore on. Rose and Siobhan had duked it out a few times with Rock, Paper, Scissors, while Huxley often debated the speed with which a person slapped the pile. In his mind, he was always the fastest, and everyone was ludicrous to say otherwise.

Huxley and Charles ended the game in a heated round of throwing down cards and smacking them with rapid speed. Ultimately Charles won the game, but that didn't stop some from contesting the results.

"I was clearly closer to the pile," Huxley said to Charles as Siobhan rounded up the cards.

"I was simply faster than you, Hux. No hard feelings." Charles leaned on the back of his chair's legs, his arms folded behind his head. He wore a smug smile that seemed to irk Huxley to no end.

Huxley pushed his sleeves up. "Round two, I think. I'll really prove who's the fastest of us all."

"You lost," Rose pointed out. She had surprised Makenna during the game. Rose had been quiet while the others were loud and boisterous, yet her hand was quick and stealthy. "Leave it be, old man."

Huxley stared at the table for a good second before his shoulders relaxed. "Another time then." He turned to Makenna, one eyebrow raised. "I hope game night lived up to your expectations."

Makenna couldn't fight the smile on her lips. "I haven't played cards in a long while. I enjoyed it very much." Tonight had been the first time since being stuck here that her mind hadn't wandered to the horrors of her fate. Perhaps this house wasn't as drab as she initially expected. There was some life here after all. "Thank you for letting me play."

Delighted, Huxley thumped the table with his fist. This man didn't mess around with game night. "That's the spirit. Just wait and see, we have many games to show you. You won't be disappointed." Standing up from the table, Huxley gave everyone a firm nod. "Ladies and gentlemen, I thank you for your time tonight, even if I did not win. I shall be retiring for the evening. See you all in the morning."

There was a chorus of goodbyes, a few others leaving as the night wound down. Soon there were only four left: Maryam, Lydia, Noah, and Makenna, the conversation flowing around the table.

"I used to play that game with my kids," Maryam said. She had taken the deck from Siobhan when the girl left. Maryam too handled the cards with precision. Again, Makenna felt incompetent.

"How many did you have?" Makenna asked. She had her head in her palms, elbows on the table in a way that would have made her mother crazy.

"Three. Two sons and a daughter. They were the most wonderful little shits to ever grace this planet." Maryam's smile warmed her face as she spoke of her children. "We lived in this house for their entire childhood. Then I got sick, and we considered selling it. The upkeep was a nightmare, and my children were lazy." There was no menace in her voice, only the fondness of someone who had loved and lost.

"Arjun did a fair bit of cleaning," Noah said, coming to one of the boys' defence.

"Because he knew I would know if he hadn't done his chores." Maryam tilted her head back and laughed. "All mothers have eyes in the back of their heads."

Noah smiled to himself as he leaned back in his chair. "He used to sweep the dirt under the front mat sometimes. But only when Nirav didn't do it himself."

"Your boys were always good to you, Mar," Lydia said. "But Dhriti was a daddy's girl."

"So she was." Maryam settled the cards on the table, and Makenna wondered if it was appropriate to ask what was about to come out of her mouth.

"How did you die?"

Maryam didn't hesitate as she answered. "Breast cancer, in 1976. I died in my room, surrounded by my family."

"I don't mean to pry, but at the end . . . were you in pain? I mean, obviously, you were, but did you suffer? Did your family's love make it any better?" Makenna wasn't sure what she was trying to ask. All she could see was her brother, sick and dying in a hospital bed.

"My dear, I was in the worst pain of my life, but I had my family with me until the very end. They are the reason I am still here, I believe – to watch over their well-being from beyond the grave. I may not be with them physically, but I will never stop being their mother, just as I will never stop being my husband's wife. They are my family, and death does not separate me from them as you would think."

Makenna felt her throat form a lump. "I'm sorry you were taken from them. No one should have to go through that."

"I am sorry, too. Sorry that I did not get to experience their lives as fully as I wanted to. But I know they lived well. I can feel it. I raised them to live their best lives, full of love, and I cannot, as a mother, ask for anything else." Maryam squeezed Makenna's hand across the table, and it felt like a tug on her chest.

Makenna sucked in a breath, trying to compose herself. "Thank you," was all she could manage.

Leaning back in her chair, Maryam thumped her chest

with her hand. "Love is limitless. It goes beyond death. I am proof of that. Never forget."

Makenna didn't think she ever would.

"Now, I am done with you all. I'm off to my room. Good night." Maryam gave them all a final wave before tottering off, singing a lullaby down the hall.

Lydia seemed to sense the heavy emotions drifting in the air, her eyes darting between Noah and Makenna. "Good game tonight, the both of you. I shall see you in the morning," she said and exited with more grace than Makenna was capable of.

Noah turned to Makenna then, his face all concern and worry. "Are you all right?" he asked. His hand came up to comfort her, but he stopped shy of her shoulder. Some small part of Makenna wished he wouldn't have stopped himself.

"My brother died of cancer a few years ago," Makenna said. The words felt hollow. They didn't seem to encompass the devastation they wrought.

Noah lowered his head, his eyes hooded. "I know. You told Huxley about it when you moved in after Rory's death, and Huxley told us. I'm so sorry, Makenna."

Of course Huxley had told them. The man couldn't hold anything back. "I just want to know Rory didn't suffer," Makenna said as she turned away from Noah. She didn't know why – he had seen her bawl her eyes out already today. This moment seemed far more intimate somehow.

Makenna couldn't stop the image of her brother's final moments, trapped in that sterile hospital room, tubes and machines poking out of his frail body to keep him alive. Had Maryam been dealt the same fate? Had they both had their humanity stripped from them one painful day at a time, until there was nothing left? What was Makenna supposed to mourn? A broken body that didn't even look like her brother anymore?

"Love is limitless," Noah said to echo Maryam's words. "Your brother was never without it."

Makenna didn't feel like sitting here anymore. She wanted away from this table and the weighted feeling now on her chest. It was ugly and clawed at her heart – had been clawing at her heart for the last two years. She was surprised to find comfort in Noah, though, sitting across from her offering his quiet support. He had a pull to him that drew her in, more magnetic than ever. It was as if she knew he would somehow assuage all her fears, or at the very least try to.

"Can we go for a walk? I don't want to go back to my room just yet."

"Of course." Noah stood from his chair and pulled Makenna's out, much like a gentleman. "Where do you want to go?"

"Anywhere but here."

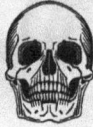

14

Three Times Too Many

The night's air was unseasonably warm for this time of year. As Noah led Makenna out into the back garden, he undid the coat he had worn in anticipation of colder weather. He peeked at Makenna to make sure she wasn't shivering. When she seemed unbothered by the cold, he went back to staring ahead as they walked. Beyond the neatly trimmed hedges and rose bushes, the garden rolled gently towards the edge of the woods, where nature took over. Towering trees and tangled undergrowth created a peaceful, hidden retreat.

"What are you thinking about?" Makenna asked. They wandered through the trees, deeper into the woods. Noah had walked this path enough times; he could do it with his eyes closed. He didn't need the light of the moon to guide him. He did appreciate it for the soft glow it cast on Makenna. She was brilliant in the sunlight, but the moon bathed her skin in an unearthly light that turned her hair silver. She was a goddess of the night.

"Just remembering my time in Edinburgh."

Makenna bobbed her head. "I went once, with my

brother and sister. Dad was supposed to come, but he got wasted the night before and was too hungover to take us. Mum was pissed but couldn't get out of work, so we went without them."

"Did you like it?" Noah asked. He missed the intricate streets. They seemed to weave and cross each other without reason. How many times had he gotten lost until he learned his way around?

"I did. I even tried haggis, and I liked it." She had a ghost of a smile on her lips.

Noah couldn't help but smile back. "If it's cooked right, it's not half bad, isn't it?"

Makenna bit her lip. "I got super drunk that night. I chucked it up later."

Noah couldn't stop the laugh from his mouth if he tried. "I'm sorry, I don't mean to laugh. I can only imagine you getting that drunk."

Waving him off, Makenna scrunched her face. "It was my sister's fault. She kept insisting on shots and beer, plus the locals kept buying us more drinks. I swear it was their sole purpose to get us wasted."

"The Scots will do that to you," Noah said with a wink. He continued to lead them down a gentle slope to where the stream began. Great trees hung over the edge, seeming to dip their leaves in the water, as if testing out the temperature. Brilliant reds and yellows blended into one another, a kaleidoscope of autumn. "Did you get along with your siblings?"

"Not so much with my sister, but I did with my brother, even if he was a momma's boy. I swear my mother forgot about Paige and me when Rory came along."

The two stopped at the edge of the water while Makenna spoke. There was an inherent sadness in her voice. Noah wasn't sure if it was for the neglect of her mother or the fact that she spoke of the dead.

"He was a good brother, an absolute shit at times but kind and carefree like most kids. When he got sick, I remember watching the innocence leave him. He was only twelve when he was diagnosed, fourteen when he died." Makenna kicked at the dirt beneath her feet, her lips pursed in a thin line. "I think my parents died when he did. My dad became a full-blown alcoholic, and my mum turned against the world. Their marriage never recovered. They split, my sister went to school, and I came here. We haven't all been together since."

Noah bowed his head. He imagined the pain of losing a child was unfathomable. It couldn't be put into words.

Makenna bent over and picked up a few stones on the shore. She tossed the first aggressively into the pond. "And now my mum has lost another child – and she doesn't even have a body to bury this time." She sent another flying into the water. This one went further.

"I'm sorry." All Noah wanted was to keep Makenna safe, and for her to live a good life without falling into the curse of this damn place. He had failed her. All the pain she had been through – and now she was trapped. "I lost someone I loved, too," he said as he picked up his own collection of smooth rocks to toss. "She was the love of my life, and I let her down."

"I doubt that," Makenna said.

"You have no idea." Noah chucked a stone as far as he could. It skimmed across the surface before succumbing to a watery grave. "And I let her down more than once."

Makenna was out of stones, having thrown the last of hers. She turned to face Noah, and the moon lit her from behind; a goddess indeed. "How did you lose her?"

Noah stalled his arm, ready to throw another rock. "She died."

It was Makenna's turn to be sorry. She shook her head before muttering, "Death is a bitch, isn't it?"

"Till death do us part," Noah said, his voice tense.

"Hey, at least you found someone, even if it was over a hundred years ago. Pretty sure I'm going to die alone. You have one up on me," Makenna said as she crouched down to hunt for more throwing stones.

Noah smacked his lips together before answering. "You aren't going to die alone."

"You seem pretty confident about that." Makenna quirked an eyebrow at him as she stood up, ready to chuck more rocks. "I'm chronically single. No one wants to date the sad girl. Doubt that will change now I'm stuck here."

"You're not sad." Noah was quick to come to her defence. "And even if you were, that doesn't make you unlovable."

Makenna's lips quirked up at the corner. "Am I now? You say that with such confidence."

"You're worth loving," Noah said as he wound his arm back to release another rock. It skimmed the surface five times before the water swallowed it up. He kept his eyes locked on the stream, though he could feel Makenna's intense stare on him.

"To be known is to be loved," she said.

"Excuse me?" Noah turned to face her, not quite prepared for the way she looked at him. He had said those words to his first love, 126 years ago. He hadn't been expecting Makenna to say them to him now.

She shrugged as she dropped eye contact. "Someone told me that once, though I can't remember who. It was so long ago. The point is, no one knows me. I never let anyone close enough to try. Therefore, I am not loved."

"People love you, more than you know. I promise you that. You are dearly loved."

Makenna let her gaze drift across the stream's length, releasing the stones she held. They tumbled to the shore before settling in their final resting place. "Do you believe what Maryam said? How we can still be connected to our loved ones even after death?" Her face screwed somewhere between hopeful and pessimistic.

Noah was out of stones. "I think death has a funny way of connecting people. It's never in the way you think." He hadn't meant to be so blunt. The instant Makenna's face fell, he regretted the words. "I just mean death is unpredictable."

"You tried it once, killing yourself in this house. That's what Huxley said." Makenna crossed her arms over her chest. "I don't mean to pry. I'm just trying to understand how this curse works. As you said, death is unpredictable. What does that mean to you?"

Everything. It meant everything.

～

OCTOBER 14, *1941*

Noah stood above her grave. Meredith's grave. His love, his life. The only joy the world had gifted him before trapping him in this hellhole. It was torturous being without her. He had mourned her death for so long. He desperately needed her comfort as he started to fade from the living, and yet the closest he could get was six feet above her grave.

"Noah, are you all right?" Lydia stood behind him. Her hand hung in the air just above his shoulder as if unsure whether to comfort him. She dropped it to wrap her maroon robe around herself when it was clear he did not want her touch.

"I don't get it." He wasn't speaking to her per se. He wasn't sure anyone could understand the whirlwind of emotion in his head right now. This situation was uniquely torturous to him and him alone. "Why did I lose her? Why am I still here?"

"I wish I could tell you." Lydia finally closed the space between them and rested her hand on his arm.

Noah shook it off, annoyed Lydia would even bother to soothe him, and she gave him the space he so desperately wanted. He was angry; beyond so. Anger wasn't heavy enough of a word. He was livid, furious, enraged. Here he stood above *her* grave, having not aged a day, yet caught in purgatory. It should have been his death. He should have been the one the ghosts buried. Not Meredith. All these years, and Noah still couldn't work out how she died. It should never have happened. None of this. He should have stayed in Edinburgh and never come to this wretched place. He had sealed their fate and there was nothing he could do about it but mourn. It was cruel with no end in sight. His suffering was eternal.

He looked up from the weathered tombstone, for he had an audience again. Rose stood at the far end of the graveyard. She had died only six months ago, her delicate hand toying with her necklace as she watched him. She wore no expression, her face as smooth as the stone with Meredith's name on it, and just as cold.

Noah barely registered crossing the well-kept graveyard – he was in front of Rose in only a few long strides. There was a vacancy in her eyes. She had had it from the moment her ghost appeared in the house. "How did you do it?" he asked. His words were to the point. He wouldn't spend another minute like this. If he couldn't have his freedom from this hell by leaving the property, he would find another way out. Maybe it would finally end the curse.

"Do what?" Rose asked. She stared at him coolly.

"Don't play with me. How? I want to know *how* you did it."

Rose's lips were tight as she spoke. "You were in the house, were you not? You saw the aftermath."

"That's not what I mean." Noah clenched his fists tightly, his heart racing furiously in his chest. It nearly clouded his vision. "*How* did you go through with it?"

Rose leaned forward as if to bestow some great secret upon Noah no one else should be privy to. "I lost something I loved."

"Your child," Noah breathed.

Rose's hand dropped to her stomach, her lips dipping ever so slightly. It was the first crack of emotion Noah had seen in her. "Twice. I didn't even get the chance to be a mother to either of them."

"And that was enough to end it all?"

"It was everything."

Noah turned his eyes to the house before coming back to Rose. He needed privacy. "I want to be buried next to her."

Rose nodded.

He didn't bother saying goodbye to Lydia. He didn't care what Huxley was doing, either. Harriet might as well have been a ghost among the dead. He wanted out, and he was going to get it now.

His room was the best place, no doubt. It would give him the privacy he desired, and it wouldn't take long for anyone to find him. Then he'd get to sleep for eternity next to Meredith. It would be peaceful and quiet and dark. How lovely that sounded. No more pain, no more loss. He wouldn't have to fight for his freedom. He'd close his eyes and drift forever.

Noah would be considerate. The tub was easy to clean. He would lie in there and wait to join Meredith, wherever the afterlife took them. Reunited at last.

Once he made it to his room, he took off his pleated jacket and rolled up his shirt sleeves. He had a blade ready to go, kept sharp and rust free after all these years. As he stepped into the tub, he felt the rage leave his body. It exhausted him as he lay down, his knees bent to accommodate his height. The porcelain was hard underneath him as he held the blade up to the light.

How many years had he been trapped here? Long enough to live another life, but this wasn't living. He might as well have been a ghost. He had no spirit left to keep him going. He didn't even have Meredith anymore. Losing a loved one twice had been enough for Rose; Noah had lost more than that. This was his way out.

He never fathomed himself capable of doing such a thing. A small voice in the back of his head cried out in alarm, but the heavy feeling in his chest drowned it. He was tired, so, so tired. He just wanted to sleep. The eternal sleep, his mother had called it.

The blade was cool against his skin, his cuts precise; one wrist, then the next. It was done. His eyelids felt heavy, and he let them close as the blood seeped out. He would think of his life outside these walls as he drifted. He would remember all the reasons he had wanted to live and the things that had given him purpose. He had lived well until he came here. Perhaps in another life, he would live well again.

His heartbeat slowed.

Stopped.

And then started again.

Noah shot up from the bathtub as if an electric current had run through his body. Every inch of him felt on fire. When he looked down, the cuts on his wrists were bloody, but slowly stitching together. He bent over, his hands trembling as he watched them heal. There weren't even scars left when they finally closed. Noah felt hot, a sweat breaking out on his skin.

No, no, no. This was Noah's last way out. He had tried everything else: the gates, the water. There was no way off this property, no way to escape this misery. He had chosen life in this frozen state for forty-two years, longer than he had ever been a free man. Now he chose death, but it rejected him.

Noah couldn't breathe as he held the blade to his throat. He pushed deep, further than he knew was recoverable. He didn't count the minutes as he bled out, for as soon as his heart stopped, it beat again.

He could see his blood before him as he came to – could feel the wound on his neck as it healed, slower than his wrists had. Noah's life force had coursed out from his injuries. It marred the tub, stained his shirt and hands – and yet here he was, alive enough to admire the abhorrence of it all.

He doubled over, his head in his hands as he let out a wretched scream. There were forty-two years of torment behind it. It shook him to his core. How unfair that death would take his lover, yet it wouldn't take him?

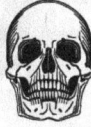

15

The Weeping Woman

The air was heavy between Noah and Makenna as he escorted her back to her room. She hadn't imagined him capable of trying something so desperate, yet she understood why he had done it as she listened to his tale. Makenna had tried it herself once, on a desperate night where life didn't seem worth it anymore. She had struggled with that feeling for years, and her brother's death only exasperated it. Both her and Noah had failed in their attempts, and now they walked together through the dark halls of the manor. Looking at him now, Makenna noted how easily he blended in with the shadows. They seemed to reach for him as he passed by. For a second, she felt the desire to slip her hand into his, to comfort him, to show him that she saw his pain and recognised it.

"Can you promise me one thing?" Noah said as they made their way to the stairs.

"I don't think I have much to give," Makenna said, "but I'll try."

Noah stopped short of the first step. His hesitancy rang something in the back of Makenna's mind. Had they had this exchange before? Why did his trepidation feel so familiar? She stared at Noah through the dark. The shadows didn't seem to reach for him anymore; they simply claimed him. It was as if he belonged to them.

"Don't try what I did. Please. I want you to remember that death picks and chooses in this house. I don't want you to risk it as a way out. Not yet."

"I won't," Makenna said, her arms wrapped tightly around her waist. It felt colder inside than it had out by the water. "I don't think of myself as stuck just yet."

Noah's shoulders relaxed, and Makenna realised how tense he had been about the whole thing. Did he know that she had tried to kill herself as well?

"Good, I just wanted to make sure you—" before Noah could finish, a low moan broke through the entrance. It grew in pitch until it sounded like a wail. Makenna's head whipped around sharply, half expecting Cody to appear with his father right behind.

"It's not Cody," Noah said quickly. His hand came up to Makenna, and instantly she moved closer to him. The wail morphed, becoming something between a sob and a scream. It was eerie how the sound seemed to bounce from one wall to the other. It felt like it circled the two before it carried on to the next room.

"What was that?" Makenna was rather close to Noah's chest. She could feel the heat of his skin through his shirt. If she moved any closer, her nose would brush his chin. Makenna nearly backpedalled, but something about being so close to him was comforting. She couldn't help the way her eyes drifted to his lips, so close to her own. The entire shape of him seemed so familiar, as if she already knew what he would taste like. All she had to do was lift up on her toes to eradicate the little space between them. Something deep within Makenna wanted her to.

Noah's hands came up along her back shoulders to bring Makenna even closer to his body. She didn't mind; his scent was warm, like clove and cinnamon. "It's Harriet. Sometimes at night, she weeps. You never see her, but you most certainly hear her."

The sounds drifted off, and Makenna was closer to Noah than she should have been. She didn't want to pull away, though. This moment was the safest she had felt since entering the house. "Why does she weep?" Makenna asked with a swallow. She could make out the dark swirls of Noah's eyes. He seemed to capture the night in all its likeness and challenge its beauty. No man should be allowed to do so.

Noah dropped his arms from Makenna to put a bit of space between them. She tried not to let the disappointment show on her face as he straightened his shirt. "She cries for what once was, her life before her death. She's been doing it for so long. I can't even remember when she started. Over a century ago."

"When did she die? How did she die?" Makenna felt far more emboldened to ask since the likeliness of her meeting Harriet was slim.

Noah cleared his throat as he directed them to the stairs again. "She died of old age shortly after I got stuck here. I think it was around 1901 – give or take a year; they all blend together."

Makenna supposed they would as the two made their way up the stairs. "After you got stuck here, what happened to the house? Was Harriet the next one in?"

"She was. After I got stuck and the living could no

longer see me, the property was sold on the assumption of my death. Harriet was a widow with great wealth. She moved in and died relatively quickly. I remember the coroners taking her body out while she stood and watched them from this very landing. Then she disappeared into the attic and hardly ever came down again."

"That must have been awful. I can't imagine."

"Harriet was a very interesting woman in life, maybe even more so in death. I think her ageing disturbed her greatly. She was always buying dresses and jewellery when she was alive, maybe to feel young again. Sometimes I think that's why she never comes down. She didn't like her old age appearance in life. Now she's stuck with it in death."

"Has she ever said that?" Makenna asked as they neared her room. Noah's hand brushed hers accidentally, sending tingles up her arm. Had Noah even noticed? His face was relatively smooth as he spoke.

"Of course not. It's just what we've surmised after all these years."

"Oh. I didn't think the dead cared about their appearances. Maybe Harriet avoids mirrors, too."

"I believe that's vampires." Noah cracked a small smile.

"Imagine if those were real," Makenna said. "Or werewolves."

"Witches, even."

Makenna's eyebrows shot up. "I'd be pissed. I never got my letter to Hogwarts."

"I don't know what those words mean," Noah said as they stopped in front of her door. "But you seem mad about it, so I'll be mad about it too. That damn Hogwarts."

Her laughter filled the hall, and she clamped a hand over her mouth. It felt wrong to laugh, knowing there was a 100-year-old ghost weeping her way through the house.

Noah let out a chuckle and reached for her hand. Makenna's heart thumped with his touch. "Please don't ever stop yourself from laughing. This house needs as much of it as it can get." Their fingers intertwined as he brought her hand down. "Shall I write a strongly worded letter to this Hogwarts and demand your letter in return?"

Makenna only giggled this time. It was much more subdued, but Noah joined in on her smile. "If you could, that would be amazing. I'd be forever grateful," she said.

Then the hall and Noah slipped from her sight, and she was somewhere else.

"IF WE COULD MAKE *it happen, I'd be forever grateful." Makenna stood in an office, a dim and brooding space with dark wood-panelled walls and bookshelves that stretched up towards the vaulted ceiling. A massive oak desk sat in the centre, a relic from a bygone era. A stone fireplace loomed nearby, holding the last embers of a dying fire.*

Noah sat at the desk, papers littering its surface in no particular order. He had ink smudged on both his hand and sleeve. As he dropped his quill, Noah pushed back his hair with messy fingers, his midnight curls bouncing back wildly. "I just worry it's not a good idea, Meredith. My mother always warned me about going to England."

"Your mother said a lot of things." The words came out of Makenna's mouth, but they were not her own. This was not her memory. It was someone else's. Someone named Meredith.

"She also did a lot of things, questionable things. I don't know if she's the best judge of character to base our entire future on. This is a fantastic opportunity – an entire manor house, already in your name. Imagine what you could do with your medicine there, all those rooms. Think of all the people you could help. And being that isolated – I

could maybe learn some magic. This is a fresh start, Noah, and it's being handed to us on a silver platter." Makenna made her way over to the desk and dropped to her elbows on it. She grabbed Noah's collar with one hand and pulled him in while the other wove through his curls. They felt like silk. His lips were even softer as she kissed him gently. He tasted of honey.

Noah returned the favour with his own hands as they crept up Makenna's sides until he held her face. He slowly rubbed his thumb along her cheekbones, her low moan encouraging him further. After a beat of self-indulgence, he broke the kiss, though he was thoroughly heated and his breathing heavy. "Can I think about it? I worry about you learning magic. It's dangerous, Meredith."

Makenna pulled back, sorely disappointed he had broken the kiss so soon. Noah looked concerned. She didn't want to do anything he was uncomfortable with, even if she was disappointed with his answer. This would be their decision together. "I know. Just think about it. That's all I ask."

Noah pulled her in close again. "I just want the best for us. A good life, you know?" he said before tasting her lips again.

The smile on Makenna's face was undeniable as she broke from him. "And a good life it shall be. For I know you, Noah Kiers, and you deserve the very best."

MAKENNA'S REALITY slammed back into her, leaving her breathless. Noah still stood in front of her, but it was not the Noah she had just been kissing. Her fingers shot to her lips, the taste of honey still in her mouth.

The smile on Noah's face wavered. "Are you all right? You look like you've just seen a ghost."

Makenna didn't know whether to laugh or cry at his statement. She was still trying to sort out the flash that had seemingly possessed her. Everything had felt so real, as if Noah had been in her arms and she in his. *Meredith*. That's what he had called her. His love from Edinburgh. Was she here? Was her ghost in the house?

"I'm fine. I just realised how tired I am." Makenna hoped Noah didn't see how badly she was shaking as she reached for the doorknob behind her. "I'll see you in the morning, yeah? Thanks for tonight." Before he could say anything, Makenna dipped into her room and gently closed the door. She felt better having a solid wall between them. Makenna had felt everything Meredith had felt: the adoration, the respect, the deep desire to never let Noah out of her sight. It was intense.

She sat down on her bed and squeezed her eyes. She could imagine Noah; the shirt he wore with the stained sleeves. An intense blush spread across her cheeks as she imagined slipping his shirt off to reveal his smooth skin beneath. She felt incredibly hot as the fantasy deepened; his hands on hers, her fingers running through his inky hair . . .

No. No, no, no.

That wasn't her. This wasn't her love she was feeling. It was Meredith's. Makenna barely knew Noah. He was a stranger.

Yet was he?

He had been watching over Makenna her entire life. A guardian angel who had tried to stop this wicked fate from befalling her. He had been kind and tender to her ever since, attentive to the point of overprotective. And he listened to her.

Makenna shook out the feeling from her fingers. Noah was a good man, and he deserved to be happy. Whoever this Meredith was, she had given him that. It was clear.

"I'm sorry," Makenna mumbled to the door, unsure if Noah was even on the other side. Losing Meredith must have been devastating. So much loss. Grief was just love with nowhere to go. No wonder he didn't want to subject Makenna to this fate. Holding on to that loss for a century would have ruined her, too. She knew he couldn't hear her, but that didn't stop her heart from breaking for him. "I'm sorry for all of it."

～

"DO you think she'll be safe? Should we tell her more?" Siobhan asked. They were in the small church located on the eastern side of the property a few hours after Makenna had gone to bed. The church was modest, but Noah liked it that way. Built of stone and timber, it rested near a copse of trees. Its arched windows and pointed roof rose gently from the earth, sagging with time. It had long ago been abandoned as a holy place and simply acted as another location to frequent when the house became repetitive.

Siobhan stretched out on one of the pews near the altar. It had toppled over long ago, and no one had bothered to set it upright.

"I thought we were avoiding that?" Charles was a few rows behind Siobhan. He leaned over the back of the pew in front of him, his head resting on his crossed arms. "So that we don't have a repeat of last time."

Noah sat down on the raised platform, his back against the toppled altar. He had no connection with any god. He hadn't been raised with one. Any religious services he had attended had been strictly to agitate his mother. "We're not telling her anything. That's final."

Charles lifted his head. "She's probably wondering what's happening to her. Shouldn't you help guide her through it?"

"Like a witch doctor or shaman," Siobhan said. She had a tennis ball in her hand. The steady rhythm of her throwing and catching it irritated Noah to no end. "Wait, no. More like a spirit guide, but you're rocking it literally."

"I am not a spirit guide, nor a witch doctor, or anything of that variety." Noah wouldn't dare associate with witch-craft ever again. "I am here to help Makenna when she asks for it. I don't want to overwhelm her. That is my only job. What else am I here for?"

"Just to suffer?" Siobhan offered. "Maybe you should help yourself first."

Noah restrained the desire to say something harsh to Siobhan. "I don't need help. *She* does. I've already accepted my fate."

Charles pushed back from the pew he leaned on. Noah had found him a few times in the church after his death in the mid-fifties. Charles said the space soothed him, even if he no longer identified with his old faith. The spirit world was bigger than any god, Charles had told Noah – and no one was holy enough to tell Charles different. Now he only visited the church when the others came, for his spirituality had moved elsewhere.

"I think you're missing the point. You should help guide her so she doesn't get overwhelmed from not know-ing. Not knowing could be just as bad as all-knowing," Charles explained. "And while you're working so hard to get her out, maybe try to get yourself out, too."

Siobhan threw the ball high enough that it hit the ceiling before falling back into her hand. Noah nearly swatted it away from her as she relaunched it. "Forget me," he said. "This isn't about me. If I tell her anything, then I risk overwhelming her when she's already overwhelmed."

Much to Noah's sanity, Siobhan flipped over so she was on her stomach. Her head rested on her fists, the ball forgotten. "So, she can either be whelmed by one thing or whelmed by another. You need to pick. I say just go for it.

How much damage can you do? She's already been here for a few days."

"Shiv." Charles's tone was harsh. "Have some respect."

The younger girl shot up. "I am. I say go for the middle. It's only logical." With a huff, she plunked herself back on the pew. "I'm not trying to be rude. I'm just saying it like it is. You guys always make me out to be such a bitch."

"No one said that," Charles soothed. "We just need a little tact here. Noah is in a very sticky situation—"

"Sticky situation? Jeez, call it like it is, grandpa. He's fucked. He needs to un-fuck it. He needs to un-fuck himself while he's at it. Otherwise, he's just rotting away with the rest of the house."

It always amazed Noah how some people could talk about him as if he wasn't even in the room. "I appreciate the feedback and suggestions, but I know what I'm doing."

"Do you?" Siobhan asked. "Is that why you look like you haven't slept in days? But you have everything perfectly under control, don't you?"

Noah, in fact, did not have everything under control. He spent his nights fretting over whether or not he'd wake up to the news he'd have to bury another body. He had to stop himself from tiptoeing across the hall and opening Makenna's door just to make sure she was still breathing. "I'm doing my best," Noah said, though even he could hear the tiredness in his voice. He would have felt much better if Makenna had been in his room, where he could keep a watchful eye on her. He wasn't sure he'd ever sleep again.

"Of course you are," Charles said. "And we'll do whatever you need of us." He cocked his head to the side, and pointedly stared at Siobhan. "Won't we?"

The girl made probably one of the top ten sighs Noah

had ever heard from her. It was both dramatic and comical, her arm shooting up and over her face. "Don't I always?"

"You have all been more than helpful," Noah said, and he meant it. Never had anyone violated his wishes when he made them clear. The ghosts had always complied. It would have been a terrible thing if an arsehole died in the house. Harriet didn't count since she never left the attic.

Siobhan sighed for a second time, though much less theatrically. "Have I been helpful? Because I just got called out for being rude *again*." Bless the teenage heart and all its angst.

"Even you." Noah stood and retrieved the ball that had rolled away from the girl. He dusted it off on the lapel of his coat and passed it back to her.

"Thanks," Siobhan said. She pursed her lips as if wanting to say something else, then sulked out of the church, leaving the ball on the floor.

"I had a tongue, too," Charles said, once again leaning on the pew in front of him. "My mother said I'd either grow out of it or grow into it. Turns out it would be the thing that killed me."

The church around them began to creak and moan. The day had been pleasant enough, but now the wind was picking up. "The thing that killed you were the men who beat you to death," Noah said as he eyed one of the windows to the left. It tended to blow open during storms. It didn't matter how many times they boarded it shut. It never hung right.

"They would have left me alone, but I just *had* to say something." Charles looked to the toppled altar before his heavy eyelids closed. "I could have walked away."

"Those men taunted you as you walked by. You weren't doing anything but your job delivering food. They were racist pigs dressed up as gardeners, and they knew what they were doing."

Charles cracked one eye open to peek at Noah. "You know what my mum told me when I was young?"

Noah shook his head.

"She told me people would say a lot of mean things to me because of the colour of my skin. She also told me to never give into it. I didn't listen. Who listens to their mum, you know? And that day, those gardeners said something so vile to me, I couldn't walk away. And then they beat the living shit out of me for it, literally."

Charles tapped the side of his head. "I felt them crack open my skull. Felt them break my bones and laugh while they did it. And then I wasn't feeling anything. I was seeing it. I watched them go at my body until a maid came out and shooed them off. She wasn't quick to call the police, either. She stood over me and fretted about what to do. And I got to watch the whole thing. Then I saw you. You were the first one to greet me."

Noah hung his head. He would never forget that day. He would never forget any of the days a new soul joined the household. Noah always had a front-row seat to their last moments of life, all while being completely useless to stop it. He had long ago decided he would make the best of anyone's passing and help ease them into their new reality. They would have a kind face to greet them as they passed through death's door and into the limbo that locked them all here. If not that, then what else could he make of his existence here?

"I'm sorry I couldn't do anything to stop it." How hard had Noah willed himself into the world of the living each time someone brushed up against death? He simply didn't have the knowhow to do so.

Charles let out a slow breath, his eyes still closed. "You

seem to be sorry for a lot of things. I never blamed you for it, and I never will. You try so hard to help all of us, but what about yourself? Siobhan is right."

"Siobhan says a lot of things. Not all of them are true."

Charles drummed his fingers on the pew in front of him. "You've become complacent in your own life here. You're stuck, yet you try so hard to help Makenna and Cody – whoever else needs it. What if you focused some of that energy on yourself? You could have a life outside these walls too, you know."

"That ship sailed long ago," Noah said, his voice tense. "I have no life, just as I will have no death. I am stuck between both, and I've made my peace with that long ago, just as you've made peace with your death."

Charles shook his head gently. "You have so much to live for. One very reason sleeps in this house as we speak. Would you not fight for yourself as much as you fight for her?"

Noah turned away from Charles, unable to meet the man's knowing eyes. Noah had grieved his own fate ages ago. The thought of what could have been, a life with someone he loved, out in the real world, was precious, but completely out of the question. Hoping for such a thing was a waste of time.

"You deserve a life," Charles said, his words striking through Noah's heart. They buried into a future he craved deeply but would never have.

"And yet this is the one I live," Noah said, right as one of the windows blasted open. It smacked hard against the stone wall of the church, its shutters rattling on impact. Noah jumped to his feet to tend to the blasted thing, glad for the interruption. He wasn't sure what had been about to come out of his mouth next.

He was surprised by the flicker of hope Charles's words instilled in him, however small. Maybe there was some truth to them. Maybe Noah did deserve to live. Maybe he *could* fight for himself, if the opportunity arose.

He just wasn't sure if that would ever happen – or what the cost would be to attain it.

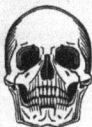

16

Old Bat

G hosts didn't sleep, but Noah sure did. It was this piece of knowledge that had Makenna creeping out of her room at the crack of dawn. She wanted to do some research of her own without him knowing. She would find a way out of this house, and she would take him with her too. Noah had been stuck in between life and death for far too long, and Makenna would be the one to break him out of it. She didn't think she could go on living outside these walls knowing he was still stuck behind.

She had dreamt all night of him, of his kindness, of the way his hand had brushed against hers in the hall. As Makenna left her room early in the morning, she felt a sense of longing as she passed his door. It was too easy to imagine opening it, padding along the cold floor to his bed and settling into his side.

Dear god, she needed to keep her mind on the task.

There had to be something that would give her answers. This manor had housed Noah for over a hundred years. There must have been something to indicate a way out during all that time. She refused to believe there wasn't.

The library seemed like the right place to start. There were more than enough books there. Maybe Makenna would find something that caught her eye. Sites like this house were always overloaded with books from bygone times. How badly she wished she could simply google his name. A search function would have been lovely about now, Makenna thought as she entered the room.

There were undoubtedly enough books to keep her occupied for years. This would be like finding a needle in a haystack. Only she wasn't even sure there was a needle to be found. But she had to start somewhere.

"What are you doing?"

In the dull morning light, Makenna hadn't noticed Cody shoved into one of the couches, poring over an X-Men comic. "Cody, good morning. It's good to see you."

The boy immediately dropped the comic book to the floor and launched off the couch. "You shouldn't be here. I shouldn't be here. I need to go." He took a giant step forward and Makenna swerved to block the door.

"Cody, wait! Please don't go. Let's talk." She held her arms out, as if to soothe a spooked animal.

"I don't want to hurt you again," he said, backing away from her. "I brough you here. I'm so sorry, Makenna. I didn't mean to." There were tears in his eyes, leaking down his round cheeks.

Makenna kept her hands up as she spoke. "Cody, I don't blame you. It wasn't your fault. I've been hearing you in my dreams for years. It was just fate that I came over on my birthday, all because of the curse, right? I never blamed you, and I pray to God that you don't blame yourself." She inched closer to him, encouraged when he didn't bolt away. His body trembled with the sobs he tried to repress.

"You're not going to hurt me, see?" She took another step in, then another, until she was close enough to reach out to him. "Look, nothing's happening." She gently wrapped her hands around his thin arm, and when he held still, pulled him in for a massive hug. "Oh god, Cody. It was never your fault. And I'm glad you're here. You remind me of my brother, and I loved him very much."

He trembled beneath her before his arms snaked around her middle, his face smooshing into her chest. "I'm glad you're okay, Makenna. I was so worried something would happen to you."

Makenna imagined the boy in her arms to be her brother, and closed her eyes shut as a wave of grief overtook her. "Shhh, none of that. I'm fine. You're fine. Everything is fine."

"Promise?" Cody's muffled voice said.

Makenna squeezed him tightly and placed a soft kiss on the top of his head. "Would I ever lie to you?"

"I don't think so."

"Good, 'cause I need your help." Dropping down to his level, Makenna looked him directly in the eye. "I need to find information on this house. Can you help me? Books, records, anything of the like. Anything I can read."

"I didn't take you for much of a reader," Cody said between sniffles.

Makenna dropped her hands from his arms to give him some breathing room. "I feel like I should be offended."

"I had a friend that didn't like to read. She was kind of dumb."

"Now I'm definitely offended," Makenna said with a small smile. "Can you help me?"

Cody stood straight as he cocked his arm into a salute, his eyes still red-rimmed. "Aye, aye, captain. What exactly do you need?"

"Good. If we can't find anything on the house, I'll take history of the local area. Anything pre-1900s would be ideal."

"I think the sixties are more fun. Did you know people did drugs back then? Heroin and LDS. I looked it up once."

"LSD," Makenna corrected him. *God forbid anyone tells him about opium.* "I did actually know that, but I want to know more about the turn of the century to be exact. People didn't have the internet back then."

"I know," Cody said dramatically. "You probably want the attic. There's a collection of books dealing with the property's history up there. But no one goes up there. That's Harriet's space. And she's really mean." He kicked a scuffed shoe against the floor. "She snatched one of my X-Men comics and tore it up a few years ago. I had to tape it together, but it's not the same. I'm not sure what she would do to you. She might scratch your face off. I wouldn't put it past her."

Makenna reached out a hand to smooth his ruffled copper hair, as she used to do to Rory. "I think I'll take my chances, thank you."

"Don't say I didn't warn you," Cody called after her as she retreated from the library. "She's really mean!"

During Huxley's tour of the house on Makenna's first day here, he had pointed out the narrow stairs that led up to the attic. He explicitly said she shouldn't go up there. Well, Makenna was going to do exactly that. She wanted answers. She hadn't woken up at the crack of dawn for anything less. Though as she stood at the bottom of the stairs, Cody's words rang in her ears. What would Harriet do to Makenna if she stumbled upon her? Could Makenna fend off a violent ghost? Did she have any better option?

It felt wrong as she tiptoed her way up the stairs, but

her mind was made. They were steep and cold, with no light to guide her, creaking under every step. The further she got, the less brave she felt. Could Harriet cause her real harm? If Makenna died up there, the two would have to haunt the attic together.

Did she call out in greeting? That felt dangerous. Maybe it was better to stick to the shadows. Could ghosts see in the dark? They were dead, not bats. Makenna popped her head into the attic first. It was an expansive space with only a few windows populating the walls, dully lit with the weak morning sun. For the most part, the room was full of random crap, and somehow dust free. These ghosts had an inclination for cleanliness, Makenna would give them that. The random crap was also well organised. Everything seemed meticulously put into place, arranged by size, colour, and functionality.

Makenna was immediately distracted by an armoire with the most luxurious coats she had ever seen. There were furs and leathers, each from a different time, and none less beautiful than the other. She was drawn to it. Her hand stretched out to touch the closest one.

"Fancy losing a hand, girl?"

Makenna spun around, her hand suctioned to her chest. Across the room stood a woman, her snow-white hair styled in an intricate chignon. Not a single hair was out of place, nor were her clothes. She wore a finely pressed, forest green dress with a tight bodice. Everything about this woman was stiff, from her posture to the cold look she gave Makenna. Her paper-thin lips were pulled down, her hands behind her back.

"I'm sorry." Makenna jumped back from the coats as if they had burned her. "They're beautiful."

"And its dirty hands like yours that will be the ruin of them."

"I didn't mean to—"

The woman moved closer to Makenna, her dress moving as stiffly as she did. "Been a long time, hasn't it?"

"I – what?" Makenna expected a good talking-to for touching things that didn't belong to her; maybe a second coming with the intensity this lady looked at her.

"Has it already been so long?" Harriet moved around Makenna to a vanity that housed a collection of makeup and brushes. Sitting down on an ornate chair, Harriet dabbed her finger into a pot and peppered her cheeks with powder. It did absolutely nothing for her complexion. The powder simply fell to the surface below.

"I don't know what you mean."

Harriet twisted in her seat, her hand resting on the back of the chair. She looked like a dowager about to dismiss a maid for some petty reason. "You grow denser every time."

It wasn't even eight in the morning, and Makenna had been insulted by not one but two ghosts. She was going to have to go hunting for a compliment after this. "Do you know me?" Makenna asked. Something about Harriet reminded Makenna of her mother. If there was one thing Jacqueline had taught her daughter, it was how to deal with difficult people. The best way was to be direct so that they couldn't jerk you around.

"Haven't been to the graveyard yet, I see," Harriet said with a cackle.

Makenna felt the floor shift beneath her. "I don't understand."

Harriet turned back around to the mirror. She had a thin brush in her hand to gloss over her hair. "Not just dense, but ignorant, too? My, my."

Somehow Makenna got her legs working again. She nearly threw herself at Harriet as she dropped to her knees in front of the woman. "Please, tell me everything. Do you know why I'm here? Who is Noah to me? Have I been here before?" A hundred questions flashed before her, and she struggled to pick one. "How do I get out of here?"

Harriet looked thoroughly repulsed that Makenna had dared to get so close to her. The old woman leaned back, her thin eyebrows nearly lost in her hair by the audacity of it all. "Has he told you nothing?" Harriet's eyebrows dropped then, her repulsion turning to something crueller. "Ignorance is bliss, girl. Surely this isn't something you want an old bat like me to tell you?"

"I want answers. I want a way out."

Harriet leaned closer, and Makenna was the one to pull away. "Death is your answer. It is the only door out of here."

"But Noah – he tried to die. He told me it didn't work."

"Of course he did. Do you honestly think death treats you as it does him? It has never shown you mercy." Harriet faced the mirror again, having said her piece to Makenna.

It wasn't good enough. Makenna was only more confused now. She got to her feet, ready to throw the brush Harriet was so preoccupied with out the window if it meant getting proper answers. "That makes no sense. What's going on?" She demanded every inch of Harriet's attention.

The old woman barely paid her any mind as she continued fussing with her appearance. "What cycle are we on now? Six or seven? I never care to count. Rinse and repeat. It's all the same."

Makenna forced herself between the vanity and Harriet so the woman could no longer look in the mirror. "I don't know what that means."

Harriet dropped the brush before giving Makenna her

full attention. "You insolent girl. Go check the cemetery. You'll find your answers there."

The air in the room felt heavy. Makenna had to actively remind herself to take a breath in and out. Harriet spoke nonsense.

"You're cruel," Makenna said as she pushed herself away from the old crone.

Harriet let out a shrill laugh that followed Makenna as she bolted from the attic. "And your time is up, girl. Nothing has changed."

~

OCTOBER 15, *1962*

The bang went off, loud but muffled. It seemed to echo through the house walls, though Noah knew the source of its origin immediately. He seemed to be moving in slow motion towards the sound. It had come from outside, in the shed. He had told May not to go in there, yet he had watched her eye it. There were fears growing in the area. Voices whispered of communism and its violent supporters. May had seen it herself in town, and she brought the concerns of it with her into this house. She didn't feel safe. She wanted protection.

"I'll protect you," Noah had told her.

It wasn't enough. May had spent the last few days scouring the house for something more substantial. She had found it. Outside in the shed were the hunting guns, long out of use and unkept. They tended to misfire, and Noah warned her about this. She hadn't listened.

He was by the shed now, where Lydia was standing outside the front door.

"Move," Noah told her.

"Noah—"

"Move," he said more forcefully.

Lydia relented. There was blood already seeping out from beneath the door. The damage was done.

. . .

NOAH SHOT up from his bed, his heart pounding as he tried to cool the panicked feeling in his chest. He had slept the morning away. Where was Makenna? Had something happened in the night? Kicking off the sheets, Noah detangled himself from his bed. Why were there so many pillows? It was unnecessary.

Noah threw on a pair of loose trousers and a navy jumper well past its prime, then left his room in haste. He nearly slammed into Lydia with his speed but caught himself before tackling her to the ground. The woman threw her hands up to slow him down, her eyebrows high in her hairline.

"Is the house on fire?"

"Is Makenna still alive?"

"Do you always answer questions with more questions?"

Noah shimmied himself around Lydia. He felt a little nauseous from jumping out of bed so fast, but he was at Makenna's door, ready to knock.

"She's alive but not there." Lydia followed Noah across the hall. "I saw her leave about two hours ago."

The heavy weight in Noah's chest lifted as he dropped his fist. Makenna had made it through the night. "You could have started with that."

"And you could learn some patience." Noah was about to open his mouth when Lydia cut him off. "I know, I know. You've been here for over a hundred years. You're a master of patience. You've been here so long, your patience has patience."

Noah pulled himself away from the door and peered down the hall. He didn't know what he was looking for. Perhaps Makenna walking towards him, her arms wide open, ready to be reunited as the soulmates they were. "I forsake patience. It's a waste of my time."

"Not sure that's how it works. Noah —" Lydia snapped her fingers in front of him. "I'm talking to you."

He didn't mean to be so distracted. Noah's dream still clouded his mind. It had been one of the bloodiest deaths. May's blood still stained the wood in the shed to this day. He had never gone in it since. "Do you know where Makenna went?"

"Last I saw, she was with Cody in the library."

Noah gave Lydia a curt nod. His feet were already flying down the stairs and into the library. He nearly kicked the door open.

"Good god, man. You nearly gave me a heart attack." Huxley sat in one of the plush chairs by the roaring fire, a cigar in his mouth. It was unlit, but the man puffed on it regardless. "Is the house on fire?"

"People need to stop asking me that." Noah did a quick scan of the room. Neither Cody nor Makenna were here. It was hard to ignore his sense of disappointment. "Have you seen Makenna?"

"Good morning to you too, young man," Huxley said around the cigar. "I swear you were taught manners, were you not?"

That was two people who called him out in less than five minutes. Noah needed to take a breather. Lydia had eyes on Makenna a short while ago. Noah wasn't here to smother the girl. He had simply been caught up in the dream. "I'm sorry. Good morning, Huxley. How are you today?"

"That's better," Huxley said, a man of propriety. "Did you hear Harriet last night? She was quite loud this time. I was out visiting my tree and heard her in the yard." Huxley's wife, Ellen, had planted the beech tree in her husband's memory after his untimely death. It now housed Cody's treehouse.

"I did hear it. Makenna did too."

"Did she now? I'm sure that would have been a fright for her. Even to this day, it still unnerves me." How silly that ghosts could unnerve other ghosts, but Noah didn't argue the point. He was about to respond when Maryam entered the room. She stood in the doorway, her face more serious than usual. She held something behind her back.

Noah cranked his neck to get a better view of it. "What do you have there, Mar?"

"I want you to keep an open mind." From behind her back, Maryam pulled out a book.

Noah's body tensed immediately. "You didn't get rid of it?"

Maryam came closer, her arm outstretched to offer the spellbook to him. He reeled back from it. "Noah, read the name on the inside of the cover."

Her tone both intrigued and worried Noah. His long fingers wrapped around the leather to take it from her. The book was frayed, damaged by years of use, the outside of the pages yellowed and bent. Flipping the cover over, Noah scanned the page until he saw it. At the bottom, in loopy cursive, was a name he hadn't seen in over a hundred years.

Constance Kiers. His mother.

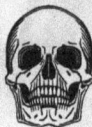

17

Dead Like Me

Makenna had heard enough of Harriet's cruel words. They had been unkind and only served to panic Makenna more than help. She didn't waste any more time in the attic. She didn't want to spend another minute with this spiteful woman, not in this dark and crowded place where truths equalled death. Harriet's laughter followed her down the stairs. How much space could Makenna put between herself and that old bat? She didn't seem to have a direction, only the need to get away from that woman.

Go check the cemetery. You'll find your answers there.

Harriet's words rang around in her head. What was Harriet on about it being the sixth or seventh? Six or seventh what? Makenna's heart raced uncontrollably, each beat pounding in her ears as her mind spiralled in a flurry of fear and confusion. She needed to get to the cemetery, *now.*

She thundered through the house, body tense as she wove through the halls and passed doors. She ran into no one, not that she'd stop for anyone. She had one mission, and nothing would deter her from it.

Finally, she was outside, where the morning sun was lost to dark grey clouds. They hung low to the ground with the threat of rain to come. Makenna paid them no mind. She kept her pace as she tried to navigate her way to the cemetery. It was further back on the property, hidden by a tangle of trees as if the graves were supposed to be a secret. A few minutes of searching, and Makenna found it.

The cemetery lay in a peaceful clearing, its weathered tombstones standing crooked and worn, surrounded by wildflowers and creeping ivy. Makenna moved through them on a well-worn path. Someone had trekked here many times, and Makenna had a feeling she knew who. She followed the worn path to the back of the cemetery to where six gravestones stood, perfectly kept and tended to. They were all dated clearly; October 1899, 1920, 1941, 1962, 1983, and 2004. All twenty-one years apart. Each of the tombs' names had been carved with the same hand; Meredith, Mallory, Millie, May, Mackenzie, Madilyn.

Makenna sunk to her knees, the grass wet beneath her. These women had died exactly twenty-one years apart. All six of them. And Makenna was the seventh. She could feel it in her bones, this sick sense of fate, of her completing the next cycle. She was the seventh. The ghosts had been warning her of it this entire time. The dreams, the memories, Makenna had been channelling these women's lives, their deaths.

She clutched at her heart as if it would stop beating in this very moment. She could imagine Noah standing over her grave, etching her name into the cool stone as she lay dead beneath. Would he mourn her as he mourned the six others? Was this the curse? Brought to the house on her twenty-first birthday, just to die?

Makenna faced the house lost to the tangle of trees. She couldn't see its foreboding walls, but she could feel it. It stood like a Grim Reaper, waiting for her fated demise to complete the seventh cycle. And then what? In another twenty-one years, a new girl would meet the same end?

Why hadn't anyone told her? Fear wrapped around her like a vice, tightening with every passing second until her throat felt dry and her legs refused to move. Liars. All of them. Deceivers of the highest degree. They had known her death was coming and had done nothing but watch.

She refused. She would not die here, not on this property. She would do what none of the other women had done before. She would surpass death.

"This one was particularly brutal."

The sound of someone speaking jarred Makenna back to reality. Rose appeared behind the most recent tomb. It was marked 'Madilyn Daws, died October 12, 2004.'

"She hanged herself that night."

Makenna's hand went to her throat. She could feel the rope digging into her skin, constricting her neck. "Why didn't anyone stop her?"

Rose picked her way around the tomb. She seemed wary of the mud as if it would dirty her shoes and sully her dress. Out of all the ghosts in the house, she looked closest to death. Her eyes were hollow, and her skin was tight over her bones.

"No one can. They're always out of reach when their time is up. We simply find them dead, bury the body, and when twenty-one years is up, another shows face again."

Makenna twisted away from the woman. She felt as if she would be sick. How many graves had Rose helped dig?

"Madilyn was special. It was the first time one willingly took their own life. I've always been curious why."

"I—" Makenna tried to sort through the building

panic. It suffocated her, as if she were drowning in her own fear, unable to focus on anything but the desperate need to escape.

Rose came closer to Makenna as the clouds began to spit. Somehow the rain never touched Rose's skin. "They've died in worse ways, but this one was the hardest for Noah. I think it's because he thought he could truly save her that time, and then she went and killed herself."

Noah. He was the constant between all of them.

"He loved them all. He loves you too, in his weird way. Madilyn really caught him off guard, though. I think he worries you'll do the same." Rose closed the distance between them. This close, Makenna could make out the thin blue veins that traced their way around Rose's limbs.

"I wouldn't—"

"Do you know what it's like to lose a child? I lost two before they were even in my arms. My husband never looked at me the same way. I wasn't a woman to him anymore. I had no purpose, he told me. And so, he left. Then I had nothing. No children, no husband, no purpose."

Rose stood straight as she looked down on Makenna. She had a strange way of speaking, her face almost still as if the words weren't coming from her mouth. "So, I slit my throat open in a bathtub, and no one looked for me. I watched my body rot for days until someone accidentally found me."

Rose's coolness had an underlying savagery to it. If hell froze over, Rose would have made a suitable queen. "You had everything, didn't you?" Rose spat at Makenna. "Your youth, your body, your lover. How many people have someone wait for them as long as he has for you? What makes you so special? You won't even last a week."

Makenna remained rooted to the ground, her clothes

damp in the frigid rain. She couldn't put into words the sense of dread Rose's words instilled in her. Six lives wasted, and this woman stood above their graves with contempt. Makenna had barely managed her brother's death, the emotional distance of her mother, and the split of her parents. This house would not claim her after everything she had survived.

When Makenna could say nothing, Rose pulled back, a humph escaping her lips. "You don't deserve to live. You tried to throw away your life once already. I know, I overheard. Life got too overwhelming, did it?" Rose's face turned cruel then. "I never got to hold my children, not even once. Two little lives gone and yet here you are. You don't appreciate life. But you'll get what you want. Death is coming for you. And who knows, maybe this will be the last time. Maybe there won't be another after you. If only God was so kind."

The rain pounded down, and Makenna was thoroughly soaked through. "I didn't choose this," she finally said. "I never asked to be trapped here. I never asked to die here. This is hell. I am linked to these women by tragedy. How dare you belittle me and their memories." Makenna shot to her feet and jabbed her hand at the gravestones. "They didn't live full lives. They were cut short every time. I don't want this. I want my life, outside these damn grounds where I don't have ghosts as my only company."

Rose tried to interrupt, but Makenna wouldn't let her speak. She had found her voice, and Rose would listen to it. "Don't you dare compare your tragedies to mine or anyone else's. We're all stuck in this hell together. The sooner you realise that, the sooner you'll move on. This house doesn't need any more bad vibes in it, including that dumbass frown permanently on your face. It doesn't do *any* favours for your complexion. And if I'm going to be stuck in this shithole until I die, I'd rather not stare at it."

For the first time since Makenna had been here, Rose showed more than contempt. There was rage behind those hollow eyes, and the woman's shoulders rounded as if she were ready to throw back another attack. Makenna had had enough of it. She didn't need a jealous spirit bringing her down. Makenna was a woman of action, not words. She wasn't going to stand around here and exchange insults; she was going to prove everyone here wrong. Makenna would break free, and she would do it today.

$\sim$

THE SPELLBOOK FELT heavy in Noah's hand. "I told you to get rid of it." He didn't look at Maryam as he spoke. His eyes were busy tracing the curvy handwriting of his mother's. It had been over a hundred years since he had seen it, yet it invoked strong memories.

He had grown up in a small cottage in the Scottish Highlands. Constance had had pages plastered all over the place, writings of what ingredients reacted with what, the magical properties of household items, and the best times to do her spellwork based on the moon phases. Constance had been a witch, and her system had been chaotic. This book before Noah was scribbled all over with her writing. Noah would recognise it anywhere.

"I was going to get rid of it, but then I noticed the name on the cover," Maryam said. She watched Noah with careful eyes, trying to anticipate his reaction. He felt incredibly drained all of a sudden. "That's your mother, isn't it?" They sat in the library, a fire on to fight the chill of the damp air.

Noah rubbed his eyes with his free hand.

Huxley perked up from the couch, having remained quiet for the entire exchange. "What do you have there, exactly?"

Noah tossed the book down on the coffee table. He didn't feel inclined to be gentle with it. "It's a spellbook. My mother's, to be specific."

"A spellbook? May I?" Huxley leaned forward to grab the item from where Noah dropped it. "How fascinating. You never mentioned your mother was into witchcraft, Noah. You always said she practised unorthodox medicine."

"It is, in a roundabout way. Magic was very exclusive back then. She wasn't supposed to practice it."

"I suppose I shouldn't be surprised spellbooks exist. We are ghosts, after all. And you are cursed." Huxley pointed to Noah as if it weren't obvious who he was talking about. "I'm surprised it took this long for you to mention witchcraft."

What would happen if Noah took the book from Huxley and threw it in the fire? It took an immeasurable amount of self-control not to. "I never mentioned it because magic is dangerous. It didn't matter either way. The dead can't use magic. I've never been able to tap into it since I faded halfway into the shadow world." Noah turned back to Maryam. "But Makenna is very much alive, and if she sees that book, she'll be tempted to use it. I know her. That book needs to be destroyed. Immediately. If you don't do it, I will." He reached for the book.

Huxley looked between Noah and Maryam as if unsure whether to relinquish the text to Noah or not. "Perhaps before we do such rash things, we take a moment to understand what it is you want to get rid of so badly," he said, taking a cue from Maryam. "There may be something of use in here yet."

Noah stalled his hand. "Huxley, do you know what magic is capable of?"

The old man shook his head.

Noah didn't want to scare the man, but he wanted his words to carry the proper caution they deserved. "I watched the most unnatural things happen, things I couldn't fathom if I tried. They weren't pleasant, always a means to an end, but they came with a price. And I watched people pay for it. I watched my mother pay for it. That book will bring Makenna nothing but harm. Please understand me when I say that."

Huxley seemed adequately alarmed. He looked down on the book as if it were about to grow teeth and bite him. "Is it really so bad?" he asked.

Noah flipped through a multitude of memories in his head. He had so many of all the times magic had gone wrong, or the price had been more than someone bargained for. "I met a man once, a sailor. He fancied himself an expert seaman. He wanted my mother to make him immune to drowning, said he was going to sail the roughest waters on the North Sea to prove his worth. She brewed a potion for a month, and when he drank it, he drowned on dry land. You can't drown in the ocean when your lungs are already filled with water, you see."

Huxley chucked the book back onto the table. It hit the wood with a thunk, shaking the vase of flowers Rose had picked a few days before.

"Huxley," Maryam chastised. She swooped in between the two and snagged the book before Noah could grab it. "You're already dead, you fool. What do you think this book can do to you?"

"Kill me twice?" Huxley said, his hands in the air. "Do what you will with it, Noah. I trust you understand more about it than any of us."

"Noah has a prejudice against magic," Maryam said, putting more space between her and Noah as if he would lunge for the book. "This could be a godsend, and if Noah is too stubborn to use it for his own good, I will."

How could they not understand the fire they were dancing with? Makenna was safe with them for now. This book, the magic it contained, was a wildcard. Noah would under no circumstance allow it to be used on her. He would protect Makenna at all costs, and right now, magic was the biggest threat. "I don't want to risk anything. Please. I have Makenna. I will keep her safe without magic. We don't need to resort to it."

Maryam was about to open her mouth when another person popped into the room. Cody stood in the doorway with his hands in tight fists. He looked visibly upset. All conversation stopped as every head in the room swivelled to him, the book momentarily forgotten.

"It's her," Cody said. "Makenna's in the pond. She's drowning."

Noah had never moved so fast in his life.

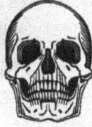

18

Just Keep Swimming

Makenna's clothes were already soaked by the time she got to the pond. It didn't matter that the rain had stopped. She didn't even pause to take her shoes off. She simply walked into the water until she could walk no further. She had been a strong swimmer as a child. It served her well as she began towards the back of the property. There was no access to it by land. She would have to go by water.

Neither Rose nor Harriet knew what they were talking about. They were bitter wisps of death. Makenna was alive and vigorous. She would prove them both wrong. Freedom was so close, just a swim away. She was halfway through the pond already. The water was frigid and pricked at her skin, but she didn't stop. Makenna would move heaven and hell to be rid of this place. No one would stop her.

OCTOBER 26, *1920*

"Stop." A man stood on the top of the landing. He held a knife in his hand. It looked dull and rusted in the hallway light, probably from

heavy use in the trenches. Mallory nearly dropped the bedding in her arms. She had tasked herself with helping the soldiers returned from war heal in the manor. Mallory had not yet become lost to the shadows like Noah had, as he had told her. She would make good use of her time here while she could.

"I'm just here to change the bedding." Mallory freed one hand and held it up. "I don't want any harm."

The soldier cocked his head as if listening to someone speak into his ear. With a nod, he turned his attention back to Mallory, his knife held high. "You're an angel of death. You will take us all."

Mallory backed up slowly as the man began to advance on her. "No. I'm not. I just want to help." Mallory had been here for the last three weeks, a nurse aiding the sick. She hadn't left the property since. She couldn't if she wanted to, though it didn't matter. There was simply too much work to be done. Her respite had been Noah, late at night, after she tended to the injured all day. He was so patient with her.

"In the night. During the day. All the moments in between. You are here, just waiting. How sneaky of you," the man said. He advanced towards her.

Mallory had been on rounds the day he was admitted – shrapnel injuries, nasty but survivable. He had been mentally unstable from the moment he took a bed. He had already lashed out at a few of the doctors and nurses. Perhaps they should have given him a private room, one where he was locked behind a door and couldn't wander the halls late at night. Mallory wasn't sure where he had even found the weapon.

"I am not death. I am alive, just as much as you are," she told him.

The soldier paused in his step, his head twisting to the side. "I am," he said to no one. "I will save them all."

Where was everyone? Usually, people populated the halls, even at this hour of the night. The sick and injured never stopped needing care. "Please. Let's go find your bed. We can worry about this in the morning when you've had a good night's sleep." Mallory backed up, though she was running out of floor space as the man continued to pursue her. Gripping the bed sheets with both hands, she raised them so they covered her chest – a small token of protection.

"No, no, no. You speak in lies. So does the devil, serpent woman."

Mallory's back hit the window at the end of the hall, its cool glass pressing into her shoulders. She wanted to scream but knew the suddenness of the gesture might spook the man and cause him to lunge. "I am no snake. I am a healer. I can help you."

The man's grip never wavered on the knife, though his eyes shifted from side to side. A cold sweat had broken out over his skin. "Yes. I'll do it for them." He didn't waste a moment more and leapt at Mallory. There was no grace in his movement, just feral anger as he raised his hand and slashed down. Mallory threw the bedding at him as she twisted out of the way. It slowed him to disentangle, just long enough for her to squeak by. Bolting down the hall, Mallory called out for help. She nearly tumbled down the stairs in all her haste. The man was right behind her, a limp to his step and his eyes crazed.

"Help. Please!" Mallory cried as she skidded into the study and threw the doors shut behind her. She locked them and turned, hoping to find something heavy to barricade the door with. The room had been cleared for more patients, their arrival expected tomorrow. With a curse, Mallory grabbed the handles, the doorknob twisting as the man on the other side tried to get in.

"Little snake, so sneaky and cruel. How many will you take before I can take you in return?" There was a thump on the door, the wood creaking as the man rammed into it from the other side. "You are far too sweet for a bringer of death. How wrong were we? I will tell them the Grim Reaper is beautiful after all. Hair spun of gold."

Mallory turned her back against the door. Her eyes screwed shut as she prayed to any divinity benevolent enough to listen. Save me. I'm not ready to die.

The force of the man breaking the door down sent Mallory flying forward. She smacked the ground hard, her head spinning as she tried to orient herself. She managed to get on her hands and knees before the soldier was on top of her. He wrapped one hand in her hair to expose her neck while the other dug the knife into her skin.

"I didn't think Grim Reapers cried," he said as he pushed the blade further into her neck.

She tried to call out, but her voice was lost as the knife slid across her throat. He let her go, and Mallory sank to the ground, blood spilling down her dress. She frantically tried to hold it in with her hands, her fingers slipping across her open wound. Slowly her vision began to fade. The last thing she saw was the satisfied smile on the soldier's face and a figure in white standing right behind him.

MAKENNA GASPED as she took in a lungful of water, the memory of another woman pulling her under. She could feel the blade as if it slit her own neck open. She was sure if she looked in the water, it would be mixed with her blood. It didn't matter. She had sucked in enough water that she couldn't catch her breath. Why did her limbs feel so heavy all of a sudden? She was alive as she swam to her freedom – but she was also dying on the floor of the study. Her body didn't seem to know which reality she was in, and it made it hard to tell her legs to kick.

She sank to the bottom of the pond slowly. It was oddly peaceful down here. The water didn't care if she lived or died. She simply just was. What an odd thought. She didn't have to decide if she wanted to fight down here. She didn't have to choose life anymore. She could just be. How many times had she thought about this peace, especially after her brother died? It had been so unreachable for so long.

Is this what her brother had felt as he died? He had been so still in the hospital bed when the monitor went flat. Makenna had been there for that very moment. Had Rory known his family surrounded him at the very end? What a shame if he had not. No one knew where Makenna was now; a tragedy, no doubt. There was beauty in death, and Makenna knew that now. She was unified with the other women. Seven lives, connected only at the very end. Poetic. But what would Noah bury if she remained at the bottom of the pond? Her grave would have to be an empty one. Makenna hoped he would be okay with that. Surely this wouldn't be the thing to break him.

Makenna wished she could tell Noah how at peace she was. She was so tired of being sad all the time, so tired of fighting for a life doomed anyway. She would be reunited with her brother soon enough. Maybe that was the price she needed to pay all along. Makenna would catch Rory up on all the years he had missed. Would he be thrilled to know their family had fallen apart after his death, that he had been the glue holding them together? He had always been a little smug. Makenna could only dream of having that impact on anyone.

How long had she been down here? It felt like an eternity. Makenna had stopped breathing long ago, she was sure of it. She couldn't feel her limbs. It was as if she floated along, caught in the current of the water. If this was death, it felt more transitional than anything – like she was caught between two things, a dream and reality.

Before she could decide she liked the dream more, something yanked her hard.

Every limb in her body tingled as the weightlessness evaporated with a spark. It didn't last long, just a flash of light in the darkness. It breathed fire in her lungs for a second before fading. How extraordinarily beautiful it had been – and warm. Makenna couldn't remember feeling such warmth. She moved towards where the spark had come from. There it was, another in the distance. It burned her lungs again in a pleasant way. She followed the light before it faded, again and again until the light was pulsating. It was a beacon, and she would follow it home.

~

THE GROUND WAS slippery as Noah sprinted across it. The rain had mixed with the fallen leaves, and he lost his footing more than once. He barely paid it any mind. Noah saw nothing but the pond before him. How fast could he get to it?

He should have known better than to leave her unattended. He had played this game enough times. Only a fool would have let her go off by herself. Noah had tried to draw the line of being protective while letting her figure things out for herself and had failed miserably.

Through the trees, he could see the pond and its grassy shore. Cody and Lydia were already by the water. The woman pointed out to the middle of it. "I saw her go down there." Ghosts couldn't move over water. They were stuck to the land they had died on. Noah was on his own.

If only he could walk on water. He settled for swimming and pumped his legs as hard as they would go as he dashed into the pond. The water wasn't too deep, but the rain had stirred it up considerably. The surface was murky with debris and soot.

"Where is she?" he yelled as he paddled to keep his head up. Cody shouted something, but it didn't carry over the wind. He frantically pointed further out, and Noah tried to gauge where on the surface he meant. His heart beat in time with the pumping of his arms. How much time had he wasted?

"Stop!" Lydia's shriek was just loud enough for him to hear over the pounding in his ears.

With a deep breath in, Noah dove beneath the surface,

his eyes stinging as he scanned the bottom for Makenna. He almost screamed when he found her, only a few feet to his left. How graceful she looked, her hair floating around her like a halo. She seemed so relaxed, so at peace in the water. Pumping his legs, Noah slammed into Makenna with all his momentum. He was quick to redirect himself as he snaked an arm around her waist. With one aggressive push off the rocky bottom, Noah kicked up until the two broke the surface.

Please be alive. Please be alive.

There was a group of spectators at the pond's edge as he dragged Makenna to the shore. Everyone except Harriet and Rose was there, but Noah could barely focus on their faces. The closer he got to land, the less sure he was that he could save Makenna. She wasn't moving at all, total dead weight in his arms. He was too late. He was always too late.

"Give them space," Huxley said as Noah found solid ground under his feet. He hooked his arms under Makenna and carried her the rest of the way out of the water. How exhausted he felt. Another cycle, another grave. He would be the one to bury her this time. She deserved that much.

Noah set her down on the edge of the pond, then leaned over and listened. It was hard to hear her breath over his own gasping. He tried to still the nerves in his body already mourning her.

Please breathe.

He tilted Makenna's head to clear her airway of any water before dropping his face to her mouth. His eyes focused on her chest for movement. It was still, so incredibly still. He checked for her heartbeat, his cold finger snaking under her jaw to find her pulse. It was almost impossible to hold back the tears when he felt nothing.

Immediately he pinched her nose and gave her five full breaths.

One, two, three, four, five.

Breathe. Please breathe.

It still wasn't enough. Noah felt numb as he began chest compressions, one minute of them before another round of breaths. Not yet; he wasn't ready to bury another body. He wasn't sure he'd survive it.

"Noah." Lydia was beside him, her arm outstretched as if to stop him. He began counting out loud – sixty seconds of compressions, five deep breaths.

"One, two, three, four, five . . ."

"Noah, honey. Stop. It's been too long. She's gone."

It hadn't been long enough. It never was. He would fight for her, fight every second of every day for the rest of his life. Noah would be her breath, and only when his stopped, would he let hers go.

". . . Fifty-eight, fifty-nine, sixty." He was about to start another cycle of breaths when Makenna coughed. Sweet heavens above, maybe there was a god after all. Noah turned Makenna over to her side with quick hands to let the water drain from her airways. She coughed violently as she spat up the pond, her body heaving in great spasms. Noah moved back to give her space while the others watched.

Maryam had fallen to her knees at some point, her hands clasped together in a silent prayer. Beside her stood Charles and Huxley, equal measures of distress and relief on both their faces. Behind them was Cody, tears in his eyes. He stood tall when Noah looked at him. Upon seeing Makenna's recovery, Siobhan was the first to leave, her face troubled as she disappeared into the house.

"You did it," Lydia breathed beside Noah. "You saved her."

Noah felt his eyes prick with the same tears that had threatened to drop earlier. He had never heard those words come out of anyone's mouth before. There was nothing on this earthly planet he would trade Makenna's safety for.

Makenna was on her hands and knees as she continued heaving. Slowly her breaths caught up with the rest of her body, and the coughing settled. She looked entirely drained, her skin paper white and ice cold as Noah pulled her into him. Death had tried them today, and for the first time in over a hundred years, they had bested it.

"Let's take her inside, gently," Maryam said. She was back on her feet, and together she and Noah helped Makenna off the ground. Charles was right behind them to offer support if needed.

Slowly they began moving towards the house, one step at a time. Noah barely noticed his soaked clothes as they stuck to his body. He wasn't even fazed by the dirt or debris digging into his skin from the shore. All he could feel was the girl under his arms and the sense of gratefulness that he would get to spend a little more time with her. Not before she passed out in his arms.

19

Madilyn

October 12, 2004

Madilyn Daws had been in this house for six exhausting days. She had learned far more than she ever imagined, the two most prominent lessons being that the dead were not quite as dead as she thought, and curses were a very real thing.

The first night had been a haze. Her springer spaniel had gotten loose and taken her on a wild goose chase – a terrible way to spend her birthday dinner. Her family hadn't cared much for the mutt, as they called him. They made it very clear that she would have to do the work herself if she wanted him back. Off with a torch, she set out to find Remy.

Further into the countryside her dog led her, over hills and through lush trees, until she came upon a manor. It was grand and foreign. She had never ventured to this part of town, had never seen this house before. There her dog was, though, on the other side of the property's ornate iron gate, barking incessantly at her.

It amazed Madilyn that her dog had managed to get

on the other side. The entire property looked gated all the way around. But the sun was starting to set, and lest Madilyn get caught trespassing, she'd have to hurry. Further ahead, she could see a latch at the gate's entrance. It didn't appear to be locked. It was easy enough to open and slip in. And then her world turned upside down.

Remy no longer barked at her on this side of the property. He was back on the road where Madilyn had just come from. Strange. She turned around to go back the way she came, but the gate was closed now. Stranger even. She didn't remember closing it behind her. When she went to open it, she found she couldn't. The latch was locked, and it wouldn't budge, not with all her might. Madilyn spent a good minute trying with brute strength to open the damn thing, all the while her dog continued to watch on the other side.

"It won't open."

Madilyn jumped a foot in the air with a shriek. Turning around, she found a man before her. He was handsome – even in the dying daylight, she could tell. He looked anything but pleased to see her. In fact, he looked rather grieved she was here at all. Such a strong emotion to look at a stranger with.

"Who are you?" Madilyn asked.

"I tried to stop you," the man said. "I called out to you, tried to warn you, but you couldn't hear me. You never do. Not until you're within the gates." His eyes were impossibly dark, his lips turned down as he spoke. He had the loveliest Scottish lilt, though his voice was rough.

Madilyn took a step back. "I don't know what you mean."

"I know, I'm sorry. I don't mean to scare you. I'll explain it all. Shall we?" He turned to the house and motioned for Madilyn to follow.

"I don't know you. I shouldn't be here." Madilyn eyed the man up and down. There was something incredibly familiar about him, as if she had seen him before.

"The gate won't open for you. I promise. You can try all you want, but it won't budge."

Madilyn twisted to look back at her dog, sitting patiently for her. This strange man and his strange words should have spooked her, but there was something in what he said that called to her. It was like a truth she hadn't realised she'd known until he said it – as if he were jogging her memory. She let her eyes drift to the pristine manor, perched on a gentle rise. It sat like a forgotten monument, its tall gables and limestone facade standing proud against the backdrop of towering elms. It had a strange draw to it, almost as if it were calling her. She didn't like the feeling.

"I can't leave my dog." She turned back to the street. Remy had not moved.

The man took a slow breath in and out. He seemed so tired. "There's nothing you can do about him. Let me explain. Please. In the house is best." He waited for her to make the first move.

The house emitted a strange energy Madilyn did not care for. She had no desire to go anywhere near it, nor hear this man out. And she most certainly wasn't going to leave Remy. "The latch is just stuck. If I can get it open, I'll be out of your way." She was back on it, trying to get the latch to move.

"It won't open because it's cursed," the man said more clearly this time. "You will never get out. Once you're on the property, you're stuck here."

This man was fifty shades of crazy. Madilyn struggled harder with the iron work. "I'm sure it just needs some elbow grease." With a grunt that wasn't very ladylike, she pushed at it from underneath, her palm slicing open with the effort. Blood welled up instantly, and she couldn't stop the expletives from her mouth if she wanted to.

The man sucked in a quick breath. It was as if he wanted to get closer to her but kept himself where he stood. "I can help. I'm medically trained. Please, just come into the house. I'll explain it all."

Blood dribbled down Madilyn's palm, crimson in the late light. She turned her hand down so that it wouldn't stain the sleeve of her baby blue raincoat. Looking at Remy, who remained faithfully in the same spot, Madilyn considered the stranger's words. The sun was nearly set now, and it was getting dark. She didn't really want to be walking around in the night all by herself. "You're not going to murder me, are you?" Her hand stung a great deal. It wouldn't do to risk an infection. If this man were truly medically trained, it would save her a trip to the nearest hospital, a good hour away.

"Of course not," the man said. "I just want to help."

"Sorry, Remy. I'll come back for you in a bit," Madilyn said to her trusty companion. "Stay close, okay?"

Leaving her beloved pet behind, Madilyn let the man escort her to the house, their walk empty of small talk. The manor itself was as impressive on the inside as it was the outside. Bright and full of decor from centuries past, the halls were littered with tapestries and paintings, with intricate carvings filling every inch of space in between. Madilyn could hear chatter from the other rooms as the man led her to a private library near the front doors. A coffee table sat in the middle of the room, flanked by two cosy couches. Medical supplies were neatly lined up and ready to go, as if he had been anticipating her injury. It stopped Madilyn in her tracks. Of all the alarm bells that should have had her running, this was by far the strangest.

"How did you know I—" she couldn't finish the

sentence before an overwhelming sense of déjà vu took her. This place, this man – she had been here before, exactly as such.

The man didn't say much as he took a seat on the couch. He glowed in the firelight that licked his dark frame as he pointed to the couch across from him. The sensation of familiarity was so extraordinary that Madilyn did as he suggested without question. She was too lost in the sense that she had been here before, with this man, in this exact room, to think otherwise.

"You know this house, don't you?" the man asked. He held out his hand, palm up. Her breath was heavy as she placed hers in his.

"Why? Why do I know this house? Who are you?" She was tempted to pull her hand back, but the man was already disinfecting it. She grimaced as he cleaned the wound, his hands careful and practised.

He didn't hesitate to answer, his words even and measured. "You know this place because you've been here before. A few times, actually. First, let me start by introducing myself. My name is Noah Kiers. I'm from Scotland, but I haven't been there in over a hundred years."

Madilyn almost yanked her hand back, but Noah tightened his grip just a smidge. He had a needle and thread in his hand, ready to go. "You and I met in Edinburgh in 1896. We spent three years there before we moved here for a better life." This man, Noah, wouldn't look at her. His face was amazingly straight as he told the sensational story. "This house belonged to my family. I thought it was a safe place for us."

"You have a very creative mind," Madilyn said quietly. His words were absurd, but somewhere, buried far down in her chest, they rang as truth.

Noah weaved the needle through her skin. She hardly

felt the pull of it as he continued. "What I didn't know about this house was that it was cursed, and the minute we stepped onto its land, we became trapped."

Madilyn felt a deep sense of sorrow. It wasn't that misplaced sorrow people liked to call sympathy. It was a sense of suffering entirely her own. It belonged to her because she *had* been trapped, here, with him – the two of them alone in this house, all those years ago.

"Being trapped was one thing. We had each other, and that would have been enough, but something tragic happened." Noah's lips pulled down at the corners. He didn't have to say the next few words. Madilyn already knew them.

"I died."

Noah nodded. "You died, and I was stuck in this house, alone. Or so I thought. There was another, a ghost. She helped me get through the worst of it, Lydia did. Over time, more people died here and got caught in the vortex of this place. And then one day, twenty-one years after you first died, you showed up again."

Madilyn had tears in her eyes. There was something about her death that didn't sit right with her. Whatever it was, it was just out of reach. She couldn't put her finger on it.

"Aye, I couldn't believe it. I thought I was going crazy, but there you were, stuck on the property just as you were all those years ago. You had no memory of your life before. You had lived an entirely new one outside this house. But we were reunited, together again."

Noah paused to collect himself. "I was so incredibly grateful you were alive, but you were – different. You were missing something, a part of yourself now." Noah was nearly done stitching her hand, the needle weaving expertly. His voice shook as he spoke. "I could feel it. All the ghosts in the house could, too. When you died and came back, you had lost a piece of your soul."

Her spirit, or a part of it, that's what was out of reach. Madilyn was missing a part of her essence.

"I didn't know how to fix it, but it didn't seem to affect you much – not at first."

"Because I died again," Madilyn said, her voice barely audible.

Noah gave a stiff nod. "It's a cycle. You come to the house, you die, and your soul is reincarnated back into the outside world. Then you're drawn to the house again on your twenty-first birthday, before you die once more."

Madilyn felt like she couldn't breathe. She had to focus hard on Noah's words to keep herself grounded.

"Every cycle, you eventually remember your previous lives. But with every death, you lose more and more of your spirit. It fragments each time."

Noah wrapped her hand in a bandage, still not meeting her eyes. Madilyn wasn't sure she could see him anyway. Her own were so full of tears. "I've tried everything to keep you from dying, from coming to this house. Nothing's worked so far." He let go of her hand, his eyes finally coming up to hers. "I've watched you die five times. But I won't let it happen again."

Madilyn struggled to find any words. This strange man she had already known. How impossible. "Why do I keep coming back?" Her voice was barely above a whisper.

"I don't know. All I do know is that it's a cycle, and you never die the same way twice. It makes it hard to protect you, but I try to keep you safe every single time." His eyes were red as he spoke.

"Why are you telling me this?" Madilyn wanted to reach forward, to run her hands through this man's hair to comfort him. She had done it before. She could feel it.

Noah bit on his bottom lip. "I thought if I told you from the beginning, maybe I could keep you safe this time. I've never been so abrupt before. I know it's a lot to put on you. I've thought about what I was going to do this time for over twenty years. This is the only thing I haven't tried, so it's worth a shot."

Madilyn wiped at her face with the back of her good hand. "I don't know you, or I shouldn't, but—" the longer she looked at him, the more real he became to her. The three years they had spent in Edinburgh over a hundred years ago – the memories were disjointed, but they were there. "I think I need to lie down."

Noah was on his feet, his hand out to help her up. "I can take you to our room – *your* room. You can rest for as long as you need. I'll be here when you're ready. I won't bother you until then."

Madilyn slipped her hand into his and let him tug her up gently. Her body was incredibly heavy, and her head swam. There were other lifetimes now, tugging at her mind – too many. They mixed and swirled together as if Noah's words had been a floodgate opening up her head. The invasiveness of it all dizzied her.

"I hope I didn't overwhelm you. In the past, your memories came back slowly, and we never have enough time together before—" he cut himself off, his eyes trained forward as he led her out of the library and up a grand staircase.

Madilyn didn't say anything. She was too busy being crushed by the lives she had lived. It seemed impossible. It should have been impossible. Why was her chest so tight?

Noah guided her down a long hall, stopping in front of a door Madilyn somehow already knew. His face wore a mix of concern and regret. "Are you going to be all right?"

"I'm fine," Madilyn breathed. She didn't wait for him

to let her in. She pushed past him into the room, gently closing the door behind her. She knew what the room would look like, how soft the bed would feel like when she lay on it. She made a beeline for the bed, threw the maroon blankets back, and curled onto the mattress.

Noah made good not to disturb her, and rightfully so. Madilyn felt quite indisposed, her head and heart being pulled in every which way. There were too many emotions, too many lifetimes to keep track of. It was difficult to manage, knowing her spirit was ruined from it all.

The night passed into day before Madilyn was ready to leave her room. She had spent most of the midnight hours tossing and turning, trying to find sleep, when instead, she was bombarded by memories. It was exhausting. The bags under her eyes were dark enough to rival the dead.

It's too much, Madilyn kept thinking as she ventured out into the house. Whose memories were from which life? Was Madilyn even herself if her spirit was torn? At least she already knew the occupants in the manor. They greeted her like old friends, a small relief in the eye of the storm.

Over the next few days, Madilyn settled into a routine with Noah. He rarely left her side. He was a comfort to her in the rush of memories that kept her up at night. Kind, gentle, always catering to her every need. His inky black hair still covered his eyes, and Madilyn delighted in pushing it back. She knew the fire he would draw upon her skin with his touch. He was Noah. He was hers, and she was his.

But death was hers as well. It would find her. It would take more of her.

It was hard to keep these thoughts at bay. With the memories of her past lives came Madilyn's past deaths. On the third night, she awoke screaming, the memory of a bullet piercing her skin driving her awake. Noah was in her room immediately. He held her in her arms as she sobbed, and he rocked her back to sleep. He slept in her room every night since.

But her nightmares didn't stop. On the fourth night, she dreamt of a great fire. It scorched her skin and suffocated her lungs. On the fifth night, she dreamt of blood. It spooled from her stomach, a river of her life force emptying onto the floor. Her cry ripped her throat as she woke. Noah didn't miss a beat. He was already whispering into her ear, his eyes filled with tears as he begged for her forgiveness. Noah hadn't meant for this to happen by bringing her memories back so quickly. He hadn't meant to cause her so much pain.

On the sixth night, Madilyn awoke from the sensation of death with little commotion. Beside her, Noah slept. He had spent their days trying to make up for the nights. It was hard to do, and she didn't want to wake him. His efforts had been valiant and loving, but Madilyn was tired. She had lived six lives already. Was this how she wanted to spend the rest of her days, waiting for death to find her?

Detangling herself from Noah's limbs and the bedsheets, Madilyn crept from her room. She needed air. Outside, the weather was rather calm for October. It hadn't rained in days. How unusual for this time of year. At least the grass felt cool beneath her feet. She was in a daze. It was tragic, this nightmare she was caught in. It was never-ending, day and night. Six lifetimes worth of pain. How did Madilyn survive it? Her mind turned to Noah, the man who had given her his heart over a century ago. She didn't deserve him. She would only cause him pain, too.

There was a lovely tree, a mature oak planted not too far from the church. Its branches were just low enough for her to climb. From the back shed, Madilyn found a garden hose. It was clunky and awkward to carry but looped around her branch of choice after a few throws. She was doing everyone a favour, she thought as she picked her way up the tree. Her injured hand burned as she climbed until she settled on the branch where the hose hung. She was doing herself an even bigger favour. These lives she kept reliving were so full of pain, and she was tired of feeling it. She just wanted some peace, and she would find it in the darkness.

With the hose securely around her neck, Madilyn dropped from the branch.

∼

SOMETHING STIRRED WITHIN NOAH. It woke him from the deep sleep he had been in. Beside him, the bed was empty. Immediately the panic set it. He was up and out of bed, a cold sweat settling over his skin.

"Madilyn?" he called out. His heart thumped painfully in his ribs as he searched. She wasn't anywhere upstairs, and the main floor was devoid of her presence. "Madilyn?" His voice was raw as he ran through the house. He had spent the last few nights waking to Madilyn's nightmares – now it was his turn to live his own. "Where are you?"

"Noah." Lydia stood in the hallway to the kitchen. Her eyes were hooded, cast in shadows. "She's outside. The back garden." Just the way she said it, Noah knew. He sank to his knees, the air in his chest gone. Lydia pulled him to his feet. "Go to her."

There was no strength left. He didn't have it in him to see Madilyn like that. He had done it too many times.

"Go to her, Noah. The oak by the church."

Whatever grief he felt faded into alarming numbness. It was enough to steady himself on his feet, to push him through the kitchen and out to the back garden.

The night was calm as Noah shuffled his way to the oak tree in a daze. The numbness that steeled his heart earlier ended abruptly when he saw her. Madilyn hung from the tree, her lifeless body caught in a noose of her own making. There was no one to keep Noah upright this time. He dropped to the ground, his head in his hands, and sobbed.

There she was, yet so far away. Unreachable. The chasm between life and death forever dividing them. The world around Noah faded into nothingness as he wept. All that remained was the crushing, unbearable weight of his loss. Seeing her so still, so silent, ripped through his heart like a blade, leaving him with nothing but the hollow ache of grief.

Another life gone. Another cycle completed.

Noah didn't know how much time had passed before a hand covered his shoulder. It was Charles, with Maryam right behind. "Do you want us to take her down?" he asked softly.

Noah tried to look at the man through the tears in his eyes. He couldn't say anything; his voice wouldn't allow it. All he had were the sobs that racked his body. Finally, Noah managed a nod, glad he didn't have to endure this moment alone any longer. It would have undone him.

Charles and Maryam went to work. Together they lowered Madilyn's body and undid the noose. They were gentle with her, Maryam resting Madilyn's head on the ground. Noah crawled his way over to her and pulled her body into his. He couldn't stop himself from wailing. The tears were hot and fevered as he cradled Madilyn, placing kisses on her forehead and eyelids.

When he could cry no longer, he let Charles and Maryam take her body from him. Huxley and Siobhan had been busy at the other end of the property, the furthest corner from the house, preparing her grave. The four would lower Madilyn's body into it, and when Noah was ready to relive the pain, he would visit her. Six headstones for Meredith now. Six too many.

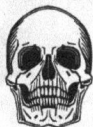

20

Lovers

Makenna's eyes flew open from the memory, Madilyn's memory.

Her memory.

Everything crashed into Makenna like a thunderstorm, ripping apart her sense of being and replacing it with something jagged and ugly: her soul, broken seven times over, until she barely recognised herself. She was not herself, but rather a collection of seven lives, thrown across the century haphazardly.

She was as much Meredith as she was Madilyn, and May, and all the others. Their memories swarmed Makenna in flashes, too much to focus, making her ill. She had loved and lost and loved again. Lived rich lives with families and goals, aspired to be someone, all for it to end in this god forsaken house each time.

Six times now. Six times too many. How did she sort through all the memories? They lambasted her, smothered her until she couldn't breathe. Makenna was being pulled in every which direction, yet at the centre of it all was one constant, one man.

Noah.

He had been her rock, her anchor in a world that demanded her death over and over again. He had fought for her, been a pillar of strength every time. He pushed for her survival when she was fated otherwise, and without his love, Makenna knew her soul would have crumbled. It barely hung together as it was, so fragmented and disjointed. How much of it was left? How many more cycles could she survive?

Makenna clutched at her chest, staring up at the dark curtains of the four-poster bed in her room. Someone must have brought her here. Her clothes were still damp from the pond. She sucked in what little air she could manage, trying to combat the memories that flooded in like a broken damn. When her body couldn't keep up, Makenna bent over the bed and puked on the floor. She heaved for a good few seconds, fingers gripping the edge of the mattress, before the door to her room burst open. Noah flew in with the swiftness of a bird, though she could barely make out his form through her tears.

"Hey, it's okay. I have you. I've got you." He perched beside her to hold her hair back until she had nothing left to puke, her chest sore from the act. "I've got you," Noah said soothingly as he helped her into an upright position, concern warping his face. He held her hands in his own, his fingers cool against her burning skin.

"Noah?" Makenna asked, tears leaking down her face. Just the way she said it, with all the weight of every past version of herself, it broke something in him. His eyes welled up instantly, his whole body shaking as he held her.

"Meredith?" His voice broke as she nodded. It was all he needed to pull her in, to wrap her fully in his arm. "Oh god," he breathed, sobs racking his chest. "Are you really back?"

Makenna squeezed her eyes shut, overwhelmed by the man in her arms. She could feel Meredith's love overcome her. It was her own, after all, locked away by the curse and only released now, despite being fragmented over the century. It was inherently confusing, but in this moment, Makenna could not hold back the desire to love this man and everything she could parcel of him from her memories. It painted a brilliant if not scrambled picture of warmth and kindness, despite the hell both had been through.

The two held each other for what seemed like an age, trying to make up for lost time in their own way. A century's worth of it. It was both joyous and painful, knowing their time was short. It always was. When at last Noah pulled back, he bore into Makenna, taking her in for everything she was worth. She knew by the way he looked at her she meant the world to him.

"I know you, don't I?" she whispered, cupping his cheek with frozen fingers. She was thrilled when he leaned into it. "I've known you this whole time." She couldn't hide the way her voice cracked, the slight sense of betrayal. "And you kept it from me."

Noah's face twisted, his hands retreating from her in shame. "I had to. After the last time – after Madilyn—" he cut himself off, unable to finish the thought right away. After taking a moment to compose himself, he continued. "The last cycle, I was upfront about everything, and it was too much." He couldn't look at her as tears dripped down his nose, his eyes focused on his hands. "I pushed you beyond what you could handle, and you ended your life because of it. I vowed that" – he took in another lungful of air, his eyes darting to the ceiling – "I vowed I would never do that again, and that the next time you came back, I would let you come to things on your own." His fingers curled into fists, squeezing until his knuckles turned white. "I'm so sorry, Makenna. It was because of me—"

"Shhh." She leaned forward to brush his cheek with a gentle kiss. The action stopped him, his eyes fluttering in surprise. "It wasn't your fault. I remember now. I—" She could feel the sense of despair Madilyn had felt. That Makenna had felt. It had been all-consuming, eating away at her soul until there was nothing left to hold on to. Nothing Noah could have said or done would have stopped her. "It wasn't you," she said quietly. "Please believe me."

Noah nodded, though his lips were trembling. She could tell he didn't quite believe her, that he would bear the responsibility of it for years to come. She searched for his hand, snaking her fingers around his as she fought to make sense of the feelings roiling up inside of her. This man before her, he was the love of her life, of her *lives*. She had spent over a century adoring him, and now he was before her, solid and real. While she might not remember everything about him, she could feel that love. There had been nothing between them that they hadn't shared, she could remember that. No secrets or misgivings, just brutal honesty. And when that was too much, unfiltered kindness.

"To be known is to be loved," she whispered, knowing now who had told her that. It was Noah, the night he had first said 'I love you' to her in Edinburgh. A century had passed since then. "And I know I love you, *mo leannan*." She leaned in again, this time pressing her lips softly against his. His lips parted, and Makenna tasted the salt of his tears as they slid down his cheeks. The kiss was tender, gentle, an unspoken promise that they would hold each other through the pain, even when words failed.

"I love you, *mo leannan*, in every form I can take you

in." He let out a nervous laugh, as if finally releasing the tension of the last twenty-one years.

"Lie with me?" Makenna asked as she tugged on Noah to bring him down on the bed. He made no argument despite their clothes being wet. It was the least of their worries. They fit so well together, like a puzzle piece finding its perfect match.

"Noah?"

"Yes?" His voice was soft, his breath gentle against her cheek.

"I know you've tried everything to save me from this house, but what about magic? Is it a possible way out? I remember as Meredith trying to learn it. Is that not something we could try?"

Noah stiffened beside her before relaxing after a beat. "We couldn't if we wanted to. We have no guidance, no spells, no nothing. Magic is just a dead end."

Makenna bit the bottom of her lip before squeezing her eyes shut. Meredith had been so adamant to learn the craft, yet what good had it done her? "Hold me, then?"

Noah's hands were uncertain as they drifted towards her waist. It was endearing how polite he had always been, still was. Makenna was quick to catch his hand before he could pull back. She settled it on her side, underneath her damp shirt. He instantly began massaging circles into her skin. She should have felt cold, but she felt only warmth as he blazed trails of fire across her body. Makenna let her own hand wander to his hair, enjoying the way his curls wound around her fingers as she ran them through his mane.

She let her eyes close, relaxed for the first time since stepping foot onto this cursed property. Noah had somehow managed to quiet the flood of memories that threatened to overwhelm her – in this very second, at least.

She wouldn't have traded it for the world, this moment of peace. Not as she drifted into a light sleep with Noah in her arms.

The two woke to the sound of light rapping on the door. It was Maryam. She gave the two a minute to open their eyes before bulldozing in. "You two, honestly, sleeping on the bed in wet clothes. I won't have it. You'll catch your deaths from the cold." She hovered like a mother hen by the end of the bed, her arms across her chest. She had tears in her eyes as she watched the two disentangle themselves from one another, a small smile on her lips. The smile quickly turned into a frown. "Noah, there's sick on the floor. Is this how you treat our guest?"

Noah rubbed at his face sheepishly. "I apologise," he said to Makenna, red spreading on his cheeks. "Let me clean it up."

"No, no. I will do it. Makenna needs a warm bath and fresh clothes. Plus the sheets need changing now. You go clean yourself up. I will deal with this." Maryam waved her hand to encompass the whole room. "Come, come. You've been in wet clothes long enough." She snapped her fingers before holding her hand out to pull Makenna from the bed. "I'll go run the bath."

She left the two of them standing in the room, their clothes clinging to their bodies. Makenna wrapped her arms around her middle, feeling the absence of Noah's body heat. She already missed his touch, the way he had guarded her from the world in their quiet moment. He stood before her, biting his bottom lip, his hair askew. She was sorely tempted to smooth it down.

"I should go wash up as well," he said, though his eyes lingered on her lips. He rocked on his heels, clearly not wanting to depart.

"Maryam would agree." Through his soaked shirt,

Makenna could make out the beat of his heart. It thumped fast, and a blush of colour still lingered across his cheeks. If she hadn't been so exhausted, she would comment on it, maybe even try and fluster him. It wasn't every day boys paid her much attention, let alone fell asleep in her arms. It wasn't every day she realised she had been in love with a man for over a hundred years.

"I should go," Noah said, hand rubbing the back of his head. "But I'll be back, if you want me here." There was a softness to him, despite his harsh colouring. His heart had always been so full of light, at least when they had first met. Makenna could feel the heaviness that weighed him down now, the words not yet said between them.

"I'll be waiting," Makenna said. She leaned forward to peck him on the cheek again, his hand coming up to touch the spot. With a gentle smile, he exited the room.

"Do you need a hand? Or shall I give you privacy?" Maryam asked as she bumbled in from the bathroom. "The bath is drawn and ready to go."

Makenna peered through the door to the tub and the clean water that steamed in it. She almost felt like refusing it. She had spent enough time in water today. "I think I'll be okay. But thank you."

"I'll be outside if you need anything." With a quick wave, Maryam left Makenna alone.

It was awkward peeling off wet clothes layer by layer from her body. Makenna felt terrible for leaving them in a soaking pile on the floor, but her teeth chattered as she stood naked in the bathroom. The bathwater felt pleasant as she climbed into the tub and dipped her body in. The heat tingled her skin.

Leaning back, Makenna closed her eyes. Despite the heat, she felt herself back in the frigid pond. Death had been all around her, and her first instinct had been to greet it as an old friend. She would have gone hand in hand with it wherever it wanted her to go.

In that moment, at the bottom of the water, Makenna had been ready to die. Only Noah had kept her from it, the pulsing light in the darkness, breathing air into her lungs. How foolish that someone could be so significant they could make you want to live. Makenna never thought of herself as dependant on anyone. She had pushed everyone way with great proficiency – until today. That was perhaps the strangest feeling of all.

The bathwater made Makenna uneasy. She no longer had the desire to sit back and dwell on life and death. She was alive, and that was good enough for now. Hastily she cleaned herself off, the shampoo and conditioner smelling of lavender, the soap of honey. It was oddly satisfying to drain the tub and watch the water slip away where it couldn't hurt her.

Maryam had thought ahead and left dry clothes on the sink. They were dreadfully dated, fashionable sometime in the eighties, but they were comfortable enough. It felt good not to have wet clothes suctioned to her body anymore.

Makenna was sure to give her hand a good clean before rewrapping it and yanking the door open. She was ready to be reunited with her saviour. She was not disappointed, for Noah bumbled around the room, trying to occupy his hands while he waited for her. He looked freshly washed, a pair of grey trousers on with a simple white shirt. He jumped at the sound of the door opening.

"How are you feeling?" he asked.

"I'm okay. Tired." Maybe not the most poetic answer, but Makenna was still processing her emotions.

Noah nodded his head, his fingers fumbling with some jewellery on the vanity. "Good."

"I didn't take you for a ring kind of guy," Makenna

said as she made her way over to the vanity. Her voice still wasn't fully recovered, but she was glad for the distraction Noah provided. She liked being near him, liked the way he didn't shy away from her closeness.

"I'm not," Noah said, his face reddening in the cheeks. That was the third time she had seen him blush today.

Before he could set the ring down, Makenna snatched it from his hand. She ignored the sting in her palm as the stitches stretched. "What's this? A family heirloom? Quite pretty, if a little audacious." The ring had a gold band with a lovely opal stone set in an antique style. Makenna slipped it onto her left middle finger only to find it didn't fit. "Too small," she said, about to take the ring off.

Noah's hand stopped her before she could take it off all the way. With a gentle grip, he slid the band from her middle to her ring finger. "It goes here," he said quietly. "A perfect fit."

Makenna's hand stilled, her body becoming stiff. Noah's eyes wouldn't meet hers. They were locked on the ring. He seemed lost in thought, his brows knit together. "Is this mine?" she half whispered. The jewel felt heavy on her finger. "Were we married?" Not all her memories had come back yet. They flew around like dizzying little birds, hard to connect which life to who. The room felt hot as she waited for his answer.

"No, betrothed. This was your engagement ring. I gave it to you the night we left Edinburgh."

"I suppose I should have known that." She couldn't hide the hurt in her voice, at the injustice of it all. "I think I'm more broken than I realise."

Noah's eyes whipped up to hers. "Don't say that. You're not broken."

"Just incomplete."

Noah shook his head. "You told me once that your

spirit was bent, not broken. We'll make it right again. I promise you that."

Makenna appreciated his enthusiasm, even if it did little to assuage her fear that she'd never be whole again.

"Can I ask you something?" Noah said after a beat.

All Makenna could do was nod. She didn't trust her voice.

"How much do you remember of your past lives?" he asked.

"Bits and pieces. I keep getting more and more as time goes by. I can feel them, or at least I have a sense of them. The details aren't clear, but I know the memories are there. It's like they're on the edge, just waiting for me to remember."

Noah nodded, his fingers now busy with a bottle of perfume on the vanity. He stared at it far too intensely. "How much do you remember of me?" he finally asked.

Makenna could feel him tense as he waited for her answer. He seemed to almost shrink in anticipation. He knew she loved him, she had told him as much. Was he worried about the gaps in her memories? That she would talk herself out of their love somehow?

"What are you worried about, Noah?"

He put on a smile and shook his head. "It's nothing. I just don't want to overwhelm you again. You took everything so hard the last time."

"I'm not worried about you," she said, though she could tell by the way his face twitched that her words didn't assuage his distress. "I promise you that." She couldn't fight the yawn that escaped her lips then. The constant influx of memories drew heavily on her energy.

"You need to rest," Noah said, his fingers coming up to tuck a loose curl behind her right ear. "Maryam changed the sheets. I'll go make you some food once you've lain down for a little bit."

Had she said something wrong? She desperately wanted to pry, but her eyelids felt so heavy. "I love you, Noah Kiers."

"I love you too, Makenna Grace." It was his time to kiss her on the cheek. He lingered for a moment, then ghosted out of the room. There was a deafening quiet in his absence, leaving a very confused Makenna in his wake. Noah had looked frightened. There was nothing else to it. And Makenna wasn't sure she had enough time to ease his mind in any way. That wasn't how the curse worked. There was simply no time at all.

It made sense now, everything clicking into place. The way Noah was so harsh towards her when she first arrived. The way Huxley had discouraged her from coming near the house on her birthday. It had all been to protect her, and yet here Makenna was – in the exact same position as Madilyn, twenty-one years ago, and all those versions of her before. Of course Noah was scared. Why wouldn't he be? Makenna was fated to die, and for once, death scared her.

❧

THE ROOF OFFERED a bird's-eye view of the property, though the woods covered most identifiable landmarks. That never stopped Noah from coming up here. He found solace in the ambiguity of the trees. Anything he dreamt of could be lying in wait under their canopy. His favourite fantasy was of the elves. They constantly bickered over whose turn it was to do the dishes. They also fought for the fairy maiden's attention in the neighbouring tree. At least three love triangles were going on.

"Boo!" Lydia said from behind Noah. When her scare was met with little fanfare, she took a seat next to him and dangled her legs over the edge. "You're a tough crowd. So, what fantasy are we indulging in today? Werewolf clan who lives by the cemetery or mermaid espionage? Wasn't there a civil war about to break out in the pond?"

Noah could tell Lydia was here for the sole purpose to liven his spirits. It was a valiant effort but sorely wasted. "The civil war ended two weeks ago. There was a coup, and the monarchy was replaced."

"Right. I shall do better next time to keep up." Lydia smacked her lips a few times when Noah didn't keep the banter alive. "Are you going to tell me what's bothering you, or am I supposed to be a mind reader?"

Where did he start? "Shall I begin with the fact that I almost lost Makenna today, or that her memories are coming back?"

"Is that not a good thing?" Lydia asked.

"You were there when we buried Madilyn, were you not?" Noah plucked at the hem of his shirt. "Makenna remembers me which means she remembers the pain associated with me. I am tied to all her deaths as much as this place is. How do I keep that pain from her? I *am* pain to her."

Lydia shook her head, not accepting Noah's words. "Nonsense. You cannot shield her from pain. And you are not her pain. You are her love. That is what she remembers of you. And that is what you will continue to be to her."

If only Noah had something small to throw off the roof. It would have been satisfying to toss it as hard as he could and watch it disappear into the trees. Maybe he'd accidentally bop an elf on the head. "I just worry if we lose her a seventh time, that will be it. She won't return.

She doesn't have much spirit left to break." Noah's shirt felt tight on his skin. Maybe he'd rip it off in frustration and throw that into the trees, clothe some homeless centaur roaming the rosebushes.

Lydia held her hands out to calm him down. "Makenna almost died today, and you saved her. That's never happened before. That has to mean something. You just need to give her a moment to process it all. Not just you; the curse, her past lives, being stuck in this house – with a horde of ghosts to boot. It's a lot for anyone. Help her sort it out. Don't get frustrated when she remembers the pain that comes with it all. This isn't just about you."

Damn it. Lydia had a way of looking at things objectively. "I know you're right, and I hate you for it," Noah said as he stretched out onto his back. His long legs dangled over the edge. "I just feel like there's a giant clock ticking over my head. I don't know how much time we have left."

"You have another means to try and stop the curse," Lydia pointed out, one fair eyebrow raised.

Noah's spine went rigid immediately. "I don't think I can. That spellbook will only bring more death." Maryam had dished out all the details to Lydia, including Noah's intense trepidation about magic. "I'm scared to use it. It could make things so much worse. I don't want to risk Makenna's life for a chance. I'm not sure she'll come back again." There was no safety net this time. No guarantee Makenna would come back if the magic went wrong and killed her.

Lydia pursed her lips. "I can't make that decision for you, Noah. But I know you'll do what's right. You always do."

Noah closed his eyes and felt the texture of the roof dig into his back. If only he could control the house like he could control his imaginings in the trees below. Noah would have it all: freedom, love, security in knowing the person he cared for most in the world would always be safe. He had none of these things. Makenna had lost everything, much the same. Her life outside the gates was untouchable to her, and her spirit was bent.

Drawing in a slow breath, Noah opened his eyes. The afternoon was as dull as the morning had been. It didn't do anything to raise his mood. As much as Lydia had tried, his despair had only shifted. Misery loved company, and both he and Makenna could be miserable together.

21

A Matter of Life and Death

There was a knock on the door. Makenna sat bolt upright on the bed. She hoped she didn't look a mess. She had been waiting for Noah to come back sooner or later, after dozing off the afternoon. In the time that had passed, her eyes remained on the ring. It felt odd to have it on her finger, yet it was fitted for her exact size. In the warm light of her room, the opal dazzled, like starlight caught in the tiny stone. She had never thought much of gemstones, but looking at it now, she decided opal was her favourite.

Of course it was. That's why Noah had picked it out for her over a hundred years ago. Makenna could feel it, the intrinsic link across time and her past selves. Meredith was Mallory, who was Millie, who was Makenna, and so on. The only distinction between them was the slow deterioration of her soul.

The realisation hit Makenna hard in the chest. It was like a giant, complicated puzzle that had finally been solved. She didn't have to be afraid of her past lives. The memories weren't there to confuse her sense of self – they were steps along her journey that led to this present moment.

Makenna felt woefully unbalanced as certain memories came back while others remained missing. It was like drinking too much the night before and the events coming back slowly the next day. It left her with a raging hangover.

But this ring on her finger helped clarify things for her. Almost dying today played on her mind, too. It was like unlocking the doors to Makenna's past. All she had to do was open them. It was just a bit of a process to get to each one. The hallway was long and winding. It would take her some time to get to all of them.

There was a knock again at the door, and Makenna realised she hadn't said anything to acknowledge it. "It's open." She patted her hair down, excited to see Noah again. He had seemed so defeated when he left.

The door kicked open with more force than necessary, and Siobhan walked in with a tray of food balanced precariously on one hand and a glass of water in the other. "I'm sure you never want to see the sight of water again, but Maryam just lectured me on dehydration and how it can affect cognitive function. To be fair, I stopped listening halfway through."

Makenna tried not to let the disappointment show when it wasn't Noah who walked in. She peeled herself from the bed, then took the food and glass from Siobhan before the girl could drop it. "Damn. I was really looking forward to a lecture on that."

"I can go get her if you're keen on it. I'm sure she'd love a new audience. We've all heard the same lectures for the last few decades. We can't even drink water."

Carrying the food and water back to the bed, Makenna plopped down and took a giant gulp from the glass. It burned her throat as it went down. "Do you know when

Noah stopped needing food and water? When should I expect it?" Makenna asked as the burning ebbed.

"He stopped needing food and water to live – or whatever that bastard's doing, his weird half-dead thing – around a few months in. He called it the Great Food Debacle of 1900. I think he got really sad when food didn't do anything for him anymore." Siobhan eyed the pasta on Makenna's plate. "I miss food too, you know. I miss a lot of things about being alive. Watching you almost die today was hard. You're very lucky you didn't croak."

Earlier, out by the water, Makenna remembered how Siobhan had looked at her when Noah brought her back to life. It had been jealousy and fear mixed on her face. "How did you die?" Makenna asked.

"Drug overdose." Siobhan smacked her lips together a few times. She was gorgeous, Makenna thought, a young girl who had had her whole life ahead of her. Thick dark lashes bordered expressive eyes. "I was really fucking dumb, and it killed me."

Not just beauty, then; she was self-aware, too. Admirable in someone her age.

"I liked this girl. She was far too cool for me, so when she showed even an ounce of interest, it was game over. All she had to do was say jump, and I'd ask her how high. Isn't that stupid? She wasn't even that nice to me."

Siobhan picked at the hem of her bright orange sleeve, her eyes on the floor. "There was one night – *the* night, I guess you could say – when she asked me to hang out. She wanted to explore this old house that no one had lived in for a few years. She said it would be the perfect place for a trip. It was far enough away from town. No one would know where we were. To be honest, I wasn't even that into drugs. I didn't care about the trip, but she wanted me there, so I went. And it was fine. We hung out, made out a little, and then she gave me more cocaine than I could handle."

Siobhan's hand went to her arm. She flexed her left hand, her lips tight. "It was awful. I couldn't stop sweating; my heartbeat wouldn't slow down. Penelope, the girl, she didn't know what to do. She held my hair as I vomited all over the floor in one of the bedrooms. And then I stopped breathing. By the time she went to get help, I was already dead."

Makenna's hands were tight on the bedsheets. It was far too easy to imagine Siobhan's end. Makenna had watched her brother die. She knew what it was like to watch a child succumb to death.

"I didn't want to die. I didn't have a death wish. I just wanted to impress a girl."

Makenna scooted closer to Siobhan and covered the girl's tiny hand with her own. "I'm sorry." The words felt shallow. It wasn't enough, but Makenna didn't know how else to convey her remorse except through the simple gesture. "My brother died young. He was very ill at the end. He didn't have a choice, either."

The air in the room was weighty as Siobhan pulled her hand out from under Makenna's. "I did have a choice," Siobhan said. "I knew Penelope was bad for me. I knew drugs were bad for me. Even this house felt bad when I stepped into it that night. So, don't compare your brother's death to mine. His wasn't avoidable. He didn't do something stupid like I did."

"Siobhan, I didn't mean it like that—"

"And watching you in the water today, watching you almost drown – you do know you're cursed, right? That doing stupid things like that will get you killed?"

Makenna pulled her hand back as if it had been

burned. "I was trying to save myself. I was fighting for my life."

"I watched my mother come here to identify my body. I watched her sob and scream as the police took me away in a body bag. You can't do things that risk your life like that. You might not come back." Siobhan pushed herself off the bed. She didn't sound angry. Her voice wasn't loud or fuelled with rage. She was upset, her eyes fighting back tears as her words tensed.

"I'm not trying to die," Makenna said. "I don't want to . . . I don't think. It's just some days—" She wasn't sure what she was trying to say. "Look, sitting here and doing nothing, I know I'll go crazy. But if I'm actively fighting it, and trying to get out, then I know I won't give in to it."

Siobhan closed the space between them and dropped to her knees. Her hands were tight on Makenna's legs as she looked up at the girl. "Please, don't give in to death. Don't let it take you. Don't even give it the chance to. It broke my mum. It broke me. It breaks Noah every time you die. All death does is take. Don't let it take you, not again."

Be strong. Makenna clenched on her back teeth as Siobhan's hands trembled.

"It's awful, Makenna. And there's no escape. I can't escape it. I'm stuck here. And every time I close my eyes, all I do is relive that night. I can't move on. You don't want that. Death is not peaceful. It's full of regret and pain. I lost my chance to live. You can't do the same." Siobhan tipped her head forward until it touched Makenna's knees, her shoulders racking as she sobbed.

Makenna wrapped her arms around the girl. Together they sat there, one lamenting the life she never got to live while the other contemplated the life she had been so ready to give up once.

~

THE BOOK FELT heavy in Noah's hand. It was as old as he, maybe even older. It was also remarkably well preserved, considering the long passage of time. After almost losing Makenna today and speaking to Lydia, Noah had changed his mind on at least destroying his mother's spellbook. Magic may be dangerous, but death was more so. Just maybe, if he could find out more about the book, it would be worth not throwing it out. He needed every bit of help he could get.

What baffled Noah the most was how the spellbook had come to be in this house in the first place. A century's worth of people coming and going meant things came and went as well. There was one place, though, where things only ever went in and never came out.

The stairs to the attic squeaked as Noah walked up them for a second time in a few days, his heart thumping erratically in his chest. What would Harriet do when he confronted her? Would she destroy something precious when he openly admitted to taking an item from her? She wouldn't dare risk harming Makenna in retaliation, would she? Noah shoved the thought aside. No ghost in this house would do such a thing, even an old bat like Harriet. And as long as Noah kept his composure and remained pleasant and apologetic, he hoped to get some answers from her. He had nowhere else to turn.

Unsurprisingly, everything was exactly as it had been the last time he came up here. Nothing was out of place – not even the frown on Harriet's face as Noah took the last step into the attic.

She stood with her arms crossed over her chest near one of the long and narrow windows, which was framed by delicate carvings and overlooked the back garden. Her face was pinched, and she looked as displeased as ever.

"Very rarely do you come to me, Kiers. What has you all up in a tizzy that you'd dare come pay me a visit?" Harriet didn't look at him. Her eyes were glued to the grounds below. She always had a way of making Noah feel like he was wasting the very air she breathed.

"I came to ask you about something." He shifted on his feet, the book still tucked under his arm.

"I suppose the girl isn't dead yet? Otherwise, you wouldn't be up here bothering me. You'd be digging a grave while you weep for a love that isn't meant to be." Harriet's lips had a small smile on them, and Noah remembered how much this woman loved being ruthless. He always seemed to forget how callous she could be.

Noah didn't bother with a response as he pulled the book out. "I want to know about this. Where did it come from, and why did you have it?" He stepped into the dim light of the few lamps Harriet kept in this dingy place.

Harriet tilted her head to make out what Noah showed her. When she realised what it was, she scoffed and turned her head back to the window. "Stealing from me again, are you now? Do you all think me so stupid I wouldn't notice anything missing?"

"Harriet, I'm sorry I took from you. I just want some answers. I'm not here for a fight."

The floor creaked as the old woman pulled herself away from the window. She let her hand dance across a table full of knick-knacks as she came closer to Noah. The move felt possessive, like a hunter taking inventory of its prey. "Out of them all, you by far are the most troublesome."

"Harriet—"

"But you have everyone wrapped around your little

finger. It's quite entertaining to watch them at your beck and call, always fawning after you and that girl. She's not the brightest, is she?" Harriet stopped at the end of the table, her thin fingers tracing a music box long forgotten from the 1930s. "She didn't have half her wits about her when she came up here looking for answers. So confused and in the dark about the whole thing."

"What did you tell her?" Noah breathed. His heartbeat thumped in his ears as his free hand tightened by his side. "Everyone here agreed to keep her in the dark, to let her come to things on her own time, as I asked. Yet here you were, just a bomb waiting to go off."

Harriet plucked open the music box, a small ballet dancer springing to life. "You never asked me any such thing. I believe you haven't paid me a visit in years. How was I to know? Besides, I simply steered her in the right direction. To the cemetery, that is."

Harriet had jeopardised everything and done it with a smile on her face. Noah shouldn't have expected anything else. "You think we wouldn't have told her unless we wanted to? You're smarter than that, Harriet. You told her because you're cruel."

Harriet's sinewy fingers gripped the music box. "I did what none of you would. Letting her run around with not a care in the world? I did you a favour. Maybe she won't be so rash and rush into dangerous situations now. Fancies herself a swimmer, does she?"

"Don't," Noah said as he tossed the book across the floor. It slid to Harriet's dress hem, the leather catching on the wood floorboards. Noah didn't care. "I'm not here for you to toy' with me. I want to know where you got this from."

It was satisfying to watch Harriet bend over to collect the book. The act felt somehow beneath her. "And why should I answer you? You lot steal from me, insult me, and then demand answers only I can give. What do I get by helping you, except to reward your poor behaviour?"

Noah kept his voice even. "It's a matter of life and death."

"Then I choose death." Harriet lobbed the book back at Noah. It hit the floor with a heavy thud near his feet.

It was Noah's turn to bend over and retrieve the book. He could feel Harriet's eyes watch him as he lowered himself to pick it up. He waited until he was at his full height before addressing her again. "Over a hundred years you have holed up in this place, alone with your things. I know you're angry about how things ended with your daughter, but you can make a difference. If you know anything—"

"Don't you dare bring her into this," Harriet seethed. The shadows around her seemed to bend with her anger. The room felt colder now. "Don't even utter her name, you imbecile."

Noah pressed on, the book tucked under his arm again. "You can make some good come out of this house, Harriet. Don't let how things ended with Effie affect the people around you, here and now."

"Out. Get out," Harriet screeched, her thin arm pointing to the door. "Get out!"

Noah didn't wait to be yelled at again. He had pressed his luck and failed. With a last look at Harriet and her seething figure, he left the way he came. He thundered down the stairs and away from the hatred he could feel vibrating off Harriet. It seemed to follow him like a cloud as he put more distance between them. It had been a risk going to see her, with nothing to show from it.

Heavens above. Noah had lost his temper and failed to do the one thing he had set out for. And now he had no answers plus the ire of a ghost who would probably burn the house down to spite him.

"No luck?" Maryam asked as Noah pounded into the drawing room she liked to frequent. The drawing room had retained its grandeur despite the passing centuries. Soft, pastel-coloured walls were contrasted by dark mahogany furniture, while an intricately woven tapestry hung above the fireplace. Maryam was nestled into one of the couches, a loose piece of paper in hand and a pen in the other. She used the back of a book to write as she scribbled on the page. Noah couldn't bring himself to words as he began pacing around the room.

"I told you you wouldn't get anything from that woman. It was a fool's errand to try."

Noah was tempted to toss his mother's book out right then and there. Actions felt better than words right now. "She was angry at me the moment I walked through the door."

"That's because Harriet is a very angry woman," Maryam pointed out. "You saw what she did to her own daughter. What she's done to us over the years. You think she'd help you?"

"No," Noah confessed, his temper dissipating now there was some distance between him and Harriet. "Didn't help that I brought Effie up, to begin with."

Maryam tsked at him, her pen still scribbling lazily on the page. She liked to write poetry to pass the time. "Rookie mistake. It's a good thing you're handsome, because sometimes I wonder about that brain of yours. I suspect it's not all there half the time."

Noah was careful to place the book on the coffee table before he did something stupid with it. "If I wanted to be insulted further, I would have stayed in the attic with Harriet."

Placing the pen and paper down on her lap, Maryam gave him her full attention. "Did your little mission result in anything useful other than confirming a suspicion of mine?"

Noah forced himself to sit down on the couch opposite Maryam. It was more to stop himself from pacing than because he needed to sit. "Harriet was the one who told Makenna to check the cemetery. That's probably why she tried to swim herself to freedom."

Maryam shook her head. "That woman – hides in her little attic all day and then disturbs the peace the moment she can. Not a good bone in her body. If only she could be useful for once."

"That's what I wanted to say," Noah agreed, dropping his head in his hands. "I shouldn't have brought up Effie. Harriet just got under my skin, and I let her. What do I do now? I'm no closer to figuring out why my mother's book is here, and I just burned the one bridge that could give us answers."

"You burned a bridge. That doesn't mean no one else can get to the other side." Maryam tapped her head as if she was all-knowing and Noah just needed to connect the dots.

"I don't understand," Noah said, suddenly very tired. The night was wearing on, and he had spent all his energy in a verbal spar with Harriet.

"You want answers. Go find someone who can get them." Maryam returned to her page, her hand scribbling words she wouldn't let anyone ever read. "Now stop bothering me unless you want me to insult you again. I have many more where that came from."

While Noah was partly curious just how many insults Maryam was capable of, he didn't want to exhaust her arsenal in one night. "Good night, Mar."

She waved him off with a flick of her pen, and Noah didn't bother to linger. He needed someone who could get from Harriet what he needed. It was beyond a matter of life and death, no matter which one Harriet chose. Makenna's soul was on the line, and that should have been enough for everyone.

22

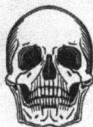

A First of Many

The house across the street was empty. Makenna had watched her mother pack up what little she had brought with her and vacate the property early in the morning. Jacqueline didn't take any of Makenna's belongings, though the police stopped by later in the day. That told Makenna two things: that she was most likely pronounced missing and that an investigation had been opened in her name. Jacqueline had probably returned to the village. Had she called Paige to let her know what happened? How did Paige feel to be the last of three children? One by one, the Grace children were being picked off. And at the rate Paige burned through drugs and alcohol, Jacqueline would have no children left.

Makenna's stomach churned with nausea. There was no goodbye as Jacqueline drove off. No last chance to say 'I love you.' Just Makenna watching her mother for possibly the last time. She didn't think she had any tears left to spare, but as she held on to the gates, her knuckles white, she managed to find a few.

How did none of them know how nefarious the house

across the street was? Makenna had been so close to it her entire life. She supposed it was the nature of the curse, to keep her away until the time was right. The house was both cunning and cruel.

"Do you miss it? Home?"

Makenna pulled her eyes from her house and settled on the boy beside her. Cody crossed his arms, just as she had, though he didn't wear the same look of concern as her. He seemed more curious than anything, like the house across the street was an odd painting in a museum he didn't quite understand.

"It's a very small house. Did you ever feel lonely being all by yourself?"

"Sometimes." Makenna let in a slow breath and closed her eyes. That house, the one she no longer could call her own, had been a place of solitude when the world had fallen beneath her feet. "Thank you for finding me in the pond," Makenna said finally. "You saved me, you know." She bumped him with her hip, a small smile on her lips.

"What do you mean?" Cody asked. "Noah was the one who pulled you from the water."

"Yeah, but you told Noah I was drowning. Without you, Noah would have never found me. And to think you were afraid of hurting me. Now, you're my hero."

Cody blushed bright red, even the tips of his ears turning crimson. "I was just out enjoying the trees when I saw you head towards the pond. Noah said we needed to keep a close eye on you, so I followed."

"And I'm still here because of you. So, thank you." She pulled him in for a tight squeeze before letting him go again. "It's strange to think I could hear you crying in my dreams all these years. We've been in each other's lives for longer than we both realise."

Cody's eyes became hooded. "I'm sorry. I didn't know you could hear me."

"No, oh no. Please don't apologise," Makenna said as she shook her head. "I'm sorry you—" She struggled to find the right words. "I'm just sorry you had to go through that. I don't know the details, but you shouldn't have been hurt like that. No one should."

Cody shrugged, though his face was pained. "He was my father, the man with the gun. There were five of us kids, and I was the youngest." Cody dug his foot into the ground, kicking up some dirt. "I killed my mother; bet you didn't know that. She died on the day I was born. My father never let me forget it. And then he snapped. He always had mental problems, but one day it was too much. He took a gun and killed every one of my siblings. I escaped the house and ran and kept running. Then I ended up here. I thought I was safe, but he followed me and—" Cody's words faded out.

Makenna pulled the boy into a tight hug. "I bet you were so brave," she whispered before letting him go. He stood tall, his eyes blazing ahead. Cody carried a strength no twelve-year-old should have had to muster. "My brother was the same way. He—"

OCTOBER 6, *1894*

"My brother, he will be delighted when he comes to visit. Look at this place," Meredith breathed as she hung on to Noah's arm. The two stood before the gates of the manor as the day slowly turned to evening. They had travelled so far to be here, given up so much for the opportunity before them now. "Look at the size of it, Noah. Think of everything we can do with the space."

"I can see your head spinning with all the ideas. Happy birthday, mo leannan." *My love, in Gaelic. Noah leaned over to kiss*

Meredith on the forehead. They were both exhausted, but in a few minutes, they would have a place to hang their coats up and celebrate – a home. How fortunate, Meredith thought. What a good life they had.

"Shall I race you?" Meredith asked, plucking the velvet top hat from Noah's head. She giggled as he lunged for it, and she took another step closer to the gate. It was locked, but Meredith had the key in her other hand, ready to go. Noah watched with a crooked grin as she placed the hat on her head, crushing her updo. Facing the gate, she fumbled with the bronze key until it slid into the lock. It clicked open instantly. "We shall make a mad dash to the house once I open this. Last one there has to carry the other across the threshold."

"You think you can carry me through the doors?" Noah asked with mock surprise. "A woman of your stature? I would surely break you. And I do not intend to break my future wife before she even gets through the doors."

The latch was stubborn to slide open, and Meredith pushed hard against the lever to make it budge. "Ouch," she said as the cool metal cut into her skin, drawing blood instantly. "Oh, now look what I've done." She held her palm up to Noah, a frown pulling her lips down. "Silly me."

He was on her instantly, his hands gentle as he wrapped a linen handkerchief around her slender fingers. "A bad omen?" He wore a smile on his lips as he kissed her knuckles. "You put me to work so quickly. We haven't even stepped foot on the property yet."

Meredith enjoyed the way he tended to her. "I am simply making sure you're up to speed on your practise. It would be poor form of me to let you slack."

"Aye. You keep me on my toes, mo leannan."

"You open the gate then. It seems the house doesn't want me here."

Noah nodded as he kissed her knuckles once more. "As you wish." He leaned around her to flick the latch. It slid up with ease, the gate swinging open.

"A knight in shining armour," Meredith said, a tease in her voice.

She was nearly over the property line before she paused to look at Noah. "The race is still on. Don't you dare think this will slow me down. Perhaps I'll spare you the embarrassment and let you win. We can't risk damaging your ego now, can we?"

Noah was quick to swipe his hat from her head and toss it onto the overgrown lawn. "I think my ego can take it." He closed the space between them, his head dropping so their lips almost touched.

Before he could make contact, Meredith leaned back. "Think of the neighbours, my love. Shall we cause a scandal so soon?"

Noah stood upright, his head turning dramatically to scan the wide space around them. Rolling hills and lush trees. Not another soul to be seen. "I have done a thorough search of the place and concluded I don't give a damn. Also, it helps there isn't anyone around. So, I shall steal this kiss from you before leaving you in the dust." His lips were light on hers, his fingers coming up to her neck. He was careful not to tangle her hair.

Meredith's heart pumped harder, and she took a step back, breaking the connection. "Oh, you'll have to race me indeed if you want to claim that prize." She stepped past the property line, ready to make a run for it.

Before Meredith could bolt, Noah passed through the gates to put himself in front of her again. "Or, I could take that prize right now." He went in for another kiss, but Meredith bolted. She had the element of surprise as she sped towards the house, kicking up grass as she went. Behind her, she could hear Noah call out in amusement. Then he was no longer behind her but in the lead, his long legs carrying him towards the house. The odds were against Meredith as she tried to speed up, limited by her restrictive day dress.

"Damn you, Kiers," Meredith said as she caught up to him. Her chest pushed uncomfortably against her corset as she tried to catch her breath.

Noah failed in hiding his smile. "I believe I am to be carried in," he said, pointing to the grand door. It towered before them, its rich wood carved by skilled hands. "But I know you have injured your hand. A gentleman would never ask that of you."

Meredith huffed as she wiped her brow dramatically. "No, no. A lady always keeps her word."

Before she could muster all her wits and lift a man taller than her through the doors, Noah stopped her with a gentle hand. "Perhaps an exchange can be made."

"Oh?" Meredith stood straight, her arms crossed over her chest, mindful of her injury. "You have my ear."

"I'd rather have your lips instead. I propose another kiss, and your loss is paid."

Meredith tried to hide the snort before it burst from her mouth. "You drive a hard bargain."

"But we have a deal?"

Meredith didn't have to think twice as she snagged him by his collar and pulled him in close. "Only if it's a good kiss."

"HE WHAT?" Cody asked beside her.

Makenna touched a hand to her lips. It had been as if Noah was standing before her now. She could see his head moving closer to hers, his top hat long forgotten somewhere in the yard. Makenna felt mildly out of breath even, as if she had just sprinted across the lawn, knowing full well Noah would beat her.

"He—" Makenna couldn't remember what she had been about to say to Cody. Her brows furrowed as she tried to bring herself back to the present. "My brother was brave, just like you."

Cody stared at her, his eyebrows knit together. "What's wrong? You froze up just now."

"I—" Makenna pointed back to the house. "I was caught in a memory, a flashback. It was like I wasn't here

238

anymore." She put a hand to her chest. Her heart raced underneath her touch.

Cody's eyes darkened. "I don't like those."

"Of course not," Makenna said as she shook the feeling. She bent down to be eye level with him then. "Cody, these flashbacks you have, do you know what triggers them?" It would be so much easier if she understood what brought them on. Maybe she'd even be able to navigate them rather than fall into the past and lose touch with the present. It was jarring to be in another place, another time.

The boy shook his head, his ginger hair falling into his bright eyes. "I don't know. They just sort of happen. It's like a bad dream I can't get out of."

Makenna smacked her lips. She didn't like prying on a subject that made Cody so uncomfortable. She just wished there was a better way to get in touch with her past lives, rather than being thrown into them.

Cody shifted his weight from foot to foot, and Makenna pulled him in close again. "I'm sorry. I didn't mean to bring it up. I won't do it again."

Pushing away from Makenna, Cody gave her a firm look. "I'm not a child. I mean, I am, but you don't have to treat me like one. I can talk about it, you know. I'm strong enough to."

He reminded her of Rory so much. The fierce determination birthed from a place of childlike indignation. Both out to prove themselves, maybe past what they were truly capable of – at least in Rory's case. He had fought against his failing body for so long. That had been the most challenging part; he had been so angry when his body failed him, and all Makenna could do was watch. Seeing Cody relive his final night alive was much the same. All Makenna could do was watch as each boy fought through their trauma.

"I know you are." Makenna ignored Cody's huff. "I didn't mean to say you weren't."

Cody squirmed beneath her pointed look, though he didn't seem as upset anymore. "We should go inside. It's going to rain soon." Makenna turned her head up to the sky. It was perhaps the clearest day since she had been here. She was about to say so, but once again, Cody was no longer in front of her.

NOVEMBER 7, *1899*

Noah stood before Meredith, his lips pulled into a frown. "We should go inside. It's going to rain soon." His shirt was untucked, his hair a mess from running his hand through it so many times. "We can't stay out here forever."

Meredith shook the gates another time. Her fingers ached from yanking on them. She had been pulling at them all afternoon and well into the night. "No. Not until we find a way out."

"Mere, you need to stop. We've tried. We've tried for a month. We can't get out." Noah's shoulders sagged. His eyes were hollow from lack of sleep. The two had spent their nights and days trying to escape. Somehow, they had become trapped, just the two of them on this massive property. "It's not going to work. You know this."

"Shame on you," Meredith spat as she dropped her hands from the bars and turned on him. "We don't just give up. We are not quitters." Scrunching up her dress, Meredith charged towards the house with Noah on her heels. "There's a way out. I know there is."

Noah kicked up his pace to put himself in front of Meredith. He stopped her in her tracks just before the entrance. "Please, Meredith, we need to rest. Let us try in the morning."

"You go to bed then. I am not done yet." Meredith sidestepped him, the hem of her grey dress dirty from the hours spent in the grass and mud searching for a way out. She hadn't changed in days. There simply was no point. She might look unkempt, but she'd be an

unkempt free woman soon enough. She could feel it in her bones. She would escape tonight, and Noah would be damned to stop her.

Noah raked his hands through his mop of black hair again, the gesture annoying Meredith. His fingers caught on the knots, and he grimaced. "What have we become? Look at us, Mere. We are better than this. Come inside, let us clean up and take a moment to breathe. We can reconvene in the morning. We aren't going anywhere."

It was hard to look at him. Meredith had never seen Noah become so undone, but neither had she let herself go this much either. She had been in a craze the last few days, zooming around the property as if she hadn't already searched every inch of it. Perhaps a moment to rest and collect their wits wasn't the worst idea. "Fine. Let us draw a bath. We can scrub off the day. Maybe we'll think of something we've missed in the quiet of it all."

Noah perked his shoulders. "Yes, that's a brilliant plan." He pulled her into a hug, his lips crushing hers briefly. It wasn't romantic. It was almost fevered in its haste. "I'll draw the bath. You give me a moment." She watched him rush into the house, his eagerness out of place in the high emotion of it all.

Noah hadn't succumbed to the anger Meredith felt being trapped in this house. He had taken on the sorrow of it all while Meredith raged and tore the place apart. At night, Noah was the one to hold her close and calm Meredith down. He counted her breaths until they were even, and she was able to drift off to sleep. She then breathed life into their mornings, ready to take on the day to find their liberation. It was a good balance. The two of them had always been that way.

Meredith looked out onto the property that had once been a beacon of hope. It hadn't taken them long before they realised their haven had turned into a unique type of hell. On the third day of coming here, Meredith had set off to get supplies, only to find she was incapable of leaving beyond the gates. She had frantically called out to Noah in the study, and he came rushing to her aid, confused as to why she was so panicked. How quickly he had learned.

Staring out across the yard now, Meredith wondered about the outside world. The lands around them were so untouched. Did anyone know they were here, unable to leave?

Above her, the sky opened up, the temperature dropping as the rain began to pour down. With a yip, Meredith scooted back under the protection of the tiled roof. No sense in waiting outside. She would do as Noah suggested and join him in a bath. The warm water would do her wonders. Perhaps taking a second to regroup would do them all some good.

Turning her back to the rain, Meredith made her way inside the house. She didn't bother to lock the door as she shut it behind her. Noah and Meredith weren't in any danger of an intruder. They hadn't seen a single soul since coming here. At least they had each other. The thought of being stuck here alone was unbearable.

Making her way up the stairs, Meredith made it to the last step before she heard the creak of the front door. Pivoting on her heel, she turned in time to see the door swing open fully, though no one occupied the foyer. Every hair on Meredith's neck stood up. "Hello?" Her voice carried across the room, though it went unanswered. The wind – it must have picked up. With slow steps, Meredith retraced her way down the stairs. She tried to ignore the feeling of someone watching her. She was, indeed, very sleep-deprived. How the brain liked to play tricks on those spent from the day.

Meredith made sure to lock the door as she closed it a second time, ignoring that the rain fell straight outside. Satisfied the door wouldn't blow open again, she began to climb the stairs once more. Noah would find humour in this, Meredith knew. He would laugh at how paranoid she had become, and she would see the silliness in it, too. She would neglect to tell him how there hadn't been any wind and that the door had opened of its own accord. That, she would keep to herself.

The stairs behind her creaked as Meredith reached the top step, forcing her to spin around hastily. There was no one behind her. She was certain. So why did it feel as if someone had brushed past her on the stairs? Meredith grabbed onto the railing, every inch of her body aware of the energy in the room. "Noah?" she called, though her voice came out barely a whisper.

Her breath hitched as a force slammed into her body from the side. It was heavy and pushed her into the railing. Meredith tried to resist, tried to scream, but the weight of it overcame her. There was no time to think as the force tipped her over and the sense of free-falling took her breath away a second time.

The ground slammed hard beneath her. It shattered what felt like every bone in her body as she lay on the floor. She could only gasp as her lungs refused to fill with air. Was this what it felt like to drown? Why did her body feel so heavy now? She couldn't move any limbs if she tried.

"Meredith?"

She could hear Noah above her. She tried to say his name, tried to see past the haze clouding her vision. His footsteps thundered down the stairs, and suddenly she was in his arms. Her name was on his lips, over and over again, caught between sobs. His tears warmed her skin. She was becoming cold fast. "Mo leannan, please, my love. Don't go. Don't leave me." Her body didn't feel heavy anymore. Her limbs felt disconnected.

My love, I don't want to leave you. The words wouldn't come out of her mouth. Nothing came out of her mouth, not even her breath.

Noah tipped his head over hers and kissed her forehead tenderly. It was the last thing she felt as the darkness swooped in. It was gentle at first, then overwhelming. It stole all her senses, and then she was nothing.

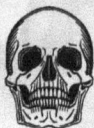

23

Everything Dies

"Absolutely not," Huxley said around the cigar in his mouth. "I do not tolerate that woman, and she suffers me just as much. You'll have to find someone else."

Noah turned to Charles. The midday afternoon light was rather bright today. It made sitting in the greenhouse pleasant for once. There wasn't rain hitting the glass roof, and the smell wasn't musty. One could almost call this an enjoyable afternoon – if Noah weren't begging the men before him to do an impossible task. "Please, Charles. You are far more agreeable than I. Harriet won't kick you out the moment she sees you. You're the only other person I can think of."

"Why not the littles? Cody or Siobhan?" Charles asked. He was sitting back in one of the lounges Maryam had dragged in a few years ago. It didn't fit with the greenhouse aesthetic, but it made for a comfy spot when the sun was just right.

Noah shook his head. "I don't want to put anything they cherish at risk – Cody's comics and Siobhan's magazines. Those are their only ties to their old lives. It doesn't feel right to risk that by throwing them to the wolves."

"But I fit the bill?" Charles asked with a raised brow.

"That's not what I mean. If I could have done it, I would have. She already kicked me out once. I need a reasonable person to ask her where the book came from."

Huxley shifted his weight in his lounge. "The book you prattled on about being cursed and dangerous? Now you want to know all about it? I can't keep my head straight with you, Kiers. Are you playing with magic or not?"

Noah pushed himself off the high table he leaned against. "If I know where the book came from, it may be a clue to all of this. It's the only source of magic I've stumbled across in my hundred-plus years here. If this book was here before me, then maybe my mum had something to do with the curse. Maybe she's the answer."

"And if the book randomly came to be here and has nothing to do with your mother, then what?" Charles asked.

Shoving his hands in his back pockets to keep them still, Noah shrugged his shoulders. "Then it's a dead end. But . . ."

Huxley pulled the cigar from his mouth and tapped it on the lounge's armrest despite it being unlit. "But what, dear boy?"

"It's too coincidental. I don't think it's a dead end."

"Have you gone through it then? Who cares if it belonged to your mother or how or when it got here? I think you're wasting your time with Harriet." Charles sat forward, his elbows on his knees. "What's stopping you from using it now if there is something of value in it?"

Noah turned to the book in question. He hadn't let it out of his sight since Makenna nearly drowned. It felt too valuable now. "I don't want to mess with magic unless I know there is a direct tie to this place. Magic is too volatile. I want a guarantee in its connection to the house before I try anything. If my mother was somehow here before me, it could mean everything."

Charles stood up from the lounge and made his way over to the book. He picked it up without hesitation. From behind him, Huxley squished into his chair as if expecting an explosion of some sort.

"All you need to know is where and when it came from?" Charles asked. He flipped the book over in his hands, feeling the leather beneath his fingers.

Noah nodded.

"All right. I guess I've been lucky enough to avoid Harriet for long enough. Suppose that luck wouldn't last forever." Setting the book back down on the table, Charles gave a nod to Huxley and Noah both. "Wish me luck, gents. And hide my books from Harriet, will you?" With a wave, Charles dipped from the room.

Noah sagged, his posture gone with Charles. Noah wasn't a religious man, but he made a silent prayer on Charles's behalf. It would be smart to pray for anyone dealing with Harriet. Maybe that's what Noah had forgotten when he made his way up to the attic last time.

"If anyone can do it, it's Charles," Huxley reassured Noah, the cigar once again in his mouth. "That man could sell water to a fish."

"Here's to hoping." Noah was about to sit himself down in Charles's seat when a very irate woman stormed her way into the greenhouse. Behind her trailed a young boy, looking very concerned, if a little guilty. "Makenna," Noah said, his posture returning instantly. His hands fluttered to button his shirt, which had been unbuttoned one past decency. "What's wrong?"

Makenna looked between him and Huxley before

zeroing in on the book where Charles had put it down. "You liar. Is that it?" she said as she made a beeline for it. The book was in her hands before Noah could stop her. She flipped through the pages as if it were a fashion catalogue and not a collection of dangerous spells that could ruin someone's life.

A visceral wave surged through Noah at the casual way Makenna handled the book. He nearly threw himself at her as he plucked it from her hands. He especially ignored her indignant yelp as he tucked it under his arm and away from her wandering fingers. "That's not a good idea," he said, twisting his body at an odd angle to avoid Makenna as she tried to take it back.

"You've had a book of spells this entire time, and you've been sleeping on me this entire time, even after I asked? I trusted you." Makenna's eyes narrowed, her words pointed.

"I have been very much awake, thank you," Noah defended himself, "and I didn't lie. Not really. Who was so bold as to tell you the book could get you out?"

All heads turned to Cody, who stood behind Makenna.

The boy worked very hard not to meet anyone's eyes. When it became apparent the spotlight wasn't going to shift from him, he finally spoke. "I didn't say that *exactly*. I just said I heard from Maryam that there was a magic book, and that it might be a way out. I didn't promise anyone anything. I swear."

Noah pinched the bridge of his nose with his free hand. "I just – ah. We were working it out." He tried to keep his tone as gentle as possible.

"You didn't see her," Cody yelled, his hands thrown up in exasperation.

Makenna held her hand up to try and calm the boy. "Cody, don't—"

"We were on the lawn, and everything was fine until it wasn't. She was just standing there, and then she was on the ground. She couldn't even move. I thought she died."

That piqued Noah's interest immensely in all the wrong ways. "What do you mean you thought she died? Did you almost die?" He turned on Makenna, the book long forgotten. "What happened? Did you have a heart attack? How are you feeling now?" He stepped closer to her, his medical training kicking in. She was clearly breathing, very much conscious if a little bit self-conscious. She seemed to shrink away from him.

"I'm fine. I got caught in a memory where I died," Makenna said, her arms tucked now. She had lost all the fire from before, and Noah stood back to give her some space.

"Which one?" he asked. It was an entirely inappropriate question, but the words were out of his mouth before he could stop them.

Makenna licked her lips. "The first one. Meredith's death."

Noah had to grip the table beside him with his free hand. That had been one of the worst nights of his life. He remembered it vividly: how devastated he had been, how lonely he became after. He had never suffered such a loss before. Afterwards, he had faded for months until the curse caught him between the living and the dead. Only then was he able to communicate with the ghosts in the house.

"I'm sorry," Noah spoke, his voice strained.

"It's fine," Makenna answered flatly. "But I'm done. I want out. I don't want to relive death anymore. I think someone—" she paused as if trying to collect her thoughts. "I don't think my soul will survive another time. If that book is a possible key, I want to try it." Makenna moved closer to Noah, and he took a panicked step back. "You lied to me. You told me we have no access to magic. But I remember. I remember your mum being a witch. I remember wanting to learn magic myself."

"I know, but it's too big of a risk right now." Noah's grip on the book tightened.

It was hard not to notice the flash of betrayal across Makenna's face. "Why? Magic, that's the answer, isn't it? We're cursed, so let's un-curse us."

"It doesn't work like that," Noah said. "Magic is dangerous, and I don't know anything about this book. It could be a dead end."

"Dangerous how? What's more dangerous than me being here, my soul fading away into nothing? I think we crossed dangerous a long time ago," Makenna snapped.

Noah felt sweat break out on his skin, his shirt too tight around the collar now. "I've seen what horrors magic can do. I've witnessed it devastate people, ruin their lives. It finds ways to take from you until you have nothing left."

"I don't have anything left!" Makenna yelled. "I'm broken, Noah. My soul is corrupted, and I don't think I'll survive another round. Do you really want to risk that? Try again in another twenty-one years and see if I come back? What if I don't? What if this is it? Are you going to think you made the right choice to not try magic when you're standing over my final grave, two decades from now, all while this book could have helped?"

The room settled with a thick tension, everyone averting their eyes from the two as Makenna searched his face.

"Are you honestly telling me that this book can't do anything? Are you ready to risk that?" Makenna's voice was hard, her eyes cold.

Noah was at a loss for words. "I – I don't know. I don't even know what's in the book. I haven't looked yet."

Makenna stepped back from him, her arms defeated by her side. "Can you help or not, Noah? Is that book a possible way out?"

She wasn't going to like his answer. "I really don't know. I need time."

Makenna's face steeled over. "I don't have time."

Her words stung, and Noah wished he knew what the right thing to say was. "I'm sorry, Makenna. I—"

"Just another dead end. Everything really does die here, doesn't it?" Makenna said. Before Noah could get another word in, she was gone, leaving a nervous Cody and silent Huxley behind.

Cody was the first to break the tense silence. "I'm sorry," he said quietly. "I just wanted to give her some hope. She looked so sad and scared when she came to, out front."

Noah tossed the book back onto the table as if it had burned him. He took a second to collect his thoughts and forced himself to relax visibly. "It's fine," he said to Cody. "We'll figure it out. I know you didn't mean any wrongdoing. It's all good." The boy scratched at his head nervously. Clearly, Noah wasn't doing a good job defusing the situation. "Really, Cody. I'm sure Makenna was glad to have you there when she came to. You did good, I mean it."

That seemed to relax the boy. Beside him, Huxley shook out his own hands as if he had been in the intense exchange himself. "All's well that ends well," he said, though his tone was a tad forced. "I daresay, I grow tired of this room. I shall retire to the house. The sun is giving me a headache. Gentleman." With a salute, Huxley disappeared, leaving the two behind.

"I think I'm going to go inside too," Cody said. "I really am sorry, Noah." With nothing else to say, the boy exited the room.

Left alone, Noah turned on his heels and let out a low groan. Already this book was causing him problems. He couldn't even imagine what would happen if its magic was let loose. He wasn't sure the potential consequences were worth the try.

~

MAKENNA'S MIND whirled with what she had seen in the memory. She didn't know how to tell Noah someone had pushed her down the stairs as Meredith. She had felt their energy, the shove that toppled her over the railing. They had sealed her fate and kicked off the cycle, beginning the horror show. Was it a ghost in the house or something more sinister? How did Makenna bring it up to Noah without upsetting him? She strained to recall which ghosts were even in the house at that time. Trying to puzzle it out was giving Makenna a headache. She needed room to breathe and think, and hiding out in the art gallery, critiquing paintings she knew nothing about, seemed like a good place to do it. Makenna both hoped and dreaded the appearance of one raven-haired man.

The paintings in the gallery were an eclectic sort. They ranged from classical to modern, the occasional abstract thrown in as well. Makenna stood in the far-right corner of the room. It was far easier to collect her thoughts when Noah wasn't around, especially as more memories of her past with him came to the surface.

"A particular favourite of mine."

Makenna's heart jolted at the sudden commentary. Beside her stood Huxley. He looked at the painting before them with a critical eye, his arms crossed over his chest and his lips pursed.

"The shading is what brings it to life, don't you agree?"

Once Makenna's soul, or what was left of it, returned to its rightful place, she leaned closer to the painting. "Uh, for sure." The picture was of a barn in a field, the weather beating down on it with heavy rain. She supposed there were more creative ways to describe it, but she had never been a writer.

"You can feel the movement of the rain. But this one . . ." The old man scooted down to a painting of a widow. A woman sat upright in an ornate chair, her black lace dress splayed out by her feet. She was older, her eyes creased and her hair white. Her gloved hands rested neatly in her lap. "This one is my absolute favourite."

Makenna moved to stand by Huxley's side again, admiring the beauty of the woman in the painting. "She looks so sad."

Huxley dropped his arms, his critical look turning to one of longing. "That's because she was. We were supposed to have our picture painted together that day."

"Is this your wife?" Makenna asked, surprised. She eyed the picture with a new sense of sentiment, trying to imagine the woman in the flesh. Indeed, she and Huxley would have made a lovely couple.

Huxley nodded, his eyes closed in a memory Makenna wasn't privy to. "A beauty, was she not? I died the day before this painting was commissioned. We had a party that night. We were to venture to the Americas a few days prior, but we didn't make our reservation on the train and the boat that should have followed. A comedy of errors, I suppose. I insisted on a party the next day to celebrate the missed opportunity and enjoy ourselves in England a little longer. And why not have our likeness painted? That boat, you may have heard of it. It famously sank a few days after its departure, in April of 1912."

"Hold up, are you saying you almost got on the

Titanic?" Makenna had had an intense *Titanic* fever back in the day, as did every young girl who lusted over Leonardo DiCaprio.

"The very same," Huxley said with a small smile.

"But you would have most likely died on the *Titanic*," Makenna pointed out. The words sounded stupid the moment they left her mouth.

Huxley seemed to catch her mistake just as fast. "The universe has a strange way of correcting itself, doesn't it? On April fifteenth, that night at the party, I died of a heart attack. I stopped breathing and was dead in minutes."

Makenna was at a loss for words before finally giving her condolences. "I'm so sorry. Your poor wife."

"I suppose there's something poetic about it. I was delighted Ellen went ahead with the scheduled painting before leaving for America. I have stared at it every day since 1912. Ellen was also an expert gardener. She planted a lovely beech tree out back in my honour, though I like to honour *her* with it instead. It is a lovely place to waste an afternoon when the weather is fair. I should like to take you to it sometime if you would. I think you'd appreciate its beauty." Huxley smiled down at Makenna, his eyes gentle and kind. "I await the day my spirit can escape this place and join her in the shadow world. That will bring me true peace."

Makenna turned away from him, unable to look upon Ellen either. "What is death like? Is it so bad?"

Huxley held a hand to his heart. "I consider myself blessed to have watched my loved one mourn for me. How many people can say that? But I also regret not seeing her live out the rest of her days with me by her side. I suppose death is a give and take. It gives you moments you can't have in the living world, but you pay a terrible price for it."

"I'm sorry you couldn't be together in the end,"

Makenna said. She had been at the very end with Rory. While that moment had torn her life apart, she wouldn't have traded it for the world.

"I suppose you are much the same way. You have been given so many chances to live, but a price must be paid each time. Always a give and take."

Makenna stood silent. Huxley's words wormed their way in her head, sinking in with a bitter truth. "What if I don't want to pay it anymore?" she finally asked. "Do I ever get an out, rather than just an end?"

She thought to Rory, who hadn't been given a choice in his end, yet had been so brave until the last second. Could Makenna do the same? She tightened her fists, nails digging into her skin as she attempted to summon the courage her brother had worn until the very end. Uncertainty in the face of death. She had a fighting chance while he had never been given one. She didn't want to waste that opportunity, not in his memory.

Huxley's eyes were full of sadness only those who had lost understood. "You'd probably have to pay a different price, would you not? It seems to be what Noah's so worried about with that magic book of his. Do you think you're ready to pay a new one?"

"I think I'm ready to find out."

~

NOAH HATED the graveyard above all places on the manor's property. He seldom came here, only once a year on October sixth – Makenna's birthday. He was a few days late this year, being a cycle year as it was, but that didn't change the harrowing nature of the visit.

He stood at the last headstone – Madilyn's – with a Scotch thistle in hand, which he placed gently above her grave. It was tradition he lay the Scottish flower over her tomb, to represent the life they should have had in Scotland, before England lured them away and stripped them of their futures.

Each of Makenna's graves had been meticulously maintained, though not by Noah. He couldn't bring himself to visit these parts of the woods except on her birthday. He had always assumed it was Charles or Maryam who did the upkeep, and he thanked them silently with a hand over his heart.

"Late, are we?"

The sound of a new voice jolted Noah's heart, and he turned sharply to find Rose hovering behind him. She didn't stand with her usual stiff back and sour expression. Rather, she held a shovel in one manicured hand and a ratty rag in the other as leaves gently brushed around her kitten heels.

"Rose. What are you doing here?"

Rose dropped the rag and proceeded to drag the shovel along the ground. It made an awful noise as she took a spot near Madilyn's grave. "I'm here to tend to the graves, make sure there aren't any vines growing over them and to wipe them down. Just the general upkeep, as I've always done."

Noah rocked back on his heels. "You upkeep the graves? I thought the others did that."

Rose lifted the shovel with a rail-thin arm and slammed it into the earth. "Since when? I have done it ever since you tried to kill yourself in the forties. Honestly, Noah. You don't know much of what goes on in this house, do you?" Leaning over, she pushed down on the handle, unearthing a small amount of compact dirt.

"What are you doing?" he asked again, rather dumbly.

"It's time to dig the next grave, seeing as you won't use

the one thing that might help you and Makenna end this cycle. Do you think this will be the last one I need to dig? I don't fancy getting dirt under my nails again, but you are rather useless, aren't you?"

Noah felt a numbing sensation spread over his body. "You're digging Makenna's grave." It wasn't a question, just a statement.

Rose sunk the shovel into the dirt again, beginning a small hole in the ground. "You refuse magic. This is the next logical step." Rose stood straight then and narrowed her eyes at Noah. "Are you just going to stand there, or are you going to help?" She thrust the shovel towards him, the bottom covered in debris. "You won't try magic, so you might as well dig her grave for her."

Noah took a step back, then another, his head shaking. "No. I'm not – that's not what I'm doing."

Rose shrugged her narrow shoulders and began working at the hard earth again, her baby-pink slip wrinkling with the motion. "If you say so. When you bring her body here, give me some notice. This will take me all day. Hopefully she'll survive until tomorrow, but after the pond, I feel her time is coming rather soon, don't you think?"

Noah's heart thumped wildly in his chest as he watched Rose plough up more dirt. She began singing a song, one that had been popular on the radio during her last year of life as she worked. Her soft voice filled the air with a haunting quality.

Stumbling back, Noah abandoned the gravesite and Rose's eerie song to lose himself in the woods. He didn't have a direction in mind, just needed to be away from her and the implication he might as well dig Makenna's grave himself.

How long had he been running? The trees around him shifted, thinning out until he came upon a small clearing that had once been used as a paddock for horses. The space didn't make him feel any better as the panic engulfed him, stealing his breath away. He had felt each strike of the shovel as Rose dug it into the ground, as if she were skewering his heart with his own guilt. Magic or death, those were the options here. Each felt as horrific as the other, but one option bore hope, even if that hope was twisted. Could Noah do it? Or would he subject Makenna to a worse fate?

Sinking down to his knees, his trousers immediately soaked by the wet fallen leaves, Noah imagined the shovel in his hands. Try magic or dig her grave. Rose had made it clear enough. Crushing his hands into fists, Noah shook his head violently, tears streaking down his face. He refused to watch her die again. He would not bury another body. He would save Makenna, and no other graves would be dug. And if magic was the price to pay for it, so be it. He would pay with his own mind, body, and soul to save her. He would pay it all.

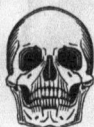

24

An Eye for an Eye

"Harriet called you a fool for trying to get someone else to do your dirty work," Charles said. He found Noah in the kitchen with Lydia. "And said if you wanted answers, to come get them yourself."

Noah sat up straight in his chair with his hands splayed out on the counter. The spellbook lay on the table before him. He had taken to it with new vigour, even if it went against every part of his soul to do so. "I did try. She kicked me out."

"Then perhaps next time, don't insult her." Charles raised an eyebrow.

"I . . . but she . . ." Noah couldn't find the right words to justify himself; he still felt shaken from Rose and the grave. "Harriet was being stubborn. This is bigger than her and her pride."

Lydia came up behind him and gave him a solid pat on the shoulder. "Why don't you go tell her that? Maybe it will change her mind? I always say, when tact fails you the first time, try being an arsehole and see where that gets you instead."

"What would be helpful is some actual advice," Noah moaned, his head in his hands. "I still don't know anything about this book, how to use it, or what it can and can't do."

"Here's some advice: just use it." Makenna entered the room.

Upon hearing her voice, Noah sat straight up, his heart instantly in his throat. He didn't like how they had last left each other.

Makenna circled the counter and plucked the book from the table before Noah could stop her. He felt almost embarrassed, retreating after trying to swipe it from her quick hands. He hadn't yet told her he had changed his mind, but that didn't mean they would proceed without caution. "I am using it." Did she hear the way his voice broke when he said it?

Makenna stilled, her fingers stiff as she held the book. "You want to use magic?" She held him down with narrow eyes, as if expecting him to change his mind again. "Why? What's changed?"

Noah couldn't hold her gaze. He didn't think telling her about Rose digging her next grave would help the situation. "Someone gave me some perspective."

"Because me dying six times wasn't enough for you?"

Noah's shoulders slumped, her words like knives in her chest. "Magic is a risk. But if you're willing to take it, then so am I."

Makenna took a deep breath in and set the book down on the counter, a painful beat passing between them. "I don't know what's changed, and quite frankly, I'm not sure I want to know. But thank you." She pushed the book towards him. "That's all I ask."

Noah collected the book from her, the leather cracked

beneath his fingertips. He hated magic with every fibre of his being. He wished Makenna understood that hatred came from a just place. "I just need some time. I need to go through it. If I'm going to do this, I want to do it properly. And I want you to know there may not be anything in here for you. This isn't a promise of freedom. This is a chance at best and a terrible consequence at worst."

Makenna held his eyes, now so full of hope. It made him sick to his stomach. That hope could be dashed very quickly if this went downhill. Noah didn't want to be the one to disappoint her, much less be the one to cause her harm. Standing back from the counter, he tucked the book under his arm. "Okay. I'll come find you when I'm ready." He couldn't look at her as he left. It felt like a weird good-bye, like a final sentencing. He had just been reunited with Makenna. Why did it feel like he'd be the one to end things this time?

～

PITLOCHRY, *Scotland*
February 23, 1890

The rain was relentless. Noah was sure the heavens were trying to drown them. It had been weeks since he'd seen the sun. That hadn't stopped his mother from sending him out on a wild goose chase, though. He had been tasked with finding some random herb that only grew next to a loch, a good half-day walk from their house. He was sopping wet and miserable when he returned. He hoped his mother would at least have some dinner prepared for him.

There was no prepared meal when he came home, and the herbs stashed in his pouch were just as wet as he was. His mother was too busy flitting around the cottage, frantically mumbling to herself as she moved. The cottage was a humble affair, the stone walls patched with mortar from years of repairs. A single chimney poked out through the slate roof, and small glass windows peered out at the surrounding moors. The heavy door was slightly ajar, the scent of peat smoke hitting Noah's nose as soon as he entered. A fire burned in the corner, boiling a pot of some strange mixture rather than the hot stew Noah so desperately craved.

"Took you long enough," Constance said as she greeted him by the door. She slipped the pouch off his frame and dug a thin hand in for the herbs. Constance had once possessed incredible vibrancy before it was dimmed by the magic she practised over time. Magic hung over her like a shadow, its darkness mixing in with her midnight locks. It deepened the hollows under her eyes, made her frame skeletal. She had most likely forgotten to eat again. Noah went to prepare some cured meats. If he was lucky, the bread he had picked up from the market a few days ago hadn't gone stale.

"Mama, please tell me you've slept since I've been gone. Tell me you took a break and had something to eat." Noah had heard his mother tampering away at the spell all night. She had been awake when he left at the crack of dawn, and he doubted she had stopped to sleep during his absence.

Constance pulled at the apron that hung on her narrow hips to tighten it. "Aye, bairn. I had a piece of bread for lunch. There's still some left for you." *Bairn*, a Scottish term for 'child'. Noah was anything but.

"That's not a meal," Noah said as he pulled out some supplies from the crooked cupboard barely hanging to the wall.

"I've had no time. I must get this spell ready for the

landlord." Constance danced around the petite kitchen where a mismatch of pots and pans hung from the ceiling. She had multiple spellbooks open on the counter. The air was full of a musty scent that had nothing to do with the rain. "This will pay our rent for the rest of the year, the landlord promised me. Then I'll only have to do small work for us to get by, and we can focus on saving for your school." Constance rounded the table to where Noah was cutting into a plate of cured meat. Coming up behind him, she wrapped her arms around his middle, all the while ignoring his wet clothes. "I promise you, I'll get you into the finest school Edinburgh has to offer. You'll be the best healer the Scots have yet to see."

"Doctor," Noah said. "Not a healer. I'm going to learn medicine."

"Of course." Constance planted a kiss on her son's cheek. He didn't get his height from his mother but rather his father, though Noah barely remembered him. He had died when Noah was young. "You'll be the best around. Now help me dry those herbs once you finish eating."

This was the way it always was: Constance finding some madman or woman to sell her magic to. When the price was right, she and Noah would be set for a while. In between, the two would struggle. The cost of these spells always took a toll on Constance. The planning was meticulous and took a tremendous amount of energy. Noah had lost count of how many times he had begged his mother to put magic to rest. He would offer to find extra work to put money away for school, but his mother would always refuse. So, she would throw herself into her spells and potions and lose a small part of her soul every time.

"There are many types of magic," she would tell him when he complained. "This is the only one I learned, for no one else would teach me the others. Women are prohibited to use magic. I even asked the elves and goblins, but they too refused me. The dark, though, it brought me spells. I am connecting with something higher, becoming closer to it the more I practice."

Elves and goblins. Hogwash. *You should be more concerned about losing yourself in your practice.* He wouldn't say it. It didn't matter. Constance wouldn't hear it. Perhaps it was much like an addiction, except this one had dire consequences.

The next day, when Noah had rested, a man came to their door. Noah had seen this man regularly, the landlord who would personally come to collect their share of the rent. He had begun accepting Constance's magic in exchange for rent months ago. Constance hoped it'd be a way to save money for Noah's education. In the beginning, it had been little things, but the man had become as much addicted to the magic as Constance had. It worried Noah every time the man came around. His requests were becoming more and more outrageous, and it was taking an immense toll on his mother to meet his demands.

"Gilbert, right on time," Constance said as she greeted the man to let him in. "I have it ready. As requested." She handed over a small glass vial to Gilbert. He was tall and wide, with wrinkles framing his beady eyes. His long, scraggly hair was often pulled back without care. His clothes were no better kept, often tattered and torn at the seams.

He smiled at Constance as he took the vial from her. "The rest of the year rent free for this, if it truly works," he said, his voice low and gravelly. He reminded Noah of a drunk, the way he held the potion in his hands. It was both seedy and possessive.

Constance bobbed her head. "You wanted to see the future, a fairly difficult potion to make. An even more dangerous thing to demand. Are you sure this is what you want?"

"Aye, who wouldn't want to know the future? I'll be a rich man, no doubt. All thanks to you." Gilbert leaned against the doorframe while the rain poured outside. The way he looked at Constance unnerved Noah. It was greedy with a perverse sense of hunger, one that could only be satiated with the touch of flesh on flesh. Noah always made sure to be present when Gilbert came around to collect.

The man's free hand crept up to Constance, and she took a step back. "Then we are bound," she said. "Once you take the potion, and you have the sight of things to come, my rent is paid, yes? You agree to the terms of this magical contract?"

Gilbert scoffed down his nose at her. "If you insist. I agree then, yes."

"Very well, but don't say I didn't warn you. Now, if that's everything, better you get home. I don't think this storm's going to let up anytime soon."

Gilbert took in a slow breath. Everything about this man screamed predatory. "I'll be leaving when I know this works and you haven't pulled a fast one on me." Biting the stopper, Gilbert pulled at it with yellowed teeth. It made a loud pop as the cork released, and he spat it across the room. Constance watched the stopper roll on the floor, her lips a thin line. "All I do is drink?" he asked, his voice nearly a growl.

"All you have to do," Constance said, her eyes hard on him.

Gilbert smiled before tipping his head back, the liquid sliding down his throat. He coughed immediately after swallowing and dropped the vial. It hit the floor with a clink as he tried to clear his throat. "Urgh," he gagged. "What in the hell did you put in that?"

Constance didn't move from her spot. The kinetic energy that had her dancing around the kitchen earlier was long gone. She was as still as the shadows that hung around her. "You didn't honestly expect it to taste good, did you?"

Gilbert bent over as he heaved, the musty smell of magic lingering in the air. It assaulted Noah's nose. "Woman, if you did anything funny, I'll—" He stopped coughing, his hands instantly going to his face as he let out the most wretched scream Noah had ever heard from a grown man. It was deep and feral. Gilbert fell to his knees as he continued to moan. "Make it stop," he howled. "Make it go away!"

Noah ran to the man, but an arm shot out to bar him from moving any further. Together, Noah and Constance watched the man squirm in pain on the ground.

"He chose his fate. Now he has to pay the price." Constance's tone was cold and unforgiving.

"What's happening to him?" Noah asked. It would be so easy to step around his mother's arm, but something kept him rooted to the spot.

"People aren't meant to know the future," Constance said. "Most can barely handle the pain of their past."

Gilbert raked his hands across his eyes. "Death, I see death. So much of it," he sobbed. "Make it stop."

Constance turned to the kitchen table and slipped something into her hand. From where Noah stood, he couldn't see what she had grabbed. Slowly she walked over to Gilbert and bent down to his level, whispering something into his ear.

Gilbert moaned and took the object from her with frenzied hands. Before Noah could comprehend what he held, Gilbert shoved a paring knife into his left eye, then his right. Noah stumbled back as blood dripped from the man's eye sockets and pooled down his chin. It splattered the floor beneath him, mixing with the rainwater from outside. Gilbert no longer screamed but rather whimpered as he huddled on the floor.

"No one can handle the sight of the future, but I warned you of that. Now be gone." Constance watched as the man picked himself off the floor and stumbled as he tried to find his feet. He said nothing as he left their home bloodied and eyeless, his carriage outside waiting for him. It wasn't long before the rain drowned out his sobs, and Constance closed the door behind him.

Noah couldn't breathe. The woman before him was no longer his mother. She had become one with the shadows. They clung to her, seeped into her skin and stole her light. He couldn't distinguish where she ended and the darkness began.

"I – you just . . ." He was lost for words, lost in his own home. He couldn't even call it that. This place reeked of magic, and it would take him as it took his mother.

"Noah, that man deserved what happened to him. You understand that, don't you?"

He couldn't think. This was just the final tipping point. Noah had seen people lose everything from the magic Constance wrought. He thought back to the girl who had asked to find someone to give her heart to. Constance's magic had ripped the girl's heart right out of her chest. Or the old man who asked for his youth back, and he de-aged until he was an infant, and then ceased to exist at all. Magic had changed his mother into something Noah didn't recognise. It warped her, and ruined lives in the process. He doubted today would be the last day something like this happened.

"What are you doing?" Constance asked, her cool

demeanour shifting as Noah began to move around the cottage. He had a sack in his hand. He barely processed the rhythmic motion of shoving clothes and supplies into it. "Stop it, Noah. Stop whatever it is you're doing."

He came to his mother last and placed a kiss on her cheek. Her skin was incredibly cold. He would miss her, or who she once was. "I love you, Mama." He didn't look back as he stole out into the rain, every step taking him further and further from the only comfort he had ever known. It wasn't long before the downpour drowned out his mother's cries as she called for her son. It was the last he would ever hear from her again.

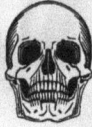

25

A Pound of Flesh

Makenna paced back and forth outside of Noah's room, with no one to keep her company as she debated speaking to him. Did she tell him she thought someone might have killed her? Did she stoke more fear in the house than there already was?

An entire day had gone by since he'd locked himself in his room to pore over the spellbook, only to come up for air once. She managed to catch him on this single outing, practically hounding him down the second his door propped open.

"Noah, I need to speak to you," she said urgently, eyeing the long expanse of the hall for any ears that might be listening.

Noah seemed to sense her urgency and pulled her into his room, shutting the door behind her quickly. His eyes were red-rimmed as he stood before her, probably from staring at the spellbook all day long. "What's wrong?"

"I think something killed me in my first life, when I was Meredith. I remember it now." Her hands were between them, flexing with the anxiety that she might be on to something. "Something pushed me over the railing. Something in this house. Or someone. I don't know."

Noah was already shaking his head, his fingers pinching the bridge of his nose. "That's impossible. We were the only ones in the house at the time. Aside from Lydia and Harriet. But they can't interact with the living."

"What if it was one of them? Harriet? My god, she would leap at a chance to kill me." Makenna's hands came up to her neck. She could remember the snap of her spine as she collided with the floor. The very thought of it made her fingers and toes tingle.

"The ghosts can't hurt the living. And as much as we all despise Harriet, she would rather sulk in her own pain than cause harm to others. Unless we invade her space. Then it's a free-for-all." Noah's hands were gentle as they came up to Makenna's so she would release her neck. He intertwined his fingers with hers, rubbing soothing circles on the backs of her palm. "Makenna, this isn't the first time you've told me this. You said it the first time you came back. I've considered it, of course. But I can assure you, it's not anyone in the house. You're always alone when you die. No ghost is ever around. It's been that way every single time."

"Then it's something else," Makenna said, squeezing his fingers in earnest. "A force knocked me over."

"And the fire that burned you alive? Did a force start that too? Or the shotgun that backfired and blew a hole through your stomach? What about the man who slit your throat? Or the time you hanged yourself?" Noah closed his eyes and bit down on his back teeth. He knew he was being cruel. Perhaps Makenna shouldn't have bothered him at all. "I'm sorry, love. I've been scouring that spellbook all day, and I can't stop thinking about all the harm my mother's magic wrought. I just – No one is out to harm you. This force, it's all part of the curse. We don't understand it. You're always alone when it happens. No one is around to save you."

"But something pushed me," she said again, her voice quiet. "I know it."

Noah dropped her hands, his jaw working as he struggled for the right words. "Do you trust me?" he finally asked.

"Of course," Makenna said, surprised by the question.

"Then trust me on this. I've exhausted every possible avenue otherwise."

Makenna couldn't help the way her lips trembled. Noah was exhausted, emotionally and physically. And he was already using the spellbook against his own wishes. Now wasn't the time to pry. "Okay," she said, shoving her hands in her back pockets.

"I know you want answers," Noah said to reassure her. "I'm doing my best."

"I know." Makenna rose on her toes to kiss him on the cheek. "I shouldn't have disturbed you. I'm sorry."

"Makenna," Noah said as she retracted herself from the room. "Makenna, please—"

She didn't stay around to hear what he had to say. She just needed time to think, to consider her deaths and everything that linked them. Noah might be exhausted, but Makenna was, too. Only she knew she wouldn't sleep. She was being haunted. She just didn't know how to prove it.

～

MAKENNA KNEW Noah detested the idea of using magic. She had no experience with it herself; only Meredith had, and that was limited at best. This entire thing felt like she was forcing Noah to do something against his will, but what other option did they have? Magic was volatile, but so was Makenna. Being cramped in this house made her reckless. She would test the limits, and unfortunately for Noah, he would help her do it. Maybe this was the only way to stop the force. She didn't know what to do otherwise.

It was late evening when Noah parted from his bedroom again, the spellbook in hand. Makenna was sitting in the library with Siobhan, Maryam, Charles, and Cody. The four ghosts had spent the last hour debating *The Twilight Saga*, which Makenna had explained in depth, more to keep them distracted while she worked away in a notebook. Any memory of her previous deaths she could recall, she scribbled down, trying to find anything that tied them together.

"That's not a real name," Cody was arguing with Siobhan when Noah came in. Makenna had her back to the doorway as she worked away on the page, squished into a corner of the couch.

"That's not the point. It's simply to honour the mother figures in her life," Siobhan said matter-of-factly.

"But she's a vampire. She doesn't have a life. She's dead, isn't she?" Cody pressed.

Siobhan lobbed a beaded pillow at the boy's head. "And what does that make you, dipshit?"

"Language," Maryam called out. "Only the adults get to say dipshit, you dipshits."

Noah cleared his throat, and all heads craned towards him.

Makenna sat bolt upright, the notebook falling to the floor. "The book. You've gone through it all?" she said.

Noah nodded. The bags under his eyes were heavy, and

the usual awkwardness he regarded her with was gone. He seemed too tired for it. "I have."

"And? Is there anything we can use?" Makenna's heart thumped in her throat. She didn't like the way she had walked away from Noah last, but this felt pivotal. What if there was nothing in there to help her?

Noah held out the book to her and she scrambled to her feet to grab it. "The page is marked." He sucked in a sharp breath as she took it from him. "There's something else, though."

Makenna paused in her haste. It felt as if the book in her hand might suddenly combust. "A good something else?"

Noah's jaw tightened as he spoke. "I found a passage that spoke of numerology in magic. Did you know that seven is a sacred number?"

"Sacred how?"

"According to this book, seven is seen as divine in many religions. In Christianity, their god created the world in seven days. There are seven chakras in Hinduism and Buddhism. The Pythagoreans believed seven was the combination of the four physical and three spiritual elements. Basically, seven means complete, whole. Another thing about magic: It isn't infinite. It requires continual life force to keep going. Without a constant source, it will end, at the natural conclusion of seven times."

Makenna stared blankly at him. "What are you saying, Noah?"

"I'm saying we're on the seventh cycle, and if this book is anything to go by, there won't be an eighth."

Makenna felt her chest tighten, her fingers gripping the book with enough tension to snap it. "So, this is it. This is our last chance. That's what you're telling me?"

Noah stared at her hard, his hands in fists by his side. "That's likely the case."

Makenna ignored the immediate need to escape the room, the way everyone now looked at her with varying levels of grief on their faces. All she wanted to do was curl up in a ball, wrapped in darkness, and cry. Was this truly her last chance? She wouldn't let the people here see her morale crack, though. Not again. So, instead, she shrugged her shoulders and hoped that her face didn't betray her every emotion as she tried to ease the tension in the room. "Well then, let's hope you found something that will work." She held the book out and flipped open to the marked page, her fingers shaking. The page was smudged, with loopy writing covering the page from top to bottom. Splotches of ink marked the corners, which had turned yellow with age. The page was titled 'Escape', though the spell became technical fast as Makenna skimmed the text. "What am I looking at? What does this mean?"

"From what I can gather, it's a freedom spell. It grants a person an escape from whatever is binding them." Noah hesitated as if the words were hard for him to get out. "I went through the thing twice, from cover to cover. It's the only thing that might help you. The rest is all resurrections, summonings, and beauty glamours."

"Noah, can I talk to you privately for a moment?" Makenna asked. Her legs felt like lead as he gave her a nod and she guided him out through the door.

They crossed into the drawing room across the hall, where Noah stood silently by the unlit fireplace. His arms crossed over his chest as Makenna closed the double doors behind them.

"I know using magic goes against your better judgement," Makenna said to him. He wasn't looking at her. His eyes were trained to the floor, his back tense as she spoke.

"But I want you to know that I wouldn't ask if there wasn't another way. If this is it, Noah – if seven is truly the last time – then we better make it count."

Makenna could see his jaw muscles working as he ground his teeth. "I know. I just—" He held her eyes before looking away again. "If things go wrong and something worse happens, I won't forgive myself."

"That's a risk we have to take. My soul is on the line here. At least with magic, we have a fighting chance." Makenna stepped towards him. "This isn't living, Noah – being stuck here. This is barely existing. You could come with me. Try the spell on yourself, too."

Noah's eyes blazed. "Is that what I've been doing? Barely existing for the last one hundred-plus years? Shame on me to think I've wasted all that time."

"Noah, that's not what I meant. I know how hard this has been on you—"

"Do you? You must really hate the company here if you're so desperate to leave."

Makenna reeled. "Don't put words in my mouth. I think you're afraid. I think this is all you've known for the past hundred years, and the unknown scares you. Magic scares you, so you chose to ignore what it could do for you – for us."

"You think I haven't thought to use magic?" Noah's eyebrows were in his hairline. "Of course I tried it after the first time you died. But I didn't have any point of reference to begin with, no spells or incantations to use. And then I stopped being able to do magic altogether. I haven't been able to since I got stuck between the living and the shadow world."

Makenna tensed. "What do you mean?"

Noah clasped his hands behind his neck, his shoulders stiff. "Magic stems from life. Life force drives it, and I've been in the shadow world for too long." His face turned to dismay. "I would have done anything to break this curse, Makenna. Even magic. Which means the only one capable of using it—"

"Is me," Makenna said. She felt cold suddenly, as if all the heat had left her body. "But my soul isn't complete."

"Doesn't matter. You're still human. At least if I was doing the magic, I could control it. I watched my mother do it for years. I know a thing or two about it. But you — magic corrupts, and I would hate myself if you corrupted yourself for the chance of freedom that isn't even guaranteed. I just want you to know the risks." All the anger that had ramped Noah up was gone. He leaned against the fireplace, his hands covering his eyes. "I watched it destroy my mother. It might hurt your soul even more."

Makenna closed the distance between them. She grabbed his hands, then lifted them from his face and brought them to her lips. She kissed them gently. He seemed surprised with the gesture.

"I remember. I remember you telling me what happened to your mother." Makenna could see the memory now. How, back in Edinburgh, Noah had confessed all his deepest fears about magic to her. He had been so vulnerable then. It broke him to leave his mother behind, to fight for a future that wasn't darkened by magic, to fight for himself.

Makenna continued. "I know it's dangerous, Noah. But whatever is trying to kill me, I want to fight it while I still have the chance." Noah had tears in his eyes as he turned away from her. She wouldn't let him do that again. Grabbing his chin firmly, Makenna brought his line of sight back to her. "Give me the chance to love you for a little while longer. Don't deny me that."

Noah's tears fell now, his shoulders shaking with the sobs that escaped his lips.

"I love you, Noah. So please, fight with me. Do what scares you because it's worth dying for. Otherwise, death will find me anyways, and it would be for nothing." She had tears in her eyes as she held his face close to hers. Their foreheads touched, and then his arms were around her, pulling her in close.

"I've missed you," he said between the sobs that shook them both. "I don't want to lose you again. That scares me more than anything."

Makenna gripped the back of his shirt, the fabric balling in her fists. She couldn't get enough of this man. They physically couldn't be closer, and yet it still wasn't enough. "Then we can be scared together. But we have to try. I wouldn't forgive myself if we don't. Will you try with me? Break free with me, with this spell," she whispered.

She could feel Noah shake around her before his body relaxed into hers. His breath was hot against her ear as he said the words she so desperately wanted to hear from him. "Magic won't work on me. I am too far gone for it. But for you – I'll fight for you. I'll always fight for you."

Fight for yourself, too. But she knew he wouldn't say those words, so she promised she'd fight on his behalf instead. She'd do it for the both of them. He just didn't know it yet.

～

"WHAT CAN I DO TO HELP?" Lydia asked as Noah zipped around the room. They were in the greenhouse, the spell-book laid out flat on the gardening table. Noah ran his fingers down the list of supplies. He was able to gather most of what he needed in here, aside from one key ingredient.

"Can you tell me where I'm going to find half an ounce of dead flesh?" Noah stared down at the book. Beside it sat his pile of collected herbs. It made most of the potion, but the last ingredient threw him off wildly.

Lydia slid the book closer to herself. "Don't suppose you fancy losing a chunk of skin, do you?"

Noah eyed her with a sharp look. "I'd die for her if it guaranteed her freedom. What's a pound of flesh?"

"So melodramatic, dear. Remember, death is overrated," Lydia hummed. "Do you think it needs to be human flesh?"

"What do you mean?"

"The spell calls for an ounce of flesh. Nowhere does it say it has to be human."

Noah's brain worked overtime to remember magic basics. Had Constance ever mentioned if 'flesh' specifically meant human?

"You think any harder, and your eyes will pop out. Unless the spell calls for it, then you're well on your way."

Noah screwed his eyes shut as he tried to think back. It was hard to remember all the lessons his mother had spouted at him over the years. There was over a hundred years of interference in the way. "I think it needs to be human."

"Does it now?" Lydia raised an eyebrow. "And how would one acquire such a thing?"

"One would need something sharp."

"How convenient all sharp objects have been rounded up and stowed away." Lydia smiled at him knowingly. "Give me a second, dear." She disappeared from the room, leaving Noah to his thoughts, until she returned with a pair of garden sheers. "Don't make too much of a mess," she said as she handed it over to him and patted his cheek. "Call me if you need me." She twirled out of the room, a mess of robes as she left Noah to himself again. One of the perks of his half-dead state meant no wound could kill him. That didn't mean it wouldn't hurt.

The shears looked sharp enough. They would get the job done. After finding a bucket, Noah placed his arm over it, a cloth ready to go at his side. He rolled up his sleeve and grabbed the shears in his left hand, angling the blades on the fattest part of his forearm. He had watched Makenna die six times. This was nothing. This was a small sacrifice for the woman he loved. With a quick squeeze, the shears sliced into his skin. He was careful to mind the moan that escaped his lips. He didn't need a lecture from anyone. This was his choice, and he made it willingly.

The pain was white-hot as he gritted his teeth and blood dripped into the bucket below in a steady stream. Noah set the shears down, then plucked the flesh severed from his body and placed it on the table with delicate fingers. The cloth he used to wrap his arm was dirty and caked with debris, but infection was the last thing on Noah's mind. His body would return to its rightful state soon enough. It was just a matter of stopping the bleeding in the meantime.

Carefully he applied pressure to the wound. One steady breath in and another out. He waited a few minutes for the bleeding to stop before peeling the towel back to peek at his wound. It was healing very slowly, Noah noted with a grimace. But he didn't want to wait any longer.

Satisfied his arm wasn't going to bleed out, Noah cleaned himself off and rolled his sleeve back down to cover the tender wound. Wrapping up the piece of flesh in an equally dirty rag, Noah proceeded into the kitchen.

"That was fast," Lydia said, eyeing his arm. Nearly everyone was in the kitchen, all except Rose and Harriet.

Noah came over to her side where she stood at the

island. Makenna sat across from them on one of the plastic barstools, with Charles and Huxley on either side. Siobhan and Cody sat in the breakfast nook. "I found a squirrel," he said, so as not to alarm Makenna.

"And you took the time to skin it, how lovely," Lydia said as she lifted the cloth to look beneath it. She gave him an approving nod. It was done. He had the ounce of dead flesh, even if the pain nearly stole his breath away.

"That's everything," he said.

"I kind of always assumed witchcraft would be more dramatic," Siobhan pipped up from her seat, her legs crossed on the table. "This seems so boring. Kind of like finding out Santa isn't real on Christmas Eve."

Cody's head whipped to the girl beside him, his eyes as big as saucers. "What do you mean, Santa isn't real?"

"Oh, come on now," Siobhan said. "Tell me you don't still believe in him?"

The boy threw his hands in the air. "This is a house full of ghosts and two very cursed people, but you're telling me Santa is the odd one out?"

"Children," Maryam called from where she stood at the head of the island. "There is a time and place for this conversation. It is not here."

"But she ruined Christmas—" Cody instantly snapped his mouth shut with the look Maryam sent him. It frightened Noah as well.

"Now what do we do?" Lydia asked to get everyone back on track.

Noah skimmed over the page again. "All we need is for Makenna to brew the potion, say the appropriate words, and smear the paste on the thing keeping her locked. If I'm correct, it will grant her freedom from the spell binding her here, and she should be able to walk out the front gates."

Makenna eyed the ingredients splayed out haphazardly on the counter. "That's it? That's all I have to do?"

Noah locked eyes with her. "That's it. You'll be free to live your life in the outside world, as it should have always been."

Makenna chewed on her bottom lip. "I could go to school. See the world. Do all sorts of things." She paused before speaking again. "But I'm not doing this alone. I'll cast the spell on the both of us. We could leave together, and you'd be free of this place, too."

Noah shook his head. "I wish, but I told you already. I've been stuck in the shadow world too long. Magic doesn't work on me."

"We could still try," Makenna argued.

"And risk it backfiring? No. We do this safely, and we get you out. Don't worry about me. I've managed over a hundred years. I can do a hundred more."

"I'm not okay with that, and neither should you be." Makenna's tone was firm. "I'm the one doing the magic, am I not? Let me try it on you too."

Noah looked around the room. Every pair of eyes was on them as they argued. "I don't want you to risk potentially damaging your soul more by using magic on the half-dead."

Makenna wouldn't take no as an answer. "You deserve your freedom too." Her previous fire had edged out, her tone soft now. "You never got to live your life fully. I'd rather take you with me than leave you behind."

Noah's throat tightened. Of course he longed to return to the outside world, but that wasn't his purpose right now. He was here to keep Makenna safe and give her back *her* freedom. Not focus on his own. Besides, the outside world had moved on without him over a century ago. He had no place in it. "It won't matter. The spell is tailored to you.

I've incorporated your essence with the pieces of hair you cut earlier. This spell won't work for anyone but you."

"Tell him he's being stubborn," Makenna said to the others. "Tell him he's squandering an opportunity here."

Maryam came around the counter and wrapped her arms around Makenna. Her chin rested on the girl's shoulder as she spoke. "My girl, the boy understands magic and has made his choice. He has chosen you. Honour that decision and don't let it go to waste."

Makenna's eyes darted to Noah, now occupying himself with the last of the spell. "But it's not fair."

"Life never is. Why would death be fair as well?"

"It's almost done," Noah said after cutting the ounce of his flesh into small pieces. He scraped the bloody bits into the bowl with the herbs and gave it a good mix. It let out a heady aroma.

"Now what?" Lydia asked from beside him. She bent over his shoulder to look at the paste, her face twisted in mild disgust.

Noah pushed the bowl across the counter towards Makenna. Her face squirmed as she looked at it. "Now we go outside and finish it." He felt a peculiar buzz creep over his skin. He struggled for a minute to identify this feeling before he found the right word: dread. It was odd to know that he'd be saying goodbye to Makenna for the seventh time. Only this time, it was done purposely.

"I guess I'll lead the way," Lydia said. "Shall we?" The others left the room, heading outside to the front gates until only Noah and Makenna remained.

"Thank you for doing this," Makenna said. "I know you think it's a bad idea, but thank you."

"Promise me one thing," Noah said. He stilled his fingers so she wouldn't see them shake.

"Of course."

"When you're free, will you come to the gates, just once when you're old and grey, and let me know you lived a good life?"

Makenna opened and closed her mouth. "Yes. Of course I will."

Noah closed his eyes. His fingers gripped the counter as he tried to imagine Makenna years down the road, with a family and having lived her best life. He let that thought centre him before he opened his eyes and looked at her. "Thank you." He cleared his throat and grabbed the spell-book, ready to head outside. Makenna stood, the bowl tucked close to her chest as if it were a lifeline. Noah supposed it was. She didn't have much time left. The curse was on the hunt for her, and if they didn't act now, it would be too late. This was their last chance for freedom before her soul degraded and she lost it entirely.

He worked to steel his heart from the pain of her potential loss. It would sting just as bad as all the others. "Shall we?"

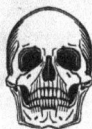

26

Oh Brother

The air was crisp as Makenna stood by the gate, looking across the road at her home. It seemed a million miles away, utterly untouchable. That was about to change.

Around her stood those who had become her companions over the last few days – previous century, if she were honest. Makenna felt like she knew every one of them intimately. It would be a loss to leave them. But her life was just beyond this very gate, and she was going to return to it. She would accept nothing else.

"Do you think you'll remember us when you leave?" Cody asked. He was the closest to Makenna, his eyes locked on the imposing iron gate. He didn't wear the same look of hopefulness as Makenna did. Instead, Cody seemed frightened, his thin arms wrapped around his body. "I heard that a person dies twice – once when they take their last breath and a second time when their name is said for the last time. Will we be forgotten?"

Huxley stood beside him and pulled Cody to his side. "My boy, do not fret. Our journey is not over yet. The shadow world still awaits us. I look forward to the day I am released from this house and am reunited with my wife, whenever that may be."

"But I don't want to be forgotten." Cody pulled himself from the man and gripped Makenna's arm. "Please don't forget me. I don't want to die twice."

"Of course not." Makenna dropped to his level. "I could never forget you, just like I'll never forget Rory. I'll take you both with me wherever I go." She wrapped her arms around him and held him. What she wouldn't give to hold her brother like this again. No, Makenna would never forget any of the ghosts. She hoped Cody understood that. She released him, rubbing his arms for extra comfort. "You be good, okay? Don't pick on Siobhan too much, and listen to Maryam when she gives you advice. It's always best to listen to mothers. They know what they're talking about, most of the time."

Cody nodded, his hands wiping at his eyes in the dramatic way only children could do.

"Huxley," Makenna said as she stood and walked over to the man. She held out a hand, as gentlemen did, but Huxley's arms were soon around her in a giant hug.

"You take the world by storm, my dear," he whispered in her ear before pulling back, tears lining his eyes. "And plant a beech tree out there somewhere for my Ellen. Just like the one she planted for me." He reached into his pocket before relinquishing a handful of seeds into Makenna's palm.

Makenna tucked them securely into the pocket of her trousers. "My first priority." It was hard to keep the waver out of her voice.

Maryam and Charles were next, each receiving equally big hugs. "Tell the next people who move in to bring new books," Charles said with an easy tone. "I need something new to read."

"And if you can, please check on my family." Maryam slipped a piece of paper into Makenna's hand. "Their names are on it. I would be so grateful."

Makenna nodded, her lips tight as she carefully put the page in her other pocket. "It's the least I can do."

Beside them stood Siobhan. The young girl fought hard to look indifferent as she rocked on her heels, her hands tucked into her back pockets. "Have a good life, I guess."

Makenna couldn't keep in the laugh as she went to embrace the girl. "I'll do my best."

Lastly stood Lydia and Noah, though Noah held back as Makenna found herself in Lydia's arms. "I'm sorry for everything. You never deserved any of this," Lydia said.

"It's okay," Makenna said as she tightened her arms around the woman. "It'll all be over soon. Thank you for everything."

"Don't thank me," Lydia said as she released Makenna, her voice strained. "Just do what you should have done over a century ago. Be free of this curse and all of us." Lydia fell back, and then there was only one person left to say goodbye to.

"I'm sorry I—" Noah started at the same time Makenna spoke.

"—I'll miss you." She felt instantly lame. Her words didn't do her feelings justice, but she felt rushed suddenly. "You first," she offered, trying to collect the right thoughts to put into words.

Noah cleared his throat. His eyes pored over Makenna as if this was the last time he'd ever see her. She supposed it was something like that. "I'm sorry I wasn't able to do this sooner. I'm sorry you had to go through this so many times. I – I wish I could have done better."

Makenna felt her heart break. This man and his words. He had always been better with them than her. He always knew what to say. "Never think that," she said as she came up to him and put a hand on his cheek. He leaned into it. "I remember what you've done for me, who you've been to me. I will love you for the rest of my life, Noah, just as all my past lives have. And I will find a way to heal my soul and bring you back to me. I will never stop trying, just as you did. I promise you that."

Noah's hand came up to rest over hers. "I'll never stop waiting. I never have, and I never will. I will always wait for you."

Makenna closed the space between them, her lips gently covering his. He tasted sweet, even through the salt of her tears. He moved his hand to the back of her neck to pull her into him. Decades had passed since they'd last held each other this often. Makenna would savour every inch of him, commit his heat to memory. She would let it stoke her fire. She would get him out and bring peace to all the souls in this house. That would be her gift to them, no matter how long it took.

"I love you, Noah Kiers."

"And I love you, Makenna Grace."

They held each other a little bit longer before separating. The loss of Noah's touch was devastating, but this was Makenna's last chance to break free from the cycle. After the seventh time, her soul would be lost.

"I'll see you again," she promised. "Now break me out before I lose my nerve," she half-joked. The tears were hot on her face as she rubbed at them with her sleeve. "Then I can save your ass and bring you into the twenty-first century. It's going to blow your mind. Just wait until you hear about TikTok."

"I have no idea why clocks make you so excited, but I look forward to it," Noah said, his fingers lingering on her skin. He seemed to not want to let her go any more than she did him. What if it didn't work? What if this was the last time he held her? "Now," he cleared his throat, his tears soaking the collar of his shirt, "go stand by the gate so we can begin."

Makenna did as told and picked up the bowl of paste. She most dearly didn't want to know what was in it. "What do I do?" she asked, turning to face everyone around her. They all gave her a good berth as Noah read the book propped in his slender hands.

"Stand by the gate and smear the lock with the paste while you repeat after me. Once you've said the words, you should be able to pass through." Noah's voice was calm, and Makenna wondered if that was for her sake or his own.

"It's that easy?" She cocked an eyebrow. "That doesn't seem very dramatic."

"As long as it works, right?"

Makenna bit down on her lower lip, a new sense of panic budding in her chest. She shoved it down. This was a risk worth dying for, she told herself. Death would find her if she stayed here, but she wouldn't be complacent. Makenna would make death chase her. It would have to fight harder than she did. Her soul was worth that much. "As long as it works."

Noah gave her a reassuring smile, though she could see the fear in his eyes. It didn't match his voice. "Be ready. Now, repeat after me. Speak very clearly. *Ithimid vi noch.*"

Makenna stumbled over the words at first until she found their rhythm. They felt awkward on her tongue, but she spoke with intention and the clarity Noah called for. "*Ithimid vi noch.*"

Noah nodded and kept going. "*Talvolgo ist ruthen.*"

The words left her mouth more easily now as Makenna dipped her hand into the paste. It was warm and chunky, but she did her best to spread it evenly over the lock.

"*Rivaren su loenth mavori,*" Noah finished.

As soon as Makenna spoke the last word, a jolt bolted through her body like hot lava. It vibrated every inch of her skin until it felt like she was on fire. Makenna couldn't tell if she was screaming, for the world around her turned dark. The only thing before her was emptiness. It was the same void that greeted her at the end of every life cycle.

~

THE EMPTINESS WAS UTTERLY EXPANSIVE. It seemed to stretch on in every direction with no end in sight. Perhaps the most concerning thing was how unalarmed Makenna felt. There was something comforting in the dark vacantness of it all. It lacked tension. There was no sadness or pain, neither was there joy or happiness. It simply just was, and a great calmness settled over her.

"You shouldn't be here," someone said from beside Makenna. As quickly as the vacantness had settled on her, the voice pulled her back to herself. Perhaps it was because this voice belonged to someone she hadn't heard speak in four years, six months, and twenty-three days. Makenna had never stopped counting from the moment he died.

"Rory."

She pivoted sharply to see him standing in the dark, his edges blurred into the shadows. He looked exactly as she remembered him the day he died, a teenage boy who had been robbed of both his youth and health. His eyes were sunken in and his body frail, with the paper-thin hospital gown draped over his bony frame. His brown hair stuck to his pale skin, and the mischief in his eyes that had ruled their childhood was gone. He looked like death.

Makenna sunk to her knees, her throat closing up. She had imagined for years that Rory's passing had been kind to him, that it would have eased his suffering. Yet here he stood before her, as sickly as the day he had died. "Rory, my god. It's you." Makenna couldn't control the sob that hitched her voice. "Is this where you've been all along?"

Rory stepped closer to her and bent down, his shadowy hand reaching out for hers. Makenna grasped at it and let out a pitiful cry when her hand passed through his. What she wouldn't give to hold him again, just this once. Not being able to was cruel.

"I'm sorry, Kenny. You shouldn't be here. You don't belong in the shadow world, not yet."

"What's happening? Why can't I touch you? Rory—" She had to get a hold of herself. Her heart beat like a drum in her chest. It made it hard to think. Now wasn't the time to fall apart. It didn't matter how much it hurt to see him like this. She needed him to know. "Rory, I love you. I never said it enough. I loved you more than life. And I'm sorry I wasn't able to save you. I'm sorry you suffered. It wasn't fair."

Rory, her Rory, looked at her with those kind eyes she had missed so much. "I know, Kenny. I love you too. It was never anyone's fault. Please don't think that."

"Were you in pain at the end?" Makenna's voice cracked as she rubbed at her face aggressively to rid herself of the tears. How many nights had she cried herself to sleep worrying over that very thought?

Rory's lips pulled down at the corners. "It wasn't easy."

Makenna felt herself break again as he spoke. She

needed to be strong for her baby brother, as strong as he had been. "And now? Have you found peace? You look so . . ." She couldn't say the words.

"I look as you remember me. But Kenny, I'm okay. I've found peace. You don't have to remember me like this. I can be whatever you want, any version of me."

Squeezing her eyes shut, Makenna fought for the memories she cherished of her brother. The time they had stolen the cake from their cousin's birthday party and made themselves sick, gorging it down. Or when they had spent a rainy afternoon outside, despite their mother begging them to come in. He had been her best friend, and she wanted to honour him as such.

Opening her eyes, Makenna looked upon her brother again. He smiled at her, his face full of light and youthful energy. He no longer looked ill and at death's door. Makenna longed to hold him in her arms, to be reassured by him that death wasn't as horrible as it seemed. "Why can't I touch you?" she asked, her voice small.

"This is the shadow world. Only the dead belong here," Rory answered her.

"I've been here before," Makenna said. "I know this place. I feel it in my bones. It's familiar."

Rory stood up, and Makenna followed, feeling light-headed as she stood. "I know. Your spirit is old. I can feel it. But you're not a spirit of the dead this time. Your soul's been separated from your body, but your body still lives. Look at how solid you are compared to me." Rory held up a hand, and Makenna saw how the shadows passed through his fingertips. Looking down at her own, she noted how the darkness seemed to repel her own flesh. She opened and closed her hands, confused.

"I don't understand."

Rory shook his head. "I don't fully understand, either.

Somehow your soul's left your body, which is why you can't stay here. You have to go back."

Makenna dropped her hand, her heart sinking with it. "But I've just found you. I can't lose you again."

Rory's eyes were wet, but he brushed away the tears. "This isn't right. If you stay here, you'll lose your connection to your body, and your entire spirit will be caught in the shadow world. There's already too much of it here."

Makenna reeled back, his words jarring her. "What do you mean?"

Rory's face fell, and he took a step to the side. Behind him, curled up on the ground, was a hunched figure – a woman, though she looked more like a skeleton. She had thin, stringy hair, and her skin was ghostly white. Her limbs poked out at odd angles, and she shook from her place on the ground. The most alarming thing about this figure was her face. She had none.

Makenna took a step back, her hand flying to her chest. "What is that?" she breathed.

"Part of your spirit," Rory said. "You keep dying, Makenna, and every time you die, a part of your soul gets trapped in the shadow world." He moved over the figure and bent down, his hand coming out to it reassuringly. "It becomes more solid, more complete with your every death. I've been taking care of it ever since I passed into the shadow world. That's why you struggle with wanting to die. Your spirit is calling out to you in the living world. There's more of it here, and it wants to be complete again."

The figure moved as if suddenly sensing Makenna. It began crawling towards her, slowly and blindly. Makenna flinched before realising she shouldn't be afraid. "This is why I want to die?" she asked. Bending down to the figure, she stretched out her hand. Her spirit reached for it in return, their fingers connecting.

It was blinding, the energy that coursed through Makenna. She had never felt so complete, so full. It was fast, for as soon as the connection was made, it vanished, and Makenna stumbled back. It felt as if a boulder hit her body when the energy evaporated. Her spirit before her shrunk, its arms covering its head protectively as if it had been wounded.

"You can't, Makenna. You're separated from your spirit by heavy magic. You have to return to the living world. It's the only place you can be reunited without dying," Rory said, putting himself between the two of them. "It's not your time yet. You need to go back."

"But I—" She was at a loss for words as she slowly picked herself up off the ground. Years she had suffered, and the thing to make her complete again was right here. "I can't just leave." She faced Rory. If her spirit was already here, and so was her brother, there was very little sense in returning to the land of the living. "I just got you back." Makenna searched Rory's face, looking for any reason as to why she would want to leave. "And there's peace here, you said so yourself."

"You have a life to live," Rory begged of her. "And this peace is for those who didn't have that chance."

Makenna shook her head fiercely. "No. That wasn't living. I died the day you did."

"No, you survived, just as your Noah survived every death of you. Death shouldn't equal more death. It should make you appreciate life, and you still have yours to live. Don't be afraid to live it."

It took every ounce of strength not to fall apart in front of Rory. Makenna had had so much fire earlier; she had been so ready to rid herself of the house that trapped her.

Where was that determination to live her life and fight for the ghosts trapped as well? It had faded the moment she saw Rory. "I'm not ready to say goodbye, not yet. It's too soon."

Rory smiled at her, though it was layered with so much anguish that it tore at Makenna's very core. "I know. And we'll have our time again, but you need to live. I'll protect your soul here, just as I always have."

"Just a little bit longer," Makenna begged. "I have so much to tell you."

"Look at you," Rory said, pointing to her hand. "You're starting to fade. You need to go before it's too late."

Rory took a step back from her, and Makenna nearly lunged at him to anchor him to the spot. "Time doesn't work the same here," he continued. "A few seconds for the dead could be years for the living. I can't risk that. I have to go." He took another step, and the air rushed out of Makenna's lungs at the thought of losing him again. "I love you, Kenny. Just remember that. Never forget." Another step and he and her spirit were gone, two wisps disappearing into the blackness as if they had never been there.

Makenna cried out, her fading hands closing on thin air. "Rory? Rory! Please. Don't leave me. Not again."

There was no response. Only the emptiness of the void.

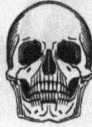

The Governess

Noah dove for Makenna as she dropped like deadweight, the spellbook tossed to the side. He reached her just before her head hit the ground and cradled her body with his.

"*Mo leannan, mo leannan*? Open your eyes." Her body lay limp in his arms, though her chest moved with shallow breaths. When he tapped her cheek gently to stir her, her skin felt cold beneath his fingers. "Makenna!"

"What happened?" Lydia asked as she rushed to his side.

"I don't understand. She's so cold." Noah pulled Makenna's body closer to his as if he could pass his heat on to her. "The spell should have worked. She should be free. I – I don't – take her," Noah said. He lifted Makenna's head and settled it in Lydia's lap. He scrambled across the grass to where he tossed the book and flipped through the pages furiously until he found the spell. "I did everything right. I don't understand," he said as he read through the instructions again.

Maryam was beside him, her eyes wary as she tugged

the book from his hands. His fingers closed on thin air, his nails digging into his skin. "Noah. Noah, look at me," she said more sternly when he ignored her the first time. "We need to get her inside. We need to warm her up, okay?"

Noah twisted from where he was on the grass. Everyone else had crowded around Makenna, intense looks of concern on their faces. "I told her it was dangerous. No one listened."

"This isn't the time, Noah. Let's get her inside." Maryam looped an arm under him and hauled Noah to his feet. "Take her inside. We can deal with this in the house."

Noah didn't feel attached to his body as he returned to Makenna, still in Lydia's lap. Makenna looked like she could have been sleeping, her blond hair splayed across the damp ground. Noah barely registered the motion as he scooped her up to carry her to the house, peppering kisses across her forehead as he went. She was weightless in his arms.

His arm throbbed as he carried Makenna, while Maryam directed him to her room. Cody had run ahead to pull back the covers of her bed so that Noah could place her in it gently. He stood back as Cody tucked her in, noting once again how peaceful Makenna looked.

"Here," Charles said to Noah, coming into the room. He handed the spellbook to Noah. "You probably want this."

Noah took it from him, careful not to use his injured arm. He didn't know what to do with the book. The spell had already gone wrong; what could they possibly do now? "I told her it was dangerous." It seemed to be the only thing Noah could say.

Charles took a deep breath. "I know. And she knew the risks. Now isn't the time to focus on that. We need to figure out what happened to her." Charles momentarily left the room before returning with two chairs. They were heavy and scraped across the hardwood floor with an awful sound. Charles sat down in one of them, then patted the seat of the other. "Sit, Noah. Walk me through the spells, all of them, page by page. We'll figure out what happened together."

Noah looked between Charles and the offending book in his hand. Why was he still holding it? It should have been destroyed when they had the chance. "I'm scared," Noah said, unable to sit down. "I don't want to lose her again."

"Then let's not. Open the book. Let's start from the beginning." Noah turned his head to the girl lying nearly lifeless in the bed. "She's not going anywhere. So, let's do for her what we can."

Charles patted the seat a second time, and Noah finally sat down. His limbs felt stiff as he settled into the plush chair and flipped opened the book.

"Good," Charles encouraged. "Now walk me through each page."

The two spent the remainder of the night combing through the text. Noah was running on pure adrenaline by the time he and Charles reached the last page, his mind as exhausted as his body when he closed the back cover.

"None of these spells indicate what's wrong with her," Noah said. "If I don't know what's wrong with her, how can I help her?" He had been trying to keep his mood in check, but each page they turned meant one less chance of saving Makenna. They were out of options. "I can't even do magic. What good am I to her, anyway?" In an impulse, Noah chucked the book across the room. It slammed into the wall and fell to the floor with a thud.

"Perhaps she just needs time," Charles said, his eyes

following the book's flight path. "And you need rest. Get some sleep. I'll watch over her."

Noah stalled in the chair. His eyes felt bloodshot, and his body was heavy with fatigue. He was almost delirious. "I don't want to leave her."

"You're not solving any problems by being over-tired," Charles said. "You can sleep here, just for a few hours. I'll wake you if anything changes." The man reached over and patted Noah on the knee. "You've done all you can for now. Sleep, Noah."

Rubbing his eyes, Noah felt how heavy they were. A few hours. He could manage that. "I'm not leaving her side." Settling himself back into the chair, Noah slumped in the plush cushion, his body exhausted. "Thank you, Charles, for everything." He gave the man a small nod before closing his eyes, lost to a dream as sleep took him.

≈

EDINBURGH, *Scotland*

August 17, 1896

The city was alive with kinetic energy, the fair weather putting everyone into a good mood. Noah had learned to love Edinburgh. Its winding streets had charmed him early on with their senseless directions. The buildings themselves were marvellous, a mash of Georgian and medieval architecture. A true sight for a boy used to the rough hills of Pitlochry.

Today, Noah's eye had been caught by the loveliest sight. He had seen this woman before. She often roamed the Royal Mile or the Princes Street Gardens, where they stood now. She wore the clothes of a respectable lady, a tall collar with elegant lines to her powder-blue dress. Her posture was straight, and her golden hair was tucked up in the latest fashion, always under a neat hat. But it wasn't her clothes nor her hair that drew Noah to her. It was the sound of her laugh.

The woman usually had a group of wee bairns in tow, and she was always telling the children fantastical stories. She would laugh along with them, and Noah delighted in the sound. He always enjoyed it when she walked by him on his lunch breaks in the park. He was ever eager to hear her laugh again.

On this particular day, the woman walked alone. There were no children tagging along behind her, and she looked entirely fussed as she passed by.

"Are you all right, miss?" The words were out of Noah's mouth before he could stop them. Both he and the woman looked surprised he had said anything, her hand flying to her chest as if he had spooked her. Rightly so; Noah supposed he had. "I'm sorry. I dinnae mean to scare you." Noah felt very hot as the woman narrowed in on him.

"I've seen you before," she said, her fuss entirely focused on him now. This wasn't how Noah had imagined their first exchange of words. She looked rather annoyed he had said anything at all. "I didn't think you were one of us, what with your medical texts you're always reading. Playing on the other side, are we?"

Certainly not what Noah had expected to come out of her mouth.

"Who exactly are you?"

He sat a little straighter on the bench. "I'm afraid I don't understand."

The woman raised an eyebrow, both hands on her hips. "You're a student at the medical school, are you not? An odd choice for a warlock. Usually, your kind sticks to more arcane ways."

Noah took a second to regain himself, entirely confused. "Warlock?"

The woman smoothed a hand over her frizzled hair, clearly annoyed with him. "You practise magic, do you not? How else would you be able to see through my glamour?"

"You're a witch?" Incredible. She looked nothing like Noah's mother. This woman was sunshine incorporated into a single human being. Noah's mother had been leeched of her light. Magic had robbed her of it.

"Well, I would be if I was allowed to practise. If you don't mind, don't mention my glamour spell to anyone, would you? I know I'm not supposed to use magic, but a man is harassing me, and I forgot some supplies at home. I just wanted to run back and get them before my charges missed me for too long." The woman twisted her hands over her skirt. All her bravado turned to nerves. "You won't tell anyone, will you?"

There was a lot to unpack here. "Someone's harassing you? Who?"

"Doesn't matter now that he can't see me. Now I need to get back, before my charges get bored and destroy the classroom."

"I – charges?"

"Yes, I'm a teacher. I educate the children of the divination professors at Alberney, the magics school. Although sometimes I take on the alchemy professors' children as well."

A lot to unpack indeed, but Noah's mind couldn't focus on just one thing. "Are women allowed to use magic?" His mother had practised it for years, though she had made it very clear she wasn't supposed to. Societal rules had always been a thorn in her side.

The woman came in closer to inspect him. Her eyes scrutinised him from head to toe as if his appearance would reveal his secrets to her. "Indeed, we are not, which is why you never saw me." She touched her nose in a knowing way, and Noah enjoyed greatly that they had this little secret binding them together now.

"Why aren't women allowed to practice magic?" His mother had never given him much of a reason.

"Imagine, a woman with any form of power. How ghastly. We've been outlawed from practising magic in Europe for centuries. Now then, who did you say you were again?"

Banned for centuries? Noah's mother had always begged him to keep her business quiet outside of working with the locals. He always thought it was because magic was too dangerous.

"Are you daft? I've asked you twice who you are. Shall I ask you a third, or will you not be answering my questions anytime soon?"

Noah pulled himself out of his memories and stuck out a hand to the woman. "Noah Kiers. From Pitlochry."

The woman reluctantly looked at his hand before giving it a fair shake. "Meredith Forbes. Of Dunbar." Meredith let go of his hand, though her eyes held his without mercy. "How long have you been in the city?"

Noah felt nervous, having her bore into him with such intensity. "This is my first year. I worked around the borders to save some money for school before coming here. Why?"

"You don't seem to know much about the magic world, do you? You ask a lot of questions."

"My mother was a witch." Something about this woman had Noah speaking all his truth. He couldn't lie to her. "She practised magic back home. It was her business. It's how we survived."

Meredith's eyes softened. "A hedge witch; far more common in the Highlands where it's easier to practice magic in secrecy. Tell me, Noah Kiers, what kind of magic did your mother practise?"

Noah shook his head. "I don't know. I left because it changed her. I didn't want the same to happen to me."

"That's the thing with hedge witches, isn't it? No formal training, so they don't know how to protect themselves from magic. I feel for you, Noah Kiers. I'm sorry you had to watch that happen."

Why did Noah feel so exposed? How could a stranger tap into his greatest misery in such little time?

"Well, I suppose I should be running. I can't leave my children for much longer. Good day, sir." She gave him a quick tilt of her head, ready to dash off in her haste as she had before Noah interrupted her.

"Wait," Noah called before she could run off. She halted in her steps, her skirts gathered in her hands. "Please, can I see you again? I don't know anyone in the magic world. I barely know anyone in the real world. May I call on you?"

Meredith hesitated before backtracking her steps. She dug a hand into one of her pockets and pulled out a crinkled calling card for him. "Yes, you may. On the weekends only, when I'm not working."

The card was plain, with Meredith's name and address printed neatly in its centre. Noah ran a thumb over the loopy writing as he said her name in his head. It was a lovely name. He was about to say so when he looked up to find her already gone. Noah felt slightly disappointed she had come and gone so quickly, but he knew deep down this wasn't the end. It was only the beginning.

～

NOAH FELT stiff in the chair as he woke, his body entirely out of tune. He had dreamt of the day he and Makenna first met. It was a day that changed his life. Looking back, he wondered if he regretted it. Perhaps if he hadn't met Meredith, the two would have never left for England. As soon as the idea crossed his mind, Noah banished it from thought. He never regretted a second spent with her.

It was hard to tell what time of day it was from the light of the room. It was pouring outside, and the bedroom was washed with dim grey light. Charles hadn't woken him in the night, which likely meant nothing had changed with Makenna. That didn't stop Noah's hope that when he opened his eyes, Makenna would be sat upright in bed, debating the merits of some movie Noah had never seen with Cody and Siobhan.

No such sight. She lay exactly as he had left her, still as stone and probably as cold as one, too. In the chair beside her sat Rose, her hands working at a piece of delicate embroidery.

"How is she?" Noah asked as he took the seat next to the thin woman. His voice was rough, and he desperately wished for a glass of water. If only he could drink it.

"Unchanged. I'd say she might as well be dead, but the dead are livelier than her at the moment." Rose's attention didn't drift from the needle and thread in her hands.

"And how did you get stuck on babysitting duty?"

"I offered."

Noah rubbed a hand over his face. "I have truly seen it all. I didn't think you cared for her. Yet you've been the one maintaining the graves this entire time."

Rose shrugged, and her hands stilled their work as she gave Noah her full attention. "Do tell me what about this girl is so special? Why have you waited over a hundred years on her?"

"Life, Rose," Noah said. "She was my life. She gave me life. She made it purposeful."

"And yet she threw it away the last time and tries so hard to escape it again this time. You are a fool, Noah Kiers."

Noah looked at Rose, a woman scorned by her own lover. "We don't get to choose what gives us purpose. And if mine comes from loving someone whose needs are not the same as mine, I accept that. It is an honour to be a part of her life, and I will do whatever I can to make hers better."

"And what does she do for you?" Rose asked. "That seems terribly one-sided."

Noah turned his attention to Makenna. "You weren't there when we met. You don't know what she gave me – what she showed me. She made me a better person, and for that, I am eternally grateful. I will do what I can to return the favour." He leaned forward, reaching across the bed to hold Makenna's. Her skin felt like ice beneath his. "She is my equal."

He could hear Rose rustle in the chair beside him. "Men don't deserve women. They will take us to the grave, somehow, someway."

Noah bowed his head. "I fear you might be right on that one."

302

"I'm always right." Rose went back to her needlework, her thin fingers making quick work of the fabric. "When she dies, what will you have of her when she doesn't come back? Will you survive it?"

When she dies again – but no, Noah wouldn't survive it. That wasn't Makenna's burden to bear, though. "I'll have her memories," he said. "And I'll know I made a difference in someone's life."

Rose cocked her head. "And when you get sad and lonely, you'll what? Just stare at the photo of her you prize above anything else? That will be enough for you?"

"The photo," Noah repeated, his body beginning to burn with realisation. "Her photo," he breathed as he bounded from the chair.

Rose sat upright with the sudden commotion. "Where are you going?"

"Watch her," Noah yelled over his shoulder as he raced out of the room, his heart pounding.

He zipped down the hall and through the house. He tore his way to the back garden and out into the relentless rain. Which tree had it been? The rain was coming down hard. It soaked his clothes, his feet numb on the ground.

Please, please, please.

He couldn't lose the one memento he had of her. He had so little of Makenna to begin with. Noah paced around furiously, scouring the trees until he found the right one. The earth before the giant oak was packed solid by a week's worth of rain. Noah sprinted to its solid base and sunk to his knees. His nails dug into the ground, pulling up as much mud as he could at a time. *As he did so, he ignored the burn from the wound in his arm where he'd cut out his own flesh. It hadn't healed as fast as previous wounds.*

Please, please, please.

He and Meredith had taken the photo on their last

night in Edinburgh. It was a reminder of where they came from and where they were going. Noah had kept that photo on or near his person spanning the century since. If he had destroyed it so thoughtlessly – he couldn't think on it.

Finally, his hands found the small slip. It was caked in sludgy earth and wrinkled from its week in a muddy grave. Noah stopped breathing as he laid the photo on his lap and wiped at the grime with trembling fingers.

His body shook as the picture lay ruined in his fingers. The film had swollen with rainwater, and mud was embedded into it, distorting the image. Noah let the picture slip from his hand as he tried to catch his breath. Not this, not the one thing he had of Meredith. He shrunk in on himself. Of course Noah would lose this small token of affection. He was the very best at that, losing things most precious to him. When did it stop?

He couldn't tell how long he'd been out here for. All he could do was stare at the photo on the ground and pity himself.

"Noah," someone called his name. He almost missed it as the rain continued its assault. In the downpour, he could soon see Siobhan, her small figure blending in with the shadows from the storm. "Noah, come inside. It's Makenna."

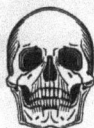

Concerning Mothers

How long had Makenna been waiting? It felt like both an eternity and as if no time had passed at all. "Rory?" she called into the abyss. Her voice seemed to echo in every direction before the darkness absorbed it. "Rory, please come back." She pivoted in another circle. The darkness was disorienting. "Rory, please—" Makenna gasped as she turned around and found a woman standing a few feet from her. "Who are you?" Makenna asked.

The woman must have been in her early forties, her dark hair shorn close to her scalp and her clothes ragged on her body. "I'm sorry," the woman said, her voice tilting in a Scottish accent. "I'm sorry for everything. Please tell him that. I'm sorry he felt he had to leave."

Makenna stood straight, her body poised for a fight as if this wisp of a woman might charge her. "Who are you?"

"Go back, before you get stuck here, and tell him I love him."

The dark hair, the Scottish accent, the love for someone who had left her behind. Everything clicked with a violent realisation. "You're her. You're Constance. Noah's mother."

Constance took a shaky step forward, her head bobbing. "You have to go. I can feel death is close to you." Her sunken eyes scanned the darkness as if seeing something Makenna could not. "It calls to you. It wants you."

Makenna took a step back. "I'm not ready yet. I'm looking for someone."

Constance's head whipped back to Makenna as if she had just remembered the girl was still there. "My Noah, please tell him I love him. And that I never hated him for leaving. Tell him that for me, will you? I can sense him on you. I know you're connected to him somehow."

"I—" Constance's words brought Makenna back to her body, and she looked down. She was almost entirely faded. Only her chest and neck were still solid. "I need to go, don't I?"

Constance nodded, her thin arms snaked around her waist. "Please, before you go; tell me he lived a good life, wherever he is now?"

Makenna froze. The coldness seeped into her bones, pulling her to the darkness with its slow hunger. "He's trapped," she said feverishly. "He has been for over a hundred years." She couldn't wait any longer. Her time was up.

The last she saw of Constance was the look of pure horror upon her face before Makenna disappeared from the world of shadows and into the one of light.

~

MAKENNA'S BODY felt as if it had been electrocuted. Every fibre in her body sizzled with energy as she bolted upright in the soft bed. It was hard to find her breath, for her lungs seemed to pump overtime to catch up with the rest of her body.

"Go get Noah," someone said.

It took a moment for the room around her to stabilise. There was still weird kinetic energy buzzing through her limbs as her eyes settled on the person beside her on the bed. Lydia had her slender hand wrapped around Makenna's, her face a mix of surprise and concern.

"Makenna, are you all right?" The blond looked at her, seemingly unsure if she should call for more help.

"I – I was there, in the shadow world." Her words were rushed, her head still foggy. "I saw my brother. He was there. I saw him." She felt almost hysterical. The bed beneath her didn't feel real. The room around her seemed like a dream. "I'm . . . Where am I?"

Lydia narrowed her eyes as she pushed her plait over her shoulder. "We brought you back to your room. Do you remember what happened? Outside, by the gate. You collapsed."

Focus, Makenna needed to focus. There were too many things pulling her attention away. It was hard to settle on one thing with all this energy bottled inside of her. "The gate?" Yes, the gate. She had been outside. They had done the spell to break her free. "I was supposed to walk out," she said slowly as the memory came back. "But I'm here. I'm still here." The pieces of the puzzle came together, if at a glacial pace.

Makenna was supposed to be free in the outside world, released from the curse. It occurred to her why this room felt wrong – why the bed beneath her seemed so off. She wasn't supposed to be here at all. "It failed," she breathed. "I'm still stuck."

"We don't know that," Lydia assured her, though her face faltered. "You never managed to try before you collapsed. It could still work." Her hand came up to soothe Makenna by stroking her hair.

The last of the weird energy seemed to dissipate from Makenna's body, and she was left absolutely exhausted. It pulled at her bones and made her want to sink into the mattress. "Why did I collapse?" Her voice came out small, edging on grief that threatened to make her weep. It should have been simple. She should have opened that latch and walked out. This had been her final shot at freedom, her last chance to save her soul, and all she had done was come one step closer to death.

"I don't know," Lydia said, close to tears, "but it was very scary. We thought you—" She averted her gaze from Makenna.

Before Makenna could say anything else, the door kicked open with a bang. It swung on its rusted hinges as Noah raced into the room. His clothes were soaked and his hands caked with dirt, but that didn't slow him. Lydia moved from her spot so that he could take it, and Noah immediately gripped Makenna in a hug that squished her chest and took her breath away.

"I thought I'd lost you again," he said, the wetness of his clothes soaking hers. His eyes were red as he moved back, though he never lost point of contact with her. He kept both hands on her arms as if she would float away from him at any moment.

"Still here," Makenna said, though she wasn't sure how to feel about it. *Here* was the very thing she had been trying to escape. She took great comfort having Noah at her side now, even if he had brought the outside in with him. His warmth was leagues above the emptiness of the shadow world.

"I don't know what happened. I knew magic was dangerous. I never wanted to try it. Oh, god, I'm so glad you're okay." He spoke a mile a minute. "What happened? Do you remember? Where did you go?"

Makenna reached for one of his dirty hands on her arm and brought it to her lap. She wove her fingers through his and focused on the feel of his skin against hers. She used it to ground herself. "I went to the shadow world. Or my spirit did, at least." She could feel Noah stiffen beneath her. "I saw my brother. He was there." She bit down on her lip, wondering whether to tell him what Rory had shown her. "So was the rest of my soul." Noah tensed, but she pressed on. "Every time I die, more of it gets left behind in the shadow world. It calls to me. It wants my death to complete itself." Her voice tapered off, her hands shaking.

Noah bit down hard on his back teeth, his hands in fists. "I won't let that happen. We'll find a way to bring it back. We'll make you complete again. Here, not in the shadow world." He leaned closer, his eyes boring into hers. "I promise you that."

Makenna could smell the rain on Noah's skin, his soaked clothes seeping onto the bed. She didn't care. "I almost didn't make it back," she whispered. "When my brother left, I waited for him to return, and I almost waited too long. I almost got stuck."

"But you came back," Noah said. "Because you weren't done living."

Did she bother telling him she had almost thrown it away, just to be with her brother for a little while longer? She decided against it. Now wasn't the time for that conversation. "Noah, he wasn't the only one I saw. Your mother was there, too."

Noah detached from her immediately, the hopeful look in his eyes gone. "What do you mean my mother was there?"

"She found me in the shadow world. She said she could feel you on me. It's what drew her to me."

"I—" Noah stood up from the bed, his back stiff as a board. "How is that possible?"

Makenna shook her head. "I don't know. She wanted me to tell you that she loved you. She never stopped loving you even after you left. She—"

"Stop," Noah said, his voice raised. He gritted his teeth before he spoke again. "Please don't play with me. Not with her. I can't handle it. Not today."

Makenna sucked in a short breath. "I'm not. She found me truly. I – I just wanted to let you know."

Noah's voice was tight, his voice coming out clipped. "Only in death does she have the courage to show me her love." His eyes were full of grief he had never let go of in over a hundred years. "I'm glad you're safe, Makenna. If you'll excuse me." He didn't waste a second longer before exiting.

The room seemed colder without his presence. "He's in shock," Lydia said. "A lot has happened today. Please forgive him."

Makenna tried to detangle herself from the sheets to go after Noah. She felt no ill will against him for his reaction as Lydia feared. Makenna had freaked out much more for far less, but she knew how Noah processed. His emotions rocked him hard, and he didn't fare well alone.

"I'm not angry," she said as she freed her legs and tried for the floor. It was too much too soon, and her legs buckled when her feet touched the ground.

Lydia instantly swooped her up and brought her back to the bed.

"I need to help him. I can't stay here."

"You need to rest," Lydia urged. "You almost died

today. I'm sure Noah will survive. He just needs a minute to process everything and calm down."

"*I* can calm him down," Makenna said.

Lydia shook a finger at her, much as a mother would when scolding a child. "You will do no such thing. You will stay here and rest. Noah will come back when he's ready. You can try the gate after."

Makenna wavered. Briefly, she wondered if she could make a break for the door, but her limbs were indeed tired. Maybe leaning back to rest and letting Noah come to her wasn't such a bad idea.

"Besides, the daft boy ruined the sheets and muddied you up. At least now I have something to do other than watch you sleep," Lydia fussed. With a thin finger, she pushed Makenna down until the girl was lying back in the bed. "You stay here while I go get fresh sheets and a cloth so you can clean off. Don't move."

Makenna didn't argue again as she gave in to the mattress.

∾

MAKENNA WAS LEFT to her own thoughts in the quiet of the room. Had the spell truly not worked? Was she still locked to these grounds, imprisoned despite the magic she had cast? Something had happened. She had gone beyond her body and into the shadow world. Did that mean she was finally able to leave the property?

She tried to rest, but after tossing and turning for an hour, Makenna could not lie still anymore. She had to know.

There were no grand goodbyes as she slipped out of the cushy bed and into the hall. No one monitored her door, expecting her up so soon. She didn't think she had the energy to say goodbye again anyway, on the chance the magic hadn't worked. She didn't want to put everyone through another grand gesture, raising and crashing their hopes like a tidal wave.

Her walk to the gate stretched on for an eternity, her limbs stiff and uncooperative. She tugged at her knitted jumper, fighting off the night's chill as she padded out the weathered front door and across the expansive lawn. She sucked in a lungful of cool air as the gate loomed before her. How could a barrier made centuries ago cause so much trouble?

She halted before the latch that blocked access to the main road, the one that had split her hand twenty-one years ago. Her fingers hovered in the air before it. *It will open.* She had done the spell ensuring her escape. Noah had walked her through it. There was no reason it wouldn't work. She would simply unlatch the bolt and pass through, free to live her life as she wanted, not as the fates had decided over a hundred years ago.

Swallowing the lump in her throat, Makenna clamped down on the old-fashioned lever and pushed up.

It didn't move.

She tried harder, pressing her lips together in all her might. When it wouldn't budge, Makenna let her hand drop, along with the hopes she had found her freedom. It was awfully quiet as she sank to her knees, tears rolling down her cheeks as she accepted her fate. The magic had not worked.

~

NOAH PACED AROUND HIS ROOM, his wet clothes sticking to his skin. In those last few years he had lived with Constance, she had succumbed to her magic as an addict did to their vice. Noah became nothing but an accessory to her spells – an errand boy to collect the ingredients Constance needed when she was too busy to fetch them herself.

The fact that she let him leave home so easily had worn away at Noah for years. What mother let their child do that? In the days after he left, he had spent time in the nearest village. He knew the people there well, and they knew him. They let him board for a few days, free of charge. A small part of him had hoped his mother would show up looking for him and demand his return home. That she would see the error in her ways and realise family meant more than magic.

No such thing had happened. Noah had waited until the villagers' hospitality wore out and he was forced to move on. His mother never came for him, and he had resented her for it for years. It wasn't until he met Meredith that he felt a sense of completion again – that the void of a family bond could be filled with a new sense of love.

How typical of Constance that her only return to him would be through magic.

He fussed around his room before cleaning off in the shower and tending to his forearm. The warm water did him good. It gave him some clarity, made him realise that he had overreacted and scorned Makenna. There she had been, freshly returned from the shadow world, and all he had done was yell in her face for delivering a message. He wasn't one to lose his temper, but he had slipped at the mention of his mother. He would apologise to Makenna, he decided as he slipped into dry clothes and wrapped his wound, which was taking longer to heal than he expected. She hadn't deserved his ire.

Satisfied he wouldn't track any more mud throughout

the house and ready for an earful for the mess he had made, he went to his door and yanked it open. He was prepared to take on the challenges of the night with his new attitude. What he wasn't ready for was the woman standing in his doorway, her expression as sour as ever.

"Harriet," Noah squeaked. Her stare could raise the dead. Or at least send the dead into a panic. "What are you doing here?" Never in his hundred-plus years here had he seen Harriet venture out of the attic. He had only ever heard her moans through the corridors late at night.

"May I come in, or do you intend to let me waste away while you pick your jaw up off the floor?" She stood straight, her hands tucked neatly on top of one another at her waist. She always made Noah feel inferior, somehow, someway.

He stared at her a second more before gathering his wits. "Uh, please. Come in."

Harriet didn't offer any pleasantries as she brushed past him. She went right for his window, her eyes staring down into the front gardens as Noah had done many times in his life. "That was quite the show you put on earlier," she said more to the window than him. "A magic spell gone awry. It seems all your worries were much warranted."

Noah felt a sudden awkwardness having Harriet in his room. He didn't know where to stand or what to do with himself. He shoved his hands into his pockets to keep them from fidgeting. "It was a risk. Everyone knew that."

"I have risked far more for much less." Harriet tucked one hand under her elbow, her other playing with the pearls around her neck. She didn't look at Noah as she spoke. "I lost my child, as you know, though it was not as spectacular as the little show you all provided tonight. There was no magic involved."

"I'm sorry. We've all lost someone," Noah said. He

knew a bit about Harriet's daughter's death, that Harriet felt extremely guilty over it. Despite all the time he and Harriet had spent trapped under the same roof, he had never gotten past her frosty exterior to learn the full story. That still hadn't stopped him from throwing that guilt in her face, just to get information about his mother's spellbook. He wasn't proud of that moment.

Harriet's eyes were cast in the shadows from the window. Finally, she shifted to look at Noah. "She was not always my daughter. I birthed a boy, and I raised a boy just the same. It wasn't until her sixteenth birthday that she confessed herself to me. She was a girl, trapped in a boy's body." Harriet's fingers picked at her necklace more aggressively. "I denied her. I denied her for years, just as the world did. I was ashamed and told her she was as good as dead to me if this was the life she chose. Do you know there is no word for a parent who loses a child? There simply is no word to describe the pain. It is unbearable. Unfathomable."

Noah listened as Harriet spoke. She had never been so vulnerable with him before.

"I told my daughter she was better off dead, and she followed my advice." Harriet's voice was cold, though Noah could hear the cracks in it, the small waver that threatened to take this force of a woman down. "All those fanciful delights in the attic," Harriet said as she continued to pick at her necklace, "all the lovely clothes and jewellery I refused my daughter to wear – I have collected them for years in my death. I know Effie would have loved them. I will take them with me when my spirit moves on from this wretched place. I will bring them to her and adorn her with them in the shadow world."

"You loved her," Noah said.

"I loved her too late." Harriet moved away from the

wall and into the light of the room. Noah could see how red her eyes were, even if her face remained as cold as stone. "And you love that girl. You've loved her as much as I could not love my Effie."

Noah forced himself to keep his face as still as Harriet's. It was nearly impossible when he imagined his love for Makenna. It ran as deep as the earth's core and as far as the heavens that spanned the universe. "I do."

Harriet moved as close to Noah as she dared. It was the closest they had ever been to each other without cursing one another out. "I cannot be the one to keep you separated. I do not know how this will help you, but that book, the one of your mother's, you asked me about it."

"Yes," Noah said, his throat tight.

"It has always been here, tucked away in the attic, longer than you or I have ever been in this place."

Noah opened his mouth, trying to process the information. "How do you know?"

Harriet tucked a hand into a pocket stitched in her clothes. From it, she pulled out a yellowed piece of paper, neatly folded and preserved. "This was in the book. A letter from a mother to her child." She handed it to Noah, who took it with shaky fingers. Constance's loopy writing stretched across the page. He would have recognised it anywhere.

"Why did you have this? Why did you keep it from me?" he asked, trying to keep any emotion out of his voice.

"Because I decided if my child couldn't know a mother's love, no other child would."

Noah's lips trembled as he unfolded the page and scanned the handwritten note. It was dated 1876, the year he had been born. "Get out," he said to Harriet, though he was unable to take his eyes off the page.

Harriet didn't move. "People are cruel, Noah. You've told me that enough times. Now you really understand it."

"Leave me." The words were barely a whisper.

"I am truly sorry." Before Noah could tell her again, Harriet exited the room.

Noah stood still for what felt like an eternity before he could move again. He tried to read the page, but it was hard with his tears. They poured freely in the solitude of his room. Sitting down on the bed, Noah prepared himself for the words to come.

SEPTEMBER 20, *1876*

Dearest Noah,

I hope to give you a better life than what has been fated here. Mistakes have been made, but I will do my best to rectify them. I will keep you safe. I write to you now to hold myself accountable for that promise. May I look back on this note when you are grown and marvel at the wonderful man you will have turned into.

Here's to living a good life.

Your loving mother,

Constance

HARRIET HAD HOARDED this letter for the love she so desperately craved for herself but had failed to deliver. If only she knew how badly Noah had needed it himself.

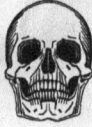

Magic Me Once, Shame on You

akenna returned to her room without running into anyone, and she was glad for it. It gave her time to settle the disappointment of the failed spell, to accept that it hadn't worked and that she needed another solution to her problem.

An hour had passed after she crawled back underneath her duvet, and when Noah did not come for her, she left to check on him.

"Noah?" she asked as she knocked on his door. The silence didn't sit right with her. She pushed into his room and waited for her eyes to adjust. All the lights were off. Only the moonlight that crept through the window illuminated the man on the bed, his head in his hands. Makenna could hear the quiet sobs that shook his shoulders.

"Noah?" she said more gently as she crossed the floor. Dropping to her knees, she wrapped her hands lightly around his to pull them from his face. "What happened?" she whispered.

Noah looked at her, his eyes red-rimmed and hair tangled. "She was here." His voice broke as he spoke.

"Who was?"

"My mother. She was here in this house when I was a babe." He sucked in a breath and pulled back from Makenna. She let him drift away from her, ready to catch him when he needed her again.

"How do you know that?"

Noah twisted to pluck something from his bed before handing it to her. Makenna scanned the handwritten letter, her gaze tracing over the date, unable to believe it was real. "Where did you get this?"

"Harriet." He spat out the name as if it burned him to speak it. "She had it this whole time. It was in my mother's spellbook. Harriet took it who knows how long ago."

"Why would she do that?" Makenna asked.

Noah's jaw tensed as his eyes darted to the window. It was as if he was seeing something Makenna could not. "To spite me."

"Oh, Noah." Dropping the note to the floor, Makenna propped herself up to wrap her arms around his shaking form. He didn't resist.

"I'm tired," he said into her shoulder. "I'm tired of all of it. I don't want to cry anymore."

Makenna loosened her grip enough to wipe at his tears. "None of that. You cry as much as you need to and then cry some more. And only when you're done crying, we'll figure out what this means."

Noah flinched from her touch, and Makenna's hands fell limply into his lap. "My mother warned me never to come to England. She spent her whole life cursing the English and begged me to never cross the border." He picked at the note Makenna had so carelessly dropped on the floor. "She was here the year I was born, but something spooked her. Something made her leave and never turn back."

"When I saw her in the shadow world," Makenna said, almost startled by the realisation, "I told her you were trapped. She was stunned, almost as if what she feared had come true."

Noah's eyes scanned the aged page again. "She knew something would happen if I came here. That's why she tried to keep me away." Noah folded the letter and tucked it into his shirt pocket. He then picked up Makenna's hands and kissed her knuckles before lifting her to her feet. "We need to speak to her."

Makenna nearly stumbled over her own feet, trying to keep up with Noah as he bolted for the door. "Noah, wait. Where are you going?"

He was out of the room and into hers before Makenna made it to the hall. She found Noah sitting on the floor in her room, an almost crazed look in his eyes as he manically flipped through the spellbook left on her bedside table. "What are you doing?"

"Here," Noah said as he found the page he so desperately sought. He beckoned for Makenna to join him as he pointed to the title on the page.

"A summoning spell?" Makenna read. "For your mum?"

"Aye. We have all the ingredients at hand," Noah said. "We can do this."

Makenna dragged the book closer to read it better. "Noah, you've spent the last few days warning me how dangerous magic is. I almost died because of it. And I'm still stuck. Now you want to use it to raise the dead? This is a huge 180 for you."

He shook his head as he ran his hand over his face. "This feels right. The spell for you did not."

"So, you're a psychic now, are you? You just know

when magic will and won't work?" Makenna tried to keep the scepticism out of her voice, but Noah's previous warning and her visit to the shadow world had spooked her greatly.

"This spell is different," Noah said firmly, and Makenna wished she could believe in his conviction as strongly as he did. "It says so here. '*To summon who you need, one must give to receive. A gift freely given: power, knowledge, love.*' We have to give one of them in order to call on death. It's an easy choice."

Makenna raised an eyebrow. "Help me out here, because I'm not sure what giving up any of those would look like. What's the easy choice here?"

"Power," Noah said, his voice unwavering. "Power means magic. You'd have to give up a part of your magic for the spell to work. Magic is all about balance. That's the cost here."

"You want me to give up a part of my magic?" Makenna asked, unsure about this now. She had spent years in Edinburgh longing to practice the craft as a governess – she remembered. Could she give up something she had wanted so badly over a hundred years ago? Was her life worth it? Noah seemed to think so. Makenna supposed it was the obvious choice.

"If you agree to it, of course. Magic is dangerous anyways. This is a double blessing in disguise, all in exchange to break the curse."

"And if we summon your mum by sacrificing a part of my magic, would I have enough to break the curse after if that's what's needed?" Makenna asked.

"This will deplete your magic, but not enough to leave us empty-handed. A summoning can't demand all of you. It wouldn't justify the cost. That's one thing my mother always taught me. Magic is about balance. And just think —" Noah reached for her hand and interlocked her fingers with his own. "If we can summon my mother, we can figure out how to break the curse, once and for all." He searched Makenna's eyes, wearing a look of utter hope she had never seen on him before. "A part of your magic for total freedom. That's the last price we have to pay. This is how we do it."

Makenna tightened her grip on his hand. "How can you promise me that?"

"I can't. But we've never known this much before. How can we not try?" Noah asked. "This could save you. It could save us both." He released her hand and moved to hold her face. His fingers were gentle on her skin, soothing and warm. "I know it's risky. I know the dangers. I watched you almost die today as I've watched you die many times before. But I refuse to do it again. If you're willing to risk your magic, we may be able to end this all."

Makenna leaned into Noah's touch, regretful she had lived her entire life without it. "I suppose I can live without magic, or however much the spell will take. I've gone without it so far. And for us, I'd give up just about anything." She bridged the space between them and let her lips taste his. They were as sweet as she remembered from decades past. How could she ever forget?

～

AFTER A RESTLESS SLEEP, Noah and Makenna spent the morning preparing the new spell. They found themselves in the drawing room with all the furniture pushed back against the upholstered walls. It seemed the most practical location; aside from the coffee table and chairs, there wasn't much in the room to destroy should things go wrong – only the ornate decorations that hung on the walls.

With his mother's book in hand, Noah stood in the centre of the room, where a circle of leaves had been drawn out. The spell called for a ring of an organic leafy substance. This was to summon the spirit in and bind it to this earthly plane. Perfect that crimson leaves had been dropping for the last few weeks.

Aside from the leafy circle, there wasn't much to the spell; only that the leaves be drizzled in with a simple mix Noah had prepared earlier. Noah worried that Makenna might struggle with the complicated words, but they had gone over it a few times already. It was truly a miracle they were going through with this. Noah felt half mad just for asking her, but what other choice did they have?

Makenna stood beside him, with an audience of ghosts in the room with them both. Most everyone in the house was eager to see this spell work, even if there were various levels of concern when Noah had proposed his new plan and what was at stake. Most were on board, though Huxley had been the most vocal about the possible drawbacks.

"She almost died yesterday, and here you are, ready to throw her into the fire again. Honestly, Noah. What's gotten into you?" Huxley huffed from the doorway, his arms crossed over his expansive chest.

"We have no other choice," Noah said, ignoring the itch at the back of his neck as he spoke. "And I'll be here the entire time if something goes wrong."

Huxley twirled his beard. His lips pulled down. "As you were the last time?"

"Huxley," Makenna said, walking over to the gentle giant. "I'm okay to do this. I want to do this. This could be our last chance."

The old man held out a large hand to Makenna and cupped her cheek as he gave her a sad smile. "You said that the last time. Forgive me if I do not believe it. I simply want the best for you both."

Makenna held his hand with her own. "I know. Thank you. I wouldn't do this if I didn't think I could handle it." Huxley nodded, though his shoulders were still tense as Makenna took her spot beside Noah. He handed her a glass vial to pour over the leaves and the book marked with the page for her to read. The potion had provided more than enough mixture. Noah wasn't worried about running out.

"If you don't want to do this, now is your last chance," he said to her.

Makenna shook her head before placing a light kiss on his cheek. "I know the cost. I'm ready to give it." Without any more words, Makenna began walking around the circle. She drizzled the mixture of crushed berries, herbs, dirt, and honey over the leaves. When she was finished, Makenna stood at the head of the room and began casting the spell. She went slow and steady, focusing on sacrificing her power as Noah directed her to. If she had any doubt using magic unpractised, she didn't show it.

"*Vivaren ith molt akda.*" The words flowed more smoothly than the last spell she had cast. Noah admired the strength with which she spoke. There was no fear on her face, no trepidation even though she had been burned by magic now. He wouldn't have asked her to do it if he could do it himself. Noah would have gladly given up his own magic, but Makenna was the only one capable.

Upon her last word, the room was filled with sudden and tense energy that nearly stole Noah's breath away, the lights flickering overhead before stabilising. Makenna kept her feet planted firmly on the ground, but sweat had broken out over her skin.

"Something's wrong," she said, her eyes focused on the page at hand. She had dropped the vial at some point, though Noah hadn't noticed when. "Something's off. I can feel it."

Noah took a step forward, but Makenna held up a hand to stop him.

"It's – it's this line, '*One* must give to receive.'" Makenna's head shot upwards, her neck twisting as she faced the others. "It's not a choice. It doesn't want just one, it's all of them – power, knowledge, love. It's an exchange. The spell requires a soul for a soul." She sunk to her knees as if holding on to the magic was becoming too much. "It's spiritual suicide," she breathed, her one hand gripping the floor. "I can feel it coming. It's pulling me into the circle."

"No!" Noah darted across the floor to anchor Makenna down. A mistake, this had been a mistake. They had openly invited the one thing they had been trying to prevent all along: Makenna losing her soul. And he had rushed her into it. Now she was about to pay the price. "Take me instead. Not you. Never you."

Makenna breathed heavily from the exertion, but she was clear when she shook her head. "Absolutely not. I will not let you." She pushed him away, and Noah felt the cold sting of desperation. "Death already wants me. I won't give it you, too."

"Don't do this, Makenna. Not for me."

"I'll do it," Huxley said from behind him. Makenna was on her hands and knees, sweat dripping from her every pore as she fought against the magic. She turned to him, her eyes red and strained.

"I can't," she said, her voice breaking. "It's not fair. I

won't let you do this." She moaned against the spell, her back arching as it pulled at her.

Huxley stood tall, his arms straight by his side. "It would be an honour to give my soul for you both. I wouldn't think twice about it."

"No," Makenna said through gritted teeth. "I won't punish you for this. You didn't deserve it."

"But I do." A woman stepped from the shadows, her thin figure emerging into the light. Harriet stood before them all, her face as frigid as ever. "I will take your place," she said to Makenna. "To repent for all my misgivings, done to you." She directed her gaze to Noah. "And to those no longer with us."

Makenna struggled to her knees, relying heavily on Noah to maintain her balance. "I can't ask that of you. I can't ask that of anyone. You're already a spirit. This isn't a second death. This is an obliteration of the soul. It means your end entirely." She barely got the last word out before arching her back in a resounding scream. Noah locked his arms around her.

Harriet moved closer to the circle. "I did not wait for you to ask. I give myself entirely. I have caused enough harm. Let me fix what I have helped break. Give me that while you can."

Makenna's nails dug into Noah's back. She searched his face as if waiting for him to stop her. No one, not a single soul in the room had anything to say against Harriet's wishes. Noah could tell the regret in Makenna's eyes as she said the words, "Then I replace myself with you, Harriet." Makenna's body collapsed as soon as the words were out of her mouth, though Noah already had her in his arms.

Makenna's eyes remained open as she watched Harriet give in to the pull of the leaves. As soon as both booted feet were across the line, there was a brilliant moment of nothing. It was as if the energy had dissipated instantly. All eyes were on Harriet. She gave no wave or nod of goodbye, just stood there with the same disappointing stare Noah had always associated her with.

"Thank you," Makenna said, and then there was a brilliant flash.

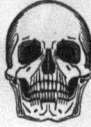

30

My Boy

It took a moment for Noah's eyes to settle after the flash of light. He kept Makenna locked tightly in his arms as he focused on the figure now standing in the circle.

She wasn't anything like he remembered. His mother had been a woman of great power, unchecked and seemingly limitless. This woman in front of him was crouched over, her midnight locks shorn short and her frame thin from malnutrition. Her raggedy clothes hung off her body, and her dark eyes seemed to sink into her skull. This was not his mother. This was a woman stripped of her power and reduced to nothing.

"My boy," Constance breathed. She moved forward but was stopped by the ring of leaves. Constance looked down at the barrier as if confused as to why she could not step over it. "Ah, a summoning spell," she whispered, connecting the dots. "How clever." She turned her head up, her eyes going directly to Noah again. "Oh, how you've changed." Her hands came to her lips as her eyes watered. "My Noah, all grown up."

Noah's throat tightened. He had dreamt of this moment for over a century. What would he say if he ever met his mother again? He had been wounded by her, torn down by her lust for magic to the detriment of their family. Yet, here and now, Noah couldn't feel any of those things. He was simply a boy who missed his mother.

"Mama." His voice was rough. Makenna moved from his arms to give him the space he didn't know he needed. "It's been so long."

"My dear boy, *m'eudail*, what happened? Tell me we aren't back in this wretched house?" Constance eyed the walls around her, grief and fear hunching up her shoulders. "I tried so hard to keep you from this fate. I didn't want this for you." Her voice came out a whisper at the end.

Noah had to look away for a moment to collect himself. He hadn't felt the touch of his mother's concern in so long. It tore at his heart. "Mama, why am I stuck here? How do we undo it?"

Constance backed up in the circle, shaking her head. Her movements were sharp and twitchy. "I tried. I tried to protect you from it. But the curse was too strong. There was too much hate. All I could do was keep you away from here and hope you never walked through the gates."

It took all Noah's strength to pull himself to his feet. "What are you talking about? What happened?"

Constance opened her mouth to speak before her eyes landed on someone else in the room. "*You.*" She pointed a stiff finger, accusation riling her face up. "You were here this entire time?"

Lydia stood in the back corner of the room, her eyes wide as she stared at Constance. "You're his mother?" Her mouth hung open, her hands gripping her silky nightgown above her chest. "I – I didn't know. I never even knew your name."

Noah's head darted between the two women. "What are you talking about, Lydia?"

The blond moved out from the corner, her face bewildered. "You made a deal with my husband around 140 years ago to bring me back from the dead."

Constance seemed to find the bit of fire that had ruled Noah's childhood. "And when you killed yourself after I brought you back, your husband cursed me."

"He did what?" Lydia choked.

Constance stood a bit straighter, her eyes spewing hate at the blond now standing just feet from her. "Your husband came to me after you died of a sickness. You had been together for twenty-one years, and he couldn't move on without you. He begged me to bring you back, but death demands payment. I told him he would have to wait another twenty-one years before I could bring you back. A year of death for a year of life together. He agreed and spent those twenty-one years hanging on to a glimmer of hope. And when the time came, I brought you back as promised."

Lydia's face twisted in agony, her nails now digging into her chest. "But I didn't want to come back. I resented my husband. Death was my escape. You pulled me from peace, my heaven."

"So, you killed yourself, in this very house, thinking heaven would take you back again. But the afterlife doesn't look kindly upon those who kill themselves," Constance said for her.

"And I became stuck." Lydia wiped frantically at the tears in her eyes, desperate to be rid of them.

Constance looked Lydia up and down. "Your husband begged me to bring you back a second time. But your betrayal of life was permanent, and when I said I could do nothing, he cursed me." She turned to Noah, who stood speechless before his mother. "He cursed me to a twenty-one-year cycle of tragedy upon the thing I loved most, which was you."

Noah felt as if the floor had opened up and swallowed him whole. Perhaps he had stopped existing entirely. He was wholly disconnected from his body.

"I tried to undo it," Constance said. She pressed against the circle's barrier as if she could break free from it. "I did everything I could, but nothing can compete with a curse made of grief and bitterness. The best I could do was localise it to this house. As long as you never stepped foot on the property, the curse would never be triggered."

Noah felt his knees go weak, but he found the will to stand. He badly needed space to think, to cope, to deal with the rising anger his mother wrought in him. She seemed to sense this and took a reluctant step back. "You knew I would be cursed if I came to this house," Noah said, his words building in fury, though it came out with a cold edge, a steel blade meant to cut his mother. "And yet you let me leave. All those years ago, you knew what was at stake, and yet you did nothing."

"I didn't think you would end up in the one place I worked so hard to keep you from. I took you far, far away from here. I forbade you to come to England." Constance's eyes were wild as she spoke, her voice rising.

"And you think that was enough? No warning, no mention of the curse. You failed in protecting me. You always failed me that way," Noah spat at her.

Constance tugged at her frayed collar as if it were choking her. "No, it was part of the curse. I couldn't speak of it. Of course I would have told you otherwise. I never meant to fail you. I am your mother, *m'eudail*, and I love you."

"You loved magic more." Noah's words rose. "And I have paid the ultimate price for it." He turned to Makenna, his eyes wide with horror. "And so have you."

Constance's head darted between the two. "What do you speak of?"

"I am trapped here. And every twenty-one years," Noah hissed, "Makenna comes back to the house and dies in some way or another before being reincarnated. Yet every time she dies, she loses a piece of her soul." His voice cracked, the weight of sorrow too much to bear. "And all I can do is sit and watch as my love loses more and more of herself, getting closer to a true death each time. And now there's nothing left to lose. We're on the seventh and last cycle. That is your legacy, Mama. That is our curse."

Constance swerved her head to Makenna, scouring her up and down, mouth agape as she realised who Makenna was to Noah. "I could never have known." She inched as close to Makenna as she could get in the ring and motioned to her. "Come here, girl. Let me look at you. Let me see the woman my boy fell in love with."

Makenna looked to Noah for approval. He had no answer for her. He only watched as she stepped forward with uncertainty, so Constance could better look at her.

"You have kind eyes, but there is fire behind them. It's diminished but there. And wisdom from so much pain; a century's worth of it. Yet your love for Noah is strong. A true match for him."

"Don't," Noah said. "Don't patronise her like that."

Constance broke her eyes from Makenna. "I do not patronise. I judge accordingly. And a witch's judgement is never wrong."

"Then you are a poor witch, for your judgement has

led to nothing but suffering in this house." Noah was stern. Any sadness or longing he felt for his mother vanished in the span of this conversation. She was exactly as he remembered her to be, conceited and blind to her own ambition.

Constance whipped back as if Noah had slapped her. "You know nothing of the things I have done to protect you, boy."

"And yet here we are. I, stuck in a house, doomed to repeat a terrible fate, and what happened to you? Did your witchy judgement spare you?"

"There are people who get paid to hunt witches," Constance growled. "And there are those who get paid to make witches suffer for practising their birthright. Deny a fish water, and it will die. I am not remorseful for using magic nor the fate it bade me. I am regretful of the fate it brought you both. That I will take with me back to the shadow world."

"Then do what we cannot and tell us how to break this curse," Noah pressed. "Fix the mistake you made."

"Were you not listening?" Constance said, her hands in the air. "I tried, all those years ago. But a curse cannot be broken unless it runs its course or the curse maker who cast it releases it. They either build a clause in the curse to end it or remove it themselves. Let me assure you, this woman's husband built no such clause. The only way to break it is for him to do it himself. That, or let the seventh cycle take her completely, fulfilling the curse."

Lydia's voice broke the intense exchange between mother and son. "That's impossible. My husband Alfred has been dead for over a hundred years."

"Then perhaps you brought back the wrong spirit." Constance stood straight. "And I know how expensive this spell is. A soul for a soul." She turned to Noah. "Are you prepared to sacrifice another for your freedom? Was I worth it in the first place?"

Unreal. There were no other words to describe how Noah felt. "I would not," he whispered. "I never expected someone to do it in the first place. I would never ask for another to make the same sacrifice." His heart sunk lower than the floor. It was beyond the ground and in the underworld. There would be no retrieving it.

"You are a far better person than I raised you to be." Constance looked at the others around the room. "I wish for a moment alone with my son." The was a chorus of disapproval, but Noah shook his head.

"Please. Give us the room." The others filed out one by one, looks of disagreement and suspicion on their faces as they left. Makenna gave Noah's hand a quick squeeze before she and Lydia were the last to leave.

"I won't stay much longer," Constance said when they were the only two in the room. "My soul itches to return to the shadow world. But before I leave, I want it to be known. I never meant to hurt you, Noah. You were the thing I loved most in this world, and I carried that with me past the grave. Please tell me you understand that?"

Noah spoke slowly. "You hurt me. In more ways than you'll ever know."

Constance pressed against the barrier, trying to get as close to her son as possible. "I failed you. And if I could ease your pain, I would. There's a spell, you know, in my book." She pointed to the floor. "It can get rid of your pain. If I can give you nothing else, let it be that."

"I don't want anything from you. I just want peace." Noah was incredibly tired now. His bones ached, and his heart throbbed more than ever.

Constance stood back from the barrier until she was

centred in the ring. "I'm sorry, *m'eudail*. I hope you'll have it in your heart to forgive me one day."

"So do I."

"Until then. May we see each other in the shadow world when the moment is right." Constance's figure began to fade. It was slow at first, her fingers becoming transparent before it moved up her arms.

"Wait," Noah said, his panic building as he realised what was happening. "Please, I'm not ready for you to leave. Not yet."

Constance smiled at him, though it was sombre and did not meet her eyes. "I know. But we will have our time. I know you won't stop until you break free of this curse. I look forward to hearing all about it when you finally join me."

"No!" Noah launched himself at the circle, but the barrier was as unpassable for him as it was for Constance. "I love you," he said to his mother as the last of her faded from the living world. He flew forward as the barrier dissolved, no longer anything to hold him up. He slammed onto his hands and knees, the leaves scattering around him. Any trace of his mother was now gone. All Noah could do was sit there, his heart pounding in his chest as he tried to collect himself.

He swore he heard her say 'I love you' back.

～

MAKENNA WATCHED as Lydia paced up and down the entrance of the house. The ghost's hands moved frantically as she mumbled to herself.

"You must calm down," Maryam said to the woman. She sat on the stairs, her arms wrapped around Cody, who was perched on a stair below her. "It was not your fault. You didn't know what Alfred had done. No one did."

That didn't calm Lydia in any way. She was lost in her daze.

"I don't understand," Cody said. "Why would Alfred curse Noah? Wasn't Noah just a baby? And what does it have to do with Makenna?"

Siobhan smacked her head. "God, you idiot. Noah is cursed to suffer; therefore, Makenna is cursed to suffer too."

"That's not fair," Cody mumbled.

"Of course not. That's why it's a curse," Siobhan said.

"Children, don't be so insensitive. Remember who's here." Maryam lifted her chin at Makenna, but Makenna barely heard the exchange. She was too focused on the door across the foyer. It didn't feel right to leave Noah alone with Constance, but he had asked for privacy, and she would not deny him that.

Charles stood beside her. "Are you all right?" he asked quietly while Siobhan and Cody continued to bicker on the stairs.

"I'm fine," Makenna said. It was an automatic response. Her eyes still focused on the door across from her. If she moved to it and listened hard enough, maybe she could cut through the noise and hear what was going on inside.

Charles crossed his arms. "It's all right to not be fine. It's all right to be sad, or angry even."

Makenna drew away from the door long enough to look at him. "What?"

Charles peered at the others buzzing around each other. He seemed so stoic compared to their constant chaos. "Injustice is cruel. We have all been dealt it. You are allowed to feel anger if that is what you indeed feel."

Makenna wasn't sure what she felt. She had been too focused on Noah. "I—" There was growing resentment in her chest, but perhaps anger wasn't the right word for it. It veered more on the heavier side. It was devastation.

It pulled at her body and made her limbs feel numb. A hundred years of her soul slowly being ripped apart, all because of the choices people had made over a century ago – choices that had nothing to do with her. There was no great reckoning. Makenna wasn't paying the price for some wrongdoing she had done. It was merely the result of falling in love with a man who had been terribly wronged. That made her feel the most uneasy, the randomness of it all. There was no prophecy, no fulfilment of fate, just random bad luck. It exhausted her more than anything.

"I should be angry," Makenna said as she pulled her jumper closer to her. "But I'm too tired to feel it right now." Her fatigue dulled the fury.

Charles gave her a kind look. "As valid a feeling as any."

"Thank you," Makenna said, preferring to feel numb than the rage that would surely come later. If only she could be alone.

"Of course." Charles seemed to sense Makenna's desire for space and moved to the stairs where a great deal of arguing was going on. The only two not involved were Huxley and Lydia. The old man stood off to the side, his hands behind his back as he watched Lydia pace. Lydia was still caught in the throes of her daze. She seemed to be running through a catalogue of emotions in rapid succession. It was almost unnerving to watch.

Lydia must have felt Makenna's eyes on her, for the woman stopped in her tracks and looked at her. "You, that's why it's you."

Makenna raised an eyebrow, but before she could say anything else, Lydia excused herself.

Maybe someone should go find her, Makenna was about to say when the doors to the study opened and Noah walked out. He looked as if he hadn't slept in days, his shoulders slumped and his face ashen. He appeared more a ghost than any of the trapped souls in the room.

Makenna beelined it for him and swept him into her arms without hesitation. He did not cry, nor did he say anything. He simply let her hold him. "Let's get some rest," Makenna whispered into his ear. A few hours of sleep, that's what her body needed so her mind could reboot. Noah needed the same.

Makenna gave the others a nod as she grabbed Noah by the hand and steered him upstairs. Together they made their way to his room, slowly, as if in a haze. Once inside, Makenna closed the door and directed Noah to the bed.

He lay down stiffly, his head hitting the cashmere pillow though his eyes stared up at the ceiling. Makenna took the spot beside him and rested on her side, her head tucked against her arm as she looked at him.

"Are you okay?" she asked as gently as she could. She wanted so badly to break down herself; the tears pressed against her eyes, but she held them back.

"It was always my mum. I should have known." Noah's tone was flat. It was more alarming than if he had been yelling.

"I don't believe that," Makenna said. "I think it was a shitty situation, and she did the best she could by you."

Makenna could see how tightly Noah clenched his jaw. "You didn't know her as I did. She never did anything good in my interest. This was no different."

"You're hurting." Makenna dared a hand on Noah's shoulder. He flinched but didn't move away from her touch. "I'm so sorry, Noah. I know it's a lot to take in. But we know how to undo the curse now." Her voice cracked at the end. She hoped he didn't notice it.

Only then did he fix his gaze on her. "And what's that? Ask one of our friends to sacrifice themselves, just to bring back a man who may or may not lift the curse? A man who has a personal vendetta against my mother?"

"Yes," Makenna said as she closed her eyes. "But we can't ask anyone to sacrifice themselves. Not ever." Her spirit wasn't worth another's destruction. She would die and complete her soul in the shadow world, as was fated.

She felt a rough thumb on her face. Noah wiped away the tears she hadn't managed to keep back. Opening her eyes, she found him staring at her. The anger was gone, and in its place was the same sense of devastation that ruined her.

"I would give up my soul for you." Noah pulled Makenna into his body until his chin rested on her head. His arms were warm around her, a fortress of comfort entirely for her.

"I won't let you do that," Makenna whispered.

"I know," Noah answered. "So, I will hold you until our time is up, *mo leannan*. I love you."

"I love you, too."

For the short time they had left, Makenna would memorise every inch of him as he surrounded her. She never wanted to forget him. Makenna would take his memory into the shadow world with her and love him from afar.

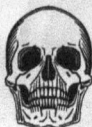

31

Haunt Me

The two lay in the bed, wrapped in each other's arms as the afternoon bled into night. Makenna didn't know how much time had passed, only that she never wanted this moment to end. She knew she was a fool for thinking such a thing. She was on a timer, and she could feel the end coming. Noah had fallen asleep at some point, though his arms still clung to her. Never did he look as peaceful as he did in his sleep. Makenna wished she could ease him of his pain. It burned her to know she could do no such thing.

Gently she ran a finger along the side of his face. She was about to kiss his lips when a low moan broke through the room. It was the same eerie cry that had rattled Makenna's bones a few nights ago. It forced her to sit straight up in the bed. Noah remained undisturbed beside her, and for a moment, Makenna wondered if she had imagined it.

No. There it was again. It carried through the room and out into the hall, but it made no sense. Harriet had sacrificed herself to the void this morning. It was impossible. Makenna shouldn't be able to hear her at all.

Detangling herself from Noah's limbs and the bed, Makenna treaded out of the room and into the hall, where the moan grew louder. She followed the sound, remembering how wretched it was. It rang of a pain Makenna didn't know how to verbalise, one she never wanted to.

The moan turned to a wail, like a ghostly breadcrumb trail that Makenna traced to the right wing of the manor. She had never ventured here yet, not in this lifetime. It was a long corridor similar to the one hers and Noah's rooms occupied. All the doors were closed, though Makenna could hear the wails coming from behind one at the very end of the hall. Every nerve in her body screamed at her to go back, but she reached for the handle regardless.

She pushed down, and the heavy door swung open. It took a moment for her eyes to adjust before Makenna could make out the basics of the room. It was much like her own, only reversed. At the four-poster bed was a figure, sat on the floor and hunched over the mattress, sobbing into her arms. Her wails filled the room as if she stood in a cave. It seemed to echo in every corner and tore through Makenna like a visible force.

"Lydia?"

The woman sat upright, her eyes red-rimmed. The wailing stopped immediately. "What are you doing here?"

Makenna looked at the woman with stark realisation. It had never been Harriet's cries who haunted the halls. It had been Lydia the entire time. "What's wrong?" Makenna asked, stepping further into the room.

"No! Don't." Lydia jumped up so fast it was nearly a blur. "Get out. Get out now."

Makenna let the door close behind her. "Why? What happened?"

Lydia scrambled to the back of the room until she hit the wall, coming into the soft light of the window. The entire left side of her head was completely blown open, blood and gore dripping down her neck and shoulder as if from a gunshot wound. Makenna swallowed the scream that bubbled up in her throat; the once beautiful woman was now a mess of tangled flesh. She had clearly reverted to her final image in death as her emotions soared. "Get out. I won't do it. I won't do it again. Now I know." Lydia pushed herself into the wall as if a great fire threatened to burn her.

"What are you talking about?" Makenna closed in on her but stopped at the bed as Lydia screamed bloody murder.

"Don't come any closer. I won't do it."

The fear in Lydia's eyes made Makenna take a step back. "I don't understand. I'm not going to hurt you."

"You don't get it," Lydia moaned, still clinging to the wall as if it were the only thing keeping her safe. "You're not the dangerous one. I am."

Makenna froze, her desire to help quickly fading to one of panic. "What do you mean?"

"I'm a part of the curse," Lydia breathed, her eyes wild. "I am Noah's curse. I am *your* curse. I am your death. Every single time."

Makenna's mind screamed at her to move, though her body was locked. "I don't get it."

"I could never stop myself, but I never knew why. Every time you've died, it's been at my hand. I have no control over it. It's as if something takes over my body and mind, and I can only watch from afar." Lydia's fingers dug into the wall as if she were fighting some force stronger than her.

"You're the figure, the figure in white that's been there every time I've died."

Lydia nodded and let out a scream as she was flung forward, her bloody hair thrown over her shoulders. "Get out. I can feel it. It's happening again."

Makenna's body seemed to snap back to reality. She whipped around and bolted for the door, only to find it locked. "I can't get out," Makenna said as she peeked over her shoulder. Lydia was on all fours, her body twisting as she fought the force dragging her across the floor towards Makenna. "Help," Makenna screamed as she pounded on the door. "Anyone!" She yanked on the handle, her injured hand burning with the movement. When the door wouldn't budge, Makenna tried kicking it. The wood creaked beneath her force, and again she kicked harder, with all the self-preservation she could muster. Behind her, she could hear Lydia wailing.

Another kick and the door splintered. Makenna targeted the weak spot and rammed into it with her full bodyweight. Her force took the door down, and she flung herself out into the hall. Twisting around, she could see Lydia, now on her feet and moaning as she picked her way through the damaged door.

Makenna scrambled to her feet and huffed it down the corridor. "Noah!" she screamed as loudly as she could. It burned her throat, but she called his name over and over as she skidded into the landing overlooking the entrance. He was there in a matter of seconds, his eyes frantic as Makenna rushed at him.

"What's wrong?" he asked, out of breath as he witnessed her pure panic.

Makenna didn't waste time. She grabbed his hand and pulled him down the stairs. Noah looked over his shoulder to see Lydia in their wake, his eyes wild with confusion. "What's happening?"

"Don't stop," Makenna yelled. They were at the front doors. Makenna yanked them open, and together they rushed out into the brisk night. She didn't know what good being outside would do them, but having its openness made her feel better. It was less restrictive when a homicidal ghost was chasing after you.

She dragged Noah around the house and into the backyard. Hesitating, Noah yanked Makenna to a stop as they neared the church. "Makenna, stop. Tell me what's going on."

She swivelled on her heel to maintain her balance. She couldn't see Lydia anymore, though the shadows played with Makenna's eyes and made every movement suspicious. "It's Lydia. She's the one who's been killing me. Each time. She told me."

Noah turned around as if half expecting Lydia to be on top of them. When it seemed clear of her, he faced Makenna again, his eyes screwed with concern. "That's impossible. You've died of freak accidents each time. There was never any foul play. I saw it with my own eyes."

"Think about it," Makenna shouted. "1899, when I tripped and fell over the railing in the entrance. I was pushed. In 1920, when that soldier killed me. He kept talking as if someone provoked him."

"But you burned in 1941," Noah said. "In the stables. It caught fire from a candle."

"A candle? Noah! She locked me in there. I remember now. She was there every single time." Makenna's memories clicked the more she thought about it. "1962, the firearm that went off. She tampered with it. 1983, when I was injured, and you had to perform surgery. You looked away for one second, and she was there. She cut my artery, and I bled out. It was all her doing."

Noah moved closer to Makenna, spooked by the rustling of some leaves. "But you killed yourself in 2004. How could she have been responsible?" His voice broke, his hands coming up to grab her arms as if she would leave him again.

"I remember," Makenna said. "I remember everything."

≈

OCTOBER 16, 2004

"It's too much," Lydia whispered in Madilyn's ear. It felt like a tickle on her cheek, but the words settled into her mind easily enough. It was far too much, Madilyn agreed. No one should have to go through this. "Whose memories are whose?" Lydia spoke again as Madilyn wandered through the halls of the manor. A good question to ask, she thought. It would drive her mad if she tried to sort through all her lives. Each memory seemed to fade into the next. It was entirely overwhelming.

Madilyn was in a routine now, on her nightly walk around the house. It was a last-minute stretch for her legs before going to bed. These walks gave her time to think. Routine was necessary to keep her from going crazy. It gave her a sense of structure while her world crumbled around her. At least she had Noah to keep her sane. He was hers, and she was his.

"But death is yours as well. It will find you. It will take more of you," Lydia said as they passed the stairs in the entrance. They were almost back at Madilyn's room. The thought made her skin itch. She didn't want to think of the inevitable. She turned her head away from Lydia as if she could make the idea disappear.

On the sixth night of being trapped in the house, Madilyn awoke from her dreams, her body covered in a cold sweat. Beside her bed stood Lydia, hidden in the shadows of the room. She bent down until she was level with Madilyn, her hand reaching out to touch the girl's cheek. Madilyn leaned into it as Lydia spoke. "You're tired. You've lived six lives already. Is this really how you want to spend the rest of your days, waiting for death to find you?" It was an extraordinary thought. Did Madilyn really want to keep living this way?

It felt hard to breathe in the room. She needed air. Madilyn wrapped herself in a robe and stole outside into the night.

Lydia followed her, her words velvety smooth as she continued to speak. "How tragic, this nightmare you're caught in. It's never-ending, day and night. Six lifetimes worth of pain. How do you survive it? And think of Noah. You don't deserve him. You will only cause him more pain."

They were outside now, in the back garden where Madilyn finally had a chance to breathe. Her mind felt foggier than ever, but Lydia was there to guide her with clarity. The ghost pointed to the garden hose, which had been wrapped up for the winter. Madilyn went to it, her hands numb as she unwound it.

"You're doing everyone a favour," Lydia encouraged her as Madilyn took the hose and dragged it to a nearby tree. It took her a few tries to loop it over, but once it was secure, Madilyn picked her way up the branches. "You're doing yourself an even bigger favour. These lives you keep reliving are so full of pain, and you're tired of feeling it."

Lydia watched from the ground as Makenna tied the hose around her neck. "You just want some peace, and you can find it in the darkness."

The words were sweet enough to make Madilyn drop.

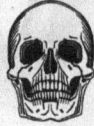

32

An Exchange

"I remember everything," Makenna said. Her eyes searched Noah's, and only then did he realise he was cruel not to believe her.

"I'll keep you safe," he said, his hand coming up to her face. "But I don't understand why she's doing this. I need to know why so I can protect you."

Makenna seemed relieved to hear his acceptance. "It's the curse. She doesn't want to do it. It takes over her body. It's happening against her will."

"Imagine my surprise the first time it happened." Lydia appeared from the trees just beyond them, her skull no longer cracked open and spilling its innards. She inched closer, her figure draped in darkness. The moonlight cut through the leaves but seemed to avoid her.

Makenna jumped back and bumped into Noah. He immediately tucked her behind him.

"It was 1899. I had been watching the two of you for days, maybe months. I don't remember. Time loses meaning in death. But I'd come to admire you both. I envied you even as you both started to unravel. So desperate to get out. All the failed magic you tried, all the escape routes. It was like a fever. It grew in the house and spawned something in me." Lydia took a step closer, a predator stalking its prey. Noah put as much of himself between her and Makenna as possible.

"Lydia, don't do this," he growled.

"And there you were, Makenna, or Meredith at the time. You were in the entrance, at the top of the stairs. That fever in me – it overwhelmed me. It took over my body, and the next thing I knew, I was pushing you over the railing. It was far too easy. As soon as you died, that fever vanished, and I cried for you. I cried for days. And then Noah became caught in the shadow world, and I cried alone no longer."

Lydia took another step, her face breaking into the moonlight. Her eyes looked foreign, as if they didn't belong to her. "And then twenty-one years later, you returned to us as Mallory. And that fever took me again – just as it did every twenty-one years after that. I never stopped crying for you, though. And tonight, I'll cry for you again once the fever leaves me. I promise you that."

Lydia lunged forward, and Noah tensed, ready to catch her and throw her down, but she was too quick, unnaturally so. He was aware of his shortcomings the moment he heard a yell behind him. Swivelling around, he watched as Lydia yanked Makenna back into the church, a wicked smile on her face as the doors slammed closed behind them.

Noah screamed as he flung himself at the doors. Again and again, he rammed his shoulder into the wood. It didn't waver, held together by some magical force he couldn't break. Noah backed up with a yell of frustration as he slammed his fists on the doors.

"Noah? By god, what's happening out here?" Huxley

asked as he appeared beside him, his face warped with concern. Behind him, Charles and Maryam sprinted up.

"Get me the book!" Noah yelled at them. "The spellbook. I need it!"

Maryam was the first to bolt. She didn't ask any questions.

"We need to get inside, now. Lydia is in there with Makenna. She's going to kill her."

Both Charles and Huxley looked at each other, almost as if they didn't believe the words coming out of Noah's mouth.

"Now!" Noah begged. They didn't need to be told a third time as both men disappeared, searching for a way in. For a terrible moment, Noah was left alone. He stared at the church doors, entirely desperate to know what was going on inside. Only did his skin crawl when the screaming began.

~

MAKENNA HIT the ground hard when Lydia smacked her down. There wasn't much time to recover. Lydia was on top of her, her hands wrapped around Makenna's throat. She tried to twist to upset Lydia's balance, but the woman didn't budge.

Think. Think. Think. It was hard when there wasn't any air getting through. All Makenna could focus on was the face of the woman pinning her down. There was almost no emotion behind it, as if Lydia had turned off and something else had taken her place.

Hips. The thought clicked in Makenna's panic-induced state, and she thrust her hips up as hard as she could. Lydia toppled forward with the momentum. It was just enough for Makenna to roll to the side and scramble to her feet before Lydia could turn back on her. The woman screamed with frustration as she found her feet. It was unsettling how slowly she moved, almost at a leisurely pace, as she stalked towards Makenna.

"Lydia, please. It's me. You don't have to do this." Makenna backed towards the wooden doors, knowing they wouldn't open. It felt better having a point of access to the outside rather than a solid wall behind her.

Rotted leaves and debris crunched underneath Lydia's feet as she continued stalking Makenna. "I don't have a choice. I will be your death as I always have been. It was my husband's will."

"I don't believe that," Makenna said as the door pressed against her back. Her hands fidgeted with the knob, but it wouldn't open, just as expected. "I don't believe your husband would want that for you." If Makenna couldn't escape, at least she could buy some time. She slid from the doors to keep Lydia following her.

Lydia's hands tensed and untensed as if she were fighting some force in her body. "Maybe he hadn't meant for me to carry out the curse specifically, but it's poetic, is it not? Alfred lost me twice. Noah's lost you how many times? Everyone suffers. Is that not the true nature of a curse?"

"Why should Noah suffer? He didn't do anything." Makenna steered Lydia away from the doors and along the pews. She wanted as much space between her and the maniac ghost counting the seconds down to her death as possible.

"Someone had to pay the price. And now Constance knows the consequences of her actions."

"So, let's end it. We've all suffered enough, haven't we?"

Lydia shook her head, and though her words were

sharp, her eyes began to water with tears. "It's a magical contract. I can't end it. Only Alfred can."

"But he's dead," Makenna said. "And the price to bring back Constance was too heavy already."

"Then you haven't suffered enough if you aren't willing to pay the price to end it." Lydia pounced, her arms out as she dove for Makenna. Makenna nearly slipped trying to pick a direction to run in, and Lydia was on her again. The ghost shoved her hard into the wall, wrapping her fingers around Makenna's throat, tighter this time, nails digging into flesh. Makenna's arms flailed as she swung at Lydia, trying to connect with anything. The woman was like stone, her hands effectively cutting off the last of Makenna's breath.

Stars clouded Makenna's vision, and she briefly wondered if she'd be reunited with her brother for a second time this week. She never found out as a loud crash pulled both women's attention behind them. It was followed by two pairs of arms wrapping around Lydia to yank her back. The woman screamed bloody murder as Charles and Huxley wrangled her away from Makenna. Collapsing to the floor, Makenna coughed violently as her lungs filled with air. It burned her throat, and her head spun as she crawled out of the pews and to the head of the church.

"Let go of me. I'm not done," Lydia howled. She had eyes for no one but Makenna, her void stare replaced by one of utter determination. Charles and Huxley kept her down as she thrashed, her legs kicking chaotically to thwart them.

"Control yourself," Huxley bellowed in her ear, and Lydia screeched in response.

There was a loud crashing sound as Noah clambered through a smashed window. It was narrow, the shutters hanging on within an inch of their life as he pulled himself through. His hands scraped on the floor as he hit the ground.

Noah's eyes sought out Makenna, and upon seeing her safely tucked by the altar, he headed straight for Lydia. "Help me make a circle with the leaves," he ordered Makenna, and the two began piling leaves in front of the unruly ghost. Lydia continued her thrashing, though her screams wavered between howls and sobs now.

There was another slew of bodies to filter through the broken window; Maryam contorted herself through the frame first, with Cody and Siobhan right behind. Maryam gripped Constance's spellbook in her hand, while Cody clutched the vial with the leftover summoning potion from earlier today. The older woman pressed the book to Makenna, a look of solidarity on her wrinkled face. The three ghosts then anchored themselves by the altar, protecting Makenna as Noah finished the circle of leaves. Their faces twisted in horror as they watched Lydia struggle against Huxley and Charles. This was their friend, though the woman before them resembled nothing but a wild beast held captive. Cody wasted no time handing the vial to Noah.

Everyone watched as he poured the potion over the leaves in a rushed fashion. He pivoted to Makenna, who was clutching the book with white knuckles. It was already marked to the page she knew he was going to ask her to read. "Are you all right?" he said, throwing her off guard.

She used the podium to steady herself and ignored the burn in her throat as she spoke. "Yes. But who?"

"It doesn't matter. Please, just read the spell."

Makenna held his eyes. She knew what he was about to do. "I can't. I won't let you."

Noah stepped closer to her, gently holding her face as

he brought her in for one last kiss. It was hastened by the wails of Lydia behind them, still trying to break free. "I love you."

He stood back to give her some space, though his eyes never left hers. She wouldn't let him do it. She had died six times already. She would give herself once more to free him. If she used herself to call Alfred forth, he could grant Noah his freedom. Then she would wait for him in death as he had waited for her all this time.

She wanted so badly to say goodbye to him, to kiss him just one more time. She couldn't control the sobs as she opened the book and spoke the words. "*Vivaren ith molt akda.*" The pull of it tugged at her immediately, and she dropped the book to the floor. The feeling was just as awful as the last time. The spell called to every fibre of her being and demanded it as payment. It was heavy and dark and inescapable, like a black hole. She would not break free of its gravity.

"Makenna," Noah begged, his finger back on her face. So soft and tender, a lover's touch. "Let it take me. Let me make right what my mother started. Please."

"No," Makenna whimpered. Hot tears flowed down her cheeks. "I can't." She stepped back from him, ready to throw herself into the ring of leaves that wanted her so badly, but there was already someone standing in it.

Huxley stood tall and proud, his hand up in a salute to his brow. "I said it would be my honour. Give me purpose in death as my wife did in life."

Makenna sank to the ground, the weight of the spell crushing her bones. "Oh, god. No. Please, Huxley."

Behind him, Maryam had taken his place, holding Lydia back. All eyes were on Huxley, his kind face holding no trace of fear. He turned in a quick circle, nodding to everyone in the room. "You have all made the past one hundred years an absolute pleasure. It was an honour knowing you all." He stopped before Makenna and Noah, his hand dropping in a final salute. "Live the best life possible, the both of you."

A second longer, and the circle would drag Makenna in. She had to let go. Holding a hand over her heart, Makenna made Huxley's promise with a nod she hoped conveyed her every piece of gratitude. "We will. Thank you." She released the spell and let it pass over to him. Noah was there to grab her before she collapsed from the sudden surge of power. The light from the spell nearly blinded her with its flash, and she wept as it took Huxley, eradicating his soul on the spot.

No man deserved such a fate. No one ever did.

33

Damn You

When the light of the flash dissipated, Makenna's eyes settled on a figure she had never seen before. In the circle stood a tall man, his broad figure draped in the finest clothes of his time. A finely cut rouge lounge suit, tailored to his every measurement. His salt-and-pepper hair was combed over to the side, and he looked entirely confused to be standing there.

"Who – who are you?" he asked, facing Makenna and Noah. He had to be nearing his sixties. His accent was posh and his posture perfect. He was entirely unlike the man Makenna pegged Lydia to marry. He didn't seem like a man capable of cursing a young mother.

Noah got to his feet, gently lifting Makenna with him. She wanted so desperately to lie down and mourn Huxley, but she wouldn't let his sacrifice go to waste.

"I am Noah Kiers," Noah said with as much confidence as someone who had just lost a close friend could muster. "And this is Makenna Grace."

The man, Alfred, looked down his large nose at them.

"Am I supposed to know who you are? Where am I? I don't understand." He turned on his booted heel to evaluate the place before his eyes stopped on Lydia. She no longer thrashed in the arms of Charles and Maryam. She was locked on her husband, her jaw unhinged.

"My dearest?" Alfred said. He immediately went for her, but the spell stopped him short of leaving the circle. "How can it be?"

The mania that seemed to cloud Lydia's eyes vanished as she gazed at her husband. "Alfred? My god." She sagged in Charles's and Maryam's arms.

"What is the meaning of this? Where am I?" he demanded. His eyes danced from his wife to everyone else in the room.

"It's my hell, Alfred. And you must undo it. You must set me free," Lydia begged. She strained in her spot as if she were fighting the fever once again.

Alfred pressed against the invisible wall. "I don't know what you're talking about. Someone, tell me what's going on."

"You are a ghost," Maryam said, her grip still tight on Lydia's arm. "But we've brought you back from the shadow world at a great personal cost. You best be worth it."

"A ghost?" Alfred stood back, offended by such a claim. "That's impossible. I am as I've always been. This is a dream."

Lydia shook her head frantically, her words pressed. "No, Alfred, it is true. You are dead, just as I am. But my soul has been trapped in the manor. Do you remember? I died here, twice."

Alfred scanned the room again, recognition finally setting in. "The church? But it's falling apart. How—"

"Time has passed," Lydia said. "So much of it. But

you must help me. I am cursed. I am a plague upon this household – all because of something you did over a hundred years ago. Can you remember? The witch you begged to bring me back when I first died? You did something to her."

Alfred stared at Lydia as if trying to connect the dots. A painful few seconds passed before it clicked. "She made me wait twenty-one years for you, then you killed yourself, and she would not bring you back a second time." All the haughtiness vanished from the man as if it had been slapped out of him. He no longer looked at his wife with confusion but instead betrayal. "You left me after I waited an eternity for you."

Lydia's sob caught in her throat. "I was in heaven. There was peace, serenity. You ripped me from it. I couldn't stand being with you our entire marriage. Death was a blessing. You did not bring me back out of love. It was possession. It always was."

"So, you shot yourself, right outside of this very church," Alfred said, his head turning to the window Noah had bulldozed his way through earlier. "I washed your blood off those walls. I took down the shutters damaged from the bullet. You died, and that witch would not bring you back. Not even after I waited all those years without you."

Lydia bit down on her lip. "She could not bring me back. There is no coming back from suicide. It is the ultimate betrayal of life. She could do nothing."

"But I could," Alfred said, his lip curling. "I cursed her name. I wished twenty-one years of tragedy upon the thing she loved most, until it too died, and would not come back. A fitting punishment for what she did to me." Alfred showed no remorse as he looked at his wife. Only dedication to the judgement he had passed.

"Alfred, you must reverse the curse. You must end it here, tonight." Lydia tried to stand, but Charles and Maryam kept her down.

"And why should I?"

"Because I am the curse. It passed on to me. That witch, the thing she loved most, was her son, the man standing behind you." Alfred peered over his shoulder at Noah, who still had Makenna in his arms. "He suffers every twenty-one years the death of his love before she is reincarnated, that girl right there. Yet every time she dies, she loses a part of her soul. And I am the one to kill her. Every single time." Lydia moved closer to the circle, dragging Maryam and Charles with her. "End the curse. Call it off, so I do not kill her a final time. Please, I beg of you. I do not want to be a murderer. Don't make me do it again."

Alfred's head went back and forth between the three as if evaluating the situation. "How many times?"

"What?" Lydia breathed, her eyes wide.

"How many times have you killed her?" He pointed to Makenna with a thick finger, though he did not look at her.

"What does it matter?" Lydia said.

Alfred kept his hand up. "How many times?"

"Six," Makenna said, detangling herself from Noah. He gave her the freedom to move, and she found herself beside Lydia. "She's killed me six times."

Lydia stared at the girl, her face a mix of horror and regret. Alfred wasn't looking at either of them. He only had eyes for Noah. "And have you suffered? Have you waited years for the love of your life, only to be greeted by her death once again? Does it burn you and make you wish death upon yourself?" He spat the words at Noah.

"I have suffered insurmountably," Noah said, his tone cold. "Over a hundred years of it. We all have."

Alfred's jaw tightened. "But she's not truly dead yet.

Lydia never came back. Why has your lover been given so many chances?"

"Alfred!" Lydia called. "Makenna is innocent. So is Noah. Do not make them pay for someone else's mistake. It was my own choice to kill myself. I should be the one you punish, not them."

Alfred turned on her, his words hot. "Then you shall get to suffer along with them for what you did to me."

"No!" Lydia screamed. "I will not. You will undo this curse. You waited twenty-one years for me. You can do this much. As your wife, I demand it."

Alfred took a step back, almost cowing under Lydia's tone. Makenna got the sense the man had rarely been spoken to this way. "You do not get to punish me anymore. I have terrorised the people here for over a century. You will end this curse, or I will make your soul suffer as you have done all of us. Noah," Lydia's voice bounced across the room with full authority. "The spellbook. Bring it here."

Noah scrambled for a moment, clearly as confused as everyone else. Finding the text, he scurried across the floor and held it out awkwardly, unsure who to hand it to.

Alfred's eyes followed the book, his posture stiff as he waited for Lydia's next move.

"You know this book, don't you?" Lydia said coolly. "It's the one the witch used to bring me back. You're a fool if you think that is all it can do. Make me haunt the living. That is nothing! Noah, find the spell."

Noah stared at Lydia. "Which one?"

"The one to damn a soul," Lydia said, her voice steely. "If my husband won't lift the curse, then we shall curse him with our own. Since we only seem to work an eye for an eye, let us do our worst." She held Alfred's gaze with the intensity of the sun. "I will damn you as you have damned me."

Noah flipped through the book and locked his finger on a page. His voice carried with authority as he began to speak.

"Stop!" Alfred's voice cut through Noah's chanting, his colour completely drained from his face. "That's enough."

"That's only the start," Lydia seethed. "Undo the curse, or we will send you to the darkest pits of hell. There they will rip your soul apart every day and stitch it back together with a hot needle. You will feel every inch of it as it burns your very being and know there is no peace from it. You will live in eternity suffering as I do here, and we will know we were each other's destruction."

Alfred backed up until he hit the back of the circle. He pressed into it to put as much distance between him and his wife as possible. "Is this how it is to be?" he said, his voice barely above a whisper. "You threaten me after the lengths I went for you?"

"I do not threaten you. I am making a promise to you." Lydia looked at him through narrow eyes. "And my patience grows thin. Undo the curse, or Noah—" She gave him a nod to start speaking again.

Noah got one word out before Alfred leapt forward. "No. I undo it. I take back my curse. I no longer wish twenty-one years of suffering on you, the witch, or whoever was affected by my words. I end it all!"

There was a moment of silence before a disturbance began. It started with a slight breeze on the floor that swirled the debris around everyone's feet. Then it grew in intensity, and seconds later, it was a great wind. It thrashed the window shutters, knocked over the pews, and nearly tumbled Makenna over. Grabbing on to one of the benches, she anchored herself down as the sound of the wind grew louder. It was as if a tornado ripped through the church.

Shutting her eyes, Makenna cried out as she felt the wind pass through her rather than at her. It tugged at her soul and burned her body before exiting out her back. Beside her, Makenna could hear Lydia scream. There was one last rush before the gale died down and dissipated completely.

Opening her eyes, Makenna relinquished the bench as she assessed the scene before her. Lydia was no longer locked in Charles's and Maryam's arms. She was on all fours, panting from the energy that had undoubtedly passed through them all. Near the altar, Noah had fallen to his knees. His hands roamed over his body as if feeling himself for the first time.

Makenna skirted the circle where Alfred stood, shocked at the power he had just unleashed. Makenna didn't care for him. If she never saw his soul again, it'd be too soon. Her only focus was the man on the floor before her.

She reached Noah and pulled him into her arms. He felt different somehow, his skin hotter, more solid. His energy seemed more realised, and the darkness that clung to him, as it did the ghosts, was gone.

"Noah?" Makenna said, her hands coming up to his face. "Are you all right?" She could feel the burn in the back of her throat as tears escaped her eyes. She knew, just knew that he was fully alive again, for the first time in over a hundred years. He no longer danced between the shadow world and the living. He belonged to her, here, where they now had their entire lives ahead of them.

"I'm okay," Noah breathed, his fingers lacing with Makenna's, though they had no strength to them. "I'm okay."

Makenna wiped at his tears with her thumbs before

kissing him hard on the lips. He tasted different than before. It was sweeter somehow, like honey and wine.

At the other end of the leaf ring, Charles and Maryam were helping Lydia to her feet. Makenna rose with Noah then, and together they circled Alfred, to stand before the blond. She retreated from them, her arm out as if in need of space. Everyone backed up from her, and she zeroed in on her husband.

"Go," Lydia barked, face twisted with rage. "Go back to whatever hell we pulled you from. Do not await me there. You will never see me again."

Alfred gritted his teeth, though his body began to fade rapidly. "You spiteful bitch. I regret those years I wasted on you."

"As do I." But the man was gone before he could hear Lydia's words. It didn't matter. Lydia stared at the spot he had stood in with contempt. "Fuck you," she said before spitting on the ground. "Fuck you and everything you've done. I am released from you. We all are." The fire in Lydia's eyes burned out quickly, and her shoulders sagged.

Maryam was the first to come up to her and wrap her arms around the blond to pull her into a hug. "It is done," Maryam said. "You are free of him. You no longer have to do his bidding." Lydia's frame shook as she began to sob, her tears heavy and angry. From over Maryam's shoulder, she looked at Noah and Makenna.

"I'm sorry," she whispered. "I'm so, so sorry."

~

NOAH STARED AT HIS HANDS. They felt different somehow. Every part of him felt different. It was as if a current of energy had charged his body. He swore if he touched anything, he would shock it.

There were new senses, too, as if his body was waking up and experiencing what it felt like to live fully again. His mouth was parched and his stomach empty. He felt cold from the wind that rushed through him earlier, and his body ached with a terrible exhaustion he had never felt before. He wanted so badly to lie down, but that energy, the one that vibrated at his core, kept him going.

Beside him stood Makenna, and he reached his fingers over to wrap his hand around hers. Her skin was hot underneath his, and as soon as their fingers touched, a jolt passed between them.

"What was that?" Makenna asked as she brought her hand up to examine it.

"I don't know." Noah retracted his hand to his chest to feel his heartbeat. It thumped vigorously, as if he had run a mile. He didn't have another moment to consider it before Lydia was upon them both. She dragged them into a tight embrace that threatened to cut his air off, her eyes red and puffy.

She let go of Noah first and focused her attention on Makenna. "You must hate me with your entire being," Lydia said, her lips warped in a frown. "I have done the most unthinkable things to you. I have tortured you and degraded your soul. I do not ask for your forgiveness. I simply ask that you understand I had no say in it. I was compelled to do it. I did not know why until now, but I have cried over it for over a hundred years."

Makenna wrapped her hands around Lydia's. She pulled them to her chest and held them there. The was nothing but compassion in her eyes as she spoke. "I don't blame you, Lydia. We've all suffered. And while there's a lot to process, I know it wasn't you. It's just going to take some time to work through everything."

"Of course," Lydia said, her smile gracious, but Noah

could see the remorse behind it. Stepping back from Makenna, Lydia went for Noah's hand next. There was no jolt of energy like there had been with Makenna. "And you, I owe you the same apology. I tried so hard to tell you, but the words would never come out of my mouth. I am sorry – both of you. I can never repay you for the pain I have caused. I'm only lucky my ruse to make Alfred lift the curse worked."

Noah squeezed her fingers, and that same sense of exhaustion weighed his body down. It felt as if he hadn't slept in a century. "It was brilliant, even if I was slow on the uptake. There is no curse to damn a soul in that book, but we sold it well," he assured her. "Please, don't take this upon yourself." His eyes flickered to the leaf circle where Alfred had stood only moments ago. "You are not the one to blame."

Lydia bent down to kiss the back of his palm. "You are too kind. All of you." She looked over his shoulder to everyone in the church. "I am truly sorry."

Cody scrambled from his spot beside Siobhan and tackled Lydia. His arms wrapped around her waist, and Lydia dropped Noah's hand to embrace the boy. "But we're still here," the boy said. "I thought when the curse was lifted, we would vanish. I thought we'd disappear like . . ." His voice drifted off, unable to say Huxley's name.

Lydia peeled the boy from her waist and sunk down until she was eye level with him. Despite the atrocities of the night, her voice was soft as she spoke. Noah did not think he would have the same strength. "Huxley was a great man. He is not lost, just like you are not. We shall remember him. He can never truly die so long as we keep his memory alive," Lydia said.

There was a moment of silence amongst everyone as they faced the circle to pay their respects. It was an unspoken agreement to remember their fallen member, the man who had given up his soul so two could live. Noah stood as tall as he could, his hand up in a salute for the absolute gentleman who had taught him more about life than Noah had ever lived. He would never forget Huxley. His sacrifice would be engraved on Noah's soul for the rest of his life.

When the moment passed, Maryam was the first to break the silence, though her voice wavered with grief as she spoke. "I need out of this dingy place. I don't know about you lot, but I never want to come in here again." With a last nod, Maryam excused herself from the church, Cody and Siobhan following suit.

Charles remained for a second, his arm up in the same salute as Noah's had been. "Old sport," he said to the air before following the others. Only Noah, Makenna, and Lydia remained.

Lydia hesitated, seemingly unsure of herself. "Before you two leave and never come back, say goodbye, will you?" She then relieved the two of her presence before they could respond.

"Oh god," Makenna said as she sunk to the floor. Her hands came up to her tangled curls, her eyes focused on the ring of leaves with utter disbelief.

Noah was by her side, his arm snaking around her shoulders to pull her into him. He rested his head on hers, enjoying the smell of her hair. He had never noticed it before. "Are you all right?" he asked, his voice sounding tired.

Makenna slumped against him. "I think I am." He could feel her shift beneath him. "I don't know. You?"

"I'm starving," he said, surprising himself. It made Makenna giggle. Her chuckle was infectious, and soon he was laughing with her. Perhaps it was the exhaustion or the absurdity of it all. Noah wasn't sure. All he knew was that he had a pain in his stomach that he hadn't felt in over a hundred years. "I forgot what being hungry felt like."

"It's a bitch," Makenna said, her eyes closing. "You tired too?"

"Incredibly."

"It's been a long day," Makenna said. "But the first of your freedom." She found his hand and kissed each knuckle slowly. "Correction, the first of ours."

Never had any words sounded sweeter.

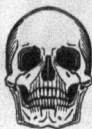

34

Don't Forget Me

The air smelt sweet, Noah noted as he and Makenna exited the church. Perhaps that wasn't the correct word for it. Fresh, maybe? He had spent so long with his senses dulled by the shadow world. He was, quite frankly, overwhelmed by everything. The stars in the sky seemed brighter, the grass crunchier beneath his feet. Even Makenna's hair seemed to reflect the moonlight with more intensity. The cut on his arm burned more intensely, too.

"I want to say our goodbyes," Makenna said as she led him to the manor, "but then I'm going to lead you out of those gates, and we're going to go to my home. There's food, a bed. Then I'm going to call my mum and tell her I'm okay."

Noah let her direct him into the house through the back kitchen. She moved with speed, and Noah tugged on her hand to slow her down. "Hold on. I need to collect a few things first. And I need to say goodbye to the house, too."

Makenna came to a stop, realising her pace had

outmatched his. "I'm so sorry. Of course." She let go of his hand. "Take your time. I'll be in the entrance."

How strange, Noah thought, as he wandered the halls for the last time. The grand corridors were vast and imposing, the high ceilings trimmed with ornate plasterwork that he had committed to memory a century ago. Would he miss the heavy velvet drapes that framed the tall windows? Would he dream of the worn stone floors and oil paintings in gilded frames?

This had been both his home and prison for so long. He had only dreamt of the day he would step foot out those front gates and never look back. He had begged for the day he never had to fear for Makenna's safety again. A miracle he had been granted both in a single night. It had come at a terrible cost.

Noah thanked Huxley once more as he passed through all the rooms, admiring the architecture. Huxley had had an eye for detail; Noah would make sure to appreciate it one last time. It felt like a small way to honour the man. It was also an excellent way to say goodbye to the walls that had kept him enclosed for so many years. Noah knew he would carry this place with him wherever he went. He would indeed walk these halls in his dreams for years to come. It would never leave him.

He moved upstairs, his hand dragging along the wooden railing as he made his way to his room. Too many nights he had spent here. Too many nights he had wandered the halls, cursing his fate and wishing for this very moment. In his room, he went for the bottom drawer of his dresser, the one he had not disturbed since the nineteenth century. He struggled against the age that had worn it down. With some effort, he popped open the drawer, and inside Noah found the vintage bag he had shoved in there in 1899.

It was the bag he had left his home with when he deemed his mother too out of control. The same one he had packed when he and Makenna left Scotland for a new life in England. It was the same bag he had shoved in this drawer on the promise only to open it when he was free to leave this house.

Gently he lifted the bag from its place of rest. It was well preserved – tanned leather and built with sturdy straps. Surveying the room, he already knew what to take. He had packed this bag a thousand times in his head. His few clothes, three of his favourite books, the picture of him and Makenna – badly damaged – and his mother's letter and spellbook. He took the time to make the bed, and with a last look, closed the door to his bedroom for a final time.

"Off then, are you?"

Startled, Noah turned around. Rose was leaning against the wall by Makenna's bedroom. "Rose," Noah acknowledged as he adjusted the strap to his pack with his good arm. "We are."

Rose's arms were crossed over her chest, her lips pressed tight. "Best of luck to you then."

"Thank you, Rose." He gave her a meaningful nod and proceeded down the hallway.

"Take care of yourself," she called after him.

He pivoted on his heel as he walked and gave her a wave, to which she returned. "You as well." He meant it.

His heart thumped in his chest as he walked onto the landing and overlooked the entrance. His eyes settled on everyone as they stood in the foyer, waiting for him. He found Makenna, her brilliant hair standing out in the mix. Had it always been so bright? He felt light-headed as he descended the stairs, knowing this was the last time he would walk down them.

He was surrounded by his family, for they had become

just that in the years he had been locked up here. They were the ones who had made it possible to survive such a cruel fate. He surely never would have done it without any of them, Huxley included. Noah would have lost his mind decades ago.

"Are you ready?" Makenna asked. She wore the clothes she had initially come to the house in all those days ago, simple leggings and her jumper. Lifetimes had passed since then.

"I am." Noah swallowed the lump in his throat. His heart felt heavy, knowing he would no longer see these beautiful souls. "But only if you all walk with us to the gates?" he said to everyone.

"Of course," Maryam said. "We'd be offended if you didn't ask."

"Can I come too? If you'll have me there after everything I've done?" Lydia asked. She was a mess; tears streamed down her face and her hair was frazzled from touching it too much.

Noah found her hand and squeezed. "Never say that. I want you all there. Especially you, Lyd."

"Okay," she said with a delicate smile. "I wouldn't miss it."

"I'll get the door!" Cody weaved through the small crowd to yank it open. One last look, Noah gave himself. One last look inside the house. His eyes danced around the room, and then he was ready. Sucking in a deep breath, he took his final few steps in the manor before he was outside. Makenna followed close behind, her hand slipping into his. He was glad for her comfort. It took far more strength than he realised to say goodbye.

Together they walked across the yard, his band of ghosts in tow. He had spent so much time waiting for this moment. Now the house was at his back and his future in front of him. All that separated Noah from his freedom was the black iron gate that had enclosed him for over a century.

He stopped short of the bars and turned to face the people he had come to love dearly. He would never forget their faces, their stories, the memories they had graciously shared with him.

"I'll miss you," he said, hugging Maryam first. "You were the mother I never had."

Maryam's embrace was warm, her words just as sweet. "Live for yourself," she said. "Live the life you always deserved." She kissed him on both cheeks and released him to take Makenna in her arms. "Keep him in line, will you? I think the outside world will be a bit of a shock for him."

Makenna laughed through the tears as Maryam peppered two kisses on her cheeks. "I'll do my best," she said as she pulled away. "Thank you for taking care of me when I couldn't do it myself."

"Nonsense," Maryam said with a wave. "You always had the strength. I just helped along the way."

"I needed it more than you knew."

"Shush. Now move along before I cry," Maryam said, her eyes beginning to water as she ushered them on. Makenna pulled her in for one more hug before she and Noah moved to Charles. He took Noah in an embrace that rivalled Maryam's. When they pulled apart, he patted Noah on the chest.

"You are a good man, Noah Kiers. Remember that."

"You're one of the best I know," Noah said in response. "You and Huxley taught me more about being a good man than anyone I know. Thank you."

Charles shook his head. "A good man doesn't need to be taught. You are kind, through and through."

Noah felt his heart beat harder. "Thank you." He

reined in the ache that tore at him as Makenna got her own hug from Charles.

"Be safe, my dear," he said to her. His hand moved to her face. "The world can be cruel, but you are a bright light in it. Never forget that."

Makenna leaned into his hand. "I hope to be just that." With a final nod, Charles moved them along.

Siobhan and Cody were next. "Shiv," Noah said by way of goodbye. She closed the distance between them and wrapped her arms around Noah's waist, her face burrowing into his chest.

"Don't do anything stupid. I mean it." His clothes muffled her voice, but Noah tightened his arms around her.

"I'll do my best."

"Not good enough," she said as she retracted from him. She wiped the back of her sleeve across her face. "Don't pull a 'me' and end up back in someplace like this. Learn from my mistakes, the both of you. Be smart and stay safe." She pointed to Makenna. "He's a big softy. Don't let the world hurt him. Only you get to tell him who's boss."

The girls embraced each other. "I am the boss, always," Makenna joked, the tears coming faster. "Thank you for reminding me, though."

"Always. Girl power." Siobhan gave her a wink as the two retracted from one another.

"Cody," Noah said, his voice wavering. He dropped down so he was level with the boy. Noah held his arms out, but Cody resisted at first. His eyes were as wet as anyone else's before he launched into Noah's arms. "My dude," Noah said, hugging him tightly, his eyes closed.

"Don't forget me," Cody said into Noah's ear, his tears free-falling.

Warm tears slipped down his cheek. "Never," he said, squeezing his eyes even tighter. "You are the strongest person I know. I could never forget you. I never will."

"It's a deal," Cody said. "You can't ever forget any of us. You're not allowed to." Cody unhooked his arms from Noah's neck and stood back, waiting for Noah to promise. For all the hardship Noah had suffered here, he had felt love as well.

"I won't ever."

Makenna took Cody in her arms next. "I have two brothers now," she said and kissed the top of his copper head. "I'm so lucky to have had both of you in my life." Her voice caught, and she kissed his head a second time, holding him close for a long moment. "Be good," she said as she let him go, and Noah could see the pain in her eyes from losing a second brother.

Cody wiped at his tears frantically. Siobhan took the cue and brought the boy into her arms – always the bigger sister.

"You two keep each other safe, will you? And look after the old folks. They can get out of hand sometimes," Noah said, making Cody giggle through his tears. Siobhan rested her head on top of Cody's and gave Noah a cheeky smile.

"We'll keep them in line," she promised.

"Good," Noah said with a small smile. "I expect nothing less."

Noah and Makenna turned to Lydia at last. She stood at the end of the line, bouncing on the balls of her feet in anticipation.

Unlike Cody, she didn't hesitate and instead threw herself at them both, bringing them into her thin arms as she sobbed. "Please, think better of me out there. Know I never wanted to hurt you. I love you both so much. Be good and keep each other safe."

Noah's hand dug into her shoulder. "I could never think poorly of you," he said into her ear. "You were by my side the entire time, Lyd. Thank you."

"You're a bright light," Makenna said to her. "We were all cursed. Now we're free. Please don't blame yourself. I don't."

Lydia's eyes were hooded as she released them, but not before giving them each a peck on the cheek. "I'll try my best. Thank you, both of you."

Makenna wiped the tears in her eyes and cleared her throat. "You were there with Noah every step of the way, through all the good and the bad. I'll never forget what you've done for him. Thank you, Lydia. I mean it."

"Stop. You're going to make me cry even harder," Lydia said with a laugh. She ran a hand over her cheeks to wipe them dry. "But thank you. I mean it." She stepped back to stand with the others.

Noah's voice wavered, but he found his strength as he faced everyone one last time. "I couldn't have done it without any of you. All these years I got to spend with you, you've each made me a better person. Thank you for that." He looked at each one of them. "I want to make a promise to you all. I will do whatever it takes to release you from this place. I will find a way to give your souls peace. That is my legacy. I promise you that."

"You just focus on yourselves," Lydia said, her arms locked with Maryam and Charles now. "That's all we ask for. Now stop stalling and go live your life outside these gates."

Noah held a hand over his heart as he bowed to them. "Thank you, every one of you. I love you all, truly."

He turned to Makenna, her fingers finding his own. He brought her hand up to his lips and kissed the back of it gently. "Ready?"

"Absolutely."

With Makenna by his side, Noah stood before the gate. His heart pounded in his chest as his fingers hovered over the latch. Without a second thought, he pulled it up. The gate swung open with ease, and both he and Makenna stepped into the outside world together.

The End

Acknowledgments

This book has a lot of support behind it, stretching across the globe and touching many lives.

I'd first like to thank my parents, who have always supported my endeavours in the arts. When I doubted myself, they were steady voices, giving me safe places to write and encourage me forward. I would also like to thank my sister for bigging me up whenever she can, even though we're oceans away. I love you all.

I would like to thank my friends in Canada who have been there since day one on this publishing journey. Nadine, you are my writing soulmate. All the hours we spent plotting, going over cover designs, book titles, and character choices, those moments are so precious to me. I love you dearly.

To my found family in Scotland, who gave me a home when I risked it all and moved across the globe, thank you. You made me feel safe enough to embrace my craft when life became chaotic. You have been there to celebrate all the wins and inspired me when I felt homesick and lost. You made me feel found. I love you all.

To Quinn, who edited the hell out of this book and made it shine while remaining dark and twisty. You are a genius, and I can't wait to work with you again.

And to Adam and Sarah, who took a chance on an unknown author and gave me the means to bring this book to life. I am so incredibly grateful you believed in me. I hope this book inspires readers as much as you have inspired me, and I can one day repay the kindness. Thank you for your support. It means the world to me.

For a book so heavily centered around death, an incredible amount of life and passion went into its pages.

Thank you all.

About the Author

Amelia Ives is a Canadian author from Calgary, Alberta but now nestled in the heart of Edinburgh. Not only a fantastical story teller Amelia also has a passion for music, while also enjoying all things nerdy. Her favourite past times include bingeing Marvel movies, watching TikToks and dreaming about fantasy worlds.

instagram.com/ameliaivesauthor

tiktok.com/ameliaivesauthor

Thank You

Thank you for reading Curse Of Midnight by Amelia Ives. If you are looking for more books to get lost in please check out our other published titles at;

www.apbeswickpublications.com.

A.P Beswick Publications
Oswaldtwistle Mills Business Centre
Clifton Mill
Pickup Street
Accrington
BB53AP